THE
TANGLED
LANDS

Paolo Bacigalupi &
Tobias S. Buckell

HEAD
ZEUS

First published in the US in 2018 by Saga Press, an imprint of Simon & Schuster, Inc.
First published in the UK in 2018 by Head of Zeus in 2018

Interior design by Brad Mead
The text for this book was set in Brioso Pro.

975312468

A catalogue record for this book is available from the British Library.

ISBN (HB): 9781788544757
ISBN (XTPB): 9781788544764
ISBN (E): 9781788544788

Printed and bound by CPI Group (UK) Ltd, Croydon, CR0 4YY

Head of Zeus Ltd
First Floor East
5–8 Hardwick Street
London EC1R 4RG

WWW.HEADOFZEUS.COM

THE TANGLED LANDS

Paolo Bacigalupi is the bestselling author of *The Windup Girl*. Tobias S. Buckell is the bestselling author of *Halo: The Cole Protocol*. Between them, they have either won or been nominated for the Locus, Hugo, Nebula, Compton Crook, and John W. Campbell awards.

CONTENTS

PART I

The Alchemist

BY PAOLO BACIGALUPI

IT'S DIFFICULT TO SELL YOUR LAST BED TO A NEIGHBOR. More difficult still when your only child clings like a spider monkey to its frame, and screams as if you were chopping off her arms with an axe every time you try to remove her.

The four men from Alacan had already arrived, hungry, and happy to make copper from the use of their muscles, and Lizca Sharma was there as well, her skirts glittering with diamond wealth, there to supervise the four-poster's removal and make sure it wasn't damaged in the transfer.

The bed was a massive piece of furniture. For a child, ridiculous. Jiala's small limbs had no need to sprawl across such a vast expanse. But the frame had been carved with images of the floating palaces of Jhandpara. Cloud dragons of old twined up its posts to the canopy where wooden claws clutched rolled nets and, with a clever copper clasp, opened on hinges to let the nets come tumbling down during the hot times to keep out mosquitoes. A beautiful bed. A fanciful bed. Imbued with the vitality of Jhandpara's lost glory. An antique made of kestrel wood—that fine red grain so long choked under bramble— and triply valuable because of it.

We would eat for months on its sale.

But to Jiala, six years old and deeply attached, who had already watched every other piece of our household furniture disappear, it was another matter.

She had watched our servants and nannies evaporate as water droplets hiss to mist on a hot griddle. She had watched draperies tumble, seen the geometries of our carpets rolled and carried out on Alacaner backs, a train of men like linked sausages marching from our marbled halls. The bed was too much. These days, our halls echoed with only our few remaining footfalls. The porticos carried no sound of music from our pianoforte, and the last bit of warmth in the house could only be found in the sulphurous stink of my workshop, where a lone fire yet blazed.

For Jiala, the disappearance of her vast and beautiful bed was her last chance to make a stand.

"NOOOOOOOO!"

I tried to cajole her, and then to drag her. But she'd grown since her days as a babe, and desperation gave her strength. As I hauled her from the mattress, she grabbed hold of one huge post and locked her arms around it. She pressed her cheek against the cloud dragon's scales and screamed again. "NOOOOOOOO!"

We all covered our ears as she hit a new crystal-shattering octave. "NOOOOOOOO!"

"Please, Jiala," I begged. "I'll buy you a new one. As soon as we have money."

"I don't want a new one!" she screamed. "I want this one!" Tears ran down her reddening face.

I tugged at her, embarrassed under the judging gaze of Mistress Lizca and the workmen behind me. I liked Lizca. And now she saw me at my most reduced. As if the empty house wasn't enough. As if this sale of my child's last belonging was not humiliating in the extreme, I now begged a child for cooperation.

"Jiala. It's only for a little while. And it will just be down the narrows at Mistress Lizca's. You can visit if you like." I looked to Lizca, hoping desperately that she wouldn't contradict. "It will be just next door."

"I can't sleep next door! This is mine! You sold everything! We don't have anything! This is mine!" Jiala's shrieks rose to new levels, and this brought on her coughing, which alternated with her screams as I tried to pry her arms free.

"I'll buy you a new one," I said. "One fit for a princess."

But she only screamed louder.

The workmen kept their hands over their ears as the gryphon shrieks continued. I cast about, desperate for a solution to her heartbreak. Desperate to stop the coughing that she was inflicting on herself with this tantrum.

Stupid. I'd been stupid. I should have asked Pila to take her out, and then ordered the workmen to come stealthy like thieves. I cast about the room, and there on the workmen's faces, I saw something unexpected. Unlike Lizca, who stood stonily irritated, the workmen showed nothing of the sort.

No impatience.

No anger.

No superiority nor disgust.

Pity.

These refugee workmen, come across the river from Lesser Khaim, pitied me. Soiled linen shirts draped off their stooped shoulders and broken leather shoes showed cold mudcaked winter toes, and yet they pitied me.

They had lost everything fleeing their own city, their last portable belongings clanking on their backs, their hounds and children squalling and snot-nosed, tangled around their ankles. Flotsam in a river of refugees come from Alacan when their mayor and majisters accepted that the city could not be held and that they must, in fact, fall back—and quickly—if they wished to escape the bramble onslaught.

Alacan men, men who had lost everything, looked at me with pity. And it filled me with rage.

I shouted at Jiala. "Well, what should I do? Should I have you starve? Should I stop feeding you and Pila? Should we all sit in the straw and gnaw mice bones through the winter so that you can have a kestrel wood bed?"

Of course, she only screamed louder. But now it was out of fear. And yet I continued to shout, my voice increasing, overwhelming hers, an animal roar, seeking to frighten and intimidate that which I could not cajole. Using my size and power to crush something small and desperate.

"Shut up!" I screamed. "We have nothing! Do you understand? Nothing! We have no choices left!"

Jiala collapsed into sobbing misery, which turned to deeper coughing, which frightened me even more, because if the coughing continued I would have to cast a spell to keep it down. Everything I did led only to something worse.

The fight went out of Jiala. I pried her away from the bed.

Lizca motioned to the Alacaners and they began the process of disassembling the great thing.

I held Jiala close, feeling her shaking and sobbing, still loud but without a fight now. I had broken her will. An ugly solution that reduced us both into something less than what the Three Faces of Mara hoped for us. Not father and daughter. Not protector and sacred charge. Monster and victim. I clutched my child to me, hating what had been conjured between us. That I had bullied her down. That she had forced me to this point.

But hating myself most of all, for I had placed us in this position.

That was the true sickness. I had dragged us into danger and want. Our house had once been so very fine. In our glory days, when Merali was still alive, I made copper pots for rich households, designed metal and glass mirrors of exquisite inlay. Blew glass bargaining bulbs for the great mustached merchants of Diamond Street to drink from as they made their contracts. I engraved vases with the Three Faces of Mara: Woman, Man, and Child, dancing.

I etched designs of cloud dragons and floating palaces. I cast gryphons in gold and bronze and copper. I inlaid forest hunts of stags and unicorns in the towering kestrel forests of the East and sculpted representations of the three hundred and thirty-three arches of Jhandpara's glorious waterfront. I traded in the nostalgic dreams of empire's many lost wonders.

And we had been rich.

Now, instead of adornments for rich households, strange devices squatted and bubbled and clanked in my workroom, and not a single one of them for sale. Curving copper tubes twisted like kraken tentacles. Our impoverished faces reflected from the brass bells of delivery nozzles. Glass bulbs glowed blue with the ethereal stamens of the lora flower, which can only be gathered in summer twilight when ember beetles beckon them open and mate within their satin petals.

And now, all day and all night, my workroom hissed and steamed with the sulphurous residues of bramble.

Burned branches and seeds and sleep-inducing spines passed through my equipment's bowels. Instead of Jhandpara's many dreams, I worked now with its singular nightmare—the plant that had destroyed an empire and now threatened to destroy us as well. Our whole house stank day and night with the smell of burning bramble and the workings of my balanthast. That was the true cause of my daughter's pitched defense of her kestrel-wood bed.

I was the one at fault. Not the girl. I had impoverished us with every decision I had made, over fifteen years. Jiala was too young to even know what the household had looked like in its true glory days. She had arrived too late for that. Never saw its flowering rose gardens and lupine beds. Didn't remember when the halls rang with servants' laughter and activity, when Pila, Saema, and Traz all lived with us, and Niaz and Romara and—some other servant whose name even I have now forgotten—swept every corner of the place for dust and kept the mice at bay. It was my fault.

I clutched my sobbing child to my breast, because I knew she was right, and I was wrong, but still I let Mistress Lizca and her Alacan workmen break the bed apart, and carry it out, piece by piece, until we were alone in an empty and cold marble room.

I had no choice. Or, more precisely, I had stripped us of our choices. I had gone too far, and circumstances were closing upon us both.

J IALA KEPT FROM ME FOR SEVERAL DAYS AFTER I SOLD HER
bed. She went out, and disappeared for hours at a time. She was
resentful, but she spoke no more to me, and seemed willing to
let me bribe her back to forgiveness with syrup crackers from Sugar
Alley. She disappeared into the cobbled streets of Khaim, and I took
advantage of the peaceful time to work.

The sale of the bed, even if it was a fabulously rare piece of art,
even if it did come from kestrel wood which no one had been able to
harvest in more than five decades as the bramble sprawl overwhelmed
its cathedral forests, would only last so long. And after the money ran
out, I would have no more options.

I felt as if I was trapped in the famous torture room of Majister
Halizak, who liked to magic his victims into a closed cell, without
door or window, and then slowly spell the whole room down from the
size of an elephant to the size of a mouse. It was said that Halizak took
great pleasure listening to people's screams. And then, as their prison
shrank beyond their ability to bear, he would place a goblet below the
tiny stone box, to catch the juices of his dying enemies and drink to
his own long health.

But I was close.

Halizak's Prison was closing down on me. But unlike Halizak's victims, I now spied a door. A gap out of my squeezing trap. We would not go without a home. Jiala and I would not be forced across the river to Lesser Khaim to live with the refugees of bramble spread.

I would be a hero. Recognized through the ages. I was going to be a hero.

Once again, I primed my balanthast.

Pila, my last faithful servant, watched from beside the fireplace. She had gone from a smiling young girl to a grown woman who now looked at me with a cocked head and a thoughtful expression as if I was already mad. She had brought in the final bits of my refashioned device, and my workshop was a new disaster of brass nails, armatures, and iron filings. The debris of inspiration.

I smiled at Pila. "This time it will work," I said.

The reek of burned neem and mint filled the air. In the glass chamber atop the balanthast, a few sprigs of mint lay with bay and lora flower and the woody shavings of the neem.

I struck a match. Its flame gleamed. I was close. So very close. But Pila had seen other failures. . . .

Pounding on the door interrupted my preparation.

I turned, annoyed. "Go answer," I told Pila. "Tell them I am busy."

I prepared again to ignite the balanthast, but premonition stayed my hand. Instead, I listened. A moment passed. And then a shriek echoed through the halls. Anguish and loss. I dropped the match and ran for the door.

Falzi the butcher stood at the threshold, cradling Jiala in his huge arms. She dangled limp, head lolling.

"I found her in a bramble," he said. "Deep in. I had to use a hook to drag her out, it was closing on her." Pila and I both reached for her, but Falzi pulled away from us. "You don't have the clothes for it." And indeed, his own leather shirt and apron were covered in pale, thready bramble hairs. They fairly seemed to quiver with wormy malevolence.

Even a few were dangerous, and Jiala's body was furred with them.

I stared, horrified. "But what was she doing there?" Jiala knew enough of bramble from my own work to avoid its beckoning vines. "She shouldn't have been anywhere near bramble."

"Street urchins . . ." Falzi looked away, embarrassed at the implication, but plunged on. "The Mayor offers a reward for bramble seeds collected in the city. To prevent the spread. A copper for a sack. Better pay than catching rats. Some children . . . if they are hungry enough, will go to the big brambles in the fields and burn it back. Then gather the seeds when the pods explode."

"My workshop," I said. "Quickly!"

Falzi carried Jiala's small body easily. Set her on the stones by the fire. "What will you do?" he asked. "The poison's already in her."

I shook my head as I used a brush to push away the bramble threads that clung to her. Redness stained her flesh wherever they touched. Poison and sleep, coursing beneath her skin. When I'd cleared a place on her throat, I pressed my fingers to her pulse, feeling for the echo of her heart.

Slow. So very slow.

"I'm so sorry, Jeoz," Falzi said. "She is too far gone."

"I have supplies that may help," I said. "Go. Thank you. But go!"

Falzi touched his heart in farewell. Shaking his head, he left us alone.

"Close the doors, Pila." I said. "And the windows."

"But—"

"Do it! And don't come within. Lock the doors."

When I first thought that I might have a method of killing bramble, it was because I noticed how it never grew around the copper mines of Kesh. Even as Alacan fell and landholders retreated all along the line of bramble's encroach, the copper mines remained pristine.

Of course, over time it became impossible to get to the mines. Bramble surrounded that strange island of immunity and continued its long march west into Alacan. The delicate strand of road that led through the bramble forest to the copper mines became impossible to defend.

But the copper mines remained safe, long after everything else was swallowed. I noticed the phenomenon on my trips there to secure new materials for my business. Keshian copper made fine urns that were much in demand from my patrons and so I made the journey often. I remembered making my careful way down that long bramble tunnel when workers still fought to keep the road to the mines open. Remembered the workers' faces sooty and sweaty with the constant chopping and burning, their leather bladder sacks with brass-nozzled burners always alight and smoking as they spread flaming paste upon the poisonous plants.

And then the copper mines, opening before me. The deep holes and scrapings of mine work, but also grasslands and trees—the huge bramble growing all around its perimeter, but none inside. An oasis.

A few majisters and scholars also noticed the Keshian copper mines' unique qualities, but by the time anyone sought the cause of the place's survival, the bramble was coming strong, and soon no one could hack their way back to that isolated place of mining tools and tailings ponds for more investigation.

Of course, people experimented.

A few people thought to beat copper into our roads, or created copper knives to cut through the bramble, thinking that the metal was bramble's bane. And certainly some people even started to call it that. Copper charms sold well for a brief time. I admit that I even trafficked in such baubles, casting amulets and beating fine urns to ward off its encroach. But soon enough, people discovered that copper gave root to bramble as easily as a farmer's tilled field and the mortar of Alacan's massive city walls. Granite was better at warding off the plant, but even that gave root eventually.

Even so, the Keshian copper mines remained in my mind, much as they likely remained in the deep bramble forest, a dream of survival, if only we could puzzle it out. And so now, from memory, I sought to reconstruct the conditions of Kesh in the environs of my workshop, experimenting with the natural interactions of flora and ore, seeking that singular formula that had stalled bramble in its march.

The door closed behind Pila. I felt again for Jiala's pulse. It was nearly gone. The drug of bramble has been used by assassins and thwarted lovers. Its poison produces an overwhelming sleep that succumbs to deeper darkness. It squeezes the heart and slows it until blood flows like cold syrup, and then stops entirely, frozen, preserving a body, sometimes for years, until rats and mice and flies burrow deep and tear the body apart from within.

And now bramble's poisonous threads covered Jiala's skin. I took a copper rod and ran it over her arms. Then touched mint to her flesh. With a pair of brass pincers, I began plucking the threads from her skin. Setting them in a pottery bowl beside me so that I wouldn't carelessly touch them myself. Working as quickly as I could. Knowing that I couldn't work fast enough. There were dozens of them, dozens and dozens. More coated her clothing but they didn't matter. Her skin was covered. Too many, and yet still I plucked.

Jiala's eyelids fluttered. She gazed up from under heavy lashes, dark eyes thick with bramble's influence.

"Do I have enough?" she murmured.

"Enough what, child?" I continued plucking threads from her skin.

"Enough . . . seeds . . . to buy back my bed."

I tried to answer, but no words came. My heart felt as if it was squeezed by Halizak's Prison, running out liquid and dead.

Jiala's eyes closed, falling into the eternal sleep. I frantically felt after her heart's echo. A slow thud against my fingertip, sugar syrup running colder. Another thud. Thicker. Colder. The sluggish call of her heart. A longer pause, then . . .

Nothing.

I stumbled away from my dying girl, sick with my failures.

My balanthast lay before me, all its parts bubbling and prepared. In desperation, I seized it and dragged it over to Jiala. I aimed its great brass bell at her inert form. Tears blurred my vision. I swept up a match, and then . . . paused.

I don't know why it came to me. It's said that the Three Faces of Mara come to us and whisper wisdom to us in our hour of need. That inspiration comes from true desperation and that the mysteries of the world can be so revealed. Certainly, Mara is the seed of life and hope.

I knelt beside Jiala and plucked a strand of hair from her head, a binding, a wish, a . . . I did not know, but suddenly I was desperate to have something of hers within the workings of the balanthast, and the bramble, too. All with the neem and mint . . . I placed her hair in the combustion chamber and struck the match. Flame rose into the combustion chamber, burning neem and mint and bramble and Jiala's black hair, smoking, blazing, now one in their burn. I prayed to Mara's Three Faces for some mercy, and then twisted the balanthast's dial. The balanthast sucked the burning embers of her hair and the writhing threads of bramble and all the other ingredients into its belly chamber.

For a moment, nothing happened. Then blue flame exploded from the bell, enveloping Jiala.

Wake up, Papa.
Wake up.
Wake.
Up.

Dim echoing words, pokes and proddings.

Wake up, Papa.
Papa?
Papa, Papa, Papapapapapa.

I opened my eyes.

Jiala knelt over me, a haziness of black hair and skinny brown limbs and blue skirts. Blurred and ethereal. Limned in an uncertain focus as light bound around her. A spirit creature from within the Hall of Judgment. Waiting for Borzai the Judge to gather her into his six arms, peer into her soul, and then pass her on to the Hall of Children, where innocents live under the protective gaze of dog-headed Kemaz.

I tried to sit up, couldn't. Lay back. The spirit creature remained, tugging at me. The workshop was a shambles, all of it blurry and unsteady, as if it lay on the plane of clouds.

All of us dead, then.

"Papa?"

I turned to her echoing voice. Stared at her. Stared again at the ravaged workroom. Something cold and sharp was pressing against my back. Not spiritlike at all.

Slowly, I dragged myself upright, leaning against the stone wall. I was lying far across the room from the fireplace. The balanthast lay beside me, its glass chambers shattered, its vacuum bulbs nothing but jagged teeth in their soldered sockets. Bent copper tubes gleamed all around me, like flower petals scattered to Mara during the planting march.

"Are you all right, Papa?" Jiala stared at me with great concern. "Your head is bloody."

I reached up and touched her small worried face. Warm. Alive. Not a spirit creature.

Whole and alive, her skin smoking with the yellow residue of bramble's ignition. Blackened threads of bramble ash covered her, her hair half melted, writhing with bramble thread's death throes still. Singed and scalded and blistery but whole and miraculously alive.

I ran my hand down her scorched cheek, wonder-struck.

"Papa?"

"I'm all right, Jiala." I started to laugh. "More than all right."

I clutched her to me and sobbed. Thanking Mara for my daughter's salvation. Grateful for this suspended execution of my soul.

And beyond it, another thought, a wider hope. That bramble, for the first time in all my experiments, had truly died, leaving not even its last residue of poison behind.

Fifteen years is not too long to seek a means to save the world.

O F COURSE, NOTHING IS AS SIMPLE AS WE WOULD WISH.
After that first wild success, I succeeded in producing
a spectacular string of failures that culminated in nearly
exploding the house. More worrying to me, even though Jiala survived
her encounter with the bramble, her cough was much worsened by
it. The winter damp spurred it on, and now she hacked and coughed
daily, her small lungs seemingly intent on closing down upon her.

She was too young to know how bad the cough had been before—
how much it had greatly concerned me. But after the bramble, blood
began staining her lips, the rouge of her lungs brought forth by the
evils that bramble had worked upon her body as it sought to drive her
down into permanent sleep.

I avoided using magic for as long as possible, but Jiala's cough worsened, digging deeper into her lungs. And it was only a small magic.
Just enough spelling to keep her alive. To close the rents in her little
lungs, and stop the blood from spackling her lips. Perhaps a sprig of
bramble would sprout in some farmer's field as a result, fertilized by
the power released into the air, but really it was such a small magic,
and Jiala's need was too great to ignore.

The chill of winter was always the worst. Khaim isn't like the northern lands, where freezes kill every living plant except bramble and lay snow over the ground in cold drifts and wind-sculpted ice. But still, the cold ate at her. And so, I took a little time away from my alchemy and the perfecting of the balanthast to work something within her.

Our secret.

Even Pila didn't know. No one could be allowed to know but us.

Jiala and I sat in the corner of my workshop, the only warm room I had left, amidst the blankets where she now slept near the fire, and I used the scribbled notes from the book of Majister Arun to make magic.

His pen was clear, even if he was long gone to the executioner's axe. His ideas on vellum. His hand reaching across time. His past carrying into our future through the wonders of ink. Rosemary and pkana flower and licorice root, and the deep soothing cream of goat's milk. Powdered together, the yellow pkana flower's petals all crackling like fire as they touched the milk. Sending up a smoke of dreams.

And then with my ring finger, long missing all three gold rings of marriage, I touched the paste to Jiala's forehead, between the thick dark hairs of her eyebrows. And then, pulling down her blouse, another at her sternum, at the center of her lungs. The pkana's yellow mark pulsed on her skin, seeming wont to ignite.

As we worked this little magic, I imagined the great majisters of Jhandpara healing crowds from their arched balconies. It was said that people came for miles to be healed. They used the stuff of magic wildly, then.

"Papa, you mustn't," Jiala whispered. Another cough caught her, jerking her forward and reaching deep, squeezing her lungs as the strongman squeezes a pomegranate to watch red blood run between his fingers.

"Of course I must," I answered. "Now be quiet."

"They will catch you, though. The smell of it—"

"Shhhh."

And then I read the ancient words of Majister Arun, sounding out the language that could never be recalled after it was spoken. Consonants burned my tongue as it tapped those words of power. The power of ancients. The dream of Jhandpara.

The sulphur smell of magic filled the room, and now round vowels of healing tumbled from my lips, spinning like pin wheels, finding their targets in the yellow paste of my fingerprints.

The magic burrowed into Jiala, and then it was gone. The pkana flower paste took on a greenish tinge as it was used up, and the room filled completely with the smoke of power unleashed. Astonishing power, all around, and only a little effort and a few words to bind it to us. Magic. The power to do anything. Destroy an empire, even.

I cracked open the shutters, and peered out onto the black cobbled streets. No one was outside, and I fanned the room quickly, clearing the stench of magic.

"Papa. What if they catch you?"

"They won't." I smiled. "This is a small magic. Not some great bridge-building project. Not even a spell of fertility. Your lungs hold small wounds. No one will ever know. And I will perfect the balanthast soon. And then no one will ever have to hold back with these small magics ever again. All will be well."

"They say that the executioner sometimes swings wild, doesn't chop a man in half with kindness. But makes him flop instead. That the Mayor pays him extra to make an example of the people who use magic."

"It's not true."

"I saw one."

"No, you didn't."

"It was last week. At the gold market. Right in the square. I was with Pila. And the crowd was so thick we couldn't leave. And Pila covered my eyes, but I could see through her fingers. And the executioner chopped and chopped and chopped and chopped and the man yelled so loud and then he stopped. Not a clean killing at all, the pig lady said. She said she's kinder to her swine."

I made myself smile. "Well, that's not our problem. Everyone does a little magic. No one will mind us. As long as we don't rub anyone's nose in it."

"I wouldn't want to see you chopped and chopped and chopped."

"Then make sure you drink Pila's licorice tea and stay out of the cold. It's a hard thing to keep secrets. But secrets are best when there are only two to know." I touched her forehead. "You and I."

I pulled my mustaches. "Tug for luck?"

But she wouldn't. And she wasn't consoled.

A month later, as the muddy rags of cruel spring snow turned to the sweet stink of wet warming earth, I made the last adjustments to the balanthast and set it loose on the bramble wall.

We left the city deep in the night, making our way east over muddy roads, the balanthast bundled on my back. Jiala, Pila, and I. With the embrace of darkness, the women of the bramble crews with their fire and hatchets were gone, and the children who gathered seeds behind them in careful lines had given up. There would be no witnesses to our experiment. The night was chill and uncomfortable. We held our torches high.

It took only two hours to reach the bramble wall, much to my surprise.

"It's moved," I muttered.

Pila nodded. "The women who sell potatoes say they've lost more fields. Some of them before they had a chance to dig up the last of their crop."

The bramble loomed above us, many tangled layers, the leading edge of an impenetrable forest that stretched all the way to fabled Jhandpara. In the light of the torches, the bramble threw off strange hungry shadows, seeming eager to tug us into its sleep-inducing embrace. I thrust my torch amongst its serpent vines. Tendrils crackled and curled in the heat, and a few seed pods, fat as milkweed, burst open, spilling new seeds onto the ground.

Tender green growths showed all along the edge where the bramble crews had been burning and pruning, but deep within, the bramble had turned woody, impenetrable, and thick. Sharp blood-letting thorns glinted in the torchlight, but more troublesome were the pale fine hairs shimmering everywhere, coating every vine's length, the venomous fibers that Jiala had so nearly succumbed to.

I took a breath, unnerved despite myself in the presence of our implacable enemy.

"Well," Pila said. "You wanted to show us."

My faith faltered. Small experiments in the workshop were one thing. But out in the open? Before my daughter and Pila? I cursed myself for my pride. I should have come to test the balanthast in private. Not like this where all my failures could be mocked or pitied.

"Well?" Pila said.

"Yes," I said. "Yes. We'll get started."

But still I delayed.

Pila gave me a look of disgust and started setting out the kestrel-wood tripod. She had grown insolent over the years, as her salary had been reduced and her responsibilities increased. Not at all the young shy girl she had been when she first came to the house. She now carried too much authority, and too much of a skeptical eye. Sometimes I suspected that I would have given up long ago on my experimentations, if not for Pila watching me with her silent judgments. It's easy to fail yourself, but failing before another, one who has watched you wager so much and so mightily on an uncertain future—well, that is too much shame to bear.

"Right," I murmured. "Of course."

I unbound the balanthast from my back. Set it upon the kestrel wood to brace it. Since my first wild success, I had managed to dampen much of the balanthast's explosive reaction, venting it from rows of newly designed chimneys that puffed like a cloud dragon's nostrils.

The balanthast now held fast and didn't topple, and didn't blow one across the room to leave a body lying bruised and dazed. I crouched and made sure that the tripod was well set in the muddy earth.

To be honest, the tripod could have been made of anything, certainly something less extravagant. But kestrel wood I loved. So hard and strong that even fire couldn't take it. The northmen of Czandia used to forge swords of kestrel wood. Lighter than steel. Just as strong. The tripod seemed to say to me that we still had a future, that we might once again stand strong, and grow the wonders of old.

Or, if you were Pila, you called it the expensive affectation of a foolish man, even as she helped me fashion its sturdy base.

I straightened and unlimbered the rest of the balanthast's components. Pila and Jiala helped me assemble its many pieces.

"No," I whispered, and then realized that I was doing so and cleared my throat. "Jiala, put the vacuum chamber so that it faces forward, toward the mouth. And please be careful. I don't have enough fire to blow another."

"I'm always careful, Papa."

At last we were ready, the brass belly chamber and curling copper tubes and glass bulbs gleamed in the silver of the moon, a strange and unearthly thing.

"It looks like something that would have come out of Jhandpara," Pila said. "So much fine artistry, put into this one object."

I primed the combustion bulb of the balanthast. Neem and bay, and mint and twilight lora flower and a bramble clipping. By torchlight, we dug into the earth, seeking the root bundle. There were many. With leather-gloved hands, I scooped out a bit of earth, bramble's vessel. Mara's fertile womb. The necessary ingredient that would contain the alchemical reaction and channel it into the deeply embedded bramble, much as Jiala's hair had bound the reaction deep into her body. Saltpeter and sulphur and charcoal to drive the concoction home, poured into the belly chamber. I slid closed the combustion bulb, twisted the brass latches tight.

With a target now chosen, I thrust the balanthast's three newly constructed nozzles into the earth beside it. Jiala covered her mouth with a tiny hand as I lit the match. I almost smiled. I set the match under the combustion bulb, and the assembled ingredients caught fire. It glowed like a firefly in its glassine chamber. Slowly the flame died. We watched. Breaths held.

And then, as if the Three Faces of Mara had inhaled all at once, the entire careful wad disappeared, sucked into the belly chamber. The primed balanthast quivered with power, elements coming together.

The reaction was so sudden that we had no chance to brace. The very earth tossed us from our feet. Yellow acrid smoke billowed over us. A desperate animal shriek filled the air, as if the swine women were amongst the pigs in a sty, wounding and bleeding a great herd and not killing a single one. We gained our feet and ran, coughing and tearing, stumbling over muddy furrows. Jiala was worst taken. Her cough ripped deep into her lungs, making me fear I'd need to use the healing magic on her again before the night was over.

Slowly the smoke dispersed, revealing our work. The balanthast quivered on its tripod, steady still where it had been jammed into the earth, but now, all around it, there was a seething mass of bramble tendrils, all writhing and smoking. The vines hissed and burned, flakes of ash falling like scales from a dragon. Another shudder ran through the earth as deep roots writhed and ripped upward—and then, all at once, the vines collapsed, falling all to soot, leaving clear earth behind.

We approached cautiously. The balanthast had not only killed the root I had chosen, but destroyed horse-lengths of bramble in every direction. It would have taken workers hours to clear so much. I held up my torch, staring. Even at the perimeter of the balanthast's destruction, the bramble growth hung limp like rags. I stepped forward, cautious. Struck a damaged plant with a gloved hand. Its vines sizzled with escaping sap, and collapsed.

I swung about, staring at the ground. "Do you see any seeds?"

We swept our torches over the earth, straining to make out any of the pods that should have sprung out and burst open in the blaze of fire's heat.

Jiala squatted in the hot smoking earth, turning it over and running it through her little gloved fingers.

"Well? Is there anything?"

Jiala looked up, amazed. "No, Papa."

"Pila?" I whispered. "Do you see any?"

"No." Astonishment marked her voice. "There are none. Not a single one."

Together, we continued our hunt. Nothing. Not a single seed disbursed from a single pod. The bramble vine had died, and left nothing of itself behind to torment us another day.

"It's magic," Pila whispered. "True magic."

I laughed at that. "Better than magic. Alchemy!"

THE NEXT MORNING, DESPITE THE PREVIOUS LATE NIGHT, we all woke with the first crowing of roosters. I laughed to find Pila and Jiala already clustered in the workroom, peering out through the shutters, waiting for enough sunlight to see the final result.

As soon as the sun cracked the horizon, we were out in the fields again, headed across the muddy furrows to the bramble wall. The first of the bramble crews were already at work, with axes and long chopping knives, wearing leather aprons to protect themselves from the sleeping spines. Smoke from bramble's burn rose into the air, coiling snakes, black and oily. Dirty children walked in careful lines through the fields with shovels and hoes, uprooting new incursions. In the dawn light, with the levee labor all at the wall, it looked like the scene of some recent battle. The smoke, the hopeless faces. But as we approached the site of my balanthast firing; a small knot of workers huddled.

We slipped close.

"Have you come to see it?" they asked.

"See what?" Pila asked.

"There's a hole in the bramble." A woman pointed. "Look how deep it goes."

Several children squatted in the earth. One of them looked up. "It's clean, Mama. No seeds at all. It's like the bramble never came at all."

I could barely restrain my glee. Pila had to drag me away to keep me from blurting out my part. We rushed back to Khaim, laughing and skipping the whole way.

Back in our home, Pila and Jiala brought out my best clothes. Pila helped me work the double buttons of my finest vest, pursing her lips at the sight of how skinny I had become since I last wore the thing in my wealth and health.

I laughed at her concern.

"Soon I'll be fat again, and you'll have your own servants and we'll be rich and the city will saved."

Pila smiled. Her face had lost its worry for the first time in years. She looked young again, and I was struck with the memory of how fine she had been in youth, and how now, despite worry and years, she still stood, unbent and unbroken by the many responsibilities she had taken on. She had stuck with our household, even as our means had faltered, even as other, richer families offered a better, more comfortable life.

"It's very good that you are not mad, after all," Pila said.

I laughed. "You're very sure I'm not mad?"

She shrugged. "Well, not about bramble, at least."

The way to the Mayor's House passes around Malvia Hill, through the clay market and then down along the river Sulong, which splits Khaim from Lesser Khaim. Along the river, the spice market runs into the potato market, runs into the copper market. Powdered spices choke the air, along with the calls of vendors with their long black mustaches that they oil and stretch with every child. Their hands are red with chilies and yellow with turmeric, and their lungs give off the scents of clove and oregano. They sit under their archways along the river, with their big hemp bags overflowing with their wares out front, and the doorways to their storehouses behind, where piled spices reach two stories high. And then it's on to the women of the potato market, where they used to sell only potatoes, but now sell any number of tubers. And then the copper families, who can beat out a pot or a tube, and who fashion brass candlesticks for the rich and cooking pots for the poor.

When I was young, there was only Khaim. At that time, there was still a bit of the old empire left. The astonishing wonders of the East and the capital of Jhandpara were gone, but still, there was Alacan and Turis and Mimastiva. At that time, Khaim was a lesser seat, valued for its place on the river, but still, a far reach from Jhandpara where great majisters had once wielded their power and wore triple diamonds on their sleeves. But with the slow encroachment of the bramble, Khaim grew. And, across from it, Lesser Khaim grew even faster.

When I was a child I could look across the river and see nothing but lemon trees and casro bushes, heavy with their dense fruit. Now refugees squatted and built mud huts there. Alacaners, who had destroyed their own homes and now insisted on destroying Khaim as well. Turis, of course, is nothing but ash. But that wasn't their fault. Raiders from Paika razed Turis, but Alacaners had only themselves to blame.

Jiala hurried along the river with me, her hand in mine. Small. So small. But now with a future. Not just a chance at life and wealth, but a chance that she would not run like the Alacaners from her home as bramble swallowed her childhood and history.

Out on the Sulong, tiny boats made their way back and forth across the water, carrying workers from Lesser Khaim into the main city. But now something else marred the vista.

A great bridge hung in the air, partially constructed. It floated there, held down by ropes so that it would not fly free. Magic. Astonishing and powerful magic coming into play. The work of Majister Scacz, the one man in the city who wielded magic with the sanction of the Mayor, and so would never fear the executioner's axe.

I paused, staring across the water to the floating bridge. Magic such as had not been seen since Jhandpara fell. Seeing it there, rising, filled me with a superstitious dread. So much magic in one place. Even the balanthast couldn't protect against that much magic.

A spice man called out to me. "You want to buy? Or are you going to block my trade?"

I tipped my velvet hat to him. "So sorry, merchantman. I was looking at the bridge."

The man spat. Eyed the floating construction. "Lot of magic, there." He spat again. Tobacco and kehm root together. Narcotic. "I hear they're already chopping bramble on the far bank. Hardly any bramble on the west side at all, and now it's growing in the wagon ruts. Next thing, we'll be like Alacan. Swallowed by bramble because our jolly wants to connect here with there. Bad enough that all these new Alacaners use their small magics. Now we have big magic too. Scacz and the Mayor pretending Khaim should be another Jhandpara with majisters and diamonds and floating castles."

"The Mayor says he wants to protect Lesser Khaim from the raiders who come from Paika."

"They're a nuisance, not a reason to build a bridge." The spice man spat more kehm root and tobacco, and eyed the bridge again. "Executioner will be busy now. Sure as bramble creep, we'll have new heads spiked on city gates. Too much big magic to let the little magics run wild."

"Maybe not," I started, but Jiala pinched my hand and I fell silent.

The spice man eyed me as if I was mad. "I had to burn an entire sack of cloves, today. Whole sack I couldn't sell. Full of bramble seeds and sprout. Someone makes his little magic, ruins my business."

I wanted to tell him that the bundle on my back would change the balance, but Jiala, at least, had sense, and so I kept my words to myself. Magic brings bramble. A project like the bridge had an inevitable cost.

I hefted my bag of implements and we carried on, around the edge of the hill and then up its face to where the Mayor's House looked down over Khaim.

We were ushered into the Mayor's gallery without fuss. Marble floors and arches stretched around us. My clothes felt poor, Jiala's as well. Even our best was now old and worn.

In the sudden cool of the gallery, her cough started. A dry hacking thing that threatened to build. I knelt and gave her a sip of water. "Are you well?"

"Yes, Papa." She watched me, solemn and trusting. "I won't cough." And then immediately her dry cough started again. It echoed about, announcing our presence to all the other petitioners.

We sat in the gallery, waiting with the women who wanted to change their household tax and the men who were petitioning to escape levee labor at the bramble wall. After an hour, the Mayor's secretary came to us, his medallion of office gleaming gold on his chest, the Axe of the Executioner crossed over the Staff of the Majister, the twin powers that the Mayor wielded for the benefit of the city. The secretary led us across another marble gallery, and thence into the Mayor's offices, and the door was shut behind us.

The Mayor wore red velvet and his own much larger medallion on a chain of gold around his neck. His fingers touched the medallion every so often, a needy gesture. And with him, the Majister Scacz. My skin prickled at the sight of one who used magic as a daily habit, passing the consequences of his activities onto the bramble crews and the children of the city who dug and burned the minor bits of bramble from between mortar stones and cobbles.

"Yes?" the Mayor asked. "You're who, then?"

"Jeoz, the alchemist," the secretary announced.

"And he reeks of magic," Majister Scacz murmured.

I made myself smile. "It is my device."

The Mayor's eyebrows rose, fuzzy gray caterpillars arching over his ruddy face. His mustache was short, no child in his history at all. An old scar puckered one side of his cheek, pulling his mouth into a slight smile. "You practice magic?" he asked sharply. "Are you mad?"

I made a placating gesture. "I do not practice, Excellency. No. Not at all." A nervous laugh escaped my lips. "I practice alchemy. It does not bring bramble. I have no dealings with the curse of Jhandpara." It was unbelievable how nervous I had become. "No need for the executioner, here. None at all." I untied my bag and began pulling out the pieces of the balanthast. "You see . . ." I screwed one of the copper ends into its main chamber. Unwrapped the combustion bulb, breathing a sigh of relief that it had survived the trip. "You see," I repeated myself, "I have created something, which your Excellency will appreciate. I think."

Beside me, Jiala coughed. Whether from sickness, or nervousness, I couldn't say. Scacz's eyes went to her. Held. I didn't like the way he stared at her, his expression thoughtful. I plunged on.

"It is a balanthast."

The Mayor examined the device. "It looks more like an arquebus."

I made myself smile. "Not at all. Though it does use the reactants of fire. But my device has properties most extraordinary." My hands were shaking. I found the mint. The neem bark. Lora flower. Set them in the chamber.

Scacz was watching closely. "Am I watching sorcery, sir? Right before myself? Unsanctioned?"

"N-no." I shook under his examination. Tried to load the balanthast.

Jiala took it away. "Here, Papa."

"Y-yes. Good. Thank you, child." I took a deep breath. "You see, a balanthast destroys bramble. And not just a little. The balanthast reaches for a bramble's root and poisons it utterly. Place it within a yard or two of a heart root, and it will destroy more than a bramble crew can destroy in half a day."

The Mayor leaned close. "You have proof of this?"

"Yes. Of course. I'm sorry." I pulled a small clay pot shrouded in burlap out of my bag and put on my leather gloves before unwrapping it.

"Bramble," I explained.

They both sucked in their breath at the sight of the potted plant. I looked up at their consternation. "We use gloves."

"You carry bramble into the city?" the Mayor asked. "Deliberately?"

I hesitated. Finally I said, "It was necessary. For the testing. The science of alchemy requires much trial and error." Their faces were heavy with disapproval. I lit my match, and touched it to the glass bulb. Clamped it closed.

"Hold your breath, Jiala." I looked apologetically at the Mayor. "The smoke is quite acrid."

The Mayor and Majister also sucked in their breaths. The balanthast shivered as its energy discharged. A ripple of death passed into the soil. The pot cracked as the bramble writhed and died.

"Magic!" Scacz cried, lunging forward. "What magic is this?"

"No, Majister! Alchemy. Magic has never been able to affect bramble. It does not sap bramble's poison, nor kill its seeds, nor burn back its branches. This is something new."

Scacz grabbed for the balanthast. "I must see this."

"It's not magic." I yanked the balanthast back, afraid that in his hurry he would destroy it. "It uses the natural properties of the neem," I said. "A special species, loved by majisters, yes, but this is merely the application of nature's principles. We vaporize the neem with a few other ingredients, force it through the tube, and with the aid of sulphur and saltpeter and charcoal, we send its essence into the earth. Even a small application does wonders. The neem essence binds with the root of the bramble. Kills it, as you see. Attracted like a fly to honey."

"And what causes neem to seek bramble?"

I shrugged. "It's difficult to say. Perhaps some magical residue or aura from the plant. I tried thousands of substances before the neem. Only the neem bark works so well."

"The neem is attracted to magic, you think?"

"Well," I hedged. "It is certainly attracted to bramble. Oil and water never mix. Neem and bramble seem the opposite. What causes the affinity . . ." I could feel myself starting to sweat under their combined gazes, not liking how Scacz was obsessed with magic. "I hesitate to say that it's magic the neem essence finds so attractive. . . ."

"You talk all around the root of the issue," Scacz said. "Worse than a priest of Assim."

"F-forgive me," I stammered. "I don't want you to think that I've been unwary in my investigations."

"He's worried we're about to send him off to the executioner," the Mayor said.

I gave the man a sickly smile. "Quite. Bramble is unique. It has qualities that we may think of as magical—its astonishing growth, its resilience, the way that magic seems to fertilize its flourishing—but who can say what unique aspect causes the neem's essence to bind with it? These questions are beyond me. I experiment, I record my results, and I experiment again.

"The alchemical response to neem is bramble death. What causes that reaction, whether it is some magical residue that leeches from the bramble root and somehow makes it vulnerable to neem, or some other quality, I can't say. But it works. And works well. There is a plot of earth that I myself have cleared into the bramble wall. In the time it takes you to clap your hands three times, I cleared more land than this office occupies."

The Mayor and Majister both straightened at the news.

"So quickly?" the Mayor asked.

I nodded vigorously. "Even today, it still shows no sign of regrowth. No seeds, you understand? Not a single one. With my device, you can arm the people and take back farmland. Push back the bramble wall. Save Khaim."

"Extraordinary," Scacz said. "Not just push the bramble back. Perhaps even reclaim the heart of the empire. Return to Jhandpara."

"Exactly." I couldn't help feeling relief as their expressions lost their skepticism.

The Mayor had begun to smile widely. He stood. "By the Three Faces of Mara, man, you've done something special!"

He motioned for Jiala and me. "Come! The two of you must have a glass of wine. This discovery is worth celebrating."

He laughed and joked with us as he guided us to a room with great windows that looked out over the city. Khaim jumbled down the hill below us. On the horizon, the sun was slowly sinking. Red sunlight filtered through the smoke and cookfires of Lesser Khaim. The half-constructed floating bridge arched across the river like a leaping cat, held in place by great hemp ropes to keep it from sailing away as they worked to extend its skeleton.

"This couldn't come at a better time," the Mayor said. "Look out there, Alchemist. Lesser Khaim grows every day. And not just from the refugees of Turis and Alacan. Others, too, small holders who have been overwhelmed by the bramble. And they bring their magics with them.

"Before they came, we were nearly in balance. We could still cut back enough bramble to offset the bits of magic use. Even the bridge would have been acceptable. But the Alacaners are profligate with their magic, and now the bramble comes hard upon us. Their habits are crushing us. Everyone has some little magic that he or she believes is justified. And then when a bit of bramble roots in a neighbor's roof beams, who can say who caused it?"

He turned to me. "You know they call me the Jolly Mayor over there? Make fun of me for my scar and my poor humor." He scowled. "Of course I'm in a poor humor. We fight bramble every day, and every day it defeats us. If this keeps on, we'll be run out of here in three sixes of years."

I startled at his words. "Surely it's not that bad."

The Mayor raised his caterpillar brows. "Oh yes." He nodded at Jiala. "Your girl will be part of a river of refugees twice the size of the one we took in from Alacan." He turned again to look west. "And where will they go then? Mpais? Loz? Turis is gone to raiders." He scowled. "Lesser Khaim is just as vulnerable. We barely fought off the raiders' last attack. Without the bridge, I cannot have a hope of defending that side of the river. And so we spend magic where we would prefer not to, and add to the problem. We're caught in Halizak's Prison, for certain."

His steward arrived with wine and goblets. I looked at the

stemmed glasses with curiosity, wondering if I myself had long ago blown their shapes, but then recognized the distinctive mark of Saara Solso. She had improved since I used to compete with her. Another reminder of how long I had been at my project.

The steward paused on the verge of uncorking the wine bottle. "Are you certain about this, Excellency?" he asked.

The Mayor laughed and pointed at me. "This man comes to us with salvation, and you worry about an old vintage?"

The steward looked doubtful, but he uncorked the bottle anyway. A joyful scent filled the room. The Mayor looked at me, eyes twinkling. "You recognize it?" he asked. "The happy bouquet of history."

I was drawn to the scent, like a child to syrup crackers. Astonished and intoxicated, wide-eyed. "What is it?"

"Wine from the hillsides of Mount Sena, the summer vineyards of the old empire," Majister Scacz said. "A rare thing, now that those hillsides are covered with bramble. Perhaps a score of bottles still exist, of which our Jolly Mayor possesses, now, two."

"Don't call me that."

Scacz bowed. "The name suits you today, Excellency."

The Mayor smiled. "For once."

The steward poured the wine into the glass bulbs.

"Currant and cinnamon and joy." Majister Scacz was watching me. "You're about to taste one of the finest pleasures of the empire. Served at spring planting, for harvest and for flowering-age ceremonies. The richest merchants had fountains of it in their floating castles, if you can credit such a thing. Magic, make no mistake. The vintner's genius bound with the majister's craft."

He caught Jiala watching, her eyes shining at the scent. "Come, girl. Taste our lost history." He poured a splash into a glass. "Not too much. You're too small to do more than taste, but I promise you, you will not forget this thing."

The Mayor held up his glass, ruby and black in the setting sun. "A toast, then, gentlemen. To our future, refound."

We drank, and the blood of the old empire coursed through our veins and made us giddy. We examined my instrument again, with the Majister and the Mayor making exclamations at the workmanship, at my methods for joining glass to copper, of metallurgy that had yielded a combustion chamber that would not crack with the power of the flames released. We talked of the difficulties of making more balanthasts and speculated how many miles we might clear of the surrounding countryside.

"It takes a great deal of trouble to make one," Scacz observed.

"Oh yes," I said fondly, patting the venting tubes that ran along its outer surface and collected the gases of the burning neem.

"How many do you think you can make?"

"At first?" I shrugged. "Perhaps it will take me a month to make another." The Mayor and Scacz both showed their consternation, and I rushed on. "But I can train other metal workers, other glass-blowers. I need not do every piece of work. With others working to my specifications. With a larger workshop, many more could be made."

"We could train the crafters who make the new arquebus," Scacz said. "Their work is obviously pointless. A weapon that can only be fired once and is so fussy. But this?"

The Mayor was nodding. "You're right. This is worth our effort. Those silly weapons are nothing to this."

Scacz took another sip of his wine, running his hand over the balanthast. A slow caress. "The potential here . . . is astonishing." He looked up at me, inquiring. "I think I would like to test it for a little while. See what it does."

"Majister?"

Scacz patted me on the back. "Don't worry. We'll be very careful with it. But I must examine it awhile. Ensure that it truly uses no magic that will come back to haunt us." He looked at me significantly. "Too many solutions to bramble have simply sought to use magic in some glancing way. To build a fire, for example, and then when the bramble is burned, it turns out that so much magic was used in the making of the fire that the bramble returns twice as strong."

"But the balanthast doesn't use magic," I protested.

Scacz looked at me. "You are a majister to know this, then? In some cases, a man will think he is not using magical principles, because he is ignorant. You yourself acknowledge that something unique is afoot with this device." He picked up the balanthast. "It's just for a little while, Alchemist. Just to be sure."

The Mayor was watching me closely. "Don't worry, Alchemist. We will not slight your due reward. But for us, the stakes are very high. If we invest our office in something which brings the doom of Takaz instead of the salvation of Mara . . . I'm sure you understand."

I wracked my mind, trying to find a reason to deny them, but my voice failed me, and at that moment, Jiala started to cough again. I glanced over at her, worried. It had the deep sound of cutting knives.

"Go on," he said. "See to your daughter's health. She is obviously tired. We will send for you quite soon."

Jiala's coughing worsened. The two most powerful men in the city looked down at her. "Poor thing," the Mayor murmured. "She seems to have the wasting cough."

I rushed to contradict. "No. It's something else. The cold is all. It starts the cough and makes it difficult to stop."

Scacz carried the balanthast away. "Go then. Take your daughter home and warm her. We will send for you, soon."

All the way home, Jiala coughed. Deep wracking seizures that folded her small body in half. By the time we arrived at our doorstep, her coughing was incessant. Pila took one look at Jiala and glared at me with astonished anger.

"The poor girl's exhausted. What took you so long?"

I shook my head. "They liked the device. And then they wanted to talk. And then to toast. And then to talk some more."

"And you couldn't bring the poor girl back?"

"What was I supposed to do?" I asked. "'Thank you so much, Mayor and Majister. I must leave, and no, the lost wines of Jhandpara are of no interest to me. Name a price and I will sell you the plans for my balanthast, good day?'"

Jiala's coughing worsened. Pila shot me a dark look and ushered her down the hall. "Come into the workshop, child. I've already lit the fire."

I watched the two of them go, feeling helpless and frustrated. What should have been a triumph had become something else. I didn't like the way Scacz behaved at the end. Everything he said had been perfectly reasonable, and yet his manner somehow disturbed me. And the way the Mayor spoke. All his words were correct. More than correct. And yet they filled me with unease.

I made my way up the stairs to my rooms, empty now except for piles of blankets and a chest of my clothes.

Was I turning paranoid? Into some sort of madman who looked beneath everyone's meaning to some darker intention? I had known a woman, once, when I was younger, who had gone mad like that. A glassblower who made wondrous jewel pendants that glittered with their own inner fire, seeming to burn from within. A genius with light. And yet there was something in her head that made her suspicious. She had suspected her husband, and then her children of plotting against her, and had finally thrown herself in the river, escaping demons from the Three Hundred Thirty-Three Halls that only she could see.

Was I now filled with the same suspicions? Was I going down her path?

The Mayor and Majister had both spoken with fair words. I unbuttoned my vest, astounded at how threadbare it had become. The red and blue stitching was old and out of mode. How broken it was. As was everything except the balanthast. It, at least, had gleamed. I had put so much hope into this idea, had spent so many years . . .

A knock sounded on my door.

"Yes?"

Pila leaned in. "It's Jiala. Her coughing won't stop. She needs you."

"Yes. Of course. I'll come soon."

Pila hesitated. "Now, I think. It's very bad. There is blood. If you don't use your spells soon, she will be broken."

I stopped in the act of fixing my buttons. A thrill of fear coursed through me. "You know?"

Pila gave me a tight smile. "I've lived with you too long not to guess." She motioned me out. "Don't worry about your fancy clothes. Your daughter doesn't care how you dress."

She hurried me down the stairs and into the workroom. We found Jiala beside the fire, curled on the flagstones, wracked by coughing. Her body contorted as another spasm took her. Blood pooled on the floor, red as roses, brighter than rubies.

"Papa . . . ," she whispered.

I turned to find Pila standing beside me with the spellbook of Majister Arun in her hands.

"You know all my secrets?" I asked.

Pila looked at me sadly. "Only the ones that matter." She handed me the rest of my spell ingredients and ran to close the shutters so no sign of our magic would be visible, reportable to the outside world.

I took the ingredients and mixed them and placed the paste on Jiala's brow, bared her bony chest. Her breathing was like a bellows, labored and loud, rich with blood and the sound of crackling leaves. My hands shook as I finished the preparations and took up Majister Arun's hand.

I spoke the words and magic flowed from me and into my child.

Slowly, her breathing eased. Her face lost its fevered glare. Her eyes became her own again, and the rattle and scrape of her breath smoothed as the bloody rents closed themselves.

Gone. As quickly and brutally as it had come, it was gone, leaving nothing but the sulphur stink of magic in the room.

Pila was staring at me, astonished. "I knew," she whispered. "But I had not seen."

I blotted Jiala's brow. "I'm sorry to have involved you."

Jiala's breathing continued to ease. Pila knelt beside me, watching over my daughter. Jiala was resting now, exhausted from what her body had used up in its healing.

"You mustn't be caught, Papa." Jiala whispered.

"It won't be much longer," I told her. "In no time at all, we'll be using magic just like the ancients and we won't have to hide a thing."

"Will we have a floating castle?"

I smiled gently. "I don't see why not. First we'll push back the bramble. Then we'll have a floating castle, and maybe one day we'll even grow wines on the slopes of Mount Sena." I tousled her hair. "But now I want you to rest and sleep and let the magic do its work."

Jiala looked up at me with her mother's dark eyes. "Can I dream of cloud castles?"

"Only if you sleep," I said.

Jiala closed her eyes, and the last tension flowed from her little body. To Pila, I said, "Open the windows, but just a little. Let the magic out slowly so no one has a chance to smell and suspect. If you are caught here, you will face the executioner's great axe with me."

Pila went and opened one of the windows and began to air the room, while I covered Jiala with blankets. We met again at the far side of the workshop.

At one time, I had had chairs in this room, for talk and for thought, but those were long gone. We sat on the floor, together.

"And now you are part of my little conspiracy," I said sadly.

Pila smiled gently. "I guessed a long time ago. She clearly has the wasting cough, but she never wastes. Most children, by this time, they are dead. And yet Jiala runs through the streets and comes home without a cough for weeks at a time. At least before she fell into bramble. The cough seemed to stay at bay unnaturally."

"Why did you not call the guards?" I asked. "There is a fine reward for people like me. You could have lived well by selling your knowledge of my foolishness."

"You don't use this magic selfishly."

"Still. It curses the city. The Mayor is right about that much. The help I visit upon Jiala means that hurt is visited upon Khaim. Some neighbor of ours may find a bit of bramble growing in his flagstones. A potato woman in the field will till up a new bramble root, attracted by my healing spells. The bramble wall marches ever closer, and cares not at all what intentions I have when I use magic. It only cares that there is magic to feed upon." I stood stiffly and went to squat by the fireplace, rolled a log so that it crackled and sent up sparks. Pila watched me. I could feel her eyes on me. I glanced back at her. "I help my child and curse my neighbor. Simple truth."

"And many of your neighbors do the same," Pila said. "Simple truth. Now come and sit."

I rejoined her, and we both watched the fire and my sleeping daughter. "I'm afraid I cannot save her," I finally said. "It will take great magic to make the cough go away, entirely. Her death is written in the dome of the Hall of Judgment, and I fear I cannot save her without great magic. Magic such as someone like Scacz wields. And he will not wield it for the sake of one little girl."

"And so you labor on the balanthast."

I shrugged. "If I can stop the bramble, then there's no reason not to use the great magics again. We can all be saved." I stared at the flames. Firewood had grown expensive since bramble started sprouting in the nearby forest. I grimaced. "We're caught in Halizak's Prison. Every move we make closes the walls down upon us."

"But the balanthast works," Pila reminded me. "You have found a solution."

I looked over at her. "I don't trust them."

"The Mayor?"

"Or the Majister. And now they have my balanthast. Another Halizakian box. I don't trust them, but they are the only ones who can save us."

Pila touched my shoulder. "I have watched you for more than fifteen years. You will discover a way."

I sighed. "When I add up the years, I feel sick. I was certain that I would have the balanthast perfected within a year or two. Within five. Within ten, for certain. In time to save Merali." I looked over at my sleeping daughter. "And now I can't help wondering if I'm too late to save even Jiala."

Pila smiled. "This time, I think you will succeed. I have never seen something like the balanthast. No one has. You have worked a miracle. What's one more, to save Jiala?"

She pushed her dark hair back, looking at me with her deep brown eyes. I started to answer, but lost my voice, struck suddenly by her proximity.

Pila . . .

With my work, I had never had time or moment to really look at her. Staring into her eyes, seeing the slight smile on her lips, I felt as if I was surfacing from some deep pool, suddenly breathing. Seeing Pila for the first time. Perhaps even seeing the world for the first time.

How long had I been gone? How long had I simply not paid attention to my growing daughter, or to Pila's care? In the firelight of the workshop, Pila was beautiful.

"Why did you stay?" I asked. "You could have gone on to other households. Could have made a family of your own. I pay you less than when you did little other than washing and cleaning, and now you run the household entire. Why not move on? I wouldn't begrudge it. Other households would welcome you. I would recommend you."

"You want to be rid of me just as you reach success?" Pila asked.

"No—" I stumbled on my own words. "I don't mean to say . . . ," I fumbled. "I mean, others all pay more."

She snorted. "A great deal more, considering that I haven't taken pay in over a year."

I looked at her, puzzled. "What do you mean?"

She gave me a sad smile. "It was a necessary economy, if we were to keep eating."

"Then why on earth didn't you leave?"

"You wished me to leave?"

"No!" All my words seemed to be wrong. "I'm in your debt. I owe you the moon. But you starve here—you can't think that I do not appreciate it. It's just that you make no sense—"

"You poor fool," Pila said. "You truly can't see farther than the bell of your balanthast."

She leaned close, and her lips brushed mine.

When she straightened, her dark eyes were deep with promise and knowledge. "I chose my place long ago," she said. "I watched you with Merali. When she was well, and when she fell ill. And I have watched you with Jiala. I would never leave one like you, one who never abandons others, even when it would be easy. You, I know."

"All my secrets," I whispered.

"All the ones that matter."

T HE NEXT DAY THE MAYOR AGAIN INVITED ME TO HIS
great house on the hill, to demonstrate the mechanics of the
balanthast.

Pila helped me with my finest once more, but now she leaned close,
smiling as she did, our cheeks almost brushing. My mustaches fairly
quivered at the proximity of this woman who had suddenly come into
view.

It was as if I had been peering through clouded glass, but now, had
finally polished a clear lens. Our fingers met on the buttons of my vest
and we laughed together, giddy with recognition, and Jiala watched
us both, smiling a secret child's smile, the one that always touched her
face when she thought she held some furtive bit of knowledge, but
which showed as clearly on her expression as the fabled rocket blos-
soms of Jhandpara showed against the stars.

At the door I hugged Jiala good-bye, then turned to Pila. I took a
step toward her, then stopped, embarrassed at my forwardness, caught
between past lives and new circumstance. Pila smiled at my uncer-
tainty, then laughed and came to me, shaking her head. We embraced
awkwardly. A new ritual. An acknowledgment that everything was

different between us, and that new customs would write themselves over old habits.

I held Pila close and felt years falling away from me. And then Jiala crashed into us, hugging us both, together. Laughing and squeezing in between. Family. Finally, family again. After too long without. The Three Faces of Mara, all of us a little more whole, and grateful.

"I think she likes us this way," Pila murmured.

"Then never leave me."

"Never."

I left that empty house feeling more full of life than I had in years. Silly and full of laughter all at once. Thinking of weddings. Of Pila as a bride. A gift I had never hoped to find again. The weight of loneliness lifted from me. Even the bramble-cutting crews didn't depress me. Men and women hacking bits of it from between the cobbles. Sweeping the city to make sure that vines didn't encroach. I smiled at them instead. With the balanthast, people would at last be safe. Could at last live their lives as they saw fit.

In ancient Jhandpara, majisters imbued carpets with magic so that they could speed from place to place, arrowing across the skies. Great wide carpets, as big as a room, with silver tea services and glass smoking vessels all set out for their friends. Crossing the empire in the blink of an eye. Flying back and forth from their floating castles and their estates in the cool north, to their seasides in the gentle south. And children did not sicken and die, and there was no wasting cough. All things were possible, except that magic made bramble, and bramble dragged flying carpets from the sky.

But now I had the solution, and I had Pila's love, and I would have Jiala forever, or for at least as long any parent can hope for a child.

Not cursed at all. Blessed.

Out on the Sulong River, work was proceeding on the floating bridge. I couldn't help imagining what it would be like to have not just the one, but perhaps even three floating bridges. We could heat our homes in the winter with green magic flames. We could speed across the land. We could reclaim Jhandpara. I laughed in the sharp spring air. Anything was possible.

As I entered the Mayor's House, the steward greeted me with quick recognition, which put me more at ease. My fears of the night before had been erased by sleep and Pila's influence and the warming spring sunshine.

The steward ushered me into the audience gallery. I was surprised to find a number of notables also there, assembled in gold and finery: magistrates of the courts, clove merchants and diamond traders, generals and old nobility who traced their lineages back to Jhandpara. Even the three ancient majisters of fallen Alacan. More people peered out from under the columned arches surrounding the gallery's marble and basalt flagstones. Much of Khaim's high and influential society, all gathered together.

I stopped, surprised. "What's this?"

Majister Scacz strode toward me, smiling a greeting. "We thought there should be a demonstration." He guided me over to a draped object in the center of the hall. From its shape, I guessed it was my balanthast.

"Is that my instrument?" I asked, concerned.

The Mayor joined us. "Of course it is. Don't be nervous, Alchemist."

"It's a delicate device."

The Mayor nodded seriously. "And we have treated it with utmost respect." Scacz patted me on the back, trying to reassure me. "These people all around us are the ones whose support we need, if we are to effect your new balanthast workshop. We must raise taxes for the initial construction, and"—he paused delicately—"some of the old nobility may be interested in patronage, in return for ancient bramble lands reclaimed. I assure you, this is a very good thing. It's easier to gain support when people whiff profit than if they simply feel they are being taxed to no purpose." He motioned me to the balanthast.

"Please, do not be nervous. All will be well. This is an opportunity for us all."

A servant brought in a huge pot containing a cutting of bramble more than seven feet tall. The thing seemed to fairly quiver in its pot, hunting malevolently for a new place to stretch its roots. They must have planted it the night before, immediately after I left, for it to have grown so large. Multiple branches sprouted from it, like great hairy tentacles.

The assembled dignitaries sucked in their breath at the sight of humanity's greatest enemy sitting in the center of the gallery. In the light of day, with its hairy tendrils and milkweedlike pods dangling, it spoke of eldritch menace. Even the pot was frightening, carved with the faces of Takaz, the Demon King, his serpent heads making offers of escape that would never be honored.

The Mayor held up his hands to the assembled. "Fear not! This is but a demonstration. Necessary for you to grasp the significance of the alchemist's achievement." He waved a hand at the servants and they lifted the drapery from my instrument.

"Behold!" the Mayor said to the throng. "The balanthast!"

The man had the gift of showmanship, I had to grant him that. The instrument had been polished, and now with sunlight pouring down from the upper galleries, it fairly blazed. Its glass chambers refracted the light, sending off rainbows. The copper bell mouths of its vents and the belly of its combustion chamber reflected the people in strange and distorted glory.

The crowd gasped in amazement.

"Has it been tampered with?" I asked.

"Of course not," Scacz said. "Just polished. That's all. I examined the workings of the thing, but took nothing apart." He paused, concerned. "Is it damaged?"

"No." But still I studied it. "And did it satisfy you? That it does not use magic? That it is not some device of the majisters pressed into new form?"

Scacz almost grinned at that. "I apologize most profusely for my suspicions, Alchemist. It seems to function entirely according to natural properties. A feat, truly. History can only bow to your singular genius." He nodded at the assembled people. "And now, will you demonstrate for our esteemed visitors?"

As I began assembling the ingredients, a general in the audience asked, "What is this instrument of yours, Scacz?"

"Salvation, Warlord."

A fat merchant out of the diamond quarter, with thick mustaches from his many children, called, "And what is the use of it?"

The Mayor smiled. "If we told you, it would spoil the astonishing surprise. You must see it as the Majister and I first did. Without preface or preamble."

I armed the balanthast, but then had to have the servants help me drag it over until it stood beside the huge bramble pot. Under the assembled gaze, it seemed to take forever to scrape the tripod over the flagstones. Despite my faith in my device, my heart was pounding. I pulled on a leather glove and pinched out a bit of the potted soil. Added it to the firing chamber. Plunged the delivery nozzles into the dirt. At last, I lit the match.

For a moment, we all watched, silent. The collected ingredients burned, and then were sucked into the combustion chamber. A pause. I held my breath, thinking that Scacz and the Mayor had somehow broken the balanthast in their ignorance. Then the balanthast shook and the snake faces of the Demon King burst wide, spilling soil as the pot shattered. The bramble toppled and hit the marble. The crowd gasped.

Yellow smoke issued from the bramble's limbs. It writhed—smoking, twisting, boiling. Sap squealed and frothed as it effervesced, a dying howl from our ancient menace.

People covered their ears as the bramble thrashed. More smoke issued from its vines. Within a minute, the bramble lay still, leaving ash and tiny blackened threads floating in the sunlight. Yellow smoke billowed slowly over the assemblage, sending people coughing and wheezing, but as the clouds dispersed, a great murmuring rose at the sight of the scorched bramble corpse.

"Inspect it!" Scacz cried. "Come to see. You must see this to believe!"

Not many cared to come close, but the general did. Unafraid, he approached and knelt. He stared, thunderstruck. "There are no seeds." His wide-eyed gaze fell upon me. "There should be seeds."

His words carried through the crowds. *No seeds. No seeds.* The lightning strike of miracle.

The Mayor laughed. Servants arrived with goblets of wine for celebration. Scacz clapped me on the back and the men and women of the great merchant houses came to stare at the cleansed soil before them. And then Scacz called out again, "One further demonstration?"

The crowd clapped and stamped their feet. Again I primed the balanthast, eager to show off the wonder of our salvation. I looked around for another pot of bramble, but none was in evidence.

"How will I demonstrate?" I asked.

"It doesn't matter," Scacz said. "Let it ignite free."

I hesitated.

The Mayor said, "Don't be shy of a bit of showmanship. Let them see the glory."

"But it can't simply be fired. It must have something to attach to. Some bit of earth at least."

"Here." Scacz took something from his sleeve. "I have something else you might try this on." He said something under his breath and suddenly, I smelled magic. The scent was different from the healing magic I had cast upon Jiala the night before. This was something special. Bright as bluebells in the summer sun, sticky as honey. He pressed a folded bit of parchment into my palm.

"Put this in your balanthast chamber," Scacz said. "It should burn well."

The whiff of bluebell honey magic clung to the paper.

I didn't want to. Didn't know what he was up to. But the Mayor was nodding, and I was surrounded by the assembled people, all those great names and powerful houses watching, and the Mayor motioned me to continue.

"Go on, Alchemist. Show us your genius. The crowd loves you. Let us see this thing fire free."

And to my everlasting regret, I did.

I braced the delivery nozzles so they poked into the air, and lit my match. The spelled parchment and the neem and all the assembled ingredients disappeared into the belly of the balanthast, and it roared.

Blue flame erupted from the nozzles, a long streak of sparkling fire. Thick yellow smoke issued with it. And something else: the sticky breath of the magic-laced parchment Scacz had given me. Flower brightness, volatilized in the belly chamber of the balanthast, and now released as smoke.

Beside me, Scacz's body began to glow an unearthly aura of blue, sharp and defined. But not just him. The Mayor as well. His steward also. I stared at my hands. Myself, even.

The fumes of the expended balanthast billowed through the room and others began to glow as well. The general. The fat diamond merchant. His wife. More women in their skirts. Men in their fine embroidered vests. But Scacz's blue-limned features were brightest of all.

"You were right," the Mayor murmured. "Look at us all."

Everyone was staring at the many people who now glowed with spirit fire, gasping at the wonder of their unearthly beauty.

Scacz smiled at me. "You were right, Alchemist. Neem loves magic. It clings to its memory like a child to her mother's skirts."

"What have you done?" I asked.

"Done?" Scacz looked around, amused. "Why, just added a bit of illumination to your neem essence. A way of seeing where your neem goes seeking. Your fine alchemy and my simple spellcraft make a lovely effect, don't you think?"

Boots thudded and steel rang around the hall. Guards appeared from behind white columns and beneath the arches. Men in scaly armor, and the tramp of more boots behind them.

"Seize them!" Scacz shouted. "All the ones who burn blue are guilty of magic's use! Every one! If they are not of the Mayor's office, they are traitors."

A babble of protest rose. Already the people who did not glow were shrinking from those that did.

The general drew his sword. "Treachery?" he asked. "This is why you bring us here?" A few others drew steel with him.

The Mayor said, "Sadly, Warlord, even you are not immune to law. You have used magic, when it is expressly forbidden. If you have some excuse, the magistrate will hear you. . . ." He paused. "Oh dear, it appears the magistrate is also guilty."

He waved to his guards. "Take them all, then."

The general roared. He raised his sword and charged for the Mayor. Guards piled atop him like wolves. Steel clashed. A man fell back. The general stumbled from within the tangle of steel. Blood streamed from half a dozen sword thrusts. For a moment I thought he would reach us, but then he fell, sprawling on the marble. And yet still he tried to reach the Mayor. Scrabbling like a beetle, leaving a maroon streak behind him.

The Mayor watched the general's struggle with distaste.

"On second thought, kill them all now. We know what they've been up to."

The guards howled and the blue-glowing nobility shrank before them. Too few were armed. They scattered, running like sheep, scrambling about the gallery as the guards hunted them down and silenced their begging. At last there were no more screams.

I stood in the midst of a massacre, clutching my balanthast.

The Mayor waved to the guards. "Drag the bodies out. Then go to seize their properties." In a louder voice he announced, "For those of you still standing, the holdings of the traitors will be sold at auction, as is custom. Your trustworthiness is proven, and you shall benefit."

He clapped Scacz on the back. "Well done, Majister. Inspired, even." His eyes fell on my own blue-glowing form. "Well. This is a pity. It seems the Majister was right in all respects. He told me he smelled magic on you when we first met, and I didn't believe him. But here you are, glowing like a lamp."

I backed away, cradling the balanthast. "You're the Demon King himself."

"Don't be absurd. Takaz would care not at all for stopping bramble."

The guards were grabbing bodies and dragging them into piles, leaving blood smears behind.

The Mayor eyed the stains. "Get someone in here to mop these tiles! Don't just leave this blood here." He glanced around. "Where's my steward disappeared to?"

Scacz cleared his throat. "I'm afraid he was caught up in the general slaughter."

"Ah." The Mayor frowned. "Inconvenient." He returned his attention to me. "Well, then. Let's have the device." He held out his hands.

"I would never—"

"Give it here."

I stared at him, filled with horror at what he had done. What I had been complicit in. In a rush, I lifted the balanthast over my head.

"No!" Scacz lunged forward.

But it was too late. I threw down the balanthast. Glass vacuum chambers shattered. Diamond fragments skittered across marble. Delicate copper and brass workings bent and snapped. I grabbed the largest part of the balanthast, and flung it from me, sending it sliding, breaking apart into even smaller parts before coming to rest in the blood of its victims.

"You fool." Scacz grabbed me. His hand closed on my throat and he forced me down. The blue glow about him intensified, magic flowing. My throat began to close, pinched tight by Scacz's hate and power.

"Join the rest of the traitors," he said.

My throat bound shut. I couldn't breathe. I couldn't even cry out.

No air passed my lips. The man was powerful. He didn't even need an inked page to spell such evil.

Darkness.

And then, abruptly, sunlight.

I could breathe. I lay on the flagstones and sucked air through my suddenly unbound throat. Majister Scacz knelt over me.

His hand lay upon my chest, resting gently. And yet, at the same time, I could feel each of his five fingers beneath my ribs. Gripping my heart. I batted weakly at his hand, trying to push him away. Scacz's fingers tightened, constraining the beat of my blood. I gave up.

I realized that the Mayor was standing over us both, watching.

"The Mayor points out that you are much too talented to waste," Scacz said. Again he squeezed my heart. "I do hope his faith proves true."

Abruptly his grip relaxed. He straightened and waved for the guards. "Take our friend to the dungeon until we have a suitable workshop for him." His eyes went to the broken balanthast. "He has many hours of labor ahead."

I found my voice. Croaked out words. "No. Not this bloodbath. I won't be a part of it."

Scacz shrugged. "You already are. And of course you will."

S HOULD I TELL YOU THAT I FOUGHT? THAT I DIDN'T BREAK?
That I resisted torture and blandishment and took no part in
the purge that followed? That I had no hand in the blood that
gushed down Khaim's alleys and poured into the Sulong? Should I tell
you that I was noble, while others pandered? That I was not party to
the terror?

In truth, I refused once.

Then Scacz brought Jiala and Pila to visit. We all sat together in the
chill of my cell, huddling under the water drip from stones, smelling
the sweet damp rot of straw, and listening to the wet bellows of Jiala's
lungs, the fourth participant in our stilted conversation.

Scacz himself said nothing at all. He simply let us sit together. He
brought wooden stools, and had a guard provide cups of mint tea and
at first I was relieved to see Jiala and Pila unharmed, but then Jiala's
coughing started and wouldn't stop, and blood spackled her lips and
she began to cry, and then I had to call the guard to take them away.
And even though the man was fast in coming, it was still too slow.

The last vision I had of Jiala was Pila carrying her small form, her
wracking cough echoing against cold stones.

And then Scacz came down to visit me again. He leaned against the wall, studying my dishevelment through the bars.

"The cold of the dungeon disagrees with her lungs," he observed.

The repair of the first balanthast was the price of Jiala and Pila's well being, but Scacz and our Jolly Mayor were not finished with me. In Jiala they had the perfect lever. In return for the magic and healing that only Scacz could provide, I created the tools and instruments they desired. My devices purchased life for myself and my family, and death for everyone else.

Blood ran in the streets. It poured down Malvia Hill. It clotted in the cobble alleys of Lesser Khaim and flooded the fields beyond the city walls. Rumors in my prison said that the Mayor's halls were redder than a sunset. That bodies burned in bramble piles, the fat of their cooking twining with the yellow smoke of bramble to fill the skies with their funeral pyres. The executioner was so busy that on some days, a second and even a third were summoned to take over the efforts of the axeman who had grown exhausted with his work. Some days, they didn't even bother with the effort of a public spectacle.

Scacz had laughed at that.

"When we couldn't find these furtive little spell casters, we needed fear to keep the magic in check," he said. "Now that we can hunt them down, it's better to let them practice for a little while, and then seize everything."

As long as I furnished the tools of the hunt, I was not harmed. Scacz and the Mayor had so many uses for me. I was a prized hawk. Free enough, within certain confines. The dynamic between us was as taut as the strings on a violin. Each of us would pluck at those strings, seeking gain, testing the other's boundaries, trying the tenor of the note, the question of its strain. The workings of my mind and its creations tugging against the value of Jiala and Pila's well-being. And so we each tugged and pulled at that catgut strand.

I was not a prisoner, precisely. More a scholar who worked all day and all night in a confined place, building better, more portable balanthasts. Constructing devices better tuned to sniffing out magic. Sometimes, I myself forgot my situation. When the work went well, I was as focused as I had ever been in my workshop.

I am ashamed to admit that there were even times when I reveled in the totality of focus that my cell provided. When there is nothing to do but work, a great deal of work can be done—and a great deal of time can pass.

"Come now. I brought sweets. You like them," Pila urged. She sat outside the bars of my workshop, offering.

I sat, staring. "I'm not hungry anymore."

"I can see that. You're getting skinny."

"I was skinny before."

Pila watched me sadly. "Please. If you won't eat for yourself, then at least eat for me. For Jiala."

Unwillingly, I stood and shuffled over to her.

"You look unwell," she said.

I shrugged. Of late, I had been having nightmares. Oftentimes I would dream of a river of my victims. Dreamed them pouring down the streets to where the executioner stood waiting, the hooded butcher chopping off heads as they flowed past, his axe swinging like a scythe, heads spinning in all directions. And I stood at the source of that river, casting each person into the flow. Illuminating them in blue fire before tossing them into the current, sending them tumbling toward that final cataract of the axe.

Pila stretched her hand through the bars, and clasped my cold fingers. Her skin showed wrinkles and her palms showed surprising dryness. I thought that maybe those hands had been soft, that she had been young once, but I could hardly remember. She clutched my hand, and against all the promises I had made myself, I collapsed against the bars, pressing her fingers to my cheek.

That I hungered for her warmth was something I could barely

stand. Majister Scacz had offered us "relief" as he called it, but he did so with such a leer that after the first time, I could do it no more, and spat in his face when he next suggested the idea. Which enraged him so much that he barred Pila from visiting for nearly six months. Only when I threatened to cut my own throat with a bulb of glass did he finally relent and allow her visits again, if only through the bars. I kissed Pila's fingers, starved for her kindness and humanity in a place that I had turned brutish and bloody.

A few feet away, a guard sat, his body ostentatiously half turned away from us, providing a semblance of privacy. This particular one was Jaiska. He had a family and his mustaches were long for his three sons, all of whom had followed him into the guards. Decent enough, and willing to give us a little privacy as we whispered to each other through the bars.

Not like Izaac, who loved to regale me with the executions he had seen, thanks to my inventions. Izaac said that within the gates of Khaim, no householder passed untested by the balanthast. Heads not only decorated the city gates, but also the broad bridge that leaped the Sulong and now linked Khaim with its lesser kin. There were so many heads that the Mayor had gotten tired of mounting trophies and now simply ordered bodies tossed into the river to float to the sea.

"How is Jiala?" I asked.

"Better than you," Pila said. "She thrives. And grows. Scacz still refuses to let me bring her, but she is well. You can trust that. Scacz is evil but he loves your work and so he cares for us."

"Other people's heads in exchange for keeping our own." I stared at my workshop. "How many now have I killed? How much blood is on my hands?"

"It's no use thinking about. They were using magic, which was always forbidden. These are not guiltless people who go to the executioner's axe."

"Don't forget that we were among them as well. Are among them, thanks to Scacz."

"There's no use thinking on it. It will only drive you mad."

I looked at her bitterly. "I've been here for two years already, and if I haven't found refuge in madness yet, I doubt I will."

She sighed. "In any case, it's slowing now. There are fewer who test the Mayor's powers of detection." She leaned close. "Some say that he now only finds magic on people who are too wealthy or powerful. Those ones he snuffs out, and confiscates their families and property."

"And no one fights?"

"A few. But he has supporters. The farmers near the bramble wall say the vines have slowed. In places, they even cut it back. For the first time in generations, they cut it back."

I scowled. "We could have cut back miles if the Mayor had simply used the balanthast as it was intended."

"It's no use thinking on." She pushed a cloth-wrapped bundle of bread through the bars. "Here," she said. "Please. Eat a little."

But I shook my head and walked away from her offering. It was a petty thing. I knew it even as I did so. But there was no one else to lash out against. A petty rebellion for the real rebellion I had no stomach for.

Pila sighed. I heard a rustling and then her words to Jaiska. "Give these to him when he changes his mind. Some for you as well. Don't let him starve himself."

And then she was gone, leaving me with my workshop and my killing devices.

"Don't scorn her," Jaiska said. "She stands by you and your daughter when she could walk away easy. Old Scacz likes to bother her. Comes and bothers her."

I turned. "What do you mean?"

He shrugged. "Bothers her."

"She doesn't say so."

"Not to you. Wouldn't want you to do something stupid."

I sighed, feeling childish for my display. "I don't deserve her."

Jaiska laughed. "No one deserves anyone. You just win 'em and hope you can hang on to 'em." He offered me the bread. "Might as well eat while it's fresh."

I took the bread and cut a slice on a worktable. Cut one for him as well. The scent of honey and rosemary, along with the reek of neem and mint and the burn of coals from my glass fire.

"It's a strange world we live in," I said, waving at my worktable. "All that time spent trying to find magic, and now, suddenly Scacz asks for balanthasts to kill bramble again. Maybe he'll finally decide to cut away the bramble wall."

Jaiska snorted. "Well. In a way." He took a bite of bread and spoke around the mouthful. "He cuts new lands into the bramble for his and the Mayor's friends. The people who inform for them. Their favored guards."

"Are you going to get new lands?"

Jaiska shrugged. "I'm just a sword. Keep my head down. Don't work magic when the hunters are out. Hope my sons all learn their sword swinging right. Don't need lands. Don't need honors. Don't do traffic with the Mayor."

I grimaced. "That's wisdom, there. I, on the other hand, thought I'd be a savior of our land."

"Bramble's mostly stopped." Jaiska said. "Hardly anyone except Scacz uses magic anymore. Not in any real way. Can't remember the last time I saw bramble sprouting in the upper city. We're saved. In a way."

"It isn't the way I hoped."

Jaiska laughed at that. "For being so clever with the devices, you're a damn silly-headed bastard."

"Pila said something similar to me once."

"Because it's true, Alchemist."

At the new voice, Jaiska leaped to his feet. "No offense, sir."

Scacz swept into view. "Go find something to do, Guardsman."

"Grace." Jaiska touched his brow and fled.

Scacz sat down on the stool that Jaiska vacated. His gaze came to rest on Pila's gift. "I'd ask you for some of that lovely bread, but I'm afraid you'd put bramble threads in it."

I shook my head. "Bramble threads would be too good for a creature like you."

"Ah. Yes. A creature. Indeed." He smiled. "A powerful creature, actually. Thanks to you. The most powerful majister in the land, now. The Majisters of Alacan all have their heads fitted to spikes." He sighed. "It really is an addiction. The feel of power flowing through . . . no one understands that. Siren song for those of us who have the knack. But then, you already knew that."

"I don't miss it," I said.

Scacz snorted. "Maybe. But the lure is certainly there. For many. For most. We could never allow the people to believe that your balanthast was actually a solution. False comfort there. As soon as they sipped a little magic from the pool, they would have demanded to drink deep. And then"—he made a motion with his hands—"willy-nilly everyone would have been spelling here and there, charming and spelling and making flying carpets, and we'd all have a lovely time. Until the bramble overwhelmed us."

"It wouldn't have," I said. "We're not stupid."

Scacz laughed. "It's not as if the people of Jhandpara—of all the old empire—were unaware of magic's unfortunate effects. From the historical manuscripts, they tried mightily to hold back their base urges. But still they thirsted for magic. For the power, some. For the thrill. For the convenience. For the salvation. For the wonderful luxury."

He made another motion and a castle appeared above his hand, glowing. It floated in clouds, with dragons of every color circling it.

"How could anyone give this up?" he asked. "The people of Jhandpara had no discipline. Even the ones who wished to control themselves lacked the necessary will. And so our empire fell."

In Scacz's hand, the castle tumbled from its clouds and crashed into deep bramble forests that appeared below. Bramble spread over arched palaces, over coliseums, over temples to the Three Faces of

Mara, growing tall and terrible. Dust and rubble clouds obscured the scene as more cloud castles fell.

Scacz brushed his hands together, obliterating the scene and knocking off a rain of dust that landed on his robes.

"Magic brings bramble," he said. "And even you, Alchemist, hungered to use it."

"Only a little. To save my daughter."

"Every spell maker has a reasonable excuse. If we grant individual mercies, we commit collective suicide. A pretty puzzle for an ethical man like you."

"You think we're the same, then?"

"Magic is magic. Bramble is bramble. I couldn't care less what hairs a philosopher splits. Now, every night, I sleep knowing that bramble will no longer encroach. So I sleep very well indeed." He stood. Nodded at my new balanthast. "Hurry with your new device, Alchemist. As always, your daughter's well-being depends upon it."

"Why not let me go?"

"Why would I do such a thing? Then you might carry this knowledge of balanthasts to some other city. Perhaps give others the illusion that discipline is no longer needed." He shook his head. "No. That would not do at all."

"Khaim is my home," I said. "I have no wish to leave. I could construct legions of balanthasts. You say you want to cut back the bramble now. At last, our goals align."

"Our goals already align, Alchemist." Scacz turned away. "Hurry with your tools. I have fiefs I wish to disburse."

"And if I refuse?"

Scacz turned back. "Then I simply will stop caring whether your daughter coughs up that river of blood of hers. The choice is yours. It always has been."

"You'll never let me go."

Scacz laughed. "I can't think why I would. You're far too useful."

~❦~

That night I lay in my bed, surrounded by the weirdly comfortable smells and drips of my prison workshop, turning the problem of the Majister over in my head. I could not bargain with the dragon mind of Scacz. And despite his words, I suspected my time was running out.

Building balanthasts to create bramble fiefdoms was not the green grass of a new beginning, but the signal smoke of a bitter end. Once a brigade of balanthasts was prepared, there would be no more need of me.

I lay listening to the night guard's snores, and began to plan. Assembling pieces and components into a larger whole. Not a plan fully formed, but still . . . an intrigue. A tangle of misdirection, and at the end of its winding way, a path, perhaps, out of my Halizakian box. I considered the alleys and angles, testing chinks in the armor of my logic.

If I was honest, there were many.

But Pila, Jiala, and I had already lived too long in the center of Khaim's bloody vortex. The storm would eventually tear us to pieces as well. Scacz might be a man of his word, but he was not a man of charity. The Mayor and Scacz thought in terms of trade, and when I had nothing left to offer, they would do away with me.

In the morning, I was up and constructing.

"Jaiska," I said. "Go find Scacz. Tell him I've had an inspiration."

When Scacz appeared, I made my proposal. "If you let me walk outside occasionally, I will make your detectors more powerful. I can extend their reach considerably, I think. And build them so that a man need not even handle them. They could run continuously, in market squares, all along the thoroughfares, at city gates."

Scacz looked at me suspiciously. "Why so amenable all of a sudden?"

"I want to live well. I want to see the sun and the sky, and I'm willing to bargain."

"You think to escape."

"From a great majister like you?" I shook my head. "I have no illusions. But I cannot live forever without fresh air." I held up an arm.

"Look at me. I'm wasting away. Look how pale I become. Shackle me how you like, but I would breathe fresh air."

"How will you improve your design?"

"Here." I rolled out parchment and dipped my quill. Scratched out the bones of a design. "It would be a bit like a torch, standing. A sentry. It would issue a slow smoke from its boiler. Anyone who walked near would be caught." I pushed the rough sketch through the bars.

"You've been holding this back."

I met Scacz's gaze. "You should realize that keeping me alive and happy has benefits."

Scacz laughed at that, liking the bargain he thought we were making. "Does your hold on survival feel tenuous, Alchemist?"

"I want assurances, Scacz. And a life. A life better than this."

"Oh? There's something else you desire?"

"I want Pila to be able to pass evenings with me again."

Scacz leered, then shook his head. "No. I think not."

"Then I will not improve your detectors."

"I could torture you."

I looked at him through the bars. "You have all the power, Majister. I ask for a favor and you return with threats. What else can I offer you? A better balanthast as well? Something that works faster and better than the ones you currently have? I can design ones that are light and portable. They could clear fields in days. Imagine the magics you could wield if bramble was hardly a threat at all."

And the hook was set. After all, what good is it to be the finest majister in the land when you cannot wield the finest, most impressive magics? Scacz's hunger to use his powers chafed against the natural limits that bramble imposed.

And so I set to work on my newly conceived balanthasts and my detectors. My workroom filled with supplies, with copper rolls, with bellows and tongs, with brass and nails, glass bulbs and vacuum tubes, and Scacz came to visit daily, eager for my promised improvements.

And Pila came to visit as well.

In the darkness we clutched close, and I murmured into her ear.

"This cannot work," she whispered.

"If it does not, you must go without me," I said.

"I won't. It will do no good."

"Do you love Jiala?"

"Of course I do."

"Then you must trust me. Trust me as much as you did when I labored for so many years to get us into this mess."

"It's madness."

"A madness I created. And I must stop it. If I cannot, you must run. Take the spell for Jiala's health and go. Run as far as you can. For if I fail, Scacz will pursue you to the very ends of the earth."

In the morning Pila left with a kiss and a copper token of my affection, bound around her wrist, a little bit of the workshop, leaving with her.

Over the course of weeks I worked, feverishly. And at night, I met with Pila and whispered formulas and processes in her ear. She listened close, her long black hair tickling like feathers on my lips, the lustrous strands cloaking us as we played at intimacy and worked at salvation.

My detectors went up in the city, gouting out foul smoke and blanketing Khaim in their reactants, and once again blood ran in the streets. Scacz was well pleased. He granted me the privilege of letting me out of my cage.

I was so unfit that I ran out of breath simply walking up the stairs out of the dungeon. And then I gasped again when we reached the grounds and gazed over the city.

The flames of the detectors glowed here and there, blue fireflies sending out scented smoke that clung to anything magical at all. The bridge to Lesser Khaim blazed astonishingly bright, a beacon of magic in the thickening darkness.

"You have wrought something beautiful," Scacz said. "Khaim will always be known as the Blue City, now. And from now on, we will grow." He pointed into the sky, and I could see where the beginnings of a castle clung to wisps of accumulating clouds.

I sucked in my breath in astonishment.

"It's damnably difficult to summon and collect the clouds," Scacz said. "But it will be quite pretty when it's completed."

I felt as if I was staring at fabled Jhandpara. I could almost hear the music and taste the joy of the Mount Sena wine I had quaffed so long ago.

When I found my voice, I said, "You must bring the old balanthasts back to me so that I can adjust them. I will have to trade out their combustion chambers for the power that they will now wield."

Scacz smiled and rubbed his hands together. "And then I will truly be able to set to work on my castle. I won't have to check my powers at all."

"The Majister of the Blue City," I said.

"Indeed."

"I'd very much like to see it when it's done."

Scacz looked over at me, thoughtful. "If these balanthasts perform as you describe them, Alchemist, then the very least I can do for you is to give you a domicile above the earth."

"A prison in the air?"

"Better than one on the ground. You will have a most astonishing view."

I laughed at that. "I won't argue. In fact, I will hurry the moment." I turned to leave, but then paused, voicing an afterthought. "When the balanthasts arrive, I'll also need several pots of bramble. To test and make sure my designs are correct."

Scacz nodded, distracted, still staring up at the triumph of his castle. "What's that?"

"Bramble," I said patiently. "For the testing."

Scacz waved an acknowledgment, and the guards led me back down to my dungeon.

~え~

Weeks later, I asked Jaiska to summon Scacz for the final demonstrations.

I had lined up a number of bramble plants in pots. "It would work better if we were at the bramble wall," I grumbled, "but this should suffice."

Along one wall, I had all the balanthasts of the city, lined up. Each one newly altered, its delivery tubes and chambers reshaped to their improved purpose. I took one of the gleaming instruments from its rank and plunged its nozzle into the bramble pot. The bramble's limbs quivered malevolently, as if it understood the evil I planned for it. The dry pods rattled as the pot shifted.

I lit the match and pressed it into the new combustion chamber. Much faster and easier to ignite now.

A low explosion. The plant thrashed briefly and then disappeared in a puff of acrid smoke. There was simply nothing left of it at all.

I laughed, delighted. "You see?"

Scacz and Jaiska stared, dumbfounded. I did it again, laughing, and now Scacz and Jaiska laughed as well.

"Well done, Alchemist! Well done!"

"And it is prepared much more quickly now," I said. "These chambers on top mix the ingredients, so that they are always at the ready. Open this valve, and . . ." I lit another match. Explosion. Vented smoke. The potted bramble soaked up the balanthast's poison and disappeared in a squeal of burning sap and writhing smoke.

I grinned. Did it again and again, working something greater than magic in my workshop. Jaiska stamped his feet and whistled. Scacz's smile widened into a greedy astonished grin. And then I, laughing and in my folly, drunk on my success, grabbed a bramble with my bare hands.

A silly, reckless thing. A moment of inattention, and all my genius was destroyed.

I yanked my hands away as if the bramble was on fire, but its threadlike hairs clung already to my bare skin. The sleeping toxins numbed my hands, spreading like fire. I fell to my knees. Tried to stand. Stumbled and crashed into the balanthast, tumbling it and knocking it over, shattering it.

"Fool!" Scacz shouted.

I tried to get up once more, but fell back instead, tangling with bramble again. Its thorns pricked me, its threads clung to my skin, poisoning, clutching and hungry for me. Burrowing sleep into my heart, pressing down upon my lungs.

Darkness closed on my vision. It was terrifyingly fast. I crawled away, stupid with the toxins, reached through the bars. Scacz and Jaiska shied from my thread-covered hands.

"Please," I whispered. "Use your magic. Save me."

Scacz shook his head, staying well away from my touch. "No magic works against bramble's sleep."

"Please," I croaked. "Jiala. Please. Keep her well."

Scacz looked at me with contempt. "There's really no point, now, is there?"

My limbs turned to water. I slumped to the flagstones, still reaching through the bars as he went blurry and distant.

The Majister stared down at me with a bemused expression.

"It's probably better this way, Alchemist. We would have had to chop your head off, eventually." He turned to Jaiska. "As soon as he's done thrashing, gather up the balanthasts. And don't be so stupid as he was."

"What about his body? Should I take him to his wife?"

"No. Dump it in the river with the rest."

I was too far gone to panic. Bramble stilled my heart.

HAVING MY FLESH BURNED WITH BLUE FLAME IS NOT my preferred method to awaken, but it is a great improvement over death.

Another gust of flame washed over me. It burned through my blood, blistered my lungs, tunneled about in my heart, and dragged me back to life. I writhed in the heat, trying to breathe. Another blast of flame.

And suddenly, I was coughing and wheezing. My skin burned, but I breathed.

"Stop," I croaked, waving weakly for mercy, praying I wouldn't be scoured again. I opened my eyes.

Pila crouched over me, a fantastic jeweled balanthast in her hands. Jiala stood beside her, worried, clutching at her skirt.

"Are you alive, Papa?" she asked.

I pushed myself upright, shaking bramble threads from my arms. Pila looked me over, brushed me with a gloved hand. "He's alive enough, child. Now hurry and get our things. It's time for us to run."

Jiala nodded obediently and ran out of my workroom. I stared after her, astonished. How she had grown! Not a small child at all, but tall and vital. So much change in the years I had been imprisoned. Pila continued to brush away the singed bramble thread. I winced at her touch.

"Don't complain," she said. "Blisters mean you're alive."

I flinched away from another round of brushing. "You found my body, it seems."

"It was a near thing. I was expecting a coffin to arrive. If Jaiska hadn't been decent enough to send word of where you'd been dumped . . ." She shrugged. "You were nearly tossed into the water with the rest of the corpses before I found you."

"Help me stand."

With her support, I made it to my feet. My old familiar workshop, but altered under Pila's influence.

"I had to replace much of the equipment," Pila explained as she braced me upright. "Even with your instruction, it was an uncertain thing."

"I'm alive, though." I looked at her balanthast. My design but her construction, noticing places where she had made changes. She held it by a leather strap that she slung over her shoulder. "You've made it quite portable," I said admiringly.

"If we're to run, it's time we did."

"More than time."

In the hall, our last belongings were stuffed into wicker baskets with harnesses to hold them upon our backs. A tiny pile of essentials. So little of my old life. A few wool blankets, food and water jugs. And yet, there also, Pila and Jiala. More than any man had any right to ask for. We slung our baskets, and I groaned at the weight in mine.

"Easy living," Pila commented. "Jiala could carry more than you."

"Not quite that bad, I hope. In any case, nothing that a long walk won't fix."

We ducked out into the streets, the three of us together, winding through the alleys. We ran as quickly as we could for the gates of Khaim, making our way toward the open fields. Inside, I felt laughter and relief bubbling up. My skin was burned, my hair was matted and melted, but I was alive, maybe for the first time in almost twenty years.

And then the wind shifted and a cloud of smoke blew across us. One of my own infernal detectors, now standing sentry on every street.

Jiala lit up like an oil lamp.

Pila sucked in her breath. "She was only treated yesterday. The magic still shows. Normally I kept her in, after Scacz spelled her."

Quick as a cat, she swept a cloak over Jiala, smothering the blue glow. And yet still it leaked out. Jiala's face shone an unearthly shade. I picked her up and buried her face in my chest. She was heavy.

"Don't show your skin, child."

We slunk through the city and out into the fields as darkness fell. We went along the muddy road, trying to hide my daughter's fatal hue. But it was useless. Farmers on the road saw and gasped and dashed away, and even as we hurried forward, we heard cries behind. People who sought to profit from turning in a user of magic.

"We aren't going to make it," Pila said.

"Run then!"

And we did, galloping and stumbling. I panted at the unaccustomed exercise. I was not meant to run. Not after years in prison. In a minute, I was gasping. In two, spots swam before my vision and I was staggering. And still we ran, now with Jiala on her own, tugging at me, dragging me forward. Healthier by far than I.

Behind us, the shouts of guardsmen echoed. They gained.

Ahead, black bramble shadows rose.

"Halt!" the guards shouted. "In the name of Khaim and the Mayor!"

On the run, Pila fired her balanthast. Lit its prime. Prepared to plunge it into the ground at the bracken root.

"No!" I gasped. "Not like that." I lifted the device so it pointed into the guts of the bracken. "Don't hurt the roots. Just the branches."

Pila glanced at me, puzzled, then nodded sharply. The balanthast roared. Blue flame lanced from the nozzle, igniting the branches. Bramble writhed and vaporized, opening a deep narrow corridor of smoking, writhing vines. We plunged into the gap. Another shout came from behind.

"Halt!"

An arrow thudded into a bramble branch. Another creased my ear. I grabbed Jiala and forced her low as Pila fired the balanthast again.

Behind us, the guardsmen were stumbling across the tilled fields, splashing through irrigated trenches. Their swords gleamed in the moonlight.

Blue flame speared the night again, and a writhing path in the bramble opened before us.

I pulled out the spell book of Majister Arun. "A match, daughter."

I struck the flame and handed it to Jiala. In its flickering unsteady light, I read spidering text by the hand of that long dead majister. A spell for sweeping.

A dust devil formed in the bracken, swirling. I waved my hand and sent it spinning down the narrow way behind us. A simple spell. A bit of household magic for a servant or a child. Nothing in comparison to the great works of Jhandpara.

But to the bramble all around, that tiny spell was like meat tossed before a tiger. The vines shivered at magic's scent and clutched after my sweeping whirlwind. I cast more small spells as Pila opened a way ahead. Bramble closed in behind, starving for the magic that I scattered like breadcrumbs, ravenous for the nurturing flavors of magic cast so close to its roots. Vines erupted from the earth, filling the path and locking us in the belly of the bramble forest.

Behind us, the guards' shouts faded and became indistinct. A few more arrows plunged into the bramble, ricocheting and clattering, but already the vines were thick and tangled behind us. We might as well have been behind a wall of oak.

Pila fired the balanthast again, and we moved deeper into the malevolent forest.

"We won't have long before they follow us," she said.

I shook my head. "No. We have time. Scacz's balanthasts will not work. I crippled them all before I left, when Scacz thought I was improving them. Only the one I used for my demonstration worked, and I made sure to shatter it."

"Where are we going, Papa?" Jiala asked.

I pulled Jiala close as I whispered another spell of dust and tidying. The little whirlwind whisked its way into the darkness, baiting bramble, closing the path behind us. When I was done, I smiled at my daughter and touched her under her chin. "Have I ever told you of the copper mines of Kesh?"

"No, Papa."

"They are truly wondrous. Not a bit of bramble populates the land, no matter how much magic is used. An island in a sea of bramble."

The blue fire of Pila's balanthast again lit the night, sending bramble writhing away from us, opening a corridor of flight. I picked up Jiala, still amazed at how heavy she had become in my years away, but unwilling to let her leave my side even for a moment, welcoming her truth and weight. We started down the corridor that Pila had opened.

Jiala gave a little cough and wiped her lips on her sleeve. "Truly?" she asked. "There is a place where you can use magic? Even for my cough?"

"As sure as balanthasts," I told her, and hugged her tight. "We only have to get there."

Another blast of blue flame lit the night, and we all forged onward.

PART II

The Executioness

BY TOBIAS S. BUCKELL

LET ME TELL YOU ABOUT THE FIRST TIME I KILLED A MAN.
On the morning of that day, my father, Anto, lay on the simple, straw-stuffed mattress that I'd dragged out to the kitchen fire, choking on his own life as a wasting sickness ate at him from the inside.

He had been like this for days now. I had watched him grow thin, watched him cough blood, and listened to him swear at the gods in a steady mumble, which I struggled to hear over the crackle of the kitchen fire.

I burned the fire to keep him warm, even though winters in Lesser Khaim were not the kind that kill men, like the ones far to the north. Winter was a cool kiss here in Lesser Khaim, and the fire kept him comfortable and happy in his last days.

"Why haven't you fetched the healer yet, you useless creature," my father hissed at me.

"Because there are none to fetch," I said firmly, gathering my skirts around my knees to crouch by his side. I put a scarred hand, the sign of my long years of slaughtering animals at the back of the butcher's shop, to his forehead. It felt hot to my old, callused palms.

There had been a healer in this neighborhood, once. A wrinkled old man who lanced boils and prescribed poultices. But he'd fled the Jolly Mayor and his city guards when he'd crossed the bridge and the smoke stained him bright blue. The old man had been lucky to flee with his life toward Paika and the lands troubled by its raiders. Though who knew how long he could live out there?

"Then bring someone who can *cure* me," my father begged. "It would be a small magic. I'm in so much pain."

His pleading tore at me. I leaned closer to him and to the crackle of the fire, which burned wood we could barely afford in these times, when refugees from Alacan crammed themselves into Lesser Khaim, eating and using everything they could get their hands on.

I sighed as I stood, my knees cracking with the pain of the movement. "Would you have me look for someone who can cast a spell for you, and then condemn us all to death when we turn blue from the Majister's smoke? It would be a heavy irony for anyone in this family to die at the blade of an executioner's axe, don't you think?"

I thought, for a moment, that he considered this. But when I looked closely at his face for a reaction, I realized he'd sunk back into his fever.

My father had returned to muttering imprecations at the gods in his sleep. A husk of a blasphemer, he took so much joy in seeing the pious void their bowels at the sight of his executioner's axe. This was the man who would lean close and whisper at the condemned through his mask, "Do you not believe you will visit the halls of the gods soon? Don't you burn favors for a god, perhaps one like Tuva, so that you will eat honey and milk from bowls that never empty, and watch and laugh at the struggles of mortals shown on the mirrors all throughout Tuva's hall? Or do you actually fear that this is truly your last moment of life?"

That was my father, the profane.

Unlike his outwardly pious victims, and despite his frequent irreverence, my father *was* a believer. He had to believe. He was an executioner. If there were no gods, then what horrible thing was it that he did?

Now he was going to find out.

It angered him that it was taking so long to slowly waste away into death. So he cursed the gods. Especially the six-armed Borzai, who would choose which hall we would spend eternity in.

My father swore at Borzai, even though he would soon meet the god. And even though that god would decide his afterlife, my father was not the sort of man who cared. He had no thoughts for the future, and he dwelled little on the past.

I always had admired that about my father. Even though I hated much about his coarseness toward me.

My oldest son, Duram, peeked around a post to look into the kitchen, his dark curly hair falling down over his brown eyes. "Is he sleeping?"

I nodded. "Are you hungry?"

"I am," Duram said. "So is Set, but he doesn't want to come down the stairs. He says it hurts."

Set had been born with a twisted foot.

"Stay quiet," I cautioned as I picked up a wooden platter. I spooned olives from a jar, tore off several large pieces of bread, cut some goat's cheese, and then lined the edges with figs.

Duram dutifully snuck back up the crude wooden stairs, and I heard the planks overhead creak as he took the food to his brother. Soon he would need to work for the family.

But for now, I sheltered him in the attic with his brother and their toys. I wanted them both to have some peace before their worlds got harder. Particularly Set's.

I opened a window and looked outside. My husband, Jorda, was supposed to be working the field. Instead he was sprawled under a gnarled tree, a wineskin lying over a blistered forearm.

There was always a wineskin. Ever since he had run away from tending the sentinel braziers along the Mayor's Bridge. Unable to scrub the sweet smell of neem and mint from his skin, or unsee the people dragged away, glowing blue and sobbing because of him.

I never passed him a single copper earned from my butchering, but he still found wine. He usually begged them from his friends among the Alacan refugees. He'd sit with them and loudly damn the collapse of Alacan, and they'd cheer him and buy him cheap wine.

With a sigh, I shut the wooden window.

My father groaned and swore in his sleep, disturbed by the cold air. I would have liked to have had a healer here. Someone who could give us bitter medicine, and hope. A kind ear for the betrayals of the body.

But for all that I may have hated the Jolly Mayor and his terrifying majister, my family's lives had depended on the Mayor over the years. My life, my two sons, my husband, and my father. For my father, skinny, frail, overtempered bastard and profaner that he was, was an executioner for Khaim and the Mayor.

We would have starved a long time ago without that money. The coin tossed in the executioner's cup by the soon-to-be-beheaded in hopes of buying a good cut. The coppers tossed into the bucket by the crowd. The Mayor's retainer.

So when the tiny bell by the door rang, it was with the authority of a thunderclap. The tiny note floated around the old house's timbers, dripping into the kitchen, and wrapping itself around me as its quivering tones faded.

This was the first time it had rung since Anto had fallen sick.

My father was being summoned, as executioner, to bring his axe to the square by the highest of noon.

Somewhere, across the inky shoving waters of the Sulong River that split Lesser Khaim and Khaim, and up on Malvia Hill and in the Mayor's House, someone had rung the executioner's bell.

The bell was magic, of course. The Mayor swore that the spells that had been cast to create the bells had been formed a long time ago, and that the bells were safe. I wondered if that was true, as I could smell magic softly in the air by the doorway whenever the bell rang. It tasted of ancient inks, herbs, and spices, and it settled deep in the back of my throat.

Once the executioner's bell was rung in the Mayor's House, Deka, the goddess of a thousand multiple roads and choices, dictated which executioner's bell rang back in sympathy. And Deka had chosen ours.

Deka was well known for her tricks. The goddess of dice throwers was playing one last little one on my father.

I looked back over my thick, wooden kitchen table toward my father. His brown eyes were wide, his brows crinkled in intense thought.

He rubbed his anemic mustache, which was a sign of his failure: that he had only ever had one child, and a daughter at that.

"The call . . . ," he said, voice breaking. "Tana. Did you hear it?"

I moved to him. "You can't go. You know that."

I wondered, as I said it, where the gentleness in my voice had come from. It had never been offered to me in my life by this old man. Not in all the years I'd cooked and chopped wood, or the long years I'd worked as a butcher.

"I know I can't go, you stupid girl," my father spat. "It is well beyond me."

The bell needed to be rung if an executioner were here. In five minutes, if there was no reply, the call would go to someone else.

In a way, that dying ring would signal the death of our family. Without my father's occasional income, we would have to sell the small house and the land. And then we would become little better than the refugees around us.

I watched him lie back down onto the bed, gazing up at the thick ceiling beams. "Where is Jorda?" my father asked.

"Sleeping," I said.

"Drunk," he spat. "Weak. Addled."

"Not everyone can see blood spilled as easily as you," I snapped at my father.

His jaw set, and he said, "I have always answered the call. Always come back with the Mayor's coin to keep us alive as the bramble creeps into our useless field. I'll slit my own throat right here and now before I hand over the executioner's bell. It is all that keeps my miserable bloodline flowing."

"What are you even talking about?" I asked.

My father coughed. "The gods hate me. Had I a son, he'd be on his way to answer the call already."

My voice jumped in anger. "Well, I'm not your son. I'm your daughter. You must live with that." And then I added, "With what little life you do have left."

My father nodded. "This is true. This is true."

And then he crawled out of his bed. The blankets slipped off to reveal his liver-spotted arms.

"What are you doing?" I asked.

He stumbled out of the kitchen to the door, sticklike legs quivering from the effort.

I realized what he was about to do and moved to stop it, but with a last wily burst of energy, he staggered forward and rang the executioner's bell before I grabbed his arm.

As the single, clear note rang out and filled the back of my throat with the faint taste of old magic, he crumpled to the floor in a heap of bones and skin, laughing at me.

"Now you *have* to go in my place, daughter of mine. Now you have no choice. Jorda is drunk, Duram too young, and Set too crippled." He panted where he lay, staring up at me with eyes sunk deep into wasted, skeletal sockets. "The Mayor would execute both of us if you try to tell him what we just did. He is not a forgiving man."

"When you face Borzai in the Hall of Judgment, he will banish you to Takaz's torture cells for eternity," I told him. "When I hear your spirit groan in the night, tortured by Takaz's demon wives, I will laugh and pretend I didn't hear it."

He flinched at that. "Do you hate me so?"

I trembled with outrage. "You bring me nothing but pain and drudgery and burden."

He thought on that for a long while. Longer than I'd seen him consider anything. "You must go just this once, then. After this, you can turn the bell in. I'll be dead soon, I can't stop you, yet you must at least cover the expense of my funeral. I'll not have my appearance in Borzai's Hall of Judgment delayed because the rites were not pleasing to him. And after that, if you wish it, it could be your trade. It is a good living, daughter. And with me gone, there will be one less body to care for, one less mouth to feed. You have no field, and butchering people will give you more than butchering pigs."

Then he sighed and crawled toward his bed. I said nothing. I helped him back to it, his body surprisingly light as I slung his arm over my neck.

"How can I kill someone who has done nothing to me?" I asked.

My father grunted. "Don't look into their eyes. Consider that the Mayor and his Majister have a reason for their death: they glow blue. Remember that if they have led a proper life, they will be sent to the right hall for eternity."

"Won't the Mayor's guards be able to tell I'm not you?"

"No," my father murmured. "I've been wasting away long enough. I'm a small figure, so are you. Wear my hood, carry my axe, and none will be able to tell the difference. It is no different than chopping wood. Raise the axe, let it fall, don't swing it, and aim the edge for the neck. You've killed enough pigs, you can do this."

And with that, he slipped away to his sleep, exhausted by all his recent efforts.

I understood he'd always wanted a son. That he'd wanted the farm to produce the crops it had when he was little, before the bramble grew to choke it. I understood that he never wanted me to marry Jorda.

I understood that maybe, he'd wanted to give me the bell a long time ago, but had been too scared to do it. Why else would he have begged and called in so many favors from old friends to make sure that I worked as a butcher?

I walked through Lesser Khaim dressed as an executioner.

Inside I was still me, Tana, weary and tired, struggling to see through the small slits in the leather hood over my face.

I'd called Duram down before I'd left, and kissed him on his forehead.

"What was that for?" he'd asked, puzzled.

"Just know that I love you and your brother. I have to leave for an errand. But I will be back home soon."

After I sent him back upstairs, I'd opened the cedar chest in my father's room and pulled out the black leather jerkin, hood, and heavy cape of his office. They fit me well enough as I pulled them on, as he had said they would. His canvas leggings slid off my waist, but a length of rope fixed that.

The axe lay in the bottom of the chest, the curved edge of the blade gleaming in the light.

It weighed less than it looked, and was well balanced in my hand. Heavier than the axe I used to chop wood with, but not anywhere as heavy as I had somehow imagined.

Now I rested the axe on my shoulder and walked through the cramped streets.

The tight alleyways of Lesser Khaim gave way to the mudbanks, stilt houses, and clumps of bramble along the river. I followed a fire crew along the stone steps toward the newly finished bridge. They wore masks and thick, double-canvas clothing. As they walked they pumped the primers on the back of their tanks, then lit the fires on the brass-tipped ends of their hoses.

When they flicked the levers, fresh flame licked out across the bramble threatening to creep over the stairs. Clumps of the thorny, thick creep withered under the assault.

Clearers followed close behind, chopping at the bramble, careful not to touch any of it lest they get pricked. Children scampered around with burlap sacks to pick up bramble seeds.

They stopped the burn when they saw me, and stepped aside to let me down the path leading toward the bridge that caused the very buildup they were burning back.

"If it's magic users you're sending to Borzai's judgment today," one of them called out from behind a mask as fearsome as mine, "then I salute you."

Others agreed in wordless grunts as they hacked at bramble with axes.

The bridge across the river reared before me, the glowing sentinel braziers that Jorda had once tended choking the air with spicy, sweet herb scents. An ominous pall of smoke caused everyone to nervously glance at one another as they set foot on the magical structure, as if the bridge's furious blue glow would stain them as well. The heads of previous victims stared down upon all as we crossed, eyes warning us of the horror that awaited those who trafficked in magic.

"It ain't those unlucky people with their petty spells causing the bramble creep," someone ahead of me muttered to a friend as he looked up at the heads. He jutted his chin up into the air. "There's the real abomination."

High above us, an unfinished castle hung in the air, the foundation resting upon wisps of cloud. The sharp smell of the magic holding the half-completed structure in the air wafted down toward the bridge: strong, tangy, and dangerous.

"Mark me," the man said as we all stepped off the bridge and into Khaim. "We'll end up like Alacan: choked with bramble and fleeing our city if Scacz keeps building that unholy thing."

But he said nothing about the magic holding up the bridge he had just crossed.

I walked through Khaim, enjoying the taller marble and stone buildings and fluted columns. Sentinel braziers glowed at every intersection, and people almost leaned against the walls to try to avoid the smoke. There were few braziers yet in Lesser Khaim. At first they had sprouted quickly, looming at every gate and market square. But of late their creation had slowed. Perhaps for lack of materials, or maybe, as some whispered, because the Jolly Mayor had mostly been interested in eliminating his velvet rivals.

But my relaxation faded as I watched people scuttle away before me in nervousness. And it fully vanished when I turned to the public square and the raised platform at the center where the executions were held.

Early crowds had already gathered. Vendors walked around selling flatbreads and fruits throughout the square.

City guards waited on the lip at the top of the platform's steps. They waved me on impatiently, and I saw the figure shimmering blue in chains between them. He turned, saw me, and his knees buckled. The guards held him up under his arms and laughed.

The Jolly Mayor himself came to the square and puffed his way up the stairs onto the platform with us. His beady eyes regarded me for only the briefest of seconds, then fixed on the blade.

He smiled and moved closer. "Make this a good one, eh, Executioner?" He chuckled before I could even think to ask what he meant. Which was a good thing, as I wasn't sure I could reach for a deeper voice. I was far too nervous.

The guards dragged the sobbing and retching prisoner up the stairs. They shackled him to the four iron rings on the floor of the platform, half bowed to the Mayor, and then retreated.

Chains tinkled as the prisoner moved, trying to look over his shoulder. "Please, please, have you no mercy? My sheep were dying of mouth rot, my family would have starved. . . ."

The Mayor did not look at the man, but instead at the crowd. He cried out for all to hear, "Khaim will *not* fall to the bramble, like the cities of the empire of Jhandpara. Their failures guide us, and we call for the gods to forgive us for what we *must* do: which is to punish those who use forbidden magic, for they threaten every last one of us."

Then the Mayor turned to me and waved his hand.

A sound like a babbling brook came from the crowd. The murmur of a hundred or so voices at once. Behind that I heard the shifting of chains, and the sobbing of a doomed man.

I imagined either of my two sons laid out like this, begging for forgiveness. I imagined my husband Jorda's scrawny body there, his burn-marked arms pulled to either side by the chains.

I had to steady myself to banish these thoughts, so I wobbled a step forward.

I raised the axe high, so that I would only need to let it fall to do its work, and as I did, the crowd quieted in anticipation.

I let the axe fall.

It swung toward the vulnerable nape of the man's neck as if the blade knew what it was doing.

And then the man shifted, ever so slightly.

I twisted the handle to compensate, just a twitch to guide the blade, and the curving edge of the axe buried itself in the man's back at an angle on the right. It sank into his shoulder and fetched up against bone with a sickening crunch.

It had all gone wrong.

Blood flew back up the handle, across my hands, and splattered against my jerkin.

The man screamed. He thrashed in the chains, a tortured animal, almost jerking the axe out of my blood-slippery hands.

"Gods, gods, gods," I said, terrified and sick. I yanked the axe free. Blood gushed down the man's back and he screamed even louder.

The crowd stared. Anonymous oval faces, hardly blinking.

I raised the axe quickly, and brought it right back down on him. It bit deep into his upper left arm, and I had to push against his body with my foot to lever it free. He screamed so loudly my ears rang, and I was crying as I raised the axe yet again.

"Borzai will surely consider this before he sends you to your hall," I said, my voice scratchy and loud inside the hood. I took a deep breath and counted to three.

I would not miss again. I would not torture this dying man any more.

I must imagine I am only chopping wood, I thought.

I let the axe fall once more. I let it guide itself, looking at where it needed to be at the end of the stroke.

The blade struck the man's neck, cleaved right through it, and buried itself in the wooden platform below.

The screaming stopped.

My breath tasted of sick. I was panting and terrified as the Mayor approached me. He leaned close, and I braced for some form of punishment for doing such a horrible thing.

"Well done!" the Mayor said. "Well done indeed. What a show, what a piece of butchery! The point has well been made!"

He shoved several hard-edged coins into my hand, and then walked over to the edge of the platform. The crowd cheered, and I yanked my axe free and made my escape.

But everywhere I turned the crowd shoved coppers into the pockets of my cape, and the guards smacked me on the back and smiled.

When I turned the corner from the square I leaned over a gutter, pulled the hood up as far as I dared, and threw up until my stomach hurt. How could my father have done this for days on end during the first purges, when blood had flooded these same gutters?

Afterward, I looked down and opened the clenched fist I had made with my free hand. Four pieces of silver gleamed back at me from the blood-soaked hand.

I wanted to toss them into the stinking gutter. But then, where would that leave my family?

Slowly I began to make my way back toward the poverty of Lesser Khaim. It was only as I approached the Mayor's Bridge that the clatter of guards sweeping past me over the bridge shook me from my stupor.

They shoved past me, rushing. I tried to see who they were pursuing. Instead, across the river, I saw rising smoke.

Raiders. Close to home.

I rushed across the bridge, fighting against the fleeing crowds seeking safety in Khaim. A screaming man smacked into me. His left arm dangled uselessly, crushed. We both fell to the ground, and he scrabbled up.

"Damn you," I grunted, "what are you doing. . . ."

"Raiders!" he shouted at me. "Run for your life! Paikans have come again."

I sat up, pulling the axe close to me, and looked down the street. More smoke seeped into the tight alleyways between buildings.

And I could hear screams in the distance.

The streets were filling with people moving quickly for the river, their eyes darting about, expecting attackers in every shadow and around every alley.

"They're here to burn us to the ground," the man said. He was originally from Turis, I could hear it in his accent. He seemed to be looking far away, maybe reliving the horrors of the raider attacks that forced him to come all the way to Lesser Khaim.

It wouldn't all burn. Not unless the water brigades failed to put out the fires. The raiders started them to distract everyone while they smashed, looted, and stole. Then they took off just as quickly as they appeared, leaving the stunned warrens of Lesser Khaim behind.

People jostled past us, a moving river of humanity headed for the riverbanks. "Where are they going?" I asked. They would drown in the river if the raiders got this far, or stumble into bramble along the banks.

"Away," the man said, and ran off with them.

I pushed through the oncoming crowds. They split apart for an executioner, and if they did not, I used the bronze-weighted butt of the axe to shove them aside.

Five streets from the river, I had to turn away from my usual route home. Smoke choked the street, black and thick, and it spat people out, who coughed and collapsed to the dirt, gasping for air.

"They set fire to the slums! Don't go down there!" a woman with a flour-covered apron shouted at me.

I ignored her and ran through alleyways. I pushed through the doors of empty houses and climbed through windows to make my way around the burning sections of town, slowly getting closer to home.

I ran past several burning wrecks of the small farms of the Lesser Estates, my boots raising dust with each step. I could see the gnarled trees behind my house writhing in flame, and as I scrambled painfully over the stone wall, I saw the timbers give way and the roof fall in on itself.

The heat forced me back when I tried to run inside. I paced around the house like a confused animal. Stone cracked from the heat, and a screaming wail came from within. I ripped my hood off and shoved it into one of my pockets so I could breathe.

"Duram?" I cried. "Set?"

A blazing figure erupted from the front door, leaping onto the dusty ground and rolling around until the flames were extinguished.

It was Anto. His blackened form lay by my feet, rasping in pain.

I dropped to my knees. "Where are Duram and Set?"

"It hurts," Anto whimpered.

I shook him. "Where are my children?" But he was too sunk in his own pain to answer. I turned to the burning house and tried to rush inside, but the building collapsed. An explosion of fire and smoke shoved me back.

I fell to the ground, sobbing my despair, ashamed of my failure to save my children. The house continued to burn. I had taken a man's life. Now mine was being taken from me.

"It hurts," Anto groaned, intruding on my grief. "Please . . ."

I stared up at the house. "Duram and Set . . ."

"With Jorda." He looked up at me, eyes startlingly white against the blackened face, begging. "Please . . ."

The smell of burned flesh filled my lungs. "You can't ask me . . ."

"Please . . . ," he whispered.

So I used the axe for the second time that day.

I found Jorda's body under the tree where he had been drinking. There was an arrow through his neck and a wineskin by his feet.

Drunkard he may have been. A disappointment to Anto, this was true. But the dirt was scuffed with footmarks. Small footmarks. He'd tried to protect my sons.

I kissed the three rings on my hand and prayed to Mara that my sons were alive, and as I did so, saw the scraped dirt of Set's dragged foot next to the hoofmarks leading off down the dirt road.

With an apology to Jorda's lifeless body, a whisper of thanks to Mara, I got up and began to follow the tracks, the executioner's axe gripped tight in both hands.

The burned remains of Lesser Khaim's southern fringe faded away into the rocky hills of sparse grass and clumps of bramble as the day passed. Weariness spread through my knees, and the miles wore at me as I doggedly moved southward.

I plowed on. I had to move faster, not pick my way around bramble if I hoped to catch the raiders. I had to hope the leather apron would also help protect me from the bramble's malevolence.

At the crest of a hill scattered with boulders, I looked back at the many burning buildings of Lesser Khaim. Tiny figures formed a line by the river, passing along buckets of water to try and douse denser areas of town. The outer sections contained many black skeletal building frames.

I turned from it all, walking down the other side of the hill, the axe weighing heavier and heavier.

At the bottom of the hill, turning onto the old cobblestoned ruins of Junpavati Road, I caught up to the raiding party. The men rode massive, barrel-chested warhorses that looked like they could pull an oxen's plough. They held their long spears in the air, like flagpoles, and their brass helmets glinted as they rode alongside a mass of humanity being herded south like sheep.

Somewhere, in that sad, roped-together crowd, were my sons.

I wondered how many other townsmen had tried to fight the raiders? And how many lay dead on the dirt roads of Lesser Khaim with pitchforks or knives in hands.

I stared at the raiders. Only four of them had been left to march their captives along. No doubt the rest had ridden on ahead.

Four trained men.

And me.

I would die, I knew. But what choice did I have? They were ripping my family away. What person would run from their own blood?

I killed already today, I thought, hefting the executioner's axe. I was dizzy from exhaustion, and the mild poison of the few bramble threads that had poked through my leggings threatened to drop me into bramble sleep. But I made my decision, and moved toward the raiders.

As I did so, I pulled the executioner's hood back over my face to protect myself from the taller clumps of bramble drooping off the rocks.

I used the rocks and boulders of the dead landscape to get close to the raider trailing the column of prisoners. I was stunned by how large the man's warhorse was. When its hooves slammed into the ground, I could feel them from twenty feet behind.

The hems of my cloak brushed bramble as I ran at the man's back, and the horse whinnied as it sensed me. The raider spun in his saddle, spear swinging down in an arc as he looked for what had spooked the horse, and he spotted me.

He realized I was inside the spear's reach, and he leaped off his horse to avoid the first high swing of my axe at his thigh, putting the horse between us. I ran in front of the giant beast to get at him, but before I could even raise the axe again, he attacked.

His red cloak flared out behind him, and the spear lashed out. I was slow, but I dodged the point. In response the man flicked it up and smacked the top of my head with the side of the shaft.

"And what do you think you're doing?" the raider demanded. He sounded unhurried and calm.

"You stole my family," I said as my knees buckled from the blow to the head. I fought to stand, and wobbled slightly. Hoofbeats thudded behind me.

The raider used the spear to hit me on the side of my head before I could even raise the axe to try and block the movement. His movements would have been too fast for me even if I hadn't been tired from chasing them, or my blood filled with bramble poison. The blow dropped me to the ground, blood running down over my eyes inside the hood, blinding me.

"What do we have here?" a second raider voice asked, as feet hit the ground. My hood was ripped clear of my head.

The two raiders bent over me, dark eyes shadowed by their bronze helmets, spears pinning my cloak, and me, to the ground.

I blinked the blood out of my eyes and waited for death.

"It's a woman," the raider I'd attacked said.

"That's quite plain," said the other. "Should we kill her or take her with us?"

"She's too old to go to the camps or to sell."

The other raider nodded. "So we kill her?"

"She doesn't need to be part of the Culling," the older-sounding raider said. He shook his head. "No, she's too old to have children. She's no threat. Cripple her so she can't follow us, then leave."

The older raider remounted his horse and left.

The remaining raider and I stared at each other, and then he reversed his spear. "The Way of the Six says that we should . . ."

I spat at him. The effort dizzied me. "I don't care about your damned Way of the Six, slaver. Do what you came to do."

He shrugged and slammed the butt of his spear into my ankle, crushing it.

As I screamed, he smacked my head. I fell back away, down into a patch of bramble, some of which pierced my clothing. The bramble threads stuck to my skin calling me down to sleep, it was enough to easily drag me away from the world.

To my shock, I woke up with a grunt in the dark, something creaking and swaying beneath me. I'd been dreaming about a younger Set, his large brown eyes looking into mine as he struggled so hard to stumble about, learning to walk. He'd fallen, and I'd rushed out, shouting at him to be careful, and then I had woken up.

I felt for my forehead, but there was no pain or bump as I expected.

My ankle felt fine. I felt fine, except for the extreme slowness that remained with me from the bramble sleep. I'd brushed against it once before, as a child. My parents had found me staggering about in the backyard and pulled the bramble threads from my skin carefully with tweezers. People fretted over me for nearly a week as I lingered on the edge of darkness.

I licked my dried lips and sat up.

The world kept creaking back and forth.

I heard wheels turning underneath me.

I was inside a covered wagon of some sort. Daylight peeked through cracks in wooden walls and top. And I could taste fish and salt hanging in the air.

A bird screeched outside, and I realized I must be near the coast.

My axe lay near me, as did my leather hood. Which meant I was somewhere safe.

In a daze I crawled toward a large flap, and as I reached it a hand flung it aside, blinding me with daylight.

"Well, hello there," someone said gently. "I was just coming to check on you."

My eyes watered, as if they hadn't seen sunlight in weeks.

Strong hands gripped my arm. "Careful, or you'll fall off."

I sat on the back of a large wagon. A small deck ran around the rim of the vehicle. A woman my age, traces of gray in her hair, held my arm. Her trader tattoos, including a striking purple figure of the elephant god Sisinak holding the triple scales of commerce, ran up and down her forearms. "I'm Anezka," she said. She squatted on the platform jutting off the back. "I was bringing you some soup. Everyone's going to be excited to hear you woke up."

I moved out onto the platform with Anezka, still amazed that my ankle wasn't hurting. Another wagon trundled along behind the one I woke up on, pulled by four massive aurochs. They looked like cattle, but far more muscular. Their long horns swooped well out before them like the prows of ships. Four aurochs also followed the back of the wagon I was on, resting from the strain of pulling. Their flanks rippled and hooves thumped the ground as they all plodded along.

Behind the wagon following us was another, and then another, and then another yet again. I counted ten before the long train of wagons curved around a bend in a fine cloud of kicked up dust. Each wagon featured its own unique mottled purple-and-green painted patterns on their wooden sides. Many had carved depictions of markets, roads, and maps of the world all expertly chipped into their sides.

"This is a caravan," I said out loud, realizing it at the same moment I spoke it.

"This is *the* caravan," Anezka said. "You're traveling the spice road on the perpetual caravan. We move along the coast starting in Paika and go all the way to Mimastiva and even a little beyond, until the bramble of the east stops us with its wall. Then we turn back around again. There used to be many, all throughout the old empire. Now: only us."

Mimastiva was on the coast, hundreds of miles from Khaim. Paika lay on the coast as well, far to the west. I knew of a few who'd visited Mimastiva. These were cities that, to me, were almost past the edge of the known world.

"You said that people would be excited I was awake," I said.

Anezka's eyes widened. "Because you're the lady executioner, who met four Paikans in mortal combat. Everyone's been talking about you up and down the line."

"I didn't fight four," I said with a frown. "I only took on one, and he beat me badly. But yes, there were four of them."

I looked down at my ankle. "How long have I been asleep?"

"You should see the roadmaster," Anezka said.

"Why is that?" I asked.

"Because this is his wagon, and you are his guest," Anezka said, somewhat formally, but quite firmly.

With her arm to steady me, I grabbed the ropes along the outside of the covered wagon's rim and we walked toward the front.

As we approached the raised platform from where the aurochs were controlled, I could see up the line of the caravan. We were near the front. Muscled men with brass arquebuses stood on a fifteen-paces-long war wagon in front of us, with hammered metal shield-walls protecting them.

Farther ahead, a wagon with a large fire crew burned bramble away from the road edges, the roar of the flame carrying back over the air to us. The stench of the burned limbs wafted past.

I was a long way from Lesser Khaim.

The roadmaster was a mountain of a successful, rich man, robes draped across the heft of his belly.

But if I thought him jolly, that was a mistake. His smile was tight, controlled, and his eyes shrewd. This man saw more miles pass under the wheels of his home in a year than most ever traveled in a life.

And judging by the lines in his face, he'd had a long life doing this. Like Anezka, trader tattoos ran up and down his forearms, and his ears dangled from his ears.

He had no mustaches, his lips were shaved clean, like a refugee from Alacan.

I'd heard tales of the caravan, and the coastal spice route. Townsmen who traveled south to markets were told tales of the great market of Mimastiva by other townsmen who ventured that far south, and here I was, sitting on a wagon with the roadmaster of the caravan himself.

"Welcome to the spice road," the roadmaster said with a twitch in the corner of his lips. He did not hold the reins himself: that was done by a young man in a loincloth with massive arms who sat nearby, the thick leather straps that lead to the aurochs were draped across his lap. The driver watched the road like an owl, his eyes never blinking.

"Thank you," I said, and moved to sit by him. Perching higher than the bramble along the road meant that a soft sea breeze cooled my skin.

From here I could see the road stretching out along the rocky coastline before us. The ocean, hundreds of feet below, slammed and boomed against the wall of brown rock. And out beyond the spray, the green waves surged around pinnacles of rock shaped like the spires of castles. And beyond the spray and foam, the sea stretched out forever: flat, unbreaking, the color of wintergreen leaves.

"It is a beautiful sight," the roadmaster said, noticing my gaze.

"I never thought I'd see it in my life," I whispered. I wondered if Duram or Set had seen this as they were being marched west.

I leaned forward to hide my face in my grief, and the roadmaster leaned close and touched my shoulder. "What is your name, Lady Executioner?"

"Tana." I swallowed. "Tana the lost. Tana the homeless. Tana the abandoned. But not Tana the lady executioner. I'm not that thing."

"I am Jal," he said softly. "Where are you from, Tana?"

"Khaim," I told him, and then I corrected myself. "Lesser Khaim."

"Ah, Khaim." He nodded. "I think I remember Khaim from when I was just a boy. I was still sitting on my father's lap when he led the last caravan through. Sometimes I think I remember the start of that journey, or the greater cities of the Jhandparan Empire. I know I remember seeing a great palace that had fallen to Earth, tilted, its foundational plane shattered like a plate! And the bramble, it gripped the city like a giant's fist, it did."

My grief broke a little, hearing his memories. "You are that old?"

Jal laughed at me. "I am that old. Yes. Hopefully old enough that I'll die before I lose the title of roadmaster to the title of bushmaster, which is what they will call me when even the spice road on this coast becomes choked by damned bramble."

I looked out on the road, and thought about what came next. "Where do you head?"

"Paika," the roadmaster said. "And you will too."

He said this so firmly, I jerked to stare at him. "What do you mean?"

"The men who delivered you here said you attacked four Paikans on your own. They said you demanded your family back and fought to the near death. So I have to imagine that a person who did that, would not then turn around and head back to where she came from."

As he spoke, he turned and looked at me with a larger smile.

"I will not be going back to Lesser Khaim," I agreed.

"The men who brought you to me thought so. Paika is the greatest city in the west, and where your family most probably will be taken. And Paika is a carefully guarded city. You cannot enter without an examination, and papers, and a writ, unless you are like me and have dispensation. The Paikans fear people like you coming in to try and find their families. Yes, a person who attacks four of them would go to Paika with someone like me, who could get you inside, I think."

I shook my head in frustration. "I didn't attack all four of the raid— I mean Paikans. The stories are wrong."

"Of course they are. They're always wrong. Stories are for the listener, Tana. And it is what the listener makes of them that truly matters. The captured men who saw you attack the Paikans, they told us they found their courage. If one woman could attack four horsemen, then they could do the same. For two days and two nights they plotted, and then finally . . . attacked!"

I couldn't believe what I heard. But it had to be true, didn't it? Or I wouldn't be here. "And they succeeded?"

"They killed three of the Paikans and took their gold, their weapons, and their horses. Then one of them rode back to find you, where you were deep in the clutches of bramble sleep."

"How long?" I asked. Jal waved a hand at me and ignored the question.

"When I saw them outside Mimastiva, they had you on a travois pulled behind a horse. They wanted to ride back to their homes along the coast as fast as they could without being slowed down, so they gave me a captive Paikan horseman in exchange for food, and coin for us to take care of you. We will ransom the raider back to Paika for good coin."

Up ahead the aurochs plodded forward. The wagon groaned and creaked along.

"How long have I slept?" I asked again, fearing the worst.

"Three weeks, I think. Maybe a month. We made bets to Deka on whether you would wake. You are lucky to return to us. Even luckier that the man who picked up your body to bury it with honors heard you still whispering in your sleep."

I rubbed my arms. "Whispering?"

"Names, I was told. Those close to you?"

"Family," I said, feeling the loss once again. Would it be possible to find my family then, after a month? Or would they be scattered to even stranger lands? I bit my lip and looked at Jal. "The stories I have heard say the caravan is an expensive place to ride. Wherever I am, you can't carry any goods for trade, right? What are you asking for the price of my passage?"

I asked that, while fearing the worst.

"I'm not after your body," Jal muttered. "The coin and the prisoner your inspired friends gave me for your safety is enough. Or we would have left you asleep by the side of the road weeks ago. But you are right: no one in the caravan lies around. Well, unless they're in a bramble sleep. I will move you to another wagon, and you will work. Everyone in the caravan helps the caravan. That is our way."

I was relieved. "In Lesser Khaim I—"

Jal held up a hand to stop me. "Our needs are different from a town's. I don't care what you used to do. The caravan is a new life for you, until we reach Paika. Anezka says we need cooks in the lagging wagons to the rear. Or firewood scroungers. We need hagglers and movers with the trading teams, inventory managers to make sure nothing is being stolen—"

Now it was my time to interrupt. I thought about my fight with the raiders, and about the future I was now thrown into. I was in a strange new land and, as Jal said, starting a new life.

I pointed at the wagon ahead of the fire crew. "Those men, with the arquebuses. Let me join them. I want to learn how to use those weapons. In Khaim there are just a handful of those weapons, in the careful guard of the Jolly Mayor. And here you have a team armed with them, it is very impressive."

Jal made a face. "Impressive? The majisters of Jhandpara would call down rocks from the skies and fly over their enemies to rain fire on them. *That* was impressive. These things are just loud tubes."

"I'm sorry," I said.

"No, no, I suppose you are right. The arquebus would be an interesting weapon for a lady . . ." and I could see the word "executioner" lurk behind his lips, but then falter as I stared coolly at him. ". . . for you to wield," he corrected himself.

I looked at the road curving off into my future, filled with ruts and ropes of bramble. "Jal. The caravan goes all the way to Paika, then back to Mimastiva. You trade with them?"

"Of course. I am a man of trade," the roadmaster said, slapping the tattoos on his forearms. "I work with anyone willing to pay a fair price for my goods, and leave me to the spice road. But my allegiance is to no single city. Most of us abandon such loyalties after years on the road, as cities rise and fall, come and go. Many of the families on the caravan have always been in the caravan, and will never rest until they reach the halls of Sisinak, if Borzai wills it and your life's trades have been judged honest. It is only there they will rest in the oasis markets, where the goods are never scarce, and the gold in your purse refills every night." Jal chuckled.

"So you are no friend of the Paikans."

"I am no one's *friend*, I am a trader," Jal said. "If you doubt me, go see the Paikan chained away in our wagon. He will remain there until we get to his city and I negotiate a good price for his freedom."

"I may well do that," I said.

Jal raised his hands and clapped them together. "So. You want to use an arquebus. I will humor you. Bojdan! Come here."

One of the warriors looked back at us, set his arquebus down, then swung over the shields to drop to the road. He waited for the road-master's wagon to approach, then climbed easily up onto the deck by us. "Yes?"

He was tall, with curled hair and a thick mustache. A massive scimitar hung on his left hip.

"This is Tana, the lady executioner. She will work with you to protect the caravan."

Bojdan looked me up, then down. "She is a woman," he said.

"Your powers of observation are astounding, Bojdan. It's a damned shame you aren't in charge of accounts, or haggling. Yes, she's a woman, it is plain for you and me to see. She is the woman who took on four Paikan soldiers by herself. Can you say the same?"

Again Bojdan regarded me. "Whatever you want, Roadmaster."

"You're correct, Bojdan. It *is* whatever I want. Take her back to a wagon with space to sleep, and teach her what she needs to know. And get out of my sight, by all the damned halls, get out of my sight."

Bojdan smiled. This was banter for them, the bluster that men exchanged. He turned around. "Let's go, Tana."

Jal cleared his throat. "Oh, and tell Anezka that Tana will not be joining them at the rear of the caravan to help out. She will be disappointed, I'm sure, but she is a capable manager, and will carry on."

I looked back at Jal. "Thank you."

"Good luck . . ." and he seemed to think about something, then smiled and said, "Executioness."

I shook my head and went back to fetch my things.

When Bojdan later saw my axe with the black stains in the handle, he nodded and smiled widely.

The muscular warrior and I stood, our backs to scrub, rock, and bramble, and waited for the caravan to pass us by.

"Do you know anything about the raiders?" I asked.

"The Paikans?" Bojdan spat. "Dogs. All of them."

I liked the large man better for the reaction. "They took my family."

"They all but own the coast and more ever north. Though I thought they would avoid the Blue City, what with your Majister Scacz and all we hear about him. Ask Jal sometime about the Paikans, he'll piss himself complaining about the extortions they rip from him to 'allow' him to keep trafficking the spice road."

"If anything they've increased their raids," I told him. "They burned my home."

"They call what they do the Culling. They believe it is their holy duty. You're lucky to live: they go after young women and children. Eliminate the breed cows, they say."

I stared at him. "How do you know all this?"

"Their preachers are all over Mimastiva these days," Bojdan said. "Things will get worse in the east, now."

"Why do they do it?" I asked. What bizarre blasphemy did they preach?

"They blame us for the bramble," Bojdan said, and pointed at a small wagon with a single auroch pulling it. "The surviving Paikan of the four you faced is in that wagon. . . ."

I cut him off. "I keep saying this and no one listens to me: I didn't face all four of them. It was just one, and he knocked me to the ground easily. They hobbled me and left me."

Bojdan nodded as we watched the wagon pass. For a moment, I thought about swinging aboard and using my axe to kill the man inside. But Bojdan saw the thought crossing my face, and he smiled. "Don't think about sneaking off in the night to come and kill him. Jal will know it was you, and you wouldn't want to experience his anger if he were to lose his ransom."

Better not to endanger my chance of getting to Paika, I thought. As the wagon passed on, I saw a glimpse of a figure sitting behind iron bars, his back to the world. I didn't recognize him as one of the two Paikans I'd seen.

"How long until we get to Paika?" I asked.

"Five weeks. Maybe six. The caravan is slow." Bojdan folded his arms. "We'll find you a place to sleep and get your axe sharpened up. And then I guess I'm the one stuck training you so that the next time you decide to take on a group of Paikans, you might at least kill one of them."

For the first two days Bojdan set me to walking alongside the caravan to get my feet back under me. We passed through more scrub and rock on the cliffs, and during those two days began to move downhill, even closer to the ocean as the land sloped. We passed coves of sand nestled in between the scallops of coast. My ankle was somewhat tender, and at night, I'd walk back to the wagon near the very end of the caravan and curse the pain.

But by the third day it was a dull ache, and Bojdan let me up into the guard wagon as we eased past a tiny fishing village perched over the ocean. Fishermen in rags raced up foothills, loudly hawking dried fish hanging from poles on their backs.

I noticed none of the other men on the guard wagon would look me in the eye. I could feel that they resented my being there.

We stood higher than all the caravan here, and I could see the five other guard wagons scattered throughout the snakelike convoy behind us.

"We used to have scouts running out ahead, beside, and lagging behind," Bojdan told me. "But Jal cannot afford it anymore. So we must be more vigilant than ever."

As he said that, he looked around at the villagers to our side that pressed close to the wagons, shouting and trying to barter as the caravan stolidly moved on.

I pointed at the gilded, brassworked arquebus Bojdan had over his shoulder. "But what about that? Isn't it a good weapon?"

"All weapons are good, if used properly," Bojdan said. He handed me the device. "It is loud, and almost anyone can use it, with some training. It sends bandits scurrying well enough."

It was heavy and clumsy in my hands. I looked down the long barrel, its surface etched with thin, serpentine dragons. "I want to learn how to use this properly. . . ."

He smiled.

I learned how to pour the powder, light the matchlock, and raise the arquebus to the side of the shieldwall to balance the ever-heavy barrel.

Powder was expensive, so Bojdan drilled me for the day without it. Over and over again I mimed putting in powder, putting in shot, tamping, then setting the gun on the ledge and aiming. I did it until my shoulders were sore.

"Look past the barrel," Bojdan urged, "to your target. That tree right over there. They are not accurate like a crossbow, or arrows, but you should still make the effort to aim."

This time the gun was loaded. The acrid burning match, pinched between the serpentine lock, had been pulled back and was ready to strike. All I had to do was pull the trigger, and the burning fuse would descend into the pan.

"Okay, fire it," Bojdan said.

I did, and the world exploded in light and smoke. "Sons of whores!" I shouted, startled, and when the smoke cleared I saw a mess of shredded leaves and some broken branches far to the right of where I had aimed. And my shoulder hurt.

Bojdan's men laughed at me. "It's got a kick, yeah?"

But Bojdan didn't laugh. "Clean it, get a new one in, try again. Same tree!"

I reloaded rapidly, but not quick enough. The tree was almost obscured by the roadmaster's wagon by the time I set the barrel on the shieldwall.

Bojdan grabbed it. "That was not bad, but not quick enough. So let's not shoot our employer with stray shot today. Shoot *that* tree."

I aimed at our sides again, and this time I was expecting the unholy roar of the weapon. Smoke burned my face, and tears stung my eyes, but pieces of shot had fanned out and hit the tree I'd aimed at.

"Good," Bojdan said.

And then it was back to walking alongside the caravan for me.

In the second week, after more drills, Bojdan decided I could handle the arquebus well enough. We had left the coastal cliffs long behind us, and wound our way through soft plains near the ocean's edge. Trees, and farther inland, woods, began to hem the road we traveled on, not just bramble and brush. "You know as much as us about the arquebus," he said. "Now it's time to think about close quarters. I will teach you to use your axe."

For this we left the caravan, once I'd retrieved the executioner's axe. We walked out into the woods as the wagons slowly rumbled past. Bojdan came with his scimitar, which was always at his side, and a small round shield he'd taken from the wagon's wall.

He looked me up and down. "You may think that because you are a woman you are not a match for my men in the caravan. But if a one-hundred-pound warrior came to me, I would not turn him away merely because my men weigh twice what he does. I would, however, have to understand how best to use him. He is a tool. Some tools are large and heavy, useful for clubbing and smashing things. Some are thin daggers, useful for stabbing quickly."

This was the longest thing I'd heard him say, and it sounded carefully thought out, like a speech. "Did you think of how you would say this all last night, as you sat sentry?" I asked him.

"Shut up. There are hard lands we will pass through, and we will be attacked, and you will protect the caravan." He pulled his shirt apart to show scars on his chest, then pushed his sleeves up to show a wicked scar that cut deep into his upper arm, biting into the muscle there. "Whether you be a trained warrior, or an old lady, the skill of fighting lies not in what you can pick up, but in how much flesh you carve, and how well you will carve it, Tana. No one cares whether the person who does this is large, small, woman, or man. Even the best die suddenly on the battlefield. Death is death."

That was a true thing. But I held the axe out in my two hands. "You want me to use this axe, not a sword? Or a scimitar like you?"

Bojdan tapped the hilt of his blade. "Do you have a sword? Have you suddenly come into money, and can afford to buy one from someone here in the caravan?"

"No," I muttered.

"Then," he said, "it will be the axe, because it is what you have. I have held it, while you were sleeping. It is well balanced. It is light, and easy to wield. Hold it two handed, just like when chopping wood. And remember, you hold a unique weapon."

He moved my hand up a little, and then the other down. "A unique weapon?" I asked.

"Most men hold their shield with the left hand. With your axe, it is easy to switch it to a left handed strike, easier than learning to use a sword with your left. And you have a swing that comes easy to their unprotected side." He held his shield up to demonstrate. "Swing slowly."

Like chopping at a tree from the left, I did, and I could see what he meant. He had to move aside to get the shield in front of him. "I'm making you move around," I said.

"You're controlling the fight. From the first swing. There are other things you can do with the axe. For example, you can swing it past them and yank back, getting their neck with the downward facing edge of the axe's point. You can stab at them with the upward point of the blade. Spike them with the side away from the blade shaped so conveniently just like a spearpoint. Use the axe as a hook, to sweep them off their feet."

There was more. And halfway through the slowly shown moves, I stopped. "You know a great deal about fighting with axes."

Bojdan paused. "It's a peasant's weapon . . . and my first."

"Why do so few use it then?" I asked. "Everyone has one."

Bojdan thought about it, as if for the first time. "It's not the weapon of a warrior, but of the low peoples. It's for chopping trees and bramble, not flesh. That is what fighters say. Did the guards in Khaim work for their meals, or do nothing but soldier?"

"No," I shook my head. "They only soldiered."

He grinned, and warmed to the subject. "So whether mercenaries or trained soldiers, it's the people who hold weapons who choose what they use the most. And they are not the same people who farm. So the axe isn't seen as a battle weapon."

I understood. "And that is good for me."

"Maybe." Bojdan shrugged. "There are many unusual weapons on the field. People who spend their lives smitten by particular weapons bring their preferred lover to the field of play. But it is not those small things that determine a battle. That is decided by things that take place long before foes meet."

I perked up. Bojdan commanded the fighting men of the caravan.

It sounded like he had seen more combat than just scaring off bandits. "Like what?"

"It is how many soldiers are raised," he said. "Your axe will do you no good against a well-aimed arrow. But an archer would have trouble escaping the jab of a sword. And so on. It is the mix of weapons and people, and how many they wield. It is how fresh they are. How healthy. Valor and intention are good for the heat of a battle, but if you are vastly outnumbered, there is only so much bravery can do."

I hefted the axe and thought about it. Bravery while charging the four Paikans had only gotten me beaten and left on the ground. "You need to win the battle before your first stroke."

Bojdan grinned. "Yes. And speaking of strokes, right there is a sapling we can take back for firewood for the cooks. Remember, chop from your left, the tree's right, to get past its shield."

"What shield?" I asked.

Bojdan walked past me even as I said that and strapped his shield to a branch that jutted out enough to be used as a temporary arm.

"Get to it!" he ordered.

And I took on the small tree as if it were a raider, swinging past the shield and biting the axe into the meat of the sapling's bark over and over again, until it toppled forward and Bojdan yanked me out of the way.

"Never get so focused that you forget what else is around you," he said, as the tree struck the ground beside us.

For four weeks we continued. Slow-moving practices against each other, and fast ones when I faced more trees. Bojdan carved a blunt axe out of wood for me and swaddled it with cloth, and then he made a light wooden scimitar padded just the same for himself.

With these we dueled in the ever-thickening woods beside the caravan. The road began to slowly move back away from the coast, into the foothills. The ever-present smell of salt faded away, and we stopped passing seaside villages.

Few towns existed here in the thick overgrowth, due to bramble.

Only a few solitary homesteads fought back, alone, becoming trapped by the increasing thicket and bramble just miles north of the road.

Occasionally dim figures watched us go past from the shadows. Our guards fingered their arquebuses, but nothing happened.

For a big man Bojdan moved damnably fast, constantly bruising my ribs and shoulders as we practiced, even slamming the padded scimitar down on my neck with swipes of his practice weapon.

Every time he hit me he'd tonelessly mutter, "Dead."

But by the fourth week, he stopped saying that and moved on to: "Maimed."

After we fought, we'd run to catch back up to the caravan, sitting on the most rearward defense wagon, panting and catching our breaths.

I slept in a bunking wagon, filled with slat beds mounted onto the walls. Ten women shared the tiny space, but I hardly knew them, even after four weeks. Except for Anezka. She'd been there as I woke up from my bramble sleep and kept to my side, helping me understand the world of the wagons.

When I had asked her why, she tapped the tattoos on her forearms. "It's an investment."

I always came to the wagon tired after Bojdan's training. I would crawl right into my bunk and fall asleep.

Bojdan and his men never saw me weaken. I'd worked among men in the butcher shops enough to know their minds. To know that to show weakness, tears, or anything other than humor and rage was to invite judgment.

But alone in the bunks, when sleep failed me and I was alone with nothing more than the sounds of snoring women and the darkness that pressed against me, then I would sometimes surrender to tears as I thought about Set and Duram.

Because of that, I feared being alone with my mind. So I trained every moment I could, worked every second I could bear.

At first the women in the bunking wagon did not speak to me, or even meet my eyes, until the oldest, a lady with a leathery weathered face called Alka, asked if maybe I was fighting with Bojdan because I was not really a woman.

"I bore two children that the Paikans took," I told her. "Torn from me like the old healer tore them from my body when they both refused to come easily. Would you have me expose myself to everyone in here to prove you wrong?"

I grabbed the hems of my skirts to raise them.

Alka shook her head quickly, scandalized, and the younger girls in the wagon laughed at her. "Of course she's a woman!" Anezka shouted at them. "She is the Executioness, remember? Not the executioner!"

I shook my head at Jal's name for me. "Don't call me that," I asked. "I am just Tana."

The women settled at Anezka's berating. Anezka was, I had found out, a quartermaster. The large mass of caravaners in the trailing edge provided the needs of the whole human train. Anezka and others like her handled accounting for supplies, and kept the trade goods under lock and key.

"There's the roadmaster," she had explained once over a stewpot hanging from the balcony of the bunking wagon as we ate, "and then there's the quartermasters. We really run it all."

The more I listened to the women chat in the wagon, the more I realized they were the grease that kept the caravan's wheels from seizing. And Anezka, with her silver-streaked dark hair, piercing dark eyes and purple tattoos, was the shadow ruler of the whole caravan.

There were questions and pieces of information constantly bandied around me between the bunks: Whose aurochs needed better feed? How fast was the caravan going? By the way, Anezka had noted a couple days ago, the flour was getting low, if they didn't get some barrels refilled, they'd run out in a week.

All these things and more these women knew.

Jal directed the caravan, but my bunkmates made the caravan a living creature.

And I was not one of them, though they all treated me with careful politeness.

At the start of the fifth week, Bojdan sent me out with Anezka and three other women for water, as one of the casks had sprung a leak.

"We are near a small river that runs beside the road," he said. "Keep a guard. It's a safe area, but be careful."

Up and down the caravan, flags whipped up onto small wooden masts at the rear of the wagons, giving the order to slow their pace.

Anezka and her three companions pulled along a two-wheeled cart that had three empty barrels on it. They laughed and joked as we moved down a narrow dirt path through the trees, out of sight of the caravan, and toward the babble of the tiny stream.

"I like to oversee where the water comes from," Anezka said. "Sometimes these three get timid and don't want to wade clear out to the center where it's freshest."

"It was just once," one of them protested.

"We all suffered for it for a week," Anezka said. She looked over at me. "Will you leave us, when we get to Paika?"

"Yes." I walked beside her, and I looked around the forest as she talked.

"That's a shame. You could spend forever in that strange city, and never find someone," she said.

"You've seen it?" I asked.

"Right after I joined the caravan to see the world, and Jal was negotiating the rights to travel in their territory," Anezka said. "Building on building crammed into mazes of leaning streets. It's on a hill, and everything looks ready to fall over on top of everything else. And it goes on and on, from the foothills and up."

We reached the river, and I helped her pull a barrel from the wagon and roll it into the river with a splash. Anezka guided it to the center, her skirts knee-deep in the strong current. "Well, if they are there to be found, I will find them. And if they are not to be found . . ."

"Then what?" Anezka asked.

"I will kill the bastards that killed them," I said quietly.

"That is good," said one of the other women. "You do what few of us can. Most of us lost families or our husbands to the Paikans. That's why we joined the caravan. What else were we to do?"

Anezka nodded. "They cull us. Or they take our youngest to large camps on some of the islands in their harbors, and off the coasts, where we can never get to them. It's there that they teach them the Paikan ways and thoughts."

Everyone nodded. "Paikan ways: they're spreading," I said.

Anezka stopped the barrel back up. I moved to help her roll it, but she pointed.

Five men had slipped out of the shadows of the trees on the opposite bank, hardly twenty feet from us. I hadn't noticed them. They held old, rusty swords and were dressed in little more than rags.

Realizing they had been seen, they splashed awkwardly across the hip-deep water at us, swords raised.

I picked up my axe. "Run for the caravan, but if they catch you, resist them any way you can!" I shouted. I saw the grins on the men's faces as their splashing steps soaked their torn clothes. "Go!"

So much for vengeance, I thought, my heart pounding. I would die slowing these attackers down enough so that Anezka and her friends could get to safety.

Well, there were worse things to spend a life on.

I only hoped my sons would forgive me.

The men did not realize I'd picked up an axe. I let my body shield it from their view.

Until they got close. I drew it from behind me and swung at the nearest man. His compatriots ran past us, leaving him alone to deal with me. I misjudged his running, and missed. Although surprised and uncertain about my axe, he attacked.

After blocking his swing, I slid the axe down the blade, then shoved it forward, puncturing his stomach with the spike at the top of the axe's curve.

We both looked surprised that it had worked, and then I shoved him free to lie in the river, crying and groaning as his stomach spilled into the formerly clean river water.

The four other men had caught themselves four struggling women and were laughing.

I ran, almost tripping over my skirts, and raised my axe up into the air and buried it into the lower spine of the first man I caught up to. Anezka, pinned underneath, screamed loudly enough the three remaining men paused. They looked over as the man on top of her rolled off. He spasmed and gushed blood after I yanked the axe free to face our attackers.

The three others shoved the women away and began to move at me.

Bojdan hadn't taught me how to take on three opponents at once.

But he had taught me that a fight was won before the fight began. Digging deep inside I calmed myself and met their gazes with a grin.

It was an anticipatory grin. As if the first two men I had just killed were no more than an appetizer, and this was about to be a course I was looking forward to.

Never mind that I had killed one half of them because he expected no real resistance, and the other because his back was turned.

"Who are you, lady?" one bandit asked.

And Anezka stepped behind me. "Can't you tell by the damned blade?" she cried out indignantly. "This is the Executioness!"

They looked at the axe, and I wiped the blood from its edge with my thumb and tested the sharpness.

When I looked back up at them, I saw I had won this battle, for there was fear there now. "The one who faced an entire party of Paikans," one of them asked.

"Yes, that one," Anezka said.

I walked forward, axe in hand, and the nearest man threw his sword at my feet. "I surrender my weapon," he said.

After a moment, the others did too.

"Pick up the swords," I ordered Anezka.

She did, and handed them to the other women. "Run for the caravan," I whispered to her. "Get Bojdan and some of his men, quick!"

"Yes," Anezka replied, wide-eyed. And then she spun and ran away.

I turned back. Were there more men out in the woods? If I let these three go, would they come back for their revenge? "You three, see those barrels?" I asked.

They nodded.

"Get them aboard that cart, and pull it over here," I ordered. They did so, quickly and with some grunting, and once the cart was in front of me, I hopped on. "Now follow those women back to the road. Do not give me any excuses to take your heads."

They again nodded.

Sitting on top of a barrel, I watched them closely as they pulled the cart through the forest to the road. I remained calm outwardly, but inside my heart raced, my breath came short, and I was terrified of every shadow in the trees.

When we broke out onto the road, the caravan was still slowly passing us by.

Bojdan and three of his men rushed up to us. They looked at my prisoners with some shock.

I leaped down from the cart, my bloodied axe over my shoulder, and grabbed Bojdan by the arm. "I would talk to you over here," I said, and lead him around to the other side of a wagon, dodging the aurochs.

Then I let my legs fold, and my breath come in staggered gasps. "Piss on them," I spat, my voice breaking with fear. "There were five of them and one of me. Five!"

Bojdan held me up. "Come, you need to go lie down," he said gently. "You've done enough."

He walked me back down the road to a bunk wagon, empty of occupants. "What are you . . ." I asked.

But he shoved me up onto the platform. "Go inside, rest for a moment, gather your thoughts. I will deal with these remaining men."

My hands shook, and I watched him pace along the wagon for a moment, then dart through the caravan and disappear.

I crept into the darkness and curled up on someone's unfamiliar-smelling bunk. I kept curling up until my body could bear being squeezed by itself no more.

When Bojdan finally came back, it might have been after half a day. All I'd done was stare at a chipped piece of wood on the wall. I'd felt that the wagon had stopped. Maybe the whole caravan had. I knew dimly something was going on, but until that moment, hadn't cared about finding out.

Bojdan said nothing, but sat in the back of the wagon and waited until I rolled over to look at him.

"It was different," I finally said. "Not like the execution, or when I went for the raider in anger."

Bojdan just sat there.

I continued. "I had to stay in control, and calm. I had to win the fight first."

"You did well," said Bojdan. "Never doubt it. You are a good fighter."

"Why did the caravan stop?" I asked. "It's not supposed to stop, right?"

Bojdan grimaced. "Our way is blocked by a scouting party. Somewhere out in the woods, north of us, a man called Jiva has been raising the discontented to fight against the Paikans. You met five of their number earlier. They're all from culled villages and towns out there."

"What do they want?"

"Food, weapons, anything we have that we can trade. Their stores ran low in the march south through bramble and forest. They look hungry enough to attack us for our stores. And Jal is reluctant to trade with them, as the Paikans will be upset. So . . . negotiation continues."

"Ah." I turned back over.

After many long moments I twisted around and found Bojdan still there.

"I will be fine," I said.

But the warrior shook his head. "Few are ever truly 'fine' after what you just did, after what we do. We can get back to being a reflection of our former self, but it's somehow not quite the same. And only another like us understands what we mean."

"I know, but I want to be left to myself for now," I told him. "Just for now."

"I will send for you when it is time for the night watch," he said. "I will need all the warriors I can fetch by my side. Particularly if Jal and the scouts can't come to an agreement."

I felt the wagon shake as he stepped out onto the road.

ANEZKA CRAWLED INTO THE WAGON AS THE SUN LEFT ITS place in the sky and woke me up. "Bojdan needs you."

"Thanks." I crawled out of bed, and before I could leave the wagon, Anezka grabbed my shoulders.

"Thank *you* for saving us," she said, and tapped her tattoos. "I would say my investment in you has been more than repaid, and that I am in your debt now."

I wasn't sure what to say, so I hugged her back. "You should carry a dagger, and practice how to stab someone," I whispered to her. "All of you should."

"We're just talliers and cooks and supply keepers, we're not . . . you, Executioness."

I sighed. "I'm just like you. I'm in the middle of my life. A mother who helped in a butcher shop. There is nothing special about me, I swear to you."

But I could see Anezka didn't believe me.

I crawled out of the wagon and got to the road, where lantern light showed a small group of muddy men in tattered peasant's clothes carrying crates of vegetables and dried meats. Trudged quickly down the road, weaving in and out of the caravan as they did so.

They all carried simple swords. I saw a single crossbowman in blue cloth farther down, surcoat slapping the backs of his knees.

Their faces did look gaunt as they slipped off into the shadows just past the caravan's edges.

At the front of the stalled caravan, Bojdan stood with Jal by the roadmaster's wagon. They welcomed me into their discussion.

"One of those scouts says there are Paikans coming down the road," Bojdan told Jal. "They are a half hour away. We need to get moving again so that everything looks normal."

"Don't fret, Bojdan. The Paikans have always respected the neutrality of the caravan. I'm more worried about Jiva's men here. If a few hungry idiots rush our wagons for stores, or loot, and we fight back, this will be an expensive mess," Jal snapped. He eyed the passing remnants of the scouts. "Is that the last of them?"

"Yes," Bojdan said.

"Good. Send the command. We're moving along. Relax, Bojdan. Relax."

"I'll relax when the Paikan party moves past us to their destination," Bojdan said. "If they know about Jiva, we don't want to get caught in the middle."

"Yes, yes," Jal said quickly. "I know. So let's get those command flags snapping, guardsman."

Bojdan ran forward, shouting orders. The fire wagon to the front lurched forward, and then Bojdan's wagon of guards followed. A green flag with a triangle in the middle lurched up the pole with a swaying lantern at the top. All along the column the same flag raised, and the caravan began to move.

I went to follow Bojdan, but Jal grabbed my shoulder.

"We have a Paikan prisoner in a wagon, and everyone in the caravan knows about it. I want you to guard him. I don't want to ransom him until we get to the city, we get more for him that way."

I lowered my voice. "I couldn't raise my hand against someone from the caravan."

Jal laughed. "Oh, you won't have to, Tana. If I let it be known the Executioness is guarding our prisoner, then I doubt anyone in the caravan will be interested."

"I don't like that name," I protested, but Jal held up a hand.

"That is too bad, it has stuck. Now take your axe and go," Jal ordered. "What in all the damned halls are we doing moving so slowly! You said it was *urgent* we get out of here, Bojdan, not something to do in our damned spare time."

"You have come around to my way, I see!" Bojdan shouted back.

Jal grumbled and climbed up on the roadmaster's wagon while I stalked back down the length of the caravan for guard duty.

After I'd climbed into the wagon and sat on the bench against the wall, the Paikan stirred. He crawled to the bars that kept him prisoner and looked out into what he could see of the night from his prison.

"I saw those scouts," he said evenly. The dull red flicker of lanterns swaying in the wagon's ceiling pulled the Paikan's figure out of the dark.

I said nothing.

The man sat, his side against the bars. "Have it your way. They are angry at us, for what we did. And yet they still haven't learned the lesson we strive to teach the world. They think they can take us in battle, but all they will do is throw away their lives."

I didn't want to talk to the man. I felt like he would force that old me, the unskilled me, the unblooded me, to reemerge from where she'd been pushed over the last weeks. The me that would be scared of him.

But I felt calm sitting there in the dark, the axe across my lap. I was a deep river, unhurried and powerful, not a frothy shallow stream. "And what lessons do you think you teach the world," I asked. "Other than your barbarism."

He jumped back. "You're a woman."

I smiled. I had control of this conversation, not him. There was no fear in my voice when I said, "Yes, so I've always been told."

He moved closer to the bars, and looked down at the axe on my lap.

"Are you *that* woman? The one I hear them call the Executioness? From the far east?"

"My name is Tana, of Lesser Khaim," I told him. I saw his shadow relax. "I was once a butcher and married to a husband called Jorda. My sons were Duram and Set. And yes, some call me the Executioness."

I could hear him draw in his breath as I claimed the name for the first time. "Are you here to kill me?"

I imagined him here in this cell, hearing that someone whose life he'd destroyed and children he'd stolen was amongst the caravan. He must have had many sleepless nights.

Which was good.

"I am here to guard you, for now." I placed the butt of the axe against the floor, and folded my hands around the top. "Killing you now would not help me understand where my family may be."

He remained quiet for a while, so I took the axe and hit the bars with it. He jumped back. "Your family is lost to you," he snapped.

"Why do you say that?" I demanded, getting off the bench I'd sat on. "I didn't come this far to turn back!"

He moved away from the bars.

I moved closer. "I will not kill you, but I think maybe I will come to maim you before we reach Paika. I think an arm would be acceptable to me. You could still talk after that, right? I don't know, because I've never tried anything like that before. But I think an arm is a fair thing, after all—what is an arm compared to a family? We can live both our lives incomplete."

The Paikan raider stepped forward to the bars. "You'd risk it all, for this quest?"

I looked him in the eyes. "Yes."

"I have nothing good to tell you," he said. "Because I doubt you'll catch your children."

"You would have sold them by now?" I asked. "Is that what you do, you twisted creatures . . . ?"

"No one young is sold," the Paikan said, a note of outrage seeping into his voice. "Their minds are moldable, they can be taught. The young can be saved."

"What are you talking about?" I demanded.

"Your sons will have been taken to the aftans of Paika. There they are taught the Way with hundreds, no thousands, of youths from all over these diseased lands, every day, until the moment their minds crack open, and the inherent truth of the Way falls upon them. It is then that they earn the right to go to the Southern Isles, far from these coasts."

"Why would they want to go there?"

"A pilgrimage. To see the lands where the Way is all. To see where we came from, long before we took the city of Paika and made it our home. Your children will be closer to the end of their time at the aftan than at the beginning, now."

I wanted to hit him with the butt of the axe, but restrained myself. He was talking. Even if I didn't want to hear it, he was talking about what was happening right now to Duram and Set.

"Why?" I asked. "Why do your people do all this? Why steal my children?"

The prisoner's voice crackled with anger. "Because you don't deserve them." He grabbed the bars. "We have them heavily guarded and protected. And when the Way gives itself over to them, they will leave for their pilgrimage. And when they return, they will bring light to this darkened land you have created."

"What are you talking about?" I sat face to face with his fiery anger.

"Look around you," he whispered. "Your towns are fallen, bramble eats and chokes at all you do. And still you can't release yourselves from the grip of the sickness that causes it."

"Magic?" I asked. "You're talking about magic. It's outlawed. That is why I was an executioner. We control it."

"You control nothing, or your greatest empire would not have fallen. You are all sick with magic's use."

"And you are not?" I said.

"No," he insisted. "Your peoples try to use fear and death to stop magic, but it will always continue. The individual will always have a use that seems to be needed, even when compared to the good of all. You have no true beliefs like the Way to guide you. Just heapings of gods that take you long after you destroy everything in *this* life. As long as your afterlives are pleasant, what reason do you have to ever stop the bramble?"

"You are all missionaries?" I asked. "Here to spread this thing you call the 'Way' by kidnapping our children? Is that what this madness is all about? Is that why you have destroyed my family and my town?"

"It is to save you from yourselves," he said sadly, as if I were a child who did not know any better. "You want to know why I came here, to this cursed land? Let me tell you. One morning, far off in the Southern Isles, I woke up and found a small, gray thorn growing in the wall around my yard. And over time its threads spread. And chopping it back did nothing, its roots continued to spread. One day my wife and my son took it upon themselves to pull up every root by hand. They slipped into the deepest sleep, and then from there to death. That is why I am here, Executioness."

He trembled, and I understood his rage. "I'm sorry to hear about your family."

The Paikan continued. "I'm here because my people forgot magic, and left it behind us when we settled the islands and left the northern coasts. I'm here because we believe Borzai judges all that we do, including what we do to this world that the gods love. I'm here because, like the people of Jhandpara, you can't help yourselves, and we suffer all together as a result. So we try to stop you from killing us, as well as yourselves."

"This is all about magic. And bramble," I said.

"What else could it be about?" the man inside the cell asked.

A trumpeting sound came from the distance.

The Paikan sucked in his breath. "The cavalry is here," he said. "That is no small Culling party, but an army. You should leave this place, and go back to where you came from. Start a new life."

"I am too old to start a new life, or family," I said.

"Then that is a shame," he said. "But there is nothing for you in Paika."

"My children are in Paika," I hissed. "There is *everything* for me there."

I could hear a distant thudding. "They're not stopping, they're not stopping," someone screamed from up the caravan.

I stepped away from the inside of the wagon and pulled myself up the side so I could look down the road.

Forms lumbered out of the dark in front of the fire crew's wagon. Elephants with armored tusks swinging from side to side as they charged forward.

They ran. And they were, indeed, not stopping.

The aurochs harnessed to the wagons up front screamed and threw themselves against their harnesses. The roadmaster's wagon toppled over as the beasts fought to get free.

Bojdan's men raised their arquebuses as one, and fired. The leading elephant shrieked and reared, then brought its massive feet down on the wagon, splintering and destroying it, throwing men from it like so much chaff in the wind.

I jumped down and ran alongside the caravan toward them, seeing more elephants moving through the large cloud of smoke left by the fired arquebuses. The dominating creatures had slowed down in the smoke. They walked three abreast, and four rows deep.

I saw Jal and Bojdan duck for cover behind the roadmaster's wagon as a sudden flurry of crossbow bolts thwacked into the wooden sides and clattered off the road.

I joined them, slamming my shoulder next to Jal's against the ruins of his wagon. "I don't understand," he repeated. "I don't understand.

They couldn't have found out we sold those rebel scouts supplies so soon, could they, Bojdan?"

The warrior shrugged. "There are many other sins they could have decided to call you on, Jal."

"But I bribed them all, Bojdan!" the roadmaster spat. "We make them rich. I use none of the magics they despise."

"Can you guarantee that no one else in this caravan ever used any magic?" Bojdan asked.

An elephant bellowed. Jal glanced over his shoulder and muttered, "Borzai be merciful when I meet you today."

Bojdan looked behind us. "We need to retreat," he said. "They're getting ready for another charge."

The remains of the guard wagon exploded and lit the entire night. The fireball blistered us with heat and roiled overhead, blunted by the now burning carcass of the roadmaster's wagon. "Arquebus powder," Bojdan explained with a sudden smile. "That will give us cover. Now run!"

Elephants shrieked, and Paikans swore loudly as they struggled to control the chaos.

Several arrows hissed by as we stood and ran. Jal gurgled, then pitched back. He looked like a pincushion: his ample body pierced from all angles by crossbow bolts. He was still alive, amazingly, crawling along the road and swearing.

Paikan crossbowmen charged us from the side of the road where they'd walked around the burning debris. Bojdan ran at them as they reloaded their devices. He began slicing arms, throats, and bellies. I buried my axe into the chest of a startled man who pointed his sword at me.

But before we could do more, the ground shook, and out from the smoke of that last great explosion, the war elephants charged once more. Crossbowmen fired down at us from wooden platforms on the elephants' backs.

A Paikan in purple robes stalked over to the roadmaster, a crossbow in hand. "You have sinned against all!" he shouted. "You have failed to keep control of your people, and failed to keep them from using that which harms us all."

"Get away from the caravan," Bojdan said, shoving me away from what was about to happen. "It's all—" He didn't finish his sentence. A bolt buried itself in his neck.

He fell. I lunged forward to go to him, but bolts struck the ground around me.

The battle is won long before the fighting, I thought. And this was a lost battle.

I spun and ran for the forest to the north of the road, where it looked thick and I thought I could lose myself.

The trumpeting of the war elephants faded as I pushed deeper into the wild. There was some bramble here, I could feel the soft threads tugging my skirts as I brushed past. But I couldn't slow down, despite the dark. I could hear the sounds of someone following me, the glow of their torch bobbing through the dark shadows far behind.

With no light, I could only walk so fast without smacking into trees and branches.

There were three torches now, I saw with a glance back. They gained on me, as they could see what was in front of them.

Every step north away from the road, every minute bumping through the scrub, took me farther from Paika, and my sons.

I began to regret the time spent enjoying the slow wend of the caravan along the road. Anezka's quiet commands and the chatter of the tallywomen. The sweet smell of the ocean. The comfort of food, and of Bojdan's company.

Yes, I missed him. It was a piece ripped away from me. Not like the piece missing inside me that was my family. But it was another cut that left me hardening up, like bramble when it wasn't totally killed.

As I ran, I hardened even further than I had before. I pushed through tall grass and broke out into a clear area on the edge of a small lake. Pebbles crunched under my feet.

How long had I kept moving through the woods? An hour?

If I kept running, the Paikans with torches would exhaust me, then easily capture me.

So I crouched low by the grass's boundary, axe readied, to make my stand.

The first man broke from the grass, his torch held high in one hand, spear in another. His spiked helmet glinted in the torchlight, as did the rest of the armor buckled to him.

I slammed the axe point first, as if it were a spear, into the face of the helmet as it turned, suddenly suspicious, in my direction.

Blood splattered the shaft of the axe, and the torch and spear clattered to the pebbles. I stepped back as the other two Paikans slowly parted the grasses on either side of me.

They looked down at their dead comrade, and kept their distance, but moved along the grass boundary to cut me off from running away. They tossed their torches down to the pebbles and gripped their spears in both hands. "You're a woman," the one to my left said, surprise in his voice. "Why do you face us?"

I backed up, my feet wetted now by the shallow water, trying to face both of them. "Because you attacked. Drop your spears and leave me be," I said.

"You killed Massiaka there," the man said, faceless behind his mask of protective bronze. "We will not turn back now."

These were Paikans, practiced and deadly, in full armor. They were not the ragged rebels I'd bested this morning, which now seemed an eternity ago. These men wore armor, and their spears gave them reach.

I'd killed their friend by surprise. They, on the other hand, would not die quickly.

I looked for some way to get out of this fight. "I was in the caravan. I did not ask to be attacked."

"It is too late," the Paikan on the right said.

My fingers loosened on the axe, getting ready for either man to attack me. The Paikans raised their spears, both of them out of reach of my axe, and they got ready to thrust them at me. But just as they stepped forward, crossbow bolts ripped out of the grass and smacked through their armor.

With grunts, they dropped to the pebble beach, armor crashing against the stone, spears clattering with them.

Five crossbowmen stepped out onto the pebbles. One of them was a short man with sweaty, raggedy hair limp over his forehead, dressed in a green robe. He slung the large wooden crossbow over his shoulder. "You are a brave woman, facing two Paikans on your own," he said with a laugh. "You may thank us for the favor we did you later."

I stared at the corpses.

"Three," I said to the man. I pointed to the dead one almost at his feet, and he pushed a torch in the body's direction to examine it.

"Well, well, well," he said.

"And you did me no damn favor," I continued. I didn't like the "thank us later" part. I wanted to make sure they would think a little further before making assumptions about me. "The caravan still burns; the Paikans still ravage the land as they please. Nothing is changed."

The man looked thoughtful. "So you *are* from the caravan?"

"Yes." I still stood apart from them, hoping that they would move on without me. I had it in my head that I would start walking west in the hopes of getting to Paika, somehow.

Though, as Jal had said, it was hard to get into the city. Without the caravaner's help, I wasn't sure how I would do it. But I would have to think of something.

The man in the green robes looked back at me, then gestured at the bloodied axe. "There is more than one man's blood on there."

"More than one man attacked me back at the caravan."

He looked thoughtful. "Did you see how many war elephants charged?"

"I saw at least twelve from the roadmaster's wagon," I said.

"Twelve!" said one of the other men. "I told you, we were sold bad information. They will rip through us like paper."

The green-robed man looked down at the stones. "We will need to recruit more men." His voice sounded bitter as he turned and looked out into the trees. "We will not try to take Paika this year, then."

"You're Jiva," I realized.

"I am Jiva," the man said. "My commanders and I here were about to go to scout the Paikan forces out there with our own eyes. We were hoping to avoid clashing with them until closer to Paika, but it seems they know we're out here."

One of the men behind Jiva spoke up. "What she says about the elephants is the same the other caravaners who escaped into the woods say. It's not worth the risk."

Jiva looked annoyed. "I know. I know. We'll return to camp."

"You have other caravaners at your camp?" I asked.

"A few survivors our scouts started finding in the woods," Jiva said. "That is what prompted us to come take a look."

I stared at him for a while, thinking about how to get to Paika. About the elephants. About what it would take to regain my children. Then I spoke without thinking. "If you are not going to use your army anytime soon, would you mind if I borrowed it to do what you wish to wait on?" I asked.

Jiva's commanders spluttered with laughter. But Jiva did not. His dark eyes narrowed, and anger surfaced in them. "Who are you to mock me?"

I rested my axe over my shoulder, hanging my arm over the shaft to balance it. "I am the Executioness."

One of the commanders stopped laughing. "You *do* exist!" he said.

Jiva glanced at him. "What idiocy are you talking about?"

"The refugees who came to us several weeks ago talk about an axe woman who faced forty Paikans on her own, defending Lesser Khaim from the Culling, until she fell from a sleeping spell they cast on her."

"Paikans don't use magic," Jiva said. "And if she is really the Executioness, she wasn't exactly killing them by the gross here, was she?"

I cleared my throat. "You interrupted me."

"Come and go back to your home, like the rest of us," Jiva said. "We will give you some water and food, what we can spare. The Alacaners will be excited to see you. Be glad you live."

"I am not glad I live!" I shouted at him. "I do not share your cowardice! The Paikans stole my family from me. They burned my home to the ground. I have nothing left. Nothing but the hope of getting to Paika."

Jiva glowered. "I am here for the same reason. To fight back against the Cullings. They took a daughter of mine, and I want my vengeance. But to call me a coward, well, it seems that you are eager to get yourself killed tonight."

"And you aren't?" I looked at the commanders around him. "The Paikans are looking for you, aren't they? My caravan was not the thing they came to destroy, was it? We were just a bonus. If you break apart to hide, it will be easier for them to take their time and seek out your parts."

Jiva's commanders looked at each other. "She is right. Once we split up, they can take their time to hunt us down one by one, like dogs."

"We have little in the way of supplies," Jiva said. "And, judging by the force that attacked your caravan, which is two hundred or so strong, with twelve war elephants you say, we are outmanned. Fighting men are in short supply throughout the lands, thanks to the Culling. We don't have many horses for cavalry. The fight is over."

I shook my head. "The fight isn't over; you are just not able to see how best to bring it to them."

"You think you are a better commander than me?"

"No," I said. "I know nothing about armies or supply trains. But I do see the things that *men* do not."

Jiva, at first furious, now snapped his fingers. "Then, tell me what you see that I do not, woman, and I'll judge your words."

I had caught him, like a fish, and had his interest. "You think about their numbers, and whether you can compare yours to theirs, like two boys seeing who can piss the farthest."

As I had intended, the warlord jerked back from my words as if slapped. "Listen, axe bitch . . ."

I spoke with a low voice, completely forcing him to stop in order to hear what I was saying. His commanders leaned forward. "The Paikans control the road. You can skulk in the woods like this, avoiding confrontation. Or you get an army so vast there is no hope for the Paikans at all."

"Since we have no vast army, but a couple hundred men, you think we should remain here, starving and hidden?" Jiva asked.

"No, starving accomplishes nothing," I said. "But with only two hundred men, you are not of much use. No, what I propose is you let me help you build an army so vast, so large, the Paikans will have no choice but to fold. They might not even choose to fight."

And, I thought, *we would win the battle before even setting foot on the field.*

Jiva folded his arms and laughed at me. "And where shall I find that army, Executioness? Shall I pull it out of my ass? Will you magic all the trees in this forest to suddenly take up my cause?"

I did not say anything, or change my expression, but waited, until one of the commanders repeated Jiva's question, "Where will you find this army?"

"The lands are short of young men, due to the Culling. But they are not short of angry, venomous mothers like me, whose families have been destroyed, and their towns scattered. And yet they live. They were the backbone of the caravan, before it was destroyed today. They haggle and trade in towns all up and down the coast. No doubt they even helped supply your army at times. There is your army, Jiva: an army of Executionesses, ready to throw themselves at the walls of Paika, like I am. No less thirsty for blood, no less able to be led into battle. No less able to kill when armed well."

Jiva unfolded his arms. "They will not fight as well as a man."

"Face me with your sword then, and find out how well a woman can fight," I said, using all my strength to banish fear from my voice.

Jiva eyed my axe. Then he pointed at one of his commanders.

The man stepped forward, and his sword flashed out, faster than I had expected, but I shoved it aside with the axe clumsily.

On the second swing I caught the blade in the curve of the axe's blade, and then spun the axe handle about to crack the man under the chin while his sword was still held away. I leaped back from his next slice, and smiled to see the blood and cracked teeth in his mouth.

He growled then, and began slashing quickly at me. I backed up farther and farther into the water as I kept the long blade away, almost tripping over my skirts in the mud that oozed under me.

We grunted, striking and clanging steel together. He was stronger, he was faster, and he would take me down.

But I refused him an easy kill.

By the end, when we both stood in hip-deep water, panting, sizing each other up, Jiva finally stood up from where he'd been squatting to watch us. "Good enough," he said. "Good enough. What will we arm this new army with?"

"Arquebuses where you can afford it," I said over my shoulder, still eyeing the commander before me. "Axes where you cannot."

"An arquebus is an expensive weapon for vain lords and the rich caravan. Do I look made of gold?" But I could hear in his voice that I had won. That he was taking me seriously.

"It took me a week to learn to shoot the arquebus. You'd have an army in that time."

"Anything else you want of me, besides what little fortune my army has amassed, then?"

With my axe still in front of me, I looked over at him. "Yes, I have another demand. We need a woman, called Anezka, from the caravan, if your scouts can find her among the survivors who are fleeing. She will be our link to getting us the supplies we need, and a new army."

I needed a quartermaster.

Jiva clapped his hands. "It will be done, if she is alive and can be found. Now both of you, come in from the water, we need to return to camp and rest. Tomorrow we need to get farther into the woods."

I held my axe in one hand, and held out my other to my opponent.

He spat a tooth out, then grinned and took the offered hand.

IT DID NOT HAPPEN AS QUICKLY AS I WANTED. BUT IT happened nonetheless.

First, with Anezka by my side, we recruited tallywomen from the remains of the caravan and hagglers from the nearby villages. They melted off into the chill of the northern forests with us, where the Paikans had to get off their horses and brave the bramble and tight brush.

Forges in half-destroyed towns built arquebus barrels, and woodsmen in the remains of once-great cities crafted stocks for us. Women all over began to carry axes, no matter where they went or what hour of day it was.

And the Paikans did not know that all throughout their lands women taught other women how to fight with an axe, or reload their arquebuses, and that those women taught others. For what men paid close attention to what women did together?

Too few.

And those few that paid too much attention, found an axe buried in their skull.

Anezka's old caravan contacts kept food and supplies moving

throughout old forest trails to us. Decimated by the lack of trade and Cullings, many were all too happy to help us in revenge for the caravan's destruction and antipathy to Paika.

Jiva slunk into a gloom after the first months. "An army of widows," he complained. "We will be laughed at and destroyed."

"So take us on raids," I told him. "Kill anyone friendly to Paikans, burn their temples. But we will keep the women in hoods, so that we don't reveal ourselves just yet. You will see how strong they are in real battle."

Jiva resisted at first, but eventually took women armed with axes. Fifty men and fifty women fell upon one of the larger towns near Paika, overwhelming the thirty or so Paikans guarding the temples there. I watched the turrets of their temple topple into the flames with grim satisfaction, and then galloped with my sisters and brothers back into the protection of the northern forests.

And that was the last time Jiva spoke of weakness. His men stopped huddling off in the corner of the camp, feeling outnumbered. They passed among the women, and ate and joked with us.

"And now we have an army," Anezka muttered to me when she saw that happen. I'd started to forget my previous life. My new life was weeks and weeks of drills, transporting the parts of arquebuses, and walking through dangerous forests.

"But do we have enough?" I wondered out loud.

"We have as many as we dare recruit," Anezka said. "Any more, my supply routes fail, or we go broke. We have a month of supplies, money, and goodwill left."

She had a long scar on her cheek, given to her when the caravan was destroyed.

It had been easy to recruit her. She'd gone from smiling caravaner to bloodthirsty soldier. Anything that would destroy Paika, or end with a Paikan's death, she enjoyed. Whenever I questioned why she stood by my side, she would once again tap her forearms and reply, "I still owe you the greatest debt." Though with all the danger we had faced together I couldn't imagine that to be true anymore.

She carried a dagger now. Along with her axe and a heavy blunderbuss on her back, carved with images of death and destruction along the stock and barrel. She even wore a silvered image of Tankan holding a spear; it hung around her neck on a leather thong. It was not the halls of the merchantmen that Anezka hoped to spend eternity in now, but the halls of a warrior god.

"Then I guess we're going to have to convince Jiva it's time to march," I said, and grabbed Anezka's forearm. "And that it's time to tear Paika down."

We swept south at first, and then westward. Jiva's men took the frontguard and fought any resistance. But there was little of that as we quickly advanced along the same spice road I'd traveled some six months ago. Just Paikan scouting parties, who usually galloped back up the road to take their reports to the city.

The road, I noticed, was more overgrown, more thick with bramble along the sides. But even that began to lessen. The woods and trees faded into hilly grasses and small farmsteads, recently abandoned.

We trudged like a normal army for the plains of Paika.

When we turned the last curve of the spice road, I gasped. The fields of Paika spread out before us, but they'd been shorn of what crops the laborers could harvest. The rest burned so that our army could not have it. Everyone had moved back behind the protective walls of the city. The sloping valley sprawled for miles on its way out to the ocean, which was a distant glimmer. To the north were hills and mountains.

It was against the foothills to the north that the stone walls of Paika made a giant U before the mountain. Behind those were several smaller rings of walls higher up the slope of the city.

What a city it was!

Rows and rows of streets and houses and windows and parapets that clung to the slope seemed to go on and on, only petering out when the hillside became so steep as to make building impossible.

Jiva laughed as he watched me from a horse that walked slowly along with us. "Do you think it still so possible to take the city now?" he asked.

"The battle was already won before we arrived," I said. Those walls would not fall easily, though.

"Maybe, maybe," Jiva said, and spurred his horse on.

"He's a bit excited," Anezka observed.

"A boy before battle," I replied.

We trickled through the empty farms and markets until we came to a stop on the edge of the fields just outside the thick walls.

An armored Paikan with a flag of negotiation flapping from a pole held in his saddle waited for us.

One of Jiva's commanders rode out to meet him.

When he came back, the commanders waved me over. Jiva threw a piece of parchment my way.

I looked down at it. I couldn't read: the words made no sense to a butcher from Lesser Khaim. So I looked back up at Jiva. "What is it?"

"The hierarch of Paika wants to talk to you," Jiva said.

"Me?"

The bitterness on Jiva's face deepened. "I think he believes the Executioness to be the mind behind the army. The word has spread before us that the great Executioness marches with us. The lady who destroyed an entire Paikan army herself, after they razed Lesser Khaim."

I ignored the sarcasm in his voice. "I know nothing about tactics or negotiations," I said. "How can I speak for us?"

"Oh, but it does make sense," Jiva said. "That this army is yours as well as mine, there is a grain of truth to that. So go. Talk to their great leader, see what he demands or wants, then come back to us. If they keep you in there, have no fear, we will come soon after to rescue you."

I pulled Anezka over to me. "You have been in the city once before, will you come with me?"

She looked at the flag over the Paikan. "Will they honor the flag?"

"I can't promise it," I told her.

She mulled it over. "I'll come. I want to see their leader's face, I want to see if he realizes that he'll see his city taken by us."

I smiled at her. "We'll each have our victories soon, Anezka. Come."

We borrowed horses and rode out across the field behind the Paikan negotiator toward the gates of Paika, where even more soldiers waited for us.

The steel doors shut once we were through, startling the horses with a loud rattle of chain as a giant weight fell down along the wall, the chains holding it yanking at pulleys and more chains that slammed the inch-thick steel doors shut. The Paikans led us through the cobbled streets, past fearful farmers camped with their livestock in what had once been markets, but were now shelters as they waited for the battle to begin.

We followed the Paikans up the steep, cramped streets, where we could hardly see the sky due to the two- and three-story buildings leaning in over us.

It reminded me slightly of Lesser Khaim, and I shivered as the horse's shoes echoed loudly around us.

At the top of Paika a final set of walls ringed an interior castle. Again, chains and weights rattled to shut the doors behind us.

The hierarch of Paika waited for us by the battlements, the wind whipping at his robes.

"The Keeper of the Way, the enforcer of the Culling, and the ruler of Paika, Hierarch Ixilon, will speak with you," the negotiator told us, and waved his hand in a bow toward the hierarch.

From up here I could look out over the city, out into the fields where our armies gathered in loose clumps around the patchwork quilts of farmland and irrigation.

"I called you here to ask what it would take for you to surrender," Ixilon said.

I folded my arms. "You could have sent a message."

"I wanted you to see I was serious." Ixilon held his hands out.

"And I wanted to see this legendary Executioness with my own eyes. I wanted to know what it would take to get you to stop this suicidal attack."

"You can give me back my children," I said simply. "Their names are Set and Duram. I have traveled from Khaim past Mimastiva, and all along the spice road on the coast to your lands. I survived the unprovoked attack on the great caravan by your people, and now I have finally arrived."

Ixilon looked down at the ground. "I did not know the names of your children. But I know that the children from Khaim, where you hailed from, have all left. They are on their way to the Southern Isles. They have chosen the Way. Their pilgrimage has begun. There is no calling them back until they are done. They have chosen the paths their lives will take them on."

"When did they leave?" I demanded.

"You will not catch them—"

"When?" I shouted at him.

The hierarch smiled. "If you were to leave now, on horseback, you might catch the last of the ships that are leaving."

I ran to the edge of the wall, looking at the roads down to the gates and out of the city. Anezka touched my arm. I turned and looked into her wide eyes.

"Will you go?" she asked me.

Would I go?

All I'd ever wanted was my family back. Could I have it by running for the harbor, far at the end of the valley?

Or was it a trick? Was it just a way for Ixilon to get me out of the way before the battle?

"You should surrender," I said, turning back to Ixilon, "if you want to offer things like guarantees that families will no longer be pulled apart. That the Cullings will stop. That you will reign peacefully over the coast. Then maybe we can discuss your future."

"I can only offer those things if you promise me that the bramble will cease appearing, or deliver me a way the bramble can be defeated through alchemical means, which my spies say the Blue City has," Ixilon said. "The Southern Isles my people hail from are small and carefully maintained. The sickness your people create from these lands floats to ours."

"Bramble cannot be destroyed, it can only be burned and hacked back," I snapped. "It is a curse we must all suffer. If you think Khaim knows otherwise, you should ask Majister Scacz."

"I have. Those envoys he returns to me in a box, missing the rest of their bodies."

"Then you have as much influence over Scacz as I have."

"So the Culling must continue, and magic use must be checked to save ourselves," Ixilon said. "And we are at an impasse. Your people have to realize that there are consequences for your actions."

"Consequences? You speak of consequences," I spat at the raider. "Come stand at your walls here and look out at the consequences of your actions. Out there is an army that *you* have created with your actions."

Ixilon did look out. Then he looked back at me. "It is hardly an army. You want me to surrender by giving me a great show of numbers. But there are barely four hundred men out there. The rest of your army is made of women. Old maids. They call it the Widow's Army, and you've only had months to train them. I will plow through them, and my elephants will scatter your old women before us like dogs."

"Indeed," I said. "I've seen the remains of wars. And the men never seem to remember the women running from the sword as they guided the army's packhorses to the frontline, and they always forget who bandaged the wounded through every skirmish. When the songs are sung about great battles, the women who helped sustain, feed, and build the army, who donated their husbands to the cause: they are always somehow forgotten. You forget that they are just as good at war as men. They fade in your memory only because they didn't share the glory of the front line, even though they often shared the losses and deaths.

"Now, these women at your walls—you've ripped their lives from them. They have nothing to live for but vengeance. Their daughters, their sons, and their husbands are gone. Their farms are burned, their means of living are nothing but rubble. They are the walking dead, and are animated for one thing only, and that is revenge."

I walked over to Ixilon and stared into the calm eyes. "These women fear death little. Far less than the men you've paid to man these walls, or the ones who fight for some distant philosophy imported from your distant islands. Will your arrows stop the walking dead? Will your walls? Remember, this army welcomes death, because at least then it means they will find some sort of peace that has been taken from them! Can you fight an army created out of the pain of all who've lost their families, Ixilon?"

I saw Ixilon's eyes flicker toward the fields outside the city, a seed of doubt in there. His face looked pale, his eyes tired, and he suddenly seemed as if he'd shrunken in on himself.

"It is a challenge to my faith that we have achieved so little here on this coast," he said. "When we first came to Paika to spread the Way, we were attacked. After we took Paika, we built it up even stronger so that we could protect our aftans and temples. And to defend ourselves, we trained larger and larger forces.

"You all were so resistant to the Way, and it was so much easier to teach to the orphans from your wars and collapsed cities, that soon it became easier to bring the collapse ourselves. It is often only in destruction that many can rebuild themselves. That is how it was with us."

Ixilon looked back from the army outside his city's walls to me, and I realized the man was shaken. "These cycles will never stop. We will always destroy ourselves."

"What in all the halls are you talking about?" I asked.

"He's talking about the Way," Anezka said. "Tell him to shut up, and let's leave."

But Ixilon ignored her. "The Five survivors found the Way. They were discovered on the southmost isle, forgotten, unable to build boats. The Five were all that remained of a whole island that had fought and killed itself, leaving the survivors to starve.

"My ancestors brought the Five back to the civilized isles. At first the Five grew fat and happy, and enjoyed the sweet breezes and palm shade. Until they observed war between the islands. They grew troubled and were beset with visions of destruction and woe. They preached their visions on the streets together and starved themselves so that their ribs were like the hulls of half-finished ships.

"They were hung for inciting riots, but their martyrdom spread their message. Their visions of the future. And the Way spread: the understanding that the island of our world was all that there was. To reach out, to fight for things that could not be shared, would only bring us cannibalism, death, and the laughter of the gods."

Ixilon looked at me now. "So I have brought destruction and chaos, but only to prevent even worse. I want to save this world."

"By destroying it first," I said.

"We are a practical people," Ixilon said. "We are taught not to love things, to live austere lives and focus on productivity and wholeness. Some things that must be done are not inherently good. Even your people recognize this. It is like a parent spanking a child. Or like one of your leaders, who must use an executioner to kill magic users. We must pass the Way on, by any means, to your lands. It must be done."

"Then you are locked into your path, and I mine," I told him. "We are tools, forged by the ripples of what has been done, quenched in the blood of our actions."

"Come," Ixilon said, walking toward a turret door. "I have something to show you."

We followed him as he opened the door into a dim room. Two guards stood inside, and at a table, a large form sat in manacles by a bowl of fruits.

"Jal, is that you?" I moved closer, and he looked up.

He raised manacle-stained wrists to shield his eyes from the light.

"Ah, the Executioness. I hear you are at the walls with an army, now. You've come far."

Ixilon stepped between us. "I could hand him back over to you. I could allow the caravan to run again."

"It's too late for that," I said. I wasn't going to suddenly change everything just because Ixilon had found Jal. He was no lover, or family member. Just an employer. An acquaintance. Ixilon had maybe thought I had been a caravaner, and that he was offering me a deal.

"I see that. Then I offer a mutual agreement. I will keep him here, safe for you," Ixilon said. "If you promise me something. Because I believe you're a person of your word."

I could hear the threat implicit. If I didn't agree, Jal would be killed. Ixilon seemed to think that would weigh heavy on me. Let him think it. I didn't care.

"What is it?" I asked.

"Do not kill the priests. Make them leave, but do not kill them. They teach the Way. They are not responsible for the Culling. That lies on me, and the others who serve with me. The moral weight of the Culling lies only with me and my soldiers. Would you agree?"

I looked back at Jal in the shadows of the room, then at Ixilon. "I will say yes. But only because I do not want to draw the judgment of Borzai for killing holy men, no matter what gods they serve. We must all walk the halls of the gods someday."

Ixilon nodded. "I'm sorry we could not come to a peace."

"You forsook it the moment you rode with soldiers against children," I told him.

We left him still standing, looking out over his city.

Back in the fold of the army I rode to Jiva. "He has nothing for us," I told the warlord.

He looked up at the city and winced. He'd been hoping for a surrender. Somehow. But now he nodded and rode off to make preparations.

I stood up on the stirrups of the horse and looked down the slope of the plains, off to the soft valley and the distant, sun-glittered ocean.

Ixilon could have been lying that my children were there. It was definitely a distraction to get me away from the battle.

Yet, I would hate myself if I didn't try to see for myself.

I turned my horse's head to ride for the harbor.

But Anezka saw the move and grabbed my horse's reins. "You can't go," she said firmly.

"My children might be getting on boats to leave," I said to her. "What would you have me do? It is the reason I came. Not to be in some great army. I came for them."

Anezka yanked on the reins to pull me alongside her. The horses huffed and sidled flank to flank. "If you leave, everyone will watch you flee for the valley. Many are here because they follow the Executioness. Your name, your reputation, has spread far and wide. If you leave, it will confuse their spirit."

"Their spirit? They are fighters. They are ready to avenge their families' deaths."

"Many of them will hear you're leaving to find your children, and run with you, hoping to find theirs," Anezka said.

I looked back at her. "As they should."

"No!" She grabbed my arm. "No. They shouldn't. Here we all stand, ready to end the Culling. Ready to stop the stealing of children, the destruction of our towns. You would throw away the chance to end all that for just your needs? You are the mother to all these fighters, you created them. You are the mother to a new generation of people who will not live under the thumb of the Paikans."

I slumped in the saddle. "I did not ask for all that. I am just Tana."

"You are not just Tana; you haven't been for months. And no one asks for the things that happen to them. You didn't ask for Lesser Khaim to be burned, any more than I asked for the caravan to be destroyed. But it has happened. And now you can stop it from all happening again."

I thought about Ixilon and his cycles of destruction, then straightened. I looked out beyond the mountain toward the slope of the land, where it carried on toward the coast, where Paikan ships would be leaving.

"I think you broke the last piece of me," I told Anezka.

"You and I were already broken," she said, and then she led my horse deeper into the camp.

The sun was orange and fat over the plains in its mid-morning bloat when the Paikans burst from their clanking gates. War elephants roared, the sound carrying out across the fields to us as we formed up.

"He should hold behind his walls," Anezka said as twenty elephants moved out onto the field, followed by a hundred Paikans on horseback. Four hundred soldiers followed the riders, each in a square group of fifty, those long spears bristling like a ship's mast from each person. We could see lines of archers up on the walls, tiny faces looking back at us. "It would take us a year to breach them."

"Ixilon knows he will eventually need to fight," I told her. "That's what Jiva says. Better to do it upfront when the men are healthy and not starving, when they still believe they are invincible and eager instead of demoralized."

We stood on foot in a cluster of eight hundred women in the field, all of them armed with both arquebuses and axes. "He still thinks one of his men is better than four of us," Anezka noted, looking at the numbers.

Two thousand total armed women had come to the field. Those not in my square of eight hundred with arquebuses carried just simple axes. Jiva's men were on their horses and ready to break for the gates from the side, preventing Ixilon from retreating back into the city.

"We'll soon find out," I said to Anezka. "I'm just grateful he's keeping his archers on the walls where they can't reach us just yet."

The ground shook as the war elephants began their charge. I turned back around to look at my own army. They shifted, nervous at the sight of the armored elephants thundering toward them.

Someone raised an arquebus, and Anezka spotted the movement

and screamed, "Keep your weapons pointed down, do not fire until the order flags go up!"

But I understood the impulse.

There were five lines of women, our most untrained recruits, that we stood with. It was quickest to teach them how to aim and shoot the arquebus. They had all been the last to join.

And breaking the Paikans depended on them more than the axe fighters.

The elephants loomed larger, their armor clanking, the ground shaking. Paikans followed behind, the charge moving quicker as they closed.

I could see the closest elephant's eyes now. The wrinkles in its long trunk that slapped back and forth as it ran.

The order flags whipped into the air, something Anezka had copied from the caravan to simplify ordering our untrained army around, and the first row of a hundred women raised their arquebuses. The entire row of newly hammered metal tubes gleamed. Slow burning fuses sparked down the line as they were lit.

The second row, the moment the first row raised, also began preparing to fire.

An elephant screamed rage and, in answer, the first line of arquebuses responded. The thunder of fire matched the earthquake of giants' hooves. Smoke rose and filled the air, and then came the second line of thunder.

Shrieks of inhuman pain pierced the smoke as the first of the elephants stumbled through the powder haze, crashed into the first line, and tumbled to the ground. Then another stumbled through.

Women dropped their arquebuses and, though untrained with their axes, fell upon the elephants like they were firewood. They hacked at both their riders and the beasts as they writhed and screamed on the ground.

"We told them to leave the elephants once they fell," I snapped, frustrated.

"They're caught up in it all," Anezka said. "There are lines behind them. It is not a problem yet."

Some were reloading though, even as the square formations of Paikans' bristling long spears came quickly through the curtain of smoke. But they were expecting to find us scattered.

Instead, they met three more rows of thunder, and then scattered pops from those in the remains of the first and second lines who had managed to reload their arquebuses.

Paikans stumbled and fell, and the impenetrable wall of spears faltered.

The axe women came from deep behind the lines and ran at the corners of the Paikan formations. They hit the spears in a bloody mangle of bodies and blades. The squares buckled and then split down their centers as the fighting degenerated into one-on-one combat.

I still stood in the second line, no more than a hundred feet away from the stalled spearmen and fighting. A wounded elephant groaned just fifty feet off to my right, a large gray hill that prevented me from seeing Paika.

I moved forward with Anezka, bringing my arquebus up only once, to sight on a raider that charged us. I fired.

He dropped, and we stepped over him to climb the dying elephant and gain a better view of the hell that we had helped design.

The clumped Paikans were slowly being overwhelmed all around me, but the well-armored soldiers on horses still milled about the gates of Paika.

I raised my axe into the air and pointed at Paika. The faces of hundreds of women who had finished reloading their guns looked up at me.

"Paika!" I screamed and waved the axe. We had stalled their spears, broken them apart, and now I wanted us to run through the open field and into the city. "Paika!"

"Paika!" they screamed back.

As I crawled down from the elephant I could hear the sound of

Jiva's horsemen moving now, galloping full tilt toward the raider horsemen.

They swept past our side and surged ahead, their way clear, and we ran after them.

Horse crashed into horse and the screams of the dying began once more. With the horsemen countered, the horde behind me swept through the Paikans as a rain of whispering arrows struck the ground all around us.

Then we poured into the city itself, arquebuses firing. We threw the long, ungainly weapons aside for our axes as we met the archers and what few Paikan soldiers had been left inside. And my words to Ixilon came true as the axe-wielding women threw themselves with grim revenge against any armed Paikan they encountered.

I ran up the streets, gasping for breath and dizzy from exertion, almost ready to pass out by the time we reached the last battlements.

Anezka had run up the hills well ahead of me.

"They never even had time to close the gate," she said.

"Then we've won!" I hadn't even bloodied my axe, and it was over. We had torn the Paikans down. "We've done it."

From up here, as I looked around, I could see smoke beginning to billow up from the city. And the field was empty of living soldiers. Only the dead and injured, lying in the mud made by our feet, lay out there like small dolls or figures in a painting regarded from a distance.

When I looked back at Anezka I did not see the same happiness. "There's something you should see," she said.

She took me into the turret I'd been in the day before. My mouth dried even before the door opened, and I looked inside.

An ashen-faced Ixilon looked back up at me, then quickly down at the table he sat at. His wrists were bound with rope. Behind him, Jal slumped. A long spear stuck out from his chest, spitting him in place.

"You killed him anyway?" I asked.

Ixilon licked his lips, and did not look up at me again. "A guard, not me."

A badly beaten guard in the corner of the room croaked, "Payback, for the whore who dared take the city."

The fury that lived inside me exploded. I grabbed my axe and crossed to where Ixilon lay with his head in his hands. I swung the axe deep, easily and precisely, toward the back of his neck.

I swerved at the last second, and buried it into the wood of the table just short of his ear.

"You failed," I told Ixilon. "You failed as a man to keep just a simple promise to me, and you failed in your attempt to foist your Way upon this land: there will be no more Cullings now. And the land will be better for it."

I had done my duty for all the other mothers in these lands. But now it was time to do something I'd yearned to do since I'd met Ixilon. I ran from the room and into Anezka. "Get me a horse. Now!"

"Please, listen to me first. Jiva's dead; you need to talk to the commanders," she said. "They need to hear from you—"

"A damned horse! Now!" I shoved past her and ran down the cobblestones with a tired limp until I saw a horseman. "Give me your horse," I demanded.

"Who are you to . . . ," he started to say, but then he saw the axe, and my face, and realized who I was, and slid off.

"Tana!" Anezka called.

"You are as much one of this army's leaders as I am!" I shouted at her. "You take care of it. In my name if you must. But you take care of it."

I galloped off as fast as the horse could manage down the hill, around the curves, and then out the gates. I pushed the creature as hard as I dared, until foam flecked its mouth and it ignored my demands.

Then I jumped down and stumbled along the empty roads of the small town that had sprung up to serve the Paikan harbor.

Eyes looked fearfully out at me from behind gaps in shuttered windows.

I staggered to the end of one of the piers and looked out at the gray sea, and in the far distance, watched a single sail slowly disappear over the edge of the ocean, headed south.

It was doubtful my sons were on that last boat. But standing there, it felt like it.

They had left me and moved on.

I crumpled to the wooden planks. I could not find tears, but my body shook as if I were trying to remember how to cry.

Anezka found me still on the edge of the pier hours later.

She said nothing, but waited at the start of the stones of the waterfront until I decided myself to turn my back to the ocean.

"What are you doing here?" I asked her.

"It was truly as much your army as it was Jiva's," she said. "We've won. And now we need to plan what comes next."

I let myself get recaptured by her, and returned to the city.

I think of philosophers as drug-addled dreamers who see only the reflections cast on their blackboards. The shadows of the world as it really exists around them. They say there is no such thing as good and evil. They talk about choice and flux, intersections and perspectives and situations.

They may well be correct. Who am I, an old peasant mother, to question those who spend their lives poring over these questions? And since I decree it, any philosopher or religion that forsakes weapons at my city's gate can come to Paika. My city. And they do so flock, like hungry sheep, to my markets.

I did this for my sons, against counsel, so that they would have a city on the coast to return to if they chose. They follow the Way, now, and I cannot bring myself to chase those who follow the same beliefs as my sons from these coasts.

I will be here, when they get back from the Southern Isles. I will be here for them, even if we might hardly recognize each other.

The thinkers say it is the way of the world for things to change. That includes people, I gather.

So even though we grow unrecognizable to each other, I am still their mother, and this is still their land.

I hold back the bramble as best I know how. At first, I did not care to hunt people in the city. But those who did not follow the Way, my own people, began using magic, and bramble began to choke our streets.

I fought the Paikans to get my children back. To stop the Culling. I had no wish to return to forcing the Way on people. And so I am forced to find the magic users, as I must, and hang them from the city's walls. On my worst days, I think I have become no better than the Jolly Mayor and Majister Scacz, hunting for every user of petty spells and spiking their heads to the city walls. And to my chagrin, the Way's priests point to the people I execute as proof that only the Way can save these lands.

I do all these things because even though I am a mother, I am also now a new person. I am the Queen of Paika, the lady of the lands in its shadow.

I am the Executioness.

And I am waiting for my children to come home.

PART III

The Children
of Khaim

BY PAOLO BACIGALUPI

MOP KNELT IN THE ASH OF BRAMBLE BURN, SEEKING bramble pods and seeds. Smoking dirt sieved between his gloved fingers. Sweat stung his eyes. Ash leaves swirled through the air, black crows' wings, tumbling and swooping, coming to rest on the scorched land.

All along the bramble wall, fires blazed.

Burnmasters sprayed flaming paste from bladder sacks while assistants worked their bellows. Poisonous tangling vines ignited and writhed. Thorny, woody trunks collapsed, crackling, hissing, and spitting sap.

The stink of dying magic washed over Mop, rancid yellow smoke, obscuring his sight. He coughed and checked again for Rain. Once again, she was lagging, a crouched form trailing behind the rest of the pickers. Leather-stitch shadow of a girl, all alone.

Mop sidled back to her. "Keep up," he whispered. "You have to keep up or they'll find someone else."

Rain peered up at him through the sewn holes of her leather cowl. Her eyes were dull and shadowed. "I'm tired," she whispered.

"You think we all aren't?" Mop motioned at the other seed pickers, women and children kneeling in still-smoking ash, humped figures laboring, working the dirt like drab curling beetles. Trains and clots and clods of them. Women with rakes. Children crawling about their mothers' skirts. All of them sifting blackened ground for bramble seeds and sprouts.

"Don't stand straight or pause," he said. "Cojzia will find others."

"How much longer until we're through?" Rain asked.

Never, Mop thought. *Never and never and never. Not until Borzai comes and gathers us into his arms for judgment.*

The burn had been going all day, and yet it seemed that their work had taken but the barest bite out of the leading edge of the bramble forest. A day's tilling cleared, perhaps, along with some peasant's stone hut that they were now fighting to disinter—a hovel of chinkstone and boulders, built generations ago, and then swallowed by bramble's encroach.

Children clambered up the hut's stone walls, lighting ancient roof beams and thatch on fire. Flame licked about the base of the hut as well, blackening stone. Just clearing the hut would take hours. Tomorrow they would be back again, doing the same work, hacking away at the encroaching bramble.

Duke Malabaz said he wanted land cleared east all the way to the old village of Kem.

"If we're lucky, we won't be done for weeks," Mop said. "Malabaz is paying, and we've got work, and that's all that matters."

He said the words, and they were true in a way, but even as he said them the forest wall of poisonous vines seemed to mock him with its loom. The bramble would never be banished. They might slash and hack and torch the thorny woods, but in the end, they sought to shove back an ocean.

No matter how much they labored, the waves of bramble would always be there, threatening to crash down upon them. Bramble reached north to green ice, and south to blue seas, and smothered all the East in thorns. It choked valleys and blanketed mountains all the way to the fabled city of Jhandpara, and yet here they pretended as if they could turn the tide.

Orange flames scrambled up spiky trunks, licking at seedpods and charring pale thready spines. Vines writhed and twisted in the heat. Bark crackled. Sores of sap spat and oozed, bubbles hissing, flaring like oil.

Leather-stitch shadows emerged and disappeared from the scabrous yellow smoke, misshapen in clothing that covered head and hair, face and limbs. Frightening dolls, stalking the bramble line, all stitched together like the legendary dog armies of Majister Calal.

When will we be done?

Never and never and never.

Beside him, Rain reached for another seedpod.

Mop smacked her hand. "Not like that!"

Rain jerked away. "What did I do now?"

"Scoop it up from under," he said. "And don't pinch it." He gently cradled the bramble pod, letting ash and clodded dirt sift through his gloved fingers. "See?"

He opened his hemp sack and held the pod over its mouth. He looked at Rain significantly, then squeezed. The pod burst like popcorn. Seeds sprayed into the bag. Dozens of obsidian orbs rattling and falling like poppy seeds.

"Don't break pods. Don't scatter seeds. If you can't learn that, we'll both be off the burn and some other Alacaner will take our places— yours for stupidity, and mine for vouching you." He glanced back to where Duke Malabaz's linemaster stood, overseeing their work. "Cojzia doesn't tolerate incompetence."

Rain shook her head tiredly and bent again to her task. "I wouldn't have squeezed like that."

"That's right, because you'll lift them from beneath."

Rain stayed stubbornly silent. Mop pressed. "You want us to starve, sister? You want us to clear the same dirt tomorrow? We're nothing, here, you understand? We have no friends. The people of

Khaim despise us, and Alacaners, too, hate our name. We are alone, here."

Rain didn't reply, but Mop was contented to see that when she scooped her next bramble pod, she did it with care.

She'd break a few anyway, because she was young and she had once been very much loved by their parents and their servants and spoiled the way young, pretty, smiling girls were often spoiled. She would chafe against his warnings, but she could not say that he hadn't warned her. He'd done what he could, and if Rain wanted to work the bramble line, she would learn its strictures.

He only prayed that her mistakes wouldn't cost his livelihood as well, if Cojzia noticed her incompetence.

The sun began its slow hunt for the horizon. Bramble burned. The peasant's home was finally freed of bramble, standing lonely in the blackened earth. Seeds and new green bramble sprouts filled pickers' sacks to bulging, were piled high in mounds and burned again. Burnmasters cradled their sloshing pig-bladder sacks, working their way down the line, squirting flaming mash from the fat bladders' brass snouts.

Fire, flying.

It splashed over vines and spines and stubborn stumps. Their assistants followed, working their bellows, encouraging the flames. Bramble sap whistled as it boiled up from deep within the wood. Seedpods burst wide in the heat. The work continued. Sweat soaked the interior of Mop's hood and slicked his hands inside his leather gloves. His face itched with sweat. His eyelids dripped water, blurring his vision. He straightened, back aching, and started to reach into his hood to dry his brow.

He froze on the verge of touching skin.

Upon his glove, a cluster of pale bramble threads clung, thin and pale. Death on his fingertips. It was a shock to see them clinging there, infinitely skinny little worms, all of them eager to kiss him down to sleep.

Mop cursed himself for old habits. It was the sort of easy, thoughtless motion that Rain might make, this touching of his skin, and here he was, about to do it. Picking seeds and bramble pods might pay better than catching rats, but there was danger, and it was too easy to let exhaustion fog him into complacency.

He carefully plucked the pale threads from his gloves and let them fall to earth.

"Malabaz don't pay you to stand straight, boy, and our friend Cojzia is watching."

Mop bent again, trying to look busy. The owner of the voice came up beside him: a woman, sooty and stoop-backed, her face shrouded by the bramble worker's leather cowl. Recognizable more by her crabbed searching movements than any physical feature.

Lizli.

She had worked the bramble all her life, and now she never stood straight. Always working, always crouching, always running her gloved hands through dirt. Mop thought she must stand like that in her hovel as well. Plucking and seeking along the flagstone edges, fingers never at rest as she sought signs of bramble's sprout.

"Don't let the battle tire you," Lizli said. "This is one we win."

"Not my battle," Mop said, waving off toward where the duke's manor stood in the far distance. "This will be Malabaz's land, not mine."

She snorted. "If you're so concerned over what is yours and what is not, you should go back to Alacan. I hear it is a lovely city."

Mop didn't take the bait. It was what Khaim people always said when Alacaners complained. He knew the pattern, how it would go.

Lizli pressed. "What? You don't want your manicured grounds and hunting forests? You don't enjoy the view from Alacan's rose granite walls?"

"Don't mock our land," Rain piped up. "It was a lovely place. Alacan was the Spring City, warm all year round, and beautiful."

"And Jhandpara's hanging gardens reached all the way up to the roof of the sky." Lizli laughed. "It's all bramble tangle, now, girl." She scooped seed pods from the ashy ground, and dropped them in her bag.

"Why do you mock us?" Mop asked.

"Mock you?" Lizli shook her head. "I wouldn't dare mock the finest of the fine."

"Who says that we are fine?"

"Your tongue has the roll. That little courtly trill. You mask it better than some, but I've seen so very many of your kind." She snorted. "But really, even if your accent didn't give you away, it's only the fine ones who complain that the land they work is not their own."

She leaned close. "I'll give you a free bit of advice, Alacaner. I don't know who you once were in that dead city of yours, but here, you are less than pig shit between a farmer's toes. Alacaner beggars. Alacaners selling their last pots and necklaces. Alacaner men in the market squares with the holes in their shoes and their mustaches cut off because they've lost their children. Alacaner women trying to sell themselves as if anyone would want their sort. All of you distilling jhalka root and smoking poppy sap and telling one another that Alacan was *the Spring City, warm all year round and beautiful.* Talking so big and wishing so long, and none of you worth a chicken's claw, because all you truly want to do is start your spelling again and drag another city down to ruin."

"We aren't that sort," Mop said.

"Not that sort?" Lizli glanced sidewise at him, skeptical. "It was someone else who choked your city down with bramble?"

"It wasn't us," Mop insisted.

Lizli hooted laughter. "Every Alacaner I have ever met tells me he cast no spell and dabbled not in the majister's trade. And every one of you speaks with great sincerity. Not a liar amongst you, I'm certain. And yet here you all are, living in Khaim, instead of Alacan. And there Alacan lies, choked dead by bramble. The greatest victim of no one since Jhandpara."

"We don't lie." Mop yanked up a new green shoot of bramble where the hateful plant was already taking root in the burned earth.

"Of course not!" Lizli held up her ash-coated gloves in mocking defense. "I meant no disrespect. I'm sure you're both as honorable as the very best of Alacan."

Mop gave her a sour look. "Malabaz gets this fief because he handed up his family for spelling. You call that honorable?"

"What do I care about those velvet intrigues? We have work and Malabaz pays, and we've pushed bramble farther back from Khaim's walls than any time in living memory. If the rich see their heads rolling the same as the poor, what care I? This is Duke Malabaz's land today. And then his head will bob in the river Sulong and Duke Halabaz will take his place, and then Balabaz, and Salabaz, all the way down the line until a pig called Palabaz roots this land for truffles. It makes no difference to me. The land is the land, and it's not covered with bramble, and I call that a gift from all the gods combined."

"I heard Malabaz even handed up his wife," Mop said.

"Oh yes." Lizli smiled eagerly. Her knotted teeth showed in the shadows of her leather hood. "He did her for land and favor and power and revenge. The velvet ones aren't people like you and I. They have no human feelings."

They bent again to their work, leaving Mop to think on Lizli's words.

The velvet ones: people with servants and courtyard homes and glass blown from Turis. People with copper bramble wards from lost Kesh. People with all the cash strings they could ever wish for.

People just the same as Mop and Rain had been.

But here, the velvet ones jostled for power in ways that Mop had never known in Alacan. Khaim's Mayor and the Majister Scacz had a genius for setting velvet ones upon one another. In the spice market, everyone talked about how Duke Malabaz had handed up his own blood.

Teoz, who gave Mop and Rain a place to sleep in his warehouse and who dealt more spices than any merchant in the city, heard all the gossip, and shared it happily.

As Teoz dipped his scales into red chili powder and yellow turmeric, his hands garish with flavor, he'd said, "Of course they were
guilty. Small magics, but all of them guilty. Love potions for the uncle
so he could mount a dozen girls and roar like a tiger. A whisper
from crystal for the sister to clear her clouding eyes. Small spellings.
Pockmarks erased from a shapely daughter, to make her marriage
better."

He'd looked up toward Malvia Hill where the wealthy of Khaim all
lived in cool marbled halls with fresh bright breezes while everyone
else sweated through the summer.

"They all do it, of course. All of them in their halls behind their
walls where Majister Scacz can't see. Send their servants out so no
one knows how blue they show."

But the duke's family had showed blue all right, all of them dragged
out under torchlight in their nightclothes, screaming as the soldiers
pulled them forth. Their house guards all standing by, watching coolly
as masters and mistresses went before Majister Scacz.

"They burned as blue as casis flies mating," Teoz said. "Saw them,
I did. Heads rolling, blood on the cobbles right in front of Mayor's
House, and all of them still afire with magic."

They'd been dumped into the river Sulong, high-born heads
floating one way, high-born bodies floating the other, without last
rites or a gift to Borzai or even a second glance. And the newly
minted Duke Malabaz strode across puddles of blood, velvet and
lace trailing red, to kneel before the Mayor and Majister Scacz and
pledge his loyalty.

And now, thanks to Malabaz's betrayals, Mop and Rain had work.

Malabaz had been given the right to clear the land. If he succeeded,
Majister Scacz and the Mayor would defend it from new bramble
intrusions, and it would belong to Malabaz so long as he swore loyalty
and refrained from dabbling in the majister's arts.

A good bargain, all around: Malabaz had new land. Khaim had
new taxes. Bramble fell back. Majister Scacz stamped out a few more

competitors in the majister's art. And Mop and Rain had money to eat for another day.

Mop bent once again to his task, scooping up bramble pods, plucking seeds and sprouts. Joining all the other laborers in the clearing of land for Malabaz.

Beside him, Rain toppled over.

MOP LEAPED TO HIS SISTER AND TORE OPEN HER LEATHER
cowl. She stared up at Mop, eyes puzzled. A pale bramble
tendril clung to her sooty cheek. Other threads tangled in
her hair. Clung to her throat. Her hood wasn't closed properly. From
the look of it, hadn't been for some time.

Rain tried to get up, her arms flailing drunkenly, then fell back.

Other workers began to gather round. First one. Then more,
increasing to a dozen, all pressing close. None of them said anything.

They all watched as the girl's eyes closed.

"She's gone," Lizli said.

"She's not!" Mop insisted. "She's my sister."

"Sister or no, she's gone. Didn't you tell her to stop working if she
caught the kiss?"

"I told her! I told her straight." He shook her. "Rain? Razica?"

He shook her again, looked desperately to the others. All of them
watched, but none of them spoke. Their faces were blank, without
judgment or anger. No pleasure or fear. They simply watched. They'd
seen this collapse before. There was nothing for it, and little point in
weeping or wailing to Borzai for some other judgment.

"If you told her, then it weren't your fault." Lizli turned away and motioned for the others to do the same. "Off with you. Give the boy his time. Seeds don't pick themselves."

As quickly as they had gathered, the laborers disbursed, leaving Mop crouched beside his sister. He could guess how it happened. She'd gotten a few threads on her skin, and then kept working anyway, despite the poison. And each bramble kiss had made her weaker and more stupid so that the next kiss was more likely. And all the while, he'd been urging her on. Mop felt nauseous with guilt.

It was easy to misjudge that first bramble kiss, to think it possible to press on. It was natural to fear starvation more than bramble sleep. And so people labored on through the welt and the burn, even as more and more poison coursed through their veins, and even as they brushed their sweating faces with bramble-laced hands and added to the kiss.

"You!" Cojzia, the linemaster, waved at Mop. "Get that body moved!"

Mop ignored him. Rain wasn't a body. She was his sister. Rain. Razica. Razica d'Almedai. A merchant's daughter out of Alacan. Famous for their exclusive contracts to distribute Mpais glasswares. They'd been rich. The d'Almedai had been a name respected, and Razica had been a girl with prospects. But they never told anyone here. Not here. Not in the city of Khaim.

Mop and Rain never named themselves here. It did no good and made no friends to brag that their courtyard had been surrounded by thirty-three arches, or that they had paid to build a temple to Kemaz out of their own pocket, and given the orphans of Alacan a place to shelter. Razica was Rain. Mapeoz was Mop. And they were safe and anonymous and no more despised than any other Alacaner who had fled to Khaim.

"Put the body over there!" Cojzia said again. "I don't want to smell it roasting when the burnmasters light these stumps."

Mop struggled to lift his sister. Limp and paralyzed, she seemed smaller. Less significant than when she'd demanded to join his work and earn. And yet now, paralyzed by bramble, she felt heavier than she'd ever been.

She'd said she was old enough, that they were past this silliness of what a man could earn and a woman could not. The d'Almedai had built themselves up from nothing, and would again, with work, she said. But only if they both labored and let go of silly illusions that she was some sort of iridescent lora flower, waiting to be opened. Those myths were for a time when they'd had courtyards and servants and marbled halls and scent gardens, and they were all gone.

Mop dragged Rain's body through the ash drifts, his feet whispering in the blackness. His arms weakened and he dropped her. He fell to his knees beside her, exhausted.

Kissed and gone. Just like Mother and Father. Just like all the rest of the d'Almedai.

"How you could you be so stupid?" he panted. "I told you."

As if in response, Rain's eyes fluttered. Mop leaned close, heart thudding wildly. "Rain?" He pinched her cheeks, trying to stir her. "Wake up!"

She'd taken less poison than he'd first thought.

With luck . . .

Her eyes closed again. Her body let out a soft sigh. She sagged, falling into deeper slumber as the bramble kiss took her completely.

Some people said it was possible to wake from bramble's deep slumber, but Mop had never seen it. It was just a lie people told themselves as they stored their family members on ornate marble slabs. They told themselves that eventually the poison would retreat and friends and family would rise again.

They said it had happened to a woman in Mpais. That a cousin's cousin-brother kissed in Kesh had wakened all in a start. They said it over and over again. Even as young boy, Mop had known it for a lie, but still they told the stories, holding on to hope the way a child holds a bit of patchwork quilt for comfort.

He remembered a dinner party his family had attended when

d'Almedai was still a name that received invitations. The Falizi family, giving them honor. Mop remembered the patriarch presiding, artfully tied to his chair so the old man didn't flop face first into each course as it was set before him.

Topaz-jeweled straps had circled the patriarch's forehead. More clasped his wrists. Another strap, barely glimpsed, around his chest and under his arms, threaded through carefully tailored holes in the back of his dinner jacket where the servants could secure him to the chair. And all around him, Falizi guests ate and drank and toasted the patriarch, everyone pretending that he was one of the living.

Mop remembered the family's embarrassment when a butterfly emerged, fluttering, from his ear.

"What are they supposed to do?" Mop's father had asked on the coach ride home.

"Accept that he is no more," Mother replied. "Accept that he is gone, even if his body slumbers here. Let him go to Borzai."

"Stick him like a pig and bleed him out?" his father asked. "Who would hold the knife?"

His mother had shrugged, as stymied as the Falizi.

The simple course was obvious, and yet the Falizi had kept their patriarch for years, kissed by bramble, asleep and gone, servants dressing him like a doll every day, plucking flies and blood beetles from nose and ears, all of them pretending that he would someday wake because no one could muster the callousness to kill him true.

Mistress Falizi conducted business in the Master's name and everyone bowed to the sleeping man and murmured to one another that he looked well.

Of course it was a failed effort. Eventually nature found its way into every bramble body's guts, Kpala's many children burrowing into defenseless flesh. Moths and maggots, centipedes and beetles eventually burst from mouth and ears and soft, soft stomach. But still, the denial ran strong. After all, the flesh was warm, even if the spirit had gone missing.

And now, Mop faced the same conundrum—but with none of the wealth or servants or security that the Falizi had enjoyed.

She's gone, Mop told himself. *It's not sleep. It's death.*

It didn't matter that Rain's body would last another dozen years. She was dead. *You can't care for her,* he thought. *It can't be done. Best to finish it now, before dogs or men come sniffing for her.*

His eyes blurred with tears as he fumbled for his knife. Clumsy leather-glove fingers. He opened her protective hood wide, revealing her dark smooth skin. Her peaceful face. He set his blade against her throat. Gleaming steel against perfect skin. Her flesh gave under the edge. He tried to press.

Do it fast. Don't think about it.

And yet he found himself imagining the blood welling out, her throat gaping open, a new grinning mouth wet and wide, her windpipe a sucking hole in red . . .

"You do yourself no favors by drawing it out."

Mop startled. Lizli had come across the ash-drifted fields to watch. "Make the mercy cut and be done," she said. "You just make it worse by waiting."

"Then you do it," Mop snapped.

Lizli laughed and shook her head. "Not me. I won't have a body strung round my neck when I go to Borzai."

"Then don't call it a mercy cut."

"Dead is dead. Mercy is mercy. Borzai judges as he will. Now hurry up and cut, and get yourself back to work. Or else go find a soft-eyed man, and profit from the girl's warmth. See if Borzai judges you any better that way. The girl's pretty enough without the soot. You'd find a buyer for a young body like that."

Mop gave her a look of disgust. "I would never do such a thing!"

"Too honorable to sell the sleeping, and too stupid to get back to work. No wonder you Alacaners are refugees. You can't see the thorns even when they're all around you."

"Mara counsels mercy," Mop said.

He put his knife away and stooped to slide his hands beneath his sister's still form. With a groan, he hefted her up and slung her over his shoulders. He staggered under the weight but managed to stand tall. "She's not dead."

A bark of surprised laughter escaped Lizli's lips. "What's this? You think to *keep* her? You think to keep the rats from her toes and the moths from her nose?"

Mop ignored the taunt. He started across the fields, stumbling under the weight.

Lizli called after him. "Shall I tell Cojzia and the burnmasters that you no longer need their coppers?"

"Tell them whatever you like."

Behind him, he heard footsteps. Lizli pursuing, catching up.

"Are you addle-brained?" she asked. "You're acting like the velvet ones. You have no servants to clean and protect her through the days. You have no way to save her. She's nothing but feed for Kpala's children. Send her on to Borzai. She's but a child. He will pass her innocence on to Kemaz's halls, and there she will play and be happy with the dog-headed one."

Mop didn't answer. He kept on, grimly trudging over the blackened fields. When he stumbled in a furrow, Lizli hooted laughter. "You'll break an ankle before you reach Khaim's gates," she said. "I'm sure your sister will thank you for that."

"She's my sister," he grunted as he resettled her over his shoulders.

"She's a body!"

Unexpectedly, Lizli reached up and yanked Rain from his shoulders. Mop spun, crying out, but it was too late. Rain hit the ground with a thump, her limbs spilling loose and awkward. Ash puffed gray around her.

"What are you doing?" He lunged at Lizli, but the crabbed woman slipped out of reach, no laughter or taunt in her face.

"I'm helping you think sense, boy."

Mop glared at the old woman. He crouched beside his sister, trying to see if she'd been wounded in her fall. She lay strangely, her face plowed deep into bramble ash. A doll discarded, blackened and sooty.

A living person would have fought to clear her mouth and nose. Rain did nothing.

Mop dug the ash away from her face and made to lift her again. Lizli put a staying hand on his shoulder. Her voice was gentle. "At least keep your place with the burnmasters, boy. Don't give Cojzia a reason to cut you from the work. He hates Alacaners enough as it is. Wait until the sun falls, then find a cart or barrow for the dragging, if you're so determined."

She looked down at Rain. "The girl won't mind the waiting. Of that you can be sure."

THE PEOPLE OF KHAIM CALLED THEIR HOME THE BLUE City. They said it with pride, but Mop thought it was half a curse, no matter how they smiled and bragged about their city's wonders.

The pride was true enough, of course: Khaim stood tall and flourished while other cities fell beneath crashing waves of bramble. Khaim's city walls still stood strong. Her people didn't spend their every waking hour burning bramble off the granite of their wharves, or prying it from between their cobbles and roof beams the way other cities did.

So, pride. Of course. For survival.

And, of a certainty, the Blue City was beautiful.

It wasn't just the wonder of a castle floating in the air, high above the highest villas on Malvia Hill. It was the copper braziers burning as blue as casis flies where they lined the thoroughfares and marked the city gates and stood sentinel on the river Sulong's docks. It was the scent of neem smoke, sweet and spicy, issuing from those braziers and winding through the city.

Khaim was arches and fountains and public squares and alleys and lanes, all of it sweating and bursting with summer trade while up on

Malvia Hill, Khaim's great marble villas looked down on the clatter and roil of the city, enjoying cool breezes.

It was the majestic flow of the river Sulong running rich and wide and full of fish, connecting Khaim to the sea trade south and the land trade north. It was the bustle of markets. Mop's family had done business in the glass market, but there was so much more: spice lanes and copper squares, diamond merchants tugging at their long mustaches and muttering deals between sips of thick-leafed tea from blown-glass bargaining bulbs from fallen Turis.

In Khaim, the Mayor commissioned fountains recalling Jhandpara, and the Majister launched fireworks from the ramparts of his floating castle on Planting Day as an offering to Mara and her Three Faces: Woman, Man, and Child.

Khaim was alive, and beautiful.

But the Blue City was other things as well.

Even as its inhabitants bragged about their city's splendors, they had the look of dogs well beaten. They sniffed the air for the scent of neem smoke that would tell them danger was approaching. People cowered from black-robed men who stalked the lanes, lazily swinging their censors.

"The smoke likes magics," Teoz had told Rain and Mop when he first took them in. "Clings to them like a lover. Lights them up like casis flies in the summer. Turns them blue and bright as a torch."

He'd pressed his finger to each of their foreheads in turn, admonishing. "You might have been able to make some small secret spellings in Alacan, but don't think you can do that sort of thing here. Majister Scacz and his censori will sniff you out, and he will chop off your heads and you'll be food for cuttle fish. Scacz has the sniff for spelling, and he has a mind as dark and sharp as Takaz the Demon King, so don't think that he can be fooled."

Mop and Rain had both nodded obediently, but whatever Teoz saw in their expressions wasn't sufficient, for he seized them and dragged them close.

"Scacz will take my family too," he whispered fiercely. "If the stink of your magic clings to us in any way, we're all bobbing in the river Sulong by nightfall. So I say again, if you spell, you will be caught. Your father did me a good favor years ago, but I will not have my family die for your foolishness, and if I catch you glowing blue, I swear by Takaz and Mara both I'll take your severed heads to Scacz myself."

After that they'd nodded more vigorously, and Teoz had been satisfied.

Wherever a visitor went in the city, whether up to the villas on Malvia Hill, or down and across the river Sulong to the sometimes raided slums of Lesser Khaim, the brazier smoke of neem and mint followed. A hungry smoke. A determined smoke. A sneaking, suspicious smoke, always sniffing for signs of magics, turning the air blue when it found the residue of spells cast, announcing it for all the world to see.

The people of Khaim stood tall with pride, and crouched in terror all in the same instant. Every inhabitant sniffed the air for neem smoke and every inhabitant lived in fear of the day when he or she would be forced to fumble at the crumbled pages of some long-dead majister's tome and attempt a spelling of their own, knowing that they baited the executioner's axe, and their chances of survival were slim.

Majister Scacz was a jealous lord. The many markets of Khaim might be open to all, but its magics were a monopoly held tight in the fist of the man who lived far above them all. In Alacan, people had been able to cast a simple spell and not fear their head would roll into the river. Trafficking in Jhandpara's Curse was against the edicts of the city, but still, there were small magics that were justifiable. Mop had been born clubfooted. Without his mother's spelling, he would never have been able to walk. Mercy dictated that sometimes spelling was needed. But in Khaim, people begged Majister Scacz for mercy, and he flipped coins like a drunken Borzai, choosing at random those he would save with his magics and those he would leave to suffering.

Mop passed under the great burning sentinel braziers and the watchful eyes of black-robed censori at the city gates. He was exhausted from the bramble work and dead with grief at the loss of Rain, but he strode with determination. If he could convince Teoz to loan him the handcart the spice man used for deliveries up to Malvia Hill, he could return to Rain and bring her back to the city, install her safely in Teoz's warehouse. It was possible.

Down Copper Lane and through the Crooked Square. It was late. The vegetable sellers were packing up the last of their day's produce. Dogs roamed the cobbles, alert to kicks and opportunities as they darted to steal rotten carrots and bits of cauliflower, slinking around fountains depicting children protected by the alertness of the Mayor.

On the far side of the Crooked Square, Mop's path wound down to the river Sulong and cut north toward Malvia Hill, slipping along the waterway that split the city into Khaim and Lesser.

Ahead, the blue arc of the Mayor's Bridge glowed bright, leaping the river like a tiger, an impossible arc of gossamer and blazing color, glowing brighter than the moon at its fullest. Magic there. Vast magics that the city's Majister had worked upon the bridge to build it, and hold it aloft, and make it last. So much magic there.

The Mayor claimed it was so that he could defend Lesser Khaim from raiding clans who came across the rolling hills to the west, but the Alacaner refugees who sheltered in Lesser Khaim all agreed that it was so he could move his soldiers and censori among them, sniffing out their needful small magics so that he and the Majister could wallow in the luxuries of the large magics.

Ahead, the river turned again, revealing the doors of the spice merchants. Lanterns hung over the doorways, giving view into dark confines where hempen sacks of chilies and turmeric and cloves were piled high.

Teoz stood impatient at this warehouse door.

"You're late."

"I'm sorry," Mop said.

"Where is Razica?" But Teoz must have seen the answer on Mop's face for his lips pursed and his hand went to his mustaches, grown long with children, as if he were trying to make a ward against the loss of them at the sight of Mop's bad luck.

"I'm sorry, Mapeoz."

Mop shook his head. "I want to use your handcart. I can fetch her and bring her back."

"Bring her back?" Teoz looked surprised. "She's bramble kissed, no?"

Mop hesitated.

"You haven't given her the mercy cut, yet?"

"She's my sister."

"She's bramble kissed," Teoz insisted. "You can't be thinking that we'll keep her here? In the warehouse?"

"She wouldn't make a sound."

Teoz gave him a sharp look. "I have enough trouble with pests without a bramble body. What will people say?"

"They don't have to know."

"Tongues wag, boy. They have no way of knowing, and yet still they wag. And when the velvet ones up on Malvia Hill hear that Teoz keeps bramble bodies with his spices? What will they do? They'll tell their house managers to order cardamom from Zalati House or Mistress Charas, and then where am I? A warehouse full of spices and a bramble body that attracts rats, and my own children starving."

"I'll keep her clean."

"Talk sense boy. I let you and your sister live here because d'Almedai did me good turns when Alacan was still a city. I do you good turns, even when my wife tells me to shove you across the river to live with the rest of the Alacaner refugees. I let you stay, and I feed you because I remember what your family once was.

"But I'm not so rich that I can simply make trouble for myself. If you and your sister can keep an eye on my warehouse and ensure that my cinnamon and lora flower don't whisper out the door, then we all benefit. But bring a bramble body home and invite the wagging tongues that go with that?" Teoz shook his head. "You ask too much."

"Just for a little while. Until I find a place for her."

"A place for her? You'll sell her to a soft-eyed man?"

"No!"

"There is no place for her, then." Teoz jerked his head toward the river Sulong. "I cannot endanger my family for a bramble body. Go out and make the mercy cut or leave her for the dogs, or do what you will." He gripped Mop's shoulder. "I'm sorry, Mapeoz. She's gone. I won't drag my family down because she was careless in her work."

"You'd do it for Mila," Mop protested. "If Rain were your daughter, you'd keep her safe. You wouldn't talk about mercy cuts. You'd keep her safe!"

But Teoz wouldn't be moved, and he wouldn't give the cart, and he wouldn't let a bramble body near.

"It would destroy me," he said, and though Mop wanted to blame the man and hate him, he knew Teoz was right.

Mop knew, too, that he would betray him.

MOP WOKE IN THE DARKNESS OF TEOZ'S SPICE WARE-
house, amongst sacks of dried chilies and powdered turmeric and cinnamon. A familiar home, even if it was less
than what they had enjoyed before—

Rain.

In his exhaustion he had fallen asleep, waiting for Teoz to close his
doors to the last of the Malvia Hill buyers. It had been torture to wait
for Teoz to finally take himself off to his wife and supper and bed in
the upper floors of the house.

And now Rain was out there in the darkness, alone and undefended.

Mop scrambled off his accidental bed. He grabbed the cart that
Teoz used to haul spice sacks up from the Sulong docks.

He'd been so stupid. How could he have fallen asleep? Rain could
already be gnawed by dogs. A scavenger for the pleasure houses might
have hauled her away to those places where soft-eyed men bought the
flesh of warm girls who could not protest their worst advances.

Sick with horror for his sister, Mop dragged the cart over to the
bolted doors. As he set his hand upon the iron latches, Mop wondered
briefly if he should feel some guilt that he now defied the one person

amongst all his father's old contacts who had been willing to care for orphans who fled out of Alacan.

"It's for Rain," he whispered, and crushed his guilt.

Rain was the last of his relations. Without her, d'Almedai was nothing and he would be alone. They were nearly all gone.

She's already gone, an unwelcome voice reminded him.

It sounded like Lizli, hounding him still. Speaking with the wisdom of someone who had seen too many fall into bramble sleep.

Mop ignored it. How could he not go to her? How could anyone turn their back on a loved one who looked so alive, who was still warm to the touch, even as she never opened her eyes or inhaled another breath?

Mop knew that desperation and hope made fools of bramble-kissed families, and yet he saw now how the foolishness gripped him as well. It was just as it had been with the apothecaries who cared for his mother and promised his distraught father that with patience and perhaps one more application of salve, she might be revived. Just one more drop of emerald philter on her tongue, and one more offering of coin and incense to Mara's Three Faces, and Mother would rise again, and Mop and Rain would have their family again.

Mop had known the apothecary for a liar, even if his father had not, and yet now he found himself in the same trap, and knew that he would follow his father's example to the very bitterest of ends. He would try to save Rain. He would protect her, and seek a cure. And if she could not be cured now, then perhaps later.

The only certain thing was death.

Everything else was possibilities.

The cart's wooden wheels rattled on the cobbles, breaking Khaim's midnight quiet, alarms announcing him as a thief and a traitor to Teoz. Mop eased the cart over each bump in the uneven alley, fighting the urge to simply dash away. Fighting to go slowly enough that he wouldn't wake the man and his family where they slumbered overhead.

The cart creaked and thumped and rattled, and Mop murmured entreaties to Kemaz.

Please let them keep sleeping, please let them keep sleeping. Praying to the dog-headed protector of children and innocents that Teoz would not suddenly appear in the open windows above the warehouse, and name Mop for the thief he was.

"I'm coming, Rain," Mop whispered. "I'm coming."

He reached the mouth of Spice Alley and sped his pace, following twists and turns through Khaim's narrow streets, hurrying across emptied market squares and past lonely fountains. Down more narrow turnings, between the high walls of merchant villas, taking advantage of every shortcut that would allow the cart to pass—

Soldiers emerged from the darkness, their red and gold livery of Mayor and Majister gleaming. And with them a shadow man came striding, a black-robed censori. He, too, bore the mark of the Mayor and Majister: gold crossed axe and staff, bright on his black velvet. But from his hands, his true mark of office hung: a censor, swinging pendulously on a copper chain.

The censor swung rhythmically, the face of Borzai the Judge engraved on each of its sides. Borzai's slitted eyes gleamed fiercely, lit by flickering blue flames within, and the god's open mouth issued a steady stream of smoke.

The smoke drifted about the black-robed censori and his retinue, filling the alley as they quested. It tested windows and doors. It rose to quest through open upper balconies. It pried at shuttered storefronts.

The smoke enveloped Mop, scents of neem and mint, cloying and close. The censori eyed Mop, and Mop was suddenly seized with an animal terror, that he himself was about to glow. That some magic that he had cast years ago still stained his skin or tangled in his hair. That the stink of it was still on him . . .

The censori and the Mayor's soldiers passed on, their eyes following the smoke where it trailed, pausing occasionally to see how it twisted and pooled within the alley.

The smoke slowly dissipated.

Mop sighed with relief and went on himself, rattling through the city gates and out into the fields beyond.

In the summer heat, barley and wheat were growing high. Apricot trees and figs lined the edges of farmers' holdings. He walked the main road out of Khaim, and then cut off along small paths, winding between farmers' fields and heading east for the bramble wall.

Moonlight turned the growing fields bright. Crickets sawed at the darkness and wooden water wheels creaked and turned, spilling water down dozens of sluices, irrigating the crops.

In the distance, Duke Malabaz's villa stood, high thick walls and small windows. A supporting cluster of hovels huddled close by it, but they were all asleep, and it was quiet except for the trickling of water. Harvest time was still far off, so there was no need for farmers to guard their fields against theft.

Mop was alone.

Ahead, the bramble wall loomed. The scents of ash and burn thickened as Mop approached the newly cleared fields of Malabaz's expanded holdings. In times past, the bramble wall had always marched closer to the city, but now, under the iron hand of Majister Scacz and his censori, few people dared loose magic upon the world. The Mayor's axe hung too low, and fell too eagerly.

When Mop complained of the horror of the Mayor and Majister and their eager executioners, Teoz had raised an eyebrow.

"You complain now, but you didn't see what it was like before the censori and all the sentry braziers were raised." Teoz said. "Instead of neem and mint, Khaim smelled of fear. Every day, we found bramble. Even inside the city walls. Even inside my own home. Even inside my bags of spice! Before Scacz, there was no hope. We knew we'd fall. Just like Mpais and Alacan and Jhandpara so long ago.

"It's an ugly thing to watch your city die. Like watching a child starve. It's ugly and there's nothing that you can say to make it beautiful. You think blue flames and sniffing smokes are bad? I tell you it's better than waking in the morning and finding a bramble sprouting in your turmeric. You think leaving all the magic to the Majister is bad? Try watching Lesser Khaim burn yet again. Instead, he burns Paikans! Pillars of fire! I've seen it!"

"But you can't even make a small healing," Mop had pointed out.

"My mother knit my feet when I was born. Two club feet when I birthed, and she whispered healing in my ear and made me walk."

He stuck out his legs to demonstrate. "Now look. Two good feet."

"Two good feet that carried you away when Alacan fell, thanks to your mother's spelling."

"It was only small magic," Mop said.

"Every Alacaner says so," Teoz said. "Small magic here. Small magic there. And now all the Alacaners live in Khaim, and bramble has swallowed Alacan entirely."

"But still, how many feet could Scacz heal if he didn't want a life in the sky?" Rain piped up, pointing at the Majister's castle where it floated high above the city. "Most people only need a little magic to live, but he keeps it all for himself and his friends."

Teoz's expression turned angry, as if Rain had taken a knife and cut off his mustaches. "Shut up, Alacaner. You know nothing. At least we don't flee our city. Here in Khaim, we push bramble back."

Mop had jostled Rain and she'd fallen silent, though she'd still looked peeved at being silenced by a man who would have been a servant to them both in past times.

Anyway, Teoz had been right, or at least, right enough. Even if the people of Khaim were all huddled down like whipped dogs, afraid to use even the smallest magics, Teoz was right about the bramble. Where it had been close, it was now miles distant from the city, and more was being burned back every day.

Mop dragged the cart through soft ashy dirt, sweating in the night's humidity. Ahead, the bramble wall loomed out of the night mists, vast and high. Malevolent woods, tangled and thick. A few large trunks still guttered with fire from the day's work, beacon fires marking the war that would never end.

Mop cast about for Rain. A lump of darkness led him toward a muddy patch, but it was only a cauldron of cured paste for the burn-master's pig bladders. He turned and continued searching.

Where was Rain?

The darkness made the fields unfamiliar. At last in the distance, he saw the cottage that they'd been excavating from bramble's embrace that morning, and he realized that he was in the wrong place. He trudged toward the cottage, eyes searching the furrows and divots of the burned land.

She wasn't anywhere to be found.

Mop fought the familiar urge to call out for her. He wanted to order her to come out from hiding, just as he used to when she hid amongst the rose and lora in their mother's night garden in the hopes of ambushing him as he walked by.

He widened his search, stomping through the newly cleared land, raising charcoal and ash in the hot night air. Clouds in moonlight. Back and forth, hither and yon, Mop searched until at last he was sure of what he had been denying: someone had taken her.

It made sense. All the burn crews had seen her fall. Any one of them could have returned ahead of him to retrieve her body, and then taken her to be sold.

Your fault.

Lizli had told him to give Rain the mercy cut, but he'd been so stubbornly certain that death was worse than sleep. He'd been wrong. There were dozens of fates that were worse than a fast cut and bleeding out in innocent sleep. He'd been a fool to think he could protect her. A fool to try to save her from something that no one had ever survived.

And if he was honest, he had been selfish to think not of Rain's protection but instead of his own lonely isolation in a city that hated their kind. He should have sent her on to Borzai and thence to Kemaz in his safe and happy hall.

That would have been true mercy, and he had failed her.

"I'll find you, Rain," he whispered as he stood alone in the blackened fields. "I swear I'll find you. And when I do, I'll do my duty as I should have done, from the start. I swear to Borzai. I swear I'll deliver you into Kemaz's halls as I should have done. And may Borzai send me to the Demon King and his brides if I fail."

YOU WANT GIRLS?" THE WOMAN ASKED.

The alley was dim, lit only by the vitreous glow of pleasure house lanterns, Naia's colors, dangling in long flickering chains outside the doors. The best of the pleasure houses twinkled with fine Turisian glass much like the d'Almedai had traded during their glory days in Alacan. But here, in the braided alleys of Lesser Khaim, there were other pleasure houses and other pleasure lanterns, and the alley stank of vomit.

Rats jostled the shadows. The orange glass of the pleasure houses was as lumpy and bubbled as if it had been fashioned by the hooves of goats. The woman came down the steps, smiling. Mop stepped back, fighting an almost-overwhelming urge to flee. He had come all this way, first returning into the Spice Alley with Teoz's cart, and then setting off in darkness across the Mayor's Bridge to Lesser Khaim. It was late now, hellishly so, yet this woman called to him, still alert, still hungry.

"I have girls," she crooned. "I have women. I have fat breasts heavy with milk. I have slim girls so delicate they could be made of spun sugar. I have boys lithe and sweet, with full lips. I have men like bulls."

Mop swallowed. "I'm not looking for that."

"We have the smoking waters of Azilah, and the wines of dream, we have khem root and the darkness and light of poppies' sap. Borzai cares not what is done here. Here, he closes his ever-watching eyes. Here you may drink deep of Naia's waters, and she will fill your empty places."

"I'm not looking for those things."

The woman laughed, low and encouraging. "I know you're not lost. No one who wanders into Naia's arms is lost. You come for your hungers. Let me satisfy them. Let me give you joy." She beckoned. "I am not your mother, I am not your master, I am not your patriarch, I am not your god. Tell me your hidden heart desires and I will feed you joy. Speak in Naia's ear and she will give."

"The dolls." Mop swallowed again. "I want to see the dolls."

"Ahh." The woman smiled. "It's hard to say those words the first time, isn't it? Hard to admit how much we hunger for girls as warm as life, and more giving than Mara. I can take you to the beauties. I can take you to the place you need."

"Is it far?"

"Not far," she said, smiling. She held out a hand. "The dolls of Jhandpara are warm as life, and yet live to muffle their complaints. They are true abandon." She cupped his hand in her own. "They are your hungers, unbounded. Come with me. Naia is no Borzai. She does not judge."

The woman was pulling him from the well-lit lane down a darker alley, down into darkness. Mop was suddenly afraid that she was leading him to cutthroats, but he was at a loss as to whether he should follow or flee.

"Is it far?" he asked again.

"Not as far as the distance you've already traveled." Her body brushed against his, softness swaying under silk. "Do not fear the path. I will help you find your match." Her hand slid up his hip.

Just as Mop sought to pull away, she said, "Here."

She tugged him up shadowed steps. An iron and plank door

creaked. Orange light spilled out. A broad muscled man loomed in the frame, arms crossed, shadowed face brooding.

"There, there, Rixus. It's only Amina, and a customer."

The guard stepped aside. A statue of Borzai waited within, its eyes blindfolded with a bit of silk. The Judge's many hands were filled with tokens.

"Pay the Judge," Amina whispered in his ear. "The smallest bit you like."

Mop put a cut copper in the god's hand.

The huge guard nodded, satisfied, and closed the door. Amina led Mop into the pleasure house, following twisting halls, pushing past men and women, heads close and murmuring, their eyes following the new arrivals. Groans of sex issued from behind curtains. Gaps in silk showed sliver glimpses of dim coitus, flexing shadows and slick skin shimmering in candlelight. The smell of excitement and sweat and poppy filled the halls.

A man pushed past Mop, so intent he didn't nod or apologize at Mop's jostling. A soft-eyed man, Mop realized. And not just one. All of them were soft-eyes. Men who sought girls like Rain.

More twisting halls. More curtains. More soft-eyed men. A whole city of them, contained within a maze of smoke and curtains.

Amina opened a door to reveal a huge room, lanterns flickering, casting shadows and light. It was filled with dolls.

Hundreds of dolls.

"Welcome to Naia's dream chamber," Amina whispered, running her hands up to his shoulders. "Tell me what you desire."

The dolls lay stacked upon the floor, piled by age and size. Girls and women, nude and clothed. Wealthy and poor. Boys and men on another wall. Tangled stacks and mounds of them, splayed and discarded.

"Ahh, you like the girls," Amina murmured. "Tell me what you need, and we will seek. Do you like the young or the old? The straw-haired, or the raven? There are many."

Mop stared at the piled bodies, shocked at the number. He saw a girl in the leather-stitch of a bramble worker, a black web of hair spilling from her hood. He ran to her with a cry, but when he knelt beside her, and turned her to meet his gaze, a stranger's face greeted him.

Amina crouched beside him. She ran her hand over the girl's face, tidying the raven hair. "You like her?"

Mop shook his head, wordless with disappointment, but Amina took his silence for something else.

"Let's take a look at her, shall we?"

She plucked at the girl's ties, and the leather jerkin fell away, showing creamy flesh. She offered no protest as Amina bared her. Amina took Mop's hand placed it upon the girl's breast. "Feel how warm she is," she whispered. "Feel how she will please you." Her other hand slipped to Mop's breeches, fumbling for his penis.

Mop scrambled away. "I don't want this!"

Amina looked confused. "You said you wanted dolls."

"I want my sister! I'm looking for my sister."

"Oh?" Amina laughed. "You want your sister?" She swept her arm. "Pick any one you like, and she'll be your sister. She'll love you as you've always dreamed she would, and she will no longer fight you."

"No! I don't want her like that! That's not what I mean."

"You have no need of protest here." Amina wagged a sly finger. "Borzai does not see us and does not judge our hungers. This is Naia's abode. This is a place for desire, not for judgment." She captured his hand again, leading him amongst the piled bodies. "Come. Look close." She lifted another girl by the hair, turning her limp head for Mop's evaluation. When Mop failed to respond, she dropped the girl with a thump and went on to another.

"We'll find your sister for you," she said. "Is she slender like this one? Or do her breasts sway lush, like this one here? Tell me her look, and we'll find her likeness." She propelled Mop to look. "Inspect to your pleasure. Some men love to simply look and imagine their pleasure, but you, when we've found your perfect match, imagine how you'll kiss her warm lips and thrust between her parted thighs." She pointed at the sprawled girls. Silk shifts, leather bramble jerkins, nude splayed limbs. "Any of these dolls would be happy to play your sister. But don't worry if none of these match your desire. We have more."

She went to a curtain and drew it aside, revealing another doorway. Beyond it, men turned, startled like cockroaches exposed to light, all of them caught in their hunt through more bodies that lay in piles and drifts beyond.

"There are many choices," Amina said.

The warren of rooms went on and on, each one full of bramble-sleeping bodies and the soft-eyed men who sought to gorge on them. The living men who fed with Kpala's appetites. All of them feverish to gorge on a pliancy that they could not beg or steal or cajole from their daily lives.

Mop turned back the way he had come, breaking into a run.

"Don't run, little lord!" Amina's voice pursued him. "I can find your sister! I can give you a harem of sisters if you tell me the look and shape! I will find them all for you! Your soft eyes are welcome here!"

Mop fled, slamming into patrons, bumping past whores. Rain was in here somewhere. He needed to stop the soft-eyed men from taking her.

He began yanking curtains aside. Men floundered and grunted atop yielding bodies. Men brandished ropes. Men lifted curved blades, steel dripping black under orange lantern light. Men fed like Kpala's children. But none of them threatened Rain. More curtains. More chambers. Fluid-smeared and broken dolls lay in corners, trash to be thrown into the Sulong before dawn.

There are always more. Amina's words whispered in his mind, telling him how little anyone cared for bramble bodies.

More and more rooms, and more and more bodies, and more and more of the soft-eyed men—

"Rain!"

His sister lay beneath a thrusting man. Mop dragged him away, only to discover that it was not Rain who was abused, but some boy with soft features. The wrong hair and the wrong face, and a history he did not know. But now the soft-eyed man was shouting outrage and reaching for a knife. Mop fled again.

In the hall, he slammed into another man hauling a naked girl slung over his shoulder. They all three fell in a tangle, the man shouting, the girl's limbs tangling them both in perverse embrace.

"You broke her head!" the man shouted. "You broke her head! I don't want one with a broken head!"

Rixus loomed, joined by other bouncers. They dragged Mop easily. "Rain!" Mop shouted as they dragged him out. "Rain!" Knowing she couldn't hear, and yet calling anyway.

The bouncers hurled him into the alley. Their fists rained down and their sandals stamped his ribs. They beat him bloody on the cobbles. His lips split and his teeth shattered and still they beat him until all that issued from his mouth was a whisper.

Rain.

He lay still. From the shadows, rats and blood beetles and gutter dogs watched, waiting to see if he would survive, or if he would become like all the other sleeping ones who were piled in the darkest alleys, the ones who lay warm and pliant even as their blood gushed hot into the mouths of Kpala's children.

MOP WOKE TO RATS CHEWING AT HIS TOES. WITH A CRY, he kicked them away.

The sky overhead was turning pink with dawn. Majister Scacz's castle gleamed with the kiss of the sun, a diamond floating against the sky, shining.

Mop dragged himself upright. The rats watched with interest, seemingly trying to decide if they still might rush him and make a meal. He staggered to his feet, leaned against a rough stone wall. The rats gave up and scuttled away, leaving him alone in the alley.

Mop spat out a shard of tooth.

Rain.

He retched dry, feeling the bruise of his ribs.

Rain.

She deserved better than whatever his selfish mercy had doomed her to. He had a duty to cut her throat with honor, to make offerings to Borzai on her behalf so that she could go quickly into the safe and happy halls of Kemaz. And yet she was lost to him.

Mop stared up at Majister Scacz's castle, gleaming high. The palace of a man who held power to himself, and kept it jealously.

There is a way. A voice whispered in his mind. *There are ways of finding needles in haystacks.*

Mop remembered his father casting simple spells, quick and furtive. The sulphur whiff of magic cast, filling a room and disbursing. He remembered his father spelling a writing quill. Remembered how the point had turned slowly, as if imbued with a life of its own.

His father had spelled the quill to seek, and it had divined a true path to a lost contract, finding where it had been tucked away with papers regarding a shipment from Turis. A small thing, a quick thing.

Tiny, useful, inconsequential magic.

Mop didn't know the spells; his father had told him that it wasn't something to be done casually, or to be assumed that it didn't have its costs. A majister's tutelage was frowned upon by the time Mop came of age. And so he hadn't been taught. But his father had grown in a different time, before Alacan was threatened so greatly by bramble. He'd had the knowledge, and with a small spelling—very nearly a child's trick—he had built friendship between quill and contract.

A small thing, a simple thing—if one had the spine to face the executioner's axe.

Mop limped slowly out of the silent alley to join the city's morning bustle. He wandered, seeking, stumbling through Khaim-Across-the-River's broken jumble of tent cities and newly rebuilt houses, through horse markets and manure, pushing between men who beaded their mustaches in the style of Mpais, and widowed Alacan women who still wore rings on three fingers, Man-Woman-Child, for the faces of Mara.

It was an odd thing to walk amongst his own people once again, to smell Alacan-style peppers on a griddle, frying, stuffed with potato, to remember how Cook had made similar concoctions, to smell the spices and see his people huddled low.

If not for Teoz's kindness, Mop would have lived among them too. Another Alacaner refugee, shoved from his home when bramble came crashing over the Spring City's walls.

Mop wasn't sure what he was looking for, but he thought he would know it when he saw it. There were whispers of such places. Much like the doll houses, there were other whispered places, and Khaim-Across-the-River was the place to hunt. He wandered through marketplaces: the travel market where copper goods came in on caravans from the west, now that Kesh was lost to bramble; the covered markets of cotton and silk; the bulk vegetable markets with bitter melon and spine fruit and chiles laying in drifts.

At last he found a simple stall, tangled amongst all the others, dried Sulong ripple fish on one side, reeking of salt and rot, smoked cats on the other, all the stalls sweltering under the market's sagging shading cattle hides. The heat under the hides was overwhelming, the scents of dry fish and sweat and mint tea pressing and mingling, adding to Mop's misery from the night's beatings and lack of food or water for breakfast.

The stall sold apothecary supplies. Tiger penises and kestrel wood shavings. Bat skins, rat tails. Serpent bile in jewel jars of yellow and green. Chests of tiny drawers lined each side of the man's carpet, draped with the skulls of rats on strings, polished white. Dung beetles in jars, climbing and falling back. Casis flies.

Mop lingered.

The apothecary eyed him.

"What do you want, boy?" His accent was Alacan, but his contempt might as well have come down from the top of Malvia Hill.

Mop stared at the man, thinking how he would have bowed and begged for Mop's business in earlier times, then shoved down the thought. "I'm looking for necessities," Mop said, then hesitated. "And instructions."

"Necessities?"

Mop leaned close. "I want magic," he murmured.

The man flinched and made a warding sign. "I sell trinkets and medicines. I traffic not in the thing you want."

"I have money."

The apothecary laughed. "Yes? So you'll buy my head and sew it back atop my shoulders after Scacz's executioner is done with me?"

"Is there no way of convincing you differently?" Mop whispered soothingly. "No payment? No favor? Nothing?"

The man's eyes went to the crowds jostling past. "What if it's true?" he said. "What if I told you it was possible still? That with the right words and right necessities, it is possible to summon the powers of lost Jhandpara." His gaze fell upon Mop, all attention now, predatory. "How much would you pay, if I told you so?"

Mop goggled. He didn't know the proper price or proper barter. "I trust you to name your fair price."

"I want three in silver, three in gold, three in copper Kesh."

"That's all I have," Mop protested, "and all I want is a simple spelling. It's nothing but a child's spell."

"A simple spell, or a spell as black and convoluted as the heart of Takaz, it makes no difference me, for it will make no difference to our dear Majister Scacz. Magic is magic, and the cost is your head if he finds out. Three and three and three," he said, "or nothing is what you get."

Reluctantly, Mop cut the cash from his string, and handed across the coins. The man weighed the money in his hand.

"Come in back."

The apothecary pushed aside a curtain and led Mop deeper into his tent, crowding into a niche claustrophobic with a desk and ledgers and loose papers, and overhung by clacking garlands of children's backbones. He squeezed behind the desk and dug under his business ledgers, eventually drew out a cracked and broken tome, pages spilling from within.

"What is the power you desire?"

"I'm seeking my sister."

"Finding, then."

He started turning the crackling pages of the tome, each one a brown fragile leaf. "Finding. Hunting. Seeking. Desiring. Pining. Hungering. Missing. Finding. Finding, finding, finding."

He lifted a page and examined it in the light of his oil lamp. "Majisters were always losing things. Losing friends and losing lives. Losing apprentices and familiars and floating castles. And of course, losing their empire. Hmmm. *Finding.*"

He looked up from the page. "I don't have all the spells of Jhandpara. Just one book. Just one hand. Majistra Kalaia's, and not her largest tome, by far."

"How does this matter?"

"You know Kalaia? You know the histories?"

Mop shrugged. "My father thought it best not to teach such things."

"Kalaia was a terrifying majistra. One of the most powerful, from a bloodline that stretched back to Jhandpara's founding. Janakgur first, and the gods, of course, before them. So she had that history in her blood. The rise of Jhandpara from the blessings of Mara, with all three faces. A lot of power, there.

"Kalaia wielded Jhandpara's armies in the north, and helped crush the forest clans. It's said she wore the skin of the rala that she hunted, and ate with her troops when they were cut off from aid in the kestrel forests for more than a year. Her soldiers were so loyal to her that the emperor feared her, and eventually had her put to death by Halizak. But even then she lived on." The apothecary shrugged. "She was powerful."

"How does this help or hinder me?" Mop asked.

The apothecary tapped the tome. "This is one of her books. Not by her hand direct, but a copy by her apprentice Torizi, and a good one. But it is but one, and it is but a sliver off the cheese of the knowledge she kept for herself in her floating villa by the sea.

"When she died, her villa crashed to rubble, and now only a slice of a portion of a bit of a crumb of her knowledge remains. It's just as it is for all the majisters and their many books and their many spellings that are lost to us. We have lost the variations, the pianissimo and the adagio, the pacings and the volume of their spellings.

"We are children where they were gods, and so we pick through their spellings and toy with the primers of their least apprentices who managed to flee from Jhandpara's Fall and the bramble onslaught.

"There is power in the surviving books, but the truth is that the majisters that survive today are nothing in comparison to the gods who ruled in Jhandpara and spread empire across sea and desert and mountain and plain."

"Except Majister Scacz," Mop said. "Scacz is different."

"Scacz?" the man laughed. "You think Scacz is powerful? Because he creates a castle that floats in the air, and stitches the pieces and parts of his enemies into loyal followers? No. Scacz is nothing in comparison to what was lost. Scacz is but a child."

He continued paging through the tome.

"The finest majisters of Jhandpara cast spelling with no effort in the least. Without book, or ingredients. They simply pressed their will upon the world. Scacz is not so much when compared to that."

He frowned as he continued examining pages. "Kalaia liked her battle magics. She burned men from within, and froze them brittle so that they shattered when her troops struck them with their swords. She turned iron swords to sheaves of wheat. She changed the nature of things. Hot to cold. Stone to water. Her power was great, but from her hand, I have but this tome, and it is a trove, but it is not the ideal— Ah." He paused. "This will do."

The apothecary took down a quill and began scratching. "It is a spell to see the things which may be hidden. Kalaia used it for detecting ambush, but with modification, it will do. Even better, this one was much concerned with finding people."

"Is it different for things?"

"Is a dog different from a cat different from your sister?" The man was scratching more notes. He studied his writings. Then pushed it across. "Can you read?"

"Of course I can."

"Some can't. I only ask. These are Kalaia's instructions."

Mop studied the words. "Why are you giving this to me?"

The man smiled. "You think I'll risk the censori? You think I wish to see myself lit up like a casis fly? You think I most desire to become another head on a spike on the wharves, with my body floating down under the Mayor's Bridge? I have no desire to visit the sea, most surely not without my head attached.

"If you wish to play at Halizak squares with Majister Scacz, that is your business. I give instructions. I sell necessities. I do not ply the majister's trade. It's dangerous enough to simply share the memories of Jhandpara's fallen names. Dangerous enough to simply admit that some of us still touch the hand of our ancestors.

"Majister Scacz is jealous for memories like the one you hold in your hand. He is desirous of every majister's power. See how many majisters he has sent to Borzai's judgment. But"—he wagged a finger—"always our Majister is careful to keep his victim's hands. Their heads go on the gates, their bodies float down the river Sulong, but their fine quill hands, those he traces with his own, and he learns from all the dead. So even if one does not turn a tongue to the curse of Jhandpara, our Majister is watching, and he his hungry for whatever traces of a majistra's hand that still remain."

He gave Mop a small leather bag, filled with ingredients.

"These will do the thing that you desire. But do your spelling far from me, and know that if you invoke the lost glories of Jhandpara, that you invoke also its great curse."

MOP CAST THE SEEKING SPELL FROM HIDING, BURROWED deep amongst sacks of Teoz's dried spices.

The instructions of the dead hand of Majistra Kalaia lay before him. Her gestures, her invocations, her words upon his lips. As if the long-dead woman blossomed and rose up within him, animating him with her power.

Mop began whispering words of magic, feeling the majistra's influence from ages past.

In its own way, the thing he did now was every bit as dark and shameful as the acts of the soft-eyed men from whom he sought to save Rain. This was the business of secrecy and shame, and fear. This looking over one's shoulder, this terror of discovery, this rot of transgression . . .

Mop traced his fingertips from a black strand of Rain's hair, to a comb that was one of her last personal belongings. The comb was a treasured thing. A memento of her own private obsessions and desires, bejeweled and made of bone, sharp tines carefully carved by a woman who specialized in such things back when Alacan's walls hadn't been overcome by bramble growth. Rain's last treasured luxury from a time when their lives had been soft and comfortable, held to her, even as their lives fell to rags.

Mop could feel power building as he traced a hand from the hair to the comb and back. A gathering of something greater than himself.

Humming quietly, holding Kalaia's words inside his head, Mop dipped his fingers in water, and carried it to turmeric he had scooped from Teoz's sacks. The water dripped, tiny gleaming jewels in candlelight. He rubbed his fingertips into the spice, turning the water and spice into a staining paste. He plucked up Rain's hair and ran it through. Dipped the comb in the paste, as well, coating its tines.

The majistra's words bubbled within him; he barely had to look at the parchment where the apothecary had written them. His lips knew the vowels and consonants, his tongue felt thick with the need to speak them. The words had their own urgency. Kalaia's voice, filling his chest, his lungs, turning his tongue, spilling from his lips. Words issued forth, sibilant. Building. Exultant. Rising. A spelling. A true spelling, full of ancient power.

Mop threaded his sister's hair through the comb, running it thrice between the tines, and then he took the hair and burned it in the oil lamp. Smoke rose. The hair sizzled and curled and burned away, spice and Rain and the whispers of his words. The acrid sulphur scent of magic coalesced around him, summoned and bound.

The flush of power was almost overwhelming. This was what it was to spell. No wonder the majisters of Jhandpara had been unable to stop.

Mop's voice rose, a thrumming chant. The power was too much. He was full of it. The flush was too fine, the pleasure too decadent. The chant began to crest. Power poured from his voice into the comb where he waved it above the flame, sifting the smoke of Rain's burned hair.

His voice rose to an ecstatic shout—

The comb flipped out of his hand.

It hit the floor, skittered about on the flagstones, flopping like a fish, first one way, then another, a thing alive and out of place, trying to find its home and direction.

It leaped into the air and shot across the room, smacked against granite stonework. It quivered against the wall, and then, slowly, it began sliding along the stones. Scraping, prying, seeking—

A crack in the door.

The comb jammed itself into the crack, wedging itself, forcing deeper, quivering and eager to find its target.

Mop barely managed to grab hold as it sank deeper into the gap. With a grunt, he hauled it back. The comb shook and twisted in his hands, slippery and sly, threatening at every moment to fly free. It trembled with the power he had imbued into it. A thing that was supposed to find ambush—

And do what?

Mop's fingers weakened with the strain of holding back the comb. What had Kalaia done when she sought her ambushers in the kestrel forests of old? Had she spelled something as innocuous as a comb?

Or had she spelled arrows and sent them ahead of her, flying like angry wasps?

The comb trembled malevolently in his hands.

Mop dragged it close, pinned it under his arm, then opened the door. He peered outside. The night was black and still and hot. If he was careful . . . He would have to avoid the braziers, and censori, but now was as good a time as any to go hunting.

The comb was dragging him already, lunging, jerking him out into the night, hauling him faster and faster as he fought to maintain his grasp on it. The comb dragging him straight for Crooked Square and its sentinel braziers.

With all his might, Mop hauled the comb back and forced it down a different alley. The comb fought him at every step, but he couldn't go close to the brazier smoke. One kiss of smoke and he'd be lit up blue, and everyone would be on him for the reward.

The comb dragged him on, faster and faster. Mop ran with it, stumbling to keep up as he was jerked around corners and galloped down alleys. The comb slammed him uncaring through the crowds on the streets, dragging him. . . .

No.

Ahead, a censori and the Mayor's guard were coming down the street.

Mop tried to turn back, but the comb kept dragging him closer. He didn't have enough strength to make it reverse course. Mop opted instead for pressing against the wall, praying to Kemaz for protection, begging the dog-headed one to push the heavy humid air away from him as the censori stalked past. The winds were in his favor. If they held, he had a chance.

The censori's feet were soft on the cobbles. Velvet sneaking shoes, inaudible amongst the tramp of the soldiers' boots who followed. His censor swung, pendulous. Smoke billowed from the bronze-cast snarl of Borzai's mouth. Blue flame flickered behind the Judge's eyes, wicked slits. Smoke issued forth, and Mop watched it, terrified that it would blow in his direction and betray his guilt.

The god seemed to stare into Mop's soul as the censori and the soldiers passed. The censori's eyes fell upon Mop. Mop ducked his head, showing respect, his hands so tight around the comb that he thought his flesh would bleed. Still the breezes favored him.

Heart pounding with fear, Mop turned and began to shuffle away from the censori, his hands cramping with the effort of restraining the terrifying comb in its hungry hunt.

He pushed past a cluster of drunken river boatmen, putting them between him and the censori, praying to Kemaz and Borzai and Mara and every god he could think of. Praying for mercy, simply praying.

The way was open ahead of him.

I'm going to make it. He realized. *I'm free of them.*

The wind shifted. Smoke blew over him. His hands blazed blue. The comb gave a sudden jerk, and it too glowed, bright as a star.

"Magic!" a soldier shouted. "There! Seize him in the name of Mayor and Majister!"

The boatmen saw Mop blaze with blue light, and made drunken grabs for him. Mop dodged and fled as above him shutters opened and people peered down to see the commotion. More drunks came out of the tavern, trying to trip him as he passed, cheering on the Mayor's hounds.

Mop skidded around a corner and collided with a woman carrying brass wares. Pots fell clattering on cobbles, ringing out. The comb skittered out of his sweat-slick hands.

"No!"

The comb ignored his anguished cry. Freed of his clutch, it arrowed down the street, then rose, arcing, flying high, a blue star, rising.

Mop followed it with his eyes, and then it was gone, over the rooftops.

The soldiers came clattering around the corner.

"There he is!"

Mop ran, his whole body aglow with the evidence of his crime. He dodged and ducked, plunging past more jeering townspeople. He reached the city gate and dove through, rolling under the portcullis as it dropped. The gate slammed down behind him, trapping the soldiers on the other side.

The soldiers cursed and shouted after him as Mop plunged on, pounding out into the darkness of peasant fields, hating that the darkness that should have been his friend was now his enemy as the bright glow of magic marked him.

Behind him, he could hear the soldiers raising the gate once more, and attempting pursuit. Slower in their armor, but dogged.

Mop ran until his lungs were raw and his legs were as weak as grass stalks, and still he stumbled on. Ahead of him, the bramble wall loomed, black and tangled. A few tall thorny trunks still guttered orange with flames, like torches lighting the walls of Mara's fortress before her last battle with the Demon King Takaz.

Ahead, he spied the cottage that he and the bramble crews had been excavating from bramble not a day before. If he could hide within . . .

Mop dove inside the chink-stone house, and tried to bury his glow in the loose dirt that had been worked by the bramble crews.

In the distance he heard the guards, calling. Coming closer. Stalking. Mop held his breath. If Kemaz favored him, he might hope to be missed. They might not see the cottage, or not dare to search it so close to bramble. Mop frantically piled more dirt atop himself.

He felt a sting and jerked his hand back. He brushed at the stinging nettle and was rewarded with a second sting. He froze. A pale strand glistened on his skin. Numbness tingled in his fingers. Carefully, holding his breath, Mop dragged his hand through the dirt. The bramble strand fell away.

But now he saw that he was surrounded. Pale wormy, threads that had survived the burning, or perhaps been blown by winds to settle within the roofless cottage, were everywhere.

Outside, the voices of the soldiers grew louder.

Mop tried to wiggle himself deeper into the dirt, anything to smother the glow that would give him away to the soldiers. He felt another sting against his bare arm, another on his neck. Bramble kisses. Numbness, spreading.

It's only a few. I can survive a few.

Not far away, the soldiers shouted as they scoured amongst cooled cauldrons of burn paste, and the saws and hatchets of the bramble crews.

Beside Mop, something moved on the moonlight. A sinuous thing, rising from the ground. A hungry tendril sprout, hatching from some uncollected seed that the pickers had missed.

Outside, he heard the soldiers calling.

Mop held his breath. The bramble vine seemed to be sniffing the air. . . .

Me. It smells me.

Mop's heart began to pound. He was stained with magic. And now the bramble was growing, attracted to him and his spelling. As hungry for him as a wolf hungered for fresh-spilled blood.

The bramble tendril quested across the dirt, slithering slowly toward him. There was more rustling. Mop spied more moonlit vines. The soil seemed to be boiling with tendrils, sinuous fingers emerging from the earth, turning this way and that, all of them seeming to sniff the air. Hungry vines, thickening, gaining strength, fertilized by the hand of Majistra Kalaia, the woman who had trafficked so ruthlessly in the curse of Jhandpara.

Mop felt a sting and then another.

Numbness spread through his body, a heavy tingling. It dragged at his face and limbs. Bramble tendrils began wrapping around his arms and legs, entombing him, questing for his bare flesh.

A vine sniffed at his face and caressed his cheek, stinging. The bramble sleep was becoming overwhelming. One sting, following another, following another. It felt as if an elephant were sitting upon his chest, forcing the breath from him.

Outside, he heard a woman's voice calling, and shouts of dismay from the soldiers. Mop fought to keep heavy lids from closing, watching, awed, as a great bramble bough eased in through a window, blotting out the moon, a branching trunk as thick as a man's waist.

The soldiers' exclamations became distant as they fled, terrified. Mop smiled tiredly. They wouldn't cut his head off, at least. Instead, the bramble would cradle him in slumberous embrace. The cottage would once again be entombed. Eventually, the burn crews might dig it out, but by then, Mop would be long past caring.

Rain. I'm sorry.

The stinging was becoming too much.

A crackling torch flared. The bramble began to burn. Mop squinted against the bright orange light. A familiar face stared down at him.

"The velvet one returns, it seems."

IT TOOK LIZLI ALMOST AN HOUR TO BURN HIM FREE, AND all that time, Mop fought lethargy. When they finally stumbled from the cottage, he leaned against her like a drunk, staggering, his vision blurred.

"You're lucky. Only a little more venom, and you'd be sleeping like your sister."

Mop struggled to move numbed lips. "W-w-w . . . w-welliwake up?"

"You've been ſpelling," Lizli said.

"L-l-l-lost Rain."

Lizli sighed. "And so you thought you'd ſpell her body to your side." She shook her head. "You, causing more bramble, just to find a dead thing." She gestured back at the stone cottage, now almost consumed by the bramble that had been fertilized by his magic.

"How many hours to burn that back again, all because a velvet one like you thinks his needs are greater than mine?"

She smacked the back of his head, a sharp correction. Mop was too bleary and exhausted to defend himself as she struck him again.

"This is why Alacan is bramble! People like you! All you Alacaners with your secret ſpecial needs!"

She grabbed his arm and tugged, nearly toppling him. "Well? Come on, then. You won't be fit for anything for hours, judging from the kisses you've taken." She eyed him with distaste. "And you've still got a bit of the glow about you. Need to get you away from the bramble. Bad enough that you spelled, but then you came here of all places. Making it worse for everyone."

"Mmm tired."

"You will be. For days, I'm sure. And we can't let you sleep tonight, or you may still not wake."

She dragged him on, relentless. Mop focused on putting his numbed feet on the ground. Forcing stony-lug feet and dead-tree-trunk legs to move. *Thump. Thump. Thump.* Clumsy weights that he dragged in counterpoint. One step at a time. *Thump. Thump.*

Lizli's crabbed hand squeezed his arm, nails digging in. He thought to complain until he realized that she was simply keeping him upright. The steps he took were not even. He swayed like a ship tossed in storm with every footfall.

If not for his leathers, he was sure that he would already be sleeping, another body to be dumped in the Sulong or sold to the soft-eyed men. His skin burned where the bramble had gifted welting kisses.

"H-h-how far?" he mumbled.

"Not far, now," Lizli said. "An easy walk when you're healthy."

In the distance, Duke Malabaz's manor glowed with candles and lantern light. Torches burned on its high walks. Mop kept his gaze focused on the light, willing his dead legs to move. Forcing himself to walk toward those flickering glows.

Quite a lot of light, for so deep in the night.

"What's this?" Lizli frowned.

Ahead, a village huddled close to the manor, the homes of the duke's servants and farmers along with assorted guards and bramble pickers. It should have been still and silent, and yet now shadow people ran and called out.

"Your hunters couldn't be seeking you here," Lizli said. "They tucked tail for the city. So who is this?"

Mop couldn't summon the energy to speculate. Only the rhythm of movement seemed to keep him upright. Dimly he was aware of the shouts and calls and running forms breaking the night stillness, but he couldn't quite summon his sodden mind to care about the activities of those who dashed amongst the village huts.

Lizli yanked him to a stop. "You still glow of magic. We can't return to my home this way."

Mop shuffled to a halt, swaying. He stared dully down at his clothes. Indeed, a faint aura still limned his body, but it was dim now. Not as before. Not the sparkling shimmering badge of shame that censori and soldiers had pursued. And now, even as he watched, the glow seemed to be sloughing from his body under the influence of the gentle night breeze.

It blew away like dust, drifting motes, like the fines of chili powders brushed from Teoz's hands after he has finished weighing orders for the velvet ones on Malvia Hill.

Mop brushed clumsily at himself. More of the spelling residue fell away, blowing clear in the night breeze. Lizli watched. She slapped her own hands together, clapping them, as if afraid that some memory of magic might cling to her own skin.

"I tried," Mop mumbled as he tried to cleanse himself. "I tried to find her. I just wanted to help her."

"And you failed. As everyone who has tried before you. Jhandpara's Curse is not something we bargain with. It is not something we undo. There is no escape from it, and you knew it when you failed to give your sister the mercy cut when you had the chance."

"It wasn't always this way," he said.

"Magic makes bramble, and bramble makes kisses, and kisses make sleep that lasts until Kpala's children tear us to pieces. It was always thus. And yet you put your yourself above the rest of us, and now all that magic blows in the breeze and brings bramble calling. Your people smothered Alacan under bramble's blanket, and now you do the same here."

"I had to find her," Mop said. "I couldn't leave her to the soft-eyed men."

Lizli gave him a disgusted look. "And see how that has served you now. You, almost kissed to join her. And a day of our work undone as well. You've had a busy night, little velvet one."

Mop stopped his protestations. He brushed again at his clothes, and the last of the magic sloughed off him.

"Well, you'll pass," Lizli judged. "Now come with me. But keep clear of whatever is brewing." She began leading him toward the noise and clamor of the village that clustered beside Malabaz's home.

The entire village was awake. For a moment, Mop was gripped with fear that more censori sought him for his spelling and searched the village. Lizli seemed to hear his mind.

"You show no blue. They cannot catch you now."

But still, the torches were alight and the village burned with awful commotion.

"It's Cojzia's house," Lizli said. "The linemaster. Malabaz's man."

"I 'member," Mop mumbled through his numbed lips.

"Can you walk in the crowd?"

"Can." Mop nodded definitively. Something about the clustered people filled him with an overwhelming urge to join them.

Lizli guided Mop into the crowd. At last they pressed through to the linemaster's open door.

"It seems we've found your sister," Lizli murmured.

Inside the hovel, Rain lay like a broken doll upon Cojzia's bed. The linemaster's body draped naked across her.

Sunk between his shoulder blades, Rain's comb lay buried. Blood dripped, soaking the bed and pooling on flagstones. The comb still quivered malevolently, smoking blue with magic's residue. People murmured all around.

"Always thought he was soft-eyed."

"You think he took Aisa, too?"

"Never liked how he looked at me when I worked."

The man had fought, it seemed. His blood was spattered around the house.

"I heard him shouting," a man said to Lizli. "Thought he was being taken by Takaz the way he howled."

"What do we do . . . with . . . that?"

"Leave it. It's cursed."

"It's a girl's comb," Lizli said. "Mayhap it came to save her."

A murmur of astonishment washed through the crowd. The comb continued to quiver, but it no longer flew, as if the war magic of Majistra Kalaia had been sated by Cojzia's blood.

Mop stumbled to his sister's side and knelt clumsily. "Rain," he whispered. "Rain."

She slept on, unbothered.

Behind him, people gasped. Mop turned at the commotion and found everyone bowing and ducking. Lizli grabbed his arm and whispered, "Bend, fool."

Duke Malabaz stood in the doorway, flanked by his guards, glowering. "What's this?"

"M-magic, m'lord," one of his guards said.

"I can see that, fool." The duke's mottled gaze swept the room. He was not a large man, or vital, but his sunken eyes glittered with malice. "Gods, the room is full of its stink. I want to know who murdered my man? Who spelled him dead?" He surveyed the bent assembly like an aged vulture. "Which one of you so despises the work that comes from my largesse?"

When no one answered, Malabaz asked, "Who knows something, and desires to thrive under my protection?"

Mop glanced worriedly at Lizli, remembering the stories of the man stepping over his headless wife, his robes trailing blood, to receive his rewards from the Mayor and Majister for turning in his relations for spelling.

And now Lizli stood to make the same reward.

"Shall I take a head and see if that loosens tongues?" Malabaz asked.

On the bed, Rain slumbered on, unbothered by the duke's threats. Unbothered by the dead linemaster who had sought to take advantage of her.

Looking at Cojzia's corpse, Mop felt a dark satisfaction that even if he had not saved his sister, he had at least avenged her. Even if Lizli gave him up, he had done his duty.

But inside the hut, no one spoke. Cojzia's blood dripped, a steady patter filling the silence.

"I can have all your heads for this," Malabaz said. "And as soon as the censori arrives, I'll catch the speller anyway."

Lizli cleared her throat. Mop braced himself for what was to come.

"It glows with magic, Lord," Lizli said.

"I can see that!"

"My meaning is that if it glows, it came from the city. To glow blue, it must needs come from the city, passing through the sentinel smokes. The sentinel smoke is only in the city, and now that . . . comb . . . glows with its touch."

A murmur of relieved agreement rippled through the farmers and bramble pickers.

"From the city. From the city."

"Yes, yes. From the Blue City."

"It glows blue. It must needs come from the Blue City."

"From Khaim?" Malabaz murmured, his eyes widening at Cojzia's corpse. "Did Cojzia have such enemies?" His anger was replaced by an anxious knitted brow.

"It's a woman's comb," Lizli supplied. "And bejeweled . . ."

Malabaz bent to study the comb. "An expensive trinket, that's true." He reached out to touch it, then seemed to think better. He drew his hand away, unconsciously wiping it on his robes. "Someone highborn, then? A woman he dallied with, who discovered his soft-eyed habits?

Disgusted with his perversions? Or is this a message from Malvia Hill to me? Magic . . . Who would risk such an . . . open . . . attack?"

Lizli cleared her throat again. "A velvet intrigue, sire. Above us and our dirt. Above our simple lives."

The others were all nodding. Malabaz didn't seem to hear—he was an ancient, fearful man still staring at the comb, looking as if all Takaz's demon wives were coming for him.

A guard took pity on them. "The workers . . . they can go, sire? If it wasn't to do with these rabble, they can go?"

Malabaz nodded absently. The pickers and peasants pushed for the door. Lizli gripped Mop's elbow to guide him out, but Mop shook her off. He approached the duke, fighting to keep his bramble-numbed tongue loose. Behind him, the others were all scrambling and shoving and scuffling to their exit, glad to flee.

"My . . . the . . . the bramble body," he mumbled thickly. He pointed at Rain. "It needs burial. Rats . . ."

Malabaz's eyes rose from the malevolent comb buried in his line-master's back. "I missed someone," he murmured. "Who did I miss? Who seeks me now? Some hidden niece?" The man's eyes were wide, haunted by the mountain of bodies he had climbed to reach his station, the enemies he had made. "Who seeks me now?"

"We should bury the body," Mop repeated.

Slowly, Malabaz's hunted look receded, and his sunken gaze centered upon Mop. "You care for this one?"

"She worked on the line. Before." Mop shrugged helplessly.

"Of course." Malabaz nodded with distaste. "And Cojzia took her for his own when she fell." He waved his hand, giving permission. "As you will. Give her the mercy cut and be done. She deserves that much kindness, anyway."

Mop clumsily tried to drag Rain from beneath Cojzia's bulk. The dead man weighed heavy. With Mop's own bramble-kissed weakness, he feared he would fail, but then, miraculously, others were gathering around, all of them silent, but all of them helping. Many hands, rolling the linemaster off the girl, and then cradling Rain.

"She is ours, too," someone murmured as they bore her out.

Outside the linemaster's house, more people gathered, lending their strength to Mop. Lizli guided them to her own house, where they laid Rain upon the old woman's bed. Many hands washed Rain and dressed her as if she were still alive, preparing her for Borzai and her final passage to Kemaz's halls, where she would live, safe and happy, with all the innocents of the world.

Finally, Mop knelt beside his sister, alone.

I'm sorry. I tried. I don't know how to save you. I'm sorry.

He accepted now what he had to do. There were too many like Cojzia in the world, and Kpala's children would come eventually. Better to send his sister on to Kemaz, where children lived in joy and were well-protected. Safer than this troubled place, in truth.

Mop fumbled for his knife. Drew the blade. He felt empty inside. He lifted the steel, preparing himself for the mercy cut.

A hand gripped his, staying his strike.

"No need for that, now." Lizli pried the knife from his hand. "We will care for her. You need have no fear, now. Look. See." She pointed to the door, where seed pickers and burnmasters pressed to see within, expressions solemn.

"I told them that it was her comb," Lizli said, "come back to save her. Come all the way from the city, to stay Cojzia's hands. She fought him even though she slumbered."

The bramble pickers and paste makers and burnmasters and apprentices entered at Lizli's invitation. Some bore candles that they lit beside her bed, others draped marigolds across Rain's body. More and more people squeezed inside the hut, all of them bearing offerings. A man laid copper coins in Rain's hands. A woman lit incense. Thick smoke began to fill the hovel. The scent reminded Mop of the temple to Kemaz that his family had endowed so long ago.

The candles burned bright around Rain's sleeping form. The piles of offerings grew.

"No one can keep her from Kpala forever, but she will be cared for," Lizli said. "As long as she lasts, she will be cared for. She is all of ours, now."

Outside, the sun was rising, light streaming in through the slitted windows of the stone hut. More and more bramble workers came to kneel in obeisance, each of them making offerings before leaving to burn the bramble wall. All of them making offerings in the hope that if they were unlucky enough to feel bramble's kiss, that they might still find shelter. That they might win protection under the hand of the sleeping girl who had defended herself, despite the permanence of bramble sleep.

PART IV

The Blacksmith's Daughter

BY TOBIAS S. BUCKELL

THE DAY MY FAMILY RAN OUT OF FOOD MY BACK ACHED from bending over the bellows. The pain had built from deep within my spine. Over the next hour it started jabbing and slashing at the muscles in my back. My arms, strong on the leather handles, had yet to give out. But oh, my poor back burned.

There was no time to rest. No time to slack. There was only the great suit of armor for the Duke Malabaz.

Or rather, his son, Savar. Who'd leered at me when he'd come in to be measured by me with my marked rope. Who kept hissing my name as I ran the rope around his body. "Sofija, Sooooﬁiijaaa . . ."

Only one person had the right to call my name like that, and it was Djoka. His family still saved coppers for the day our two humble houses would join. Then Djoka and I would stand under the Three Faces of Mara and he would offer me three rings and three vows for Woman, Man, and Child, dancing.

A straw dummy stood in the corner of the forge with a melon for a head and broomstick skeleton. We draped the armor as we pieced it together.

It was a bargain with one of Takaz's demon wives to take on a commission like this. Call on a demon, it was said, and you could maybe bend it to your will. But you always ended up paying a price you didn't expect, even if you got what you wanted.

Our family got the prestige of making the duke's armor. But we were struggling to finish it.

"We used to cast a spell at the bellows that made them belch fire for hours," I complained out loud as I stood and stretched, finally unable to stand the pain any longer. "My back feels like it is being stabbed with one of those spears!" I pointed at two of the longer city guard's spears hanging from the rafters above me. Unfinished, the tips were only wooden, to remind my father of the size the captain demanded. There wasn't enough metal, or time, to make them right now.

I pushed hard on my lower back with my thumbs, shoving them deep into the muscle under the skin until my eyes watered. Kneading the knots out. Leaning from side to side.

My mother stopped tapping fine gold inlay into the set of greaves she had on the old wooden bench in front of her. She'd been following a finely laid-out groove my father had carved into the metal with the pattern of the Malabaz house sigil: a tiger with wicked claws grasping a money cord. My father had hammered out the lines with a glowing hot chisel and evenly weighted hammer for the last week, and sworn every time his hand had slipped and touched the lower part of the chisel. "I'll take a hand."

"Your neck will hurt more than your back if we ever choose to spell the bellows again," my father said quietly, moving the breastplate in front of him back over the fire, then picking up the larger hammer.

The sound of metal against metal filled the workshop. My father had a rhythm to his strikes, one that sounded near-musical in its precision.

As a child I'd curled up on cold nights near the fires of the forge, lulled to sleep by that steady, strong clank. Now, dripping sweat and swaying in place, my back offering up thanks to Mara in all her faces for the ability to stand straight, I could feel myself slipping as the steady strikes took me away into meditation.

"I might be taking the bellows!" my mother shouted, breaking me out of my lull. "But you don't get to just stand there like a statue. Make yourself useful and go fetch wood from the pile."

I jumped in place. I hadn't realized my eyes were half closed with exhaustion.

My mother grimaced when I looked at her, and I knew that if my back hurt, hers hurt more. Youth had left her somewhere early in my memories of learning how to walk, with her scolding me away from the fires and slapping my hands away from tools. Where my arms were brown, with veins like ropes when I grabbed the hammer, she had gone to pale and her veins were green, like ink under a spelled parchment.

Still, she had the strength to cuff my head hard enough to make my eyes water if she wanted. Even an old, slowed-down blacksmith was stronger than any other tradeswoman.

I scurried out of the forge with a nod.

Rain so soft it hung in the air like gauzy curtains swept across the cool air of the packed-dirt road. The family forge was on the other side of the Sulong from Khaim, and in between the jeweler's and ferrier's huts I could see the brown water of the large river lazily flowing away.

And Khaim, the Blue City, on the other side.

The blue light, even in the late midday, came from the hundreds of alchemical braziers that cast the city in blue smoke. The magical blue clung to anything—and more importantly, anyone—that used magic.

That was why we couldn't spell the bellows even though I'd complained about it. If we used magic, which only the great Majister Scacz could do, we would lose our heads to the executioner's blade.

Or worse.

I picked up several pieces of wood, checking them first to make sure there was no bramble that could prick me hidden away in the dark crevices of the pile. Very little survived inside the city walls, but some still crept in here or there. I stepped back into the choking heat of the forge. It was a simple place, a large round house with the main forge at the center. Open, warm, and filled with our tools on benches or hanging from the walls. The shelves held scraps of metal. They used to hold things we'd made for the people of Lesser Khaim, but since accepting the duke's commission, we'd made nothing but pieces of armor.

We slept in alcoves against the outer wall, though my parents had a thick curtain over their bedding. My mother would cook over the forge fire, using tongs to pull simple cakes out of the coals the same as she would a bar of metal that had been heated to be beaten.

I leaned over, my lower back complaining, and took the handles of the bellows from my mother and started pumping. The fire rose, and my father grunted with approval. He wouldn't have to leave the metal in as long for it to turn pliable now. We'd finish the basic shaping of the breast plate faster.

When we broke for dinner my linens were soaked through with sweat, my back again in agony, and I drank an entire pitcher of watered wine from the casket by our foodstuff table so fast I dizzied and the room spun around me.

My father and I sat near each other at the roughly hewn table, my father drinking just as heavily and noisily from a pitcher, spilling some of the watered wine down his thick, hairy arms.

"Is it enough?" I asked. Something caught in my throat. "And what will the duke think?"

My father looked away from me toward the forge and stroked his mustaches. "We will see after tonight's work," he said. "When we glaze the breastplate and helmet."

What he left unsaid was . . . if *we glaze it.*

I knew we only had enough for one attempt.

My mother sat down, and we split the last loaf of our gritty bread between the three of us. And after that, we seized the head-sized melon that had been the dummy's head in the forge.

That was how I knew we had run out everything to eat, and that all our family's money had been tied into the making of Savar's armor, hoping to impress the duke.

An unfinished suit, no less.

I stabbed my piece of melon angrily, imagining it was Savar's sneering face. But after that was done, all that was left was hunger. We hadn't had any meat in days, and there was a pit in my stomach. Bread and melon would not fill it, and every stroke of the bellows made it yawn larger.

I was hungry. And I knew that after that last piece of slightly dried-out, tasteless melon, there was nothing left. If the duke was not happy tomorrow, we would starve.

Or worse.

Lakil, the rag-boy, told me several days back about two brothers he'd known who'd been approached for a well-paying, mysterious job in one of the new estates in northern Khaim, carved out of the bramble in fresh new fields. They'd been blindfolded and taken in a covered cart to the estate, and lived inside for two whole months, their jobs to recite incantations and spells, covered in foul smelling mints and jhordril leaves, until they were blue and stinking with magic.

Then they spent a month hiding in a clearing room with other boys, slowly waiting until the sulphuric smell of magic had dissipated. They were paid, and then blindfolded again, and dumped out in Lesser Khaim.

But the one brother had gone back, sure he could remember the twists and turns of their trip. Hunting for the blue that would let him turn in the velvet lord he was sure he worked magic for, thinking that turning them in would make his fortune.

They found his body in the river Sulong two days later with his throat cut.

That was the way it was for the people of Lesser Khaim. We meant nothing to those who lived across the river.

We began the glazing after the sun set, once the last gleaming lines of light faded away from the inside of the forge. The evil red glow of the coals glimmered as we took out five vials.

"Vitreous ndeza," my mother murmured, putting two of them by my father's bench.

I took the three containing the yellow iron oxide and set them down as well.

My father used mortar and pestle to carefully mix the ingredients into a sickly yellow paste. Once smoothed, with not a single bit of grit left in the mix, he scooped the ingredients out and transferred them into a larger wooden bowl.

And now we added the other liquids. Translucent fikik tree sap that was normally used to coat cogs and axles, songbird oil, distilled water. The paste built into a slurry, and then a smooth, slightly yellow broth.

"It isn't glowing," I said, my voice wavering slightly.

"Won't until it's fired," my mother reassured me, putting a hand on my shoulder. She'd been putting the fire under the kiln, bringing the heat up. There'd been a small blaze glowing under it as we'd eaten the last of our food for dinner, now it burned bright with all the wood I'd brought inside earlier crackling underneath.

We'd had to rent it from a potter, for no small fee, and have it delivered. Test objects in it. Fire small pieces of armor with the vitreous ndeza mixture.

These were not normally things blacksmiths did, but the duke had been quite clear about what he wanted from us.

And my father had agreed.

Though now I knew he regretted it. I could see it in his dark eyes when he thought we were not watching. The moments when he hung his head, or pushed the heel of his hand against his brow.

He continued to whisk the mixture as the kiln heated. The pot-bellied chamber glowed, the air around it rippled, and after what seemed a minor eternity, my mother finally nodded.

My father turned to me with a fine, horsehair brush in his hands, holding it almost like he would a newborn in his massive, calloused palms.

"Here," he said. And no more.

My mother put a hand on my forearm. "You are good with the brush. Do not doubt yourself."

Of course, her telling me made me do just that. I took a deep breath. We should have been able to dip the breastplate in a vat of the nasty smelling yellow liquid, then transfer it to the kiln. But we simply didn't have any more than the bowl in front of us. The ndeza came from a far off mine, via caravans on the old roads, created back when Jhandpara was a vast empire and Khaim nothing more than a sleepy roadside stop on the way to the sea cliffs of Rusajka.

Ndeza was highly prized by the sign makers in Khaim, farther up the hill and close to the Mayor's Palace. With their various mixtures they could create glowing signs that fetched a premium price. Particularly, my dad said, for signs to places that I shouldn't know anything about.

As if children didn't also fear the kiss of bramble, and being sold by families who couldn't afford to care for their ever-sleeping bodies to the brothels for the men of Khaim to do whatever they wanted to young, unmoving bodies.

"Get the helm ready, Mother," I said. I grabbed the brush from my father, my hand shaking slightly, and dipped it into the bowl. I bit my lip, swirled the brush around, and then began to paint the breastplate with the light touch I'd been practicing for weeks, using milk-water to delicately paint whitewash onto bone, metal, or any substance I could find to practice the skill that might make or break us. *Mara, steady my hand,* I prayed. *For Mother, Father, Child.*

Eyes narrowed, I laid the bare minimum of a yellow glaze down, the brush a feather in my fingers. A breath of yellow on the fine steel my father had spent so much time hammering, smoothing, polishing.

My mother passed the helmet over. A fearsome thing, patterned to resemble the face of Takaz, with many serpent-headed faces thrust forth out of the helm. Fangs jutted out from it, and my father had tapped out fine scales throughout the entire surface.

A more difficult surface to paint, and I had to twist my hand to dab, tap, daub, and pack glaze into the crevices and crooks of the helm.

And then, all too soon, there was nothing left in the tiny bowl.

"Did I do it?" I asked, setting the brush down.

Neither of my parents answered me. They moved as one toward the kiln, holding each object in tongs. The breastplate they lowered in first, canted up on its side. Should it fall over, all this would have been for nothing.

Next to it soon sat the demon-faced helmet, only a hair's width apart, and then they shut the door as gently as they could.

There was nothing to do but sit and stare at it. To watch over the next hour as the vitreous ndeza and yellow iron oxides burned hot in the furious fires, and a dull yellow gleam began to seep around the edges of the kiln's door.

My father laughed out loud and clapped his large hands together. "We did it." He grabbed both me and my mother by the shoulders and pulled us in close. "I told you the extra coin we gave to Assim were worth it."

He smiled. *That coin would have fed us*, I thought as my stomach grumbled. But I had gone with him to the Temple of the Merciful and Sly Assim, where the four prophets slept. We had left the coins with a monk by the steps, and my father had said his prayers.

My mother usually fought about my father's adherence to the monks. Assim had not saved their town or families from the creeping bramble, she would say. But tonight, tonight she said nothing and just smiled.

Hugged together against them both by the fires of our furnace, the searing heat of the kiln playing across our backs, I could close my eyes for a moment and feel safe and happy.

When we pulled the two pieces out after they had cooled in the early dark of morning, they still glowed a malevolent yellow. My father set them on the straw dummy. My mother wrapped an old cloth into a ball, and then ran twine around it to create a linen head we could put the helm on.

We sat and looked at our weeks of work.

The breastplate, shiny and muscular, was a new addition to Jhandparan armor. An imitation of the exotic kestrel-made armor the Czandians wore, each piece carved to mirror the human body it fit. Our breastplate sat over the Coat of a Thousand Nails. A hundred years ago, the coat would have been made out of silk so strong and light, men could run easily across a field while wearing a long armored coat. Today we sowed each protective armor plate into a coat of linen.

It was heavy, but Savar did not stand all that much taller than me. I had pulled the coat on myself to test the weight. I could move quickly enough around the forge, and raise my hands over my head with a forge hammer still in hand. And dance in half circles around the fire, the heavy waist of the coat slapping against my legs.

The gloves and steel sleeves, the greaves, and the entire coat remained poignantly dull and unlit. It was almost worse to have glazed what we could, I thought in the gloom. It highlighted what we were not able to glaze. What we couldn't afford to glaze without more money from the duke.

"Why yellow?" I asked, staring at the three quarters finished armor. I hadn't dared asked Savar or the duke himself. I'd forgotten to ask until now, staring at it. "Isn't their house color green?"

My parents turned as one to look at me as if I had turned into a river-gull and burst scrawking through the doors of the forge.

"Girl, what do you think the color of yellow mixed with blue makes?" my father asked slowly.

"Green," I said.

Obviously.

I stood there and stared at my parents, and they stared back.

Then the flame rushed to my head, and my eyes widened with hot understanding. "*Blue,*" I said.

"Blue," my mother repeated.

The blue from the magical sentinel braziers of Khaim, across the great river. Blue that clung to anyone using magic, fingered them for anyone to turn in to the Majister. The same blue that had clung to the corpses of Malabaz's uncles, cousins, and nephews when he turned them over to the Majister. A color that turned to purple as his robes dragged across the blood of his family's as he rose to become the head of his own house and lands.

Malabaz was a hungry duke, eager to expand his lands. He jostled with the other velvet families of Khaim. Sometimes they would spill blood in the streets, out in the dark, away from the prying eyes of the Mayor and the ever more powerful Majister Scacz.

If Malabaz wanted to protect his son, why not a suit that would glow with his house's color when tainted with the mark of blue?

"By the faces of Mara," I muttered. "If the Majister ever finds out we did this . . ."

For a moment I imagined being thrown out of the half-built floating palace that hung over the highest point of Khaim, its stone bulk held aloft by the clouds beneath it that glowed blue whenever the winds were still and the smoke of the braziers became pillars that rose toward their heights.

"Malabaz is favored by Majister Scacz," my father said flatly. "There was no way to refuse him."

"We could have taken what we had and run for the trade roads," I suggested.

My mother's face darkened. "And risk raiders?"

"They haven't had the strength to reach Lesser Khaim in many years, not since the rise of the Executioness," I snapped.

"Or face roads choked with bramble," my father added softly.

And just like that, he pulled the winds out of the two storms brewing in the room.

"Do not forget," my father said, his voice soft like flour and silk. "When you were just a tiny thing we could carry you around, we watched the bramble grow and grow until it choked the town we lived in. People fell into sleep every day. Just a touch, you *know* just a touch, would leave you bereft of sense. And then another touch, and then another, because it lurks in the corners of your pantry, or under the door latch. Brothers, aunts, uncles—they would all sleep. The curse of Jhandpara lies all over the lands beyond the two Khaims, Daughter. Never forget that. And never forget that the Majister has beaten it back, now. This isn't like Alacan, where they magicked themselves to death, spreading the bramble around because they couldn't stop themselves from risking magic's curse. The Majister and his favored are strong and powerful men, but they have made a great city for us that is safe. Do *not* forget that."

I flinched from the steely anger in his voice. "I do not forget." I could never forget. My parents never let me forget.

"Good." He relaxed, seeing his words take root in me. "Now go get some sleep. You've been working through the night. The duke and his son will be here soon enough. And then we will see where we stand."

I thrashed and kicked when I felt a hand on my brow. My mother pulled back from my bed, hands raised against my fists. "Hush," she said, "it's just me. Hush. The duke has arrived."

Wild-eyed with fear, I took a moment to hug my blankets close to me and looked at her. "I'm sorry," I said. "My dreams tore at me."

I rubbed at my crusty eyes. In some ways, just getting a few hours of sleep hurt more than if I'd just stayed up. Maybe that was why such horrors had come to me.

"What did you dream?" my mother asked.

For a moment I didn't want to tell her. But then I swallowed. "I dreamed about measuring Savar."

Her face darkened, but she tried to make light of it for a moment. "But your father and I have been talking to Ivica and Anshoula. At your request! If we should be talking to the duke . . ."

But I was no mood for her false smiles. She'd named Djoka's parents, the man I'd hoped to join our houses with. Djoka was a large man, larger than my father. Born of a long line of farriers, he was large enough wrestle an unruly horse that objected to being shoed.

Djoka's family lived at the far end of the street, and just sitting under their roof often made me feel safe. Like I had journeyed to a land of giants. Like the stories of Okenaide, who had hurled boulders at the army of Jhandpara during the conquest of the northern forests.

"Savar leered at me. All I did was dream of it. He didn't touch me." I shrugged. "I dreamed that he leered at me, and then cut my throat and threw me into the Sulong. I dreamed I was lying there, drifting under the great bridge and the blue smoke. Bleeding into the dark, cold water. My head bobbing along just like the head of Malabaz's wife. You know he betrayed her to Majister Scacz for magic, right? Even as she stood amongst the rest of her family's bodies?"

"By all the gods, child. Don't say such things." My mother's smile burned away, replaced with worry. "Get out to the forge with me. We will stand by your father and see what the duke's word brings."

I grabbed my heavy leather apron from the hook on my side of the common room and shouldered it on. My mother cracked the thick and heavy door to the forge, and I heard the duke's word right away.

"You idiot," he snarled at my father. He pointed at the armor standing in the corner of the forge like a straw man-at-arms. "I don't care about your coin problems. I *gave* you *gold*, Blacksmith. I gave you all the gold you said you needed to make my son a suit of armor."

"My Duke," my father said, bowing as far as his protective leather apron would let him. It boiled my blood to see him do it. But what choice did he have?

"My Duke, my Duke," Savar mocked him by repeating the words. "That won't bring you mercy, Blacksmith."

"Please, lords," my mother said, also bowing as she stepped forward. Malabaz looked at us, seeing us for the first time. His lip curled slightly and my heart beat faster with fear. I felt like a rabbit cornered between a patch of bramble and a dog when he looked at me.

His pale, wrinkled skin sagged under his ratlike eyes as he looked my mother up and down. "What?" he spat.

"We cannot buy vitreous ndeza easily in the city, not in the amounts you need. It's not about the gold, it's about how little of the yellow we can make. You know that it is harder and harder to get things from the other cities. Bramble chokes the roads, kills the sources of what we need. The last shipment of ndeza arrived a month ago, the sign makers hoard it. We purchased all we could, but the price rises each week. We need the other half of the promised pay for the armor, and even then, we will not break even, but craft this armor in your honor. Please, my child goes hungry."

Malabaz sneered. "I don't care about your brat. Your inability to run your business effectively is not my problem."

Savar moved to look over at the armor. And leaned in to see the fine engraving and detail. The house sigil's swoops of gold.

His lust showed clearly in the sickly yellow light.

Ever sensitive to the manner of a sale, my father leaned in. Seeing opportunity, he became a merchant artisan again. My pride bloomed. "Look at the craftmanship your son admires, my Duke. That fine work, you won't get that anywhere else. I'm a strong blacksmith, and I can tame the heavy metals. But my wife's family were jewelers who hailed from Paika, and together, no one can make finer, stronger things than our small house. And my daughter's hand has been trained by both of us."

"Takaz pisses on your bloodlines," Malabaz snapped while Savar laughed, turning and watching on. Malabaz simmered, and I struggled to understand his rage. The offer my parents made was fair. He could see for himself that most of the armor stood before him. It was true we feared the velvet folk on Malvia Hill. But now that I saw a human, and a wrinkled old one at that, before me, the awe had fled.

Yet, this flabby-skinned creature could kill us all. There was an evil mind there.

And as I struggled to understand it, that same cruel face pinned me with sudden attention.

"Your daughter, your daughter," Duke Malabaz whined. "You keep mewling about her. But there's your solution."

The anger in his eyes changed to satisfaction as his lips quirked.

"My Duke?" my father asked.

Duke Malabaz pointed at me. "Sell your daughter."

My mother blurted a wail that she quickly stifled, and my father shook his head. "I don't understand. You want to buy my daughter?"

"That's why I'm a duke, and you're a tradesman," Malabaz hissed. "You're slow in the head. Sell your daughter. She's squat and muscled like stone, you'll hardly get a good bride price. Sell her to the soft men. Prick her one night with bramble, and she won't even notice. She'll fall asleep, and there will be hard men who want a stone troll like that. Like the ones who clear my fields of bramble. No one will blame you when they see her in the bramble sleep."

Savar snorted and looked at his father.

"It won't be the first time a family has done this," Savar said with a knowing smirk, "for the chance to stay alive on this side of the river."

My father opened his mouth, but I put my hand on his forearm.

Malabaz was pleased with his solution. "I will be back in two sunrises, blacksmith. There is no more gold for you. You will complete the armor. There is a *deadline*. If you do not, I will have your head decorating a pike. I will ask it of *Majister Scacz* himself."

My father shrank back from the invocation of that name.

"Good," Malabaz said. "I see you know who I mean. Scacz will be here in Lesser Khaim, to oversee the clearing of some land that he will be gifting the Duke Borka for his new hold. If my armor is not ready, you will die at the hands of the Majister himself. I promise you this."

He slid his way out of the house, and Savar, with one last look at the armor, followed him.

I closed and barred the door behind the trailing edge of Savar's cloak.

We all looked at anything in the forge but one another, or the armor.

"He spoke pure truth when he said there was no more gold for me. He never intended to pay the other half for the armor," my father muttered to himself, a realization spilling out of him. "That's why he was so angered we came so close but could not finish, and why he refuses to give us any more."

My mother brushed at the tears on her cheeks. "He is a murderous bastard son of a lesser duke who married his way into power. Borzai piss on *his* bloodlines."

"I'm a fool," my father said, sitting on his bench heavily. "I'm a fool."

"Just to have come even would have been a boon," my mother reassured him. "How could we ignore it? We never had a choice, he was a duke."

I watched them, but didn't join. My own family suddenly didn't feel like a warm and safe place for me. I could only think of the prick of the bramble brushing against my skin in the late night, for what other choices might my parents have? "I have a thought," I said.

And they turned as one to look at me, a faint sliver of hope in their eyes.

I SAT AT IVICA AND ANSHOULA'S FORGE. IVICA SCRATCHED at one of his mustaches thoughtfully while Anshoula poured red wine into crude wooden cups. It muddled my head a little, as I hadn't eaten today yet, and the red was not watered down at all.

Djoka sat with his legs wrapped around a wooden bench, it creaked as he shifted.

"Why aren't Cedomill and Natazia here to ask?" Ivica finally asked me in his deep rumble of a voice, naming my father and then mother. His voice sounded like a poker being drawn across iron coals to me.

"They don't know I'm here," I lied, trying to look him in the eye. "It is my idea."

Anshoula sat next to me. "Oh, my little berry."

Djoka remained a mountain of calm, his corded forearms wrapped around his oak-barrel chest, drinking me in. I had to look away from those eyes. It had been just a week since I sat watching the Sulong, confessing my fears about my father's latest project to him.

"It's never a good idea to take up with the velvet ones," Djoka had said then, with a conviction stronger than the deep, dark currents of the Sulong.

Now his eyes showed that his worst fears had come true.

But there was no anger. Only sadness.

"We can't do this," Anshoula said to me, so very sadly but firmly. There was agreement in Ivica's face. "We give alms to Mara, as parents, to ensure that you will be parents as well. It's not coin for you. It's coin for the god. Not everyone can save this gift, and they risk bad judgment for eternity, a risk we who are less fortunate take. And that is why this is so special, and why I can't give it to you knowing what your family will do with it."

I balled my hands into fists and dug my fingers into my palms to keep my composure. Anshoula saw it, and made it worse by leaning forward and wrapping me in a giant hug.

She enveloped me, and I didn't hug her back.

Feeling my resistance, she let me go. "You will move in here, with us. Now," she said.

"No." I shook my head.

"You must leave your family," Djoka finally said. "And join with ours. There is nothing we can do for your parents, but we can save you."

"And you are worth saving, little berry," Anshoula said. "It took a great deal of bravery to come to us without your parents knowing. Now you need to find the bravery to stay with us and not look behind you."

I still shook my head.

They were family. My mother and father. *Mother, father, child.* The three faces of Mara. All the world could tell me to leave them, but I would stand against that great stinking wind.

After all, only Borzai could judge me in the end.

Not them.

I stood up, somewhat unsteadily. "I must go."

Ivica spoke up. Quiet all this time as Anshoula had held the reins, he now sought to reach through and shake me from my path. "Your mother and father are dead, child. Understand this. It is as sure as if they had fallen into bramble, and someone is coming to give them the mercy cut. Their lungs may fill and empty, but they are dead. They just don't know it yet."

If I had wavered, I now strengthened. "Then I am dead as well," I told him. "And it is *you* who just doesn't understand this."

He nodded. "Yes. That is what I will tell Djoka when you walk out of these doors."

Djoka stood up, the bench barely able to withstand the sudden explosion of movement. "Father!"

Anshoula took a long pull of wine and said, "It is not necessary to give bad news with the smell of bramble sap, when you can deliver it with fresh mint, Husband."

"But it is true, and you all know it." Ivica turned his back to me, and looked into his wife's eyes. "You of all people should know what comes of working for the velvet ones."

She poured more wine with an unsteady hand, and I left them to whatever bitter cloud hung in the room that had stolen their hearts.

Djoka ran outside after me. "Sofija! Sofija! Wait."

He had to run to get in front of me. I stopped, a puff of dust kicking up around our knees because I had to halt hard to avoid hitting him.

"What?"

Djoka caught his breath. "Please . . ."

"I can't."

He grabbed my shoulders. Leaned down to move his face closer to mine. "He isn't wrong, you know."

"What is it that eats you inside?" I asked. "What is it you won't talk about?"

Djoka looked around. Then he lowered his voice. "My parents used to live on Malvia Hill. My father was blacksmith for a duke. Until one night. And now, neither my mother nor father will talk about it. You make of it what you will, but we left the next morning for Lesser Khaim, and we never talk about it. And we never deal with the velvet ones. Ever."

His voice wavered at the end. Anger, humiliation.

And defeat.

He handed me a small leather pouch. It clinked. Copper. I could tell the sound of the metal.

Loose copper, not even wound to a string yet for counting.

What good would it do me?

"Keep it," I told him, while damning my pride. "Keep it because it's not enough to help me, and so you might as well give me toy wooden coins. It will give you something to remember me by. As well as this." I handed him back his bracelet, which he'd given me when he'd promised that we would join houses.

Because what use did I have for a husband who couldn't help me right now? Who didn't at least counsel that we run away with my parents? Or offer to fight, even if he didn't really mean it? Maybe the red wine was speaking, and I was not thinking correctly. But I made the decision—it was iron and strong, and I'd forged it well within myself.

He may have been a mountain of a man, but I demolished him. Like a magician of Jhandpara destroyed hills in their way to create flat plains for their summer cities. He dropped the pouch in the dust, slunk back into his family's forge, and shut the door heavily behind him.

After a long moment, I picked up the pouch of coppers and began the walk home.

Halfway home I stopped where the dirt road met cobblestones. A clatter echoed through a nearby alley, and the screams of little children pierced the air.

Two censori strode out from the alley, swinging their brass boxes. The holes vomited neem smoke, and they waved them from side to side as they moved quickly and efficiently on. A gaggle of street children followed along, dancing in the smoke.

The children were hoping to spot anyone who glowed blue, and to catch the reward for turning them in. Because sometimes the marked ones ran. Along the street, merchants looked up from their tents and stalls and stiffened as the censori approached.

The whole street held its breath as the censori threw smoke between the tables and canvas, over the boxes of breadfruit, gooseberries, honey apples, and into the faces of the flies on the butcher's tables.

But no one took blue today, and the censori continued quickly on into the distance.

I turned onto the street, away from my home. I should take the coppers home and see what we could buy with them. But I wasn't stupid. The fifteen or so coins in my hand would do nothing. They were no answer to our problems.

I wandered the streets of Lesser Khaim and saw them for the first time. Always I'd been passing through, my jaw firm and my destination in mind. I was always going to somewhere, from somewhere else.

Now I wandered aimlessly.

The Xun weavers begged me to feel the tight fibers of their bold red-and-yellow squared carpets, and I stopped to eat fresh cooked lamb sliced right from the leg over a sizzling fire in the Amber Aisle. I passed the soft streets, and heard the moans from behind the barred windows.

Would I ever make sounds like that again? When Djoka stood with me behind my parent's forge he'd slid his fingers under my linens. I'd made that sound, and pushed myself down while kissing him so hard our teeth hurt.

I'd thrown that behind me.

Somewhere near the spice merchants, where the curry was mixed with dust and carried through the air, I stopped and just breathed.

"You look lost," a voice said.

"I'm near the spice streets," I told it. "I am not lost."

"Not that sort of lost," the voice said.

A beggar sat in the dirt. An Alacan refugee with his mustaches cut off, the reek of poppy around him. At his long, curled toes, a bowl for alms or food.

"I remember looking like that, the day after my city fell," he said. And I heard a note of pity in it. I stood on a street, with a beggar giving me pity. "My whole world fell apart, and what I thought was up was down. Down became up. I once could hold handfuls of gold and wore only the finest silks, now I wear rags, beg for copper. I once commanded thirty servants. Now I am lucky to empty a lord's night-soil buckets. I once ran up the side of a mountain, now I'm sickly with bramble cough. It made no sense to me to see these things change, just as right now, the world makes no sense to you."

He was right.

I sighed. "What should I do?" I asked.

The beggar snorted. "Piss on it all if I know. I once would have lectured to you about the treatises of Zizabar, and of how you should approach your life via the quadrant of righteous harmonies. But knowing that did little to prevent hunger in my case. I'm just praying you'll give me one of those coppers you have in your leather there."

"Praying," I said as I bent to give him a copper. "I've been praying for so long. Why would the gods start answering now, when they haven't all this week yet?"

"Well, they just answered *my* prayer," the beggar said. He stood up, flipped the copper, and turned to leave.

"Alacaner," I said to his back. "When your city fell, what were the roads like? What was it like out there past Khaim?" I'd heard about the trade caravans that trundled through the old roads and fought to keep them clear of the bramble, so that trade could live. And I knew about the legend of the Executioness, who had thrown every Paikan raider from the high city walls until the blood ran through their fields and their crops grew in bright red. Some said the sea-facing cities still thrived, but who really knew?

Maybe this beggar had actually seen such things.

He paused. Thought about it. He didn't turn back to face me, but I could hear memory strong in his voice. "There was a lot of bramble.

Not enough clean roads. Many died. There used to be raiders." He shrugged. "I made it here, at least."

I didn't sleep at home that night. For a few coppers I rented a locked bed in the Mudflats. The old building perched next to the Sulong's banks on eroded pillars that looked like a sap-sniffer's crooked teeth, next to another ancient, stilted mansion that had slumped over into the mud. The ruins of the riverside vacation homes of the mighty Jhandpara, now turned into housing for hundreds of refugees.

Tradesmen had ripped the inner walls out of the old stilt house. Then carpenters built wooden cages not much larger than chicken crates when viewed from the front. But they extended back seven feet. Hundreds of them, stacked fifteen high, crammed and bolted into any spare nook or crevice in the ancient swooping walls.

Like coffins, I thought as I climbed up a ladder to my numbered cage.

The front doors of my cage shut solid when I slid myself down onto the straw, and the bar I dropped from the inside was as thick as my forearm.

The warmth of hundreds of other bodies choked the air.

Did I fear my parents would prick me with bramble and sell me to the soft-eyed men? I didn't know. And that scared me. *Because I couldn't say for sure.*

Like the beggar, my life was turning upside down.

I didn't think they would do such a thing. But I knew nothing.

When I woke up to the bustle of cooks shouting in the common room, the smell of cinnamon and stewed fruit hitting my nose, I sat up to smack my face into the wooden ceiling just a foot above my nose. But this was why I'd come here.

Refugees fresh from the road stayed here, if they had any means. Men, women, and children from the outer towns and fallen cities of the world. The constant sound of bramble cough floated in the air, and many had a far-off look to their eyes that terrified me.

The families huddled together with their fearful children as I sat on the row benches next to a green-eyed girl who stared at my steaming bowl of noodles. Recognizing the hunger, I slid it over, and her parents gushed with gratitude at the sudden kindness, but eyed me warily at the same time.

"I just want to ask you about the roads," I said.

"You want to *leave* Khaim?" they asked, shocked as their child slurped noodles. "Do you understand what the bramble has done to the land?"

I didn't explain my business, but I poked them with questions until their child finished my bribe of food and they fell to quiet. And then the censori arrived, the crowd of smelly, hopeless humanity parting before them in fear.

"They come every morning and wave those metal boxes," the little girl said. "Yesterday some men from Tussetia lit up all blue, and the men in the robes and swords cut them in half, right there. I saw it."

She pointed at a spot among the tables where the dirty wooden floor planks were splotched brown.

City guardsmen followed the censori through the crowds of hungry refugees. It made sense, to come here every day. These would be the people most likely to still be in the habit of using small magics. The censori would break them of that habit quickly enough.

So I moved on to other recent arrivals and ignored the smoke. I looked for the hungry children and repeated the act four more times, until the tables cleared and the food stopped, and people left the stilt house to seek work or beg. The censori, maybe slightly disappointed, also left. They left behind a faint lingering of smoke and neem in the air as a sign of their passage.

My parents looked up when I entered the forge, and my mother wept openly when she saw me. "You shouldn't have come back," she said.

That terrified me, for a moment. Fear spilled out of me that they would hold me down and apply bramble's tendrils to my arm.

But that wasn't what my mother meant. "You can leave us. Stay with Djoka's family. Leave your father and me to our fate. Don't burden yourself with what comes next."

Now I cried with them. "You spent what little you had saved for Borzai's gift on the armor. I can't watch you condemned to risk judgment for eternity. . . ."

"Let us worry about the judgment our lives might bring," my father said. "We lived honorable lives! How much should we fear judgment? And dry your tears, child, we are not dead just yet."

I looked up.

"You were right," my mother said. "When you said we should run, you were right. We were hoping you would stay with Djoka, and by the time you found out we had left it would be too late. We are going to leave the city this hour. We spent our night packing what we could not live without into a small cart. It holds enough bricks to make a simple village forge and the most basic tools."

"I can't go back to Djoka," I said, and held up my bare forearm.

My mother swept me into a hug, and I didn't fear it. I relaxed into it. "Oh, my child," she whispered, and kissed my hair and pulled me even tighter.

"I've talked to the refugees in the Mudflats about the roads," I said. "I think I know some clear ways, and the names of some towns. There may be need for blacksmiths, when so many have fled. And I have some coppers to help our way. Please let me come with you."

They nodded, then helped me bundle my own tools and put them in the small cart. For the first time in days a small smile flickered around my lips. But it was snuffed when I realized we'd all been walking around the edges of something in the room: the dummy made of straw, draped in a Coat of a Thousand Nails, muscular breast gleaming its evil yellow.

"What about the armor?" I asked. The gold hammered into its lines would be enough for us to make our way through the world outside Lesser Khaim with full bellies and comfortable rooms. "We should take some of the gold."

It had been my father's plan to earn enough off making it to change our lives. Why not let it do just that? If we were going to run, why did we think we had to leave the armor for the duke?

My father shook his head. "The duke never intended to pay us the other half, he wanted his armor cheap. But we are not thieves. Leave it for him. Let's be just be on our way."

"Thieves?" my mother spat as she stared at my father angrily. "Cedomill, we spent weeks and weeks on this armor and have nothing, and we are to leave with nothing?"

My father slumped slightly. "I know. I know," he muttered.

My mother walked up to the straw dummy, and pulled the gauntlets off. "Sofija is right. So are you. We are not thieves," she said. "So we will take only what we are owed and no less."

We wrapped the gauntlets in oily rags and threw pig iron in with them, to confuse any one who looked through the contents of our cart. We left in the noon, the sun high overhead. The last of the forge's fire guttered as we shut the door. It felt strange to watch the last swirls of smoke from its mouth of embers escape the chimney, then scatter on the wind.

My father pulled the cart swiftly down the dirt, and then onto cobblestones. We passed beggars and censori, smelled spice on the wind, and paid it little attention. We had a direction and purpose. The three of us moved as one. Mother, father, child: a family under Mara's gaze.

NO GATES MARKED THE EDGE OF LESSER KHAIM. NO
River Sulong cut it off like at the edge of Khaim. Instead,
Lesser Khaim exhausted itself and trailed away into smaller
and smaller claims as we walked on through the afternoon. The outer
farms, with men hunched over plows and fields, was often rimmed by
the ghost-white tangle of bramble.

The one hard edge of Lesser Khaim, the new estates, were being
carved back out of the bramble that choked around the main trade
road. We could see the glow of fire in the fields as teams of hundreds
burned back more bramble in their lines. They were far enough away
that they looked like the little figurines given to the Ahadita, the ones
with the purple dye daubed on the spot you begged a healing for.

My father sweated in the sun, but we were used to sweating in
forge heat. We sipped watered wine that I had purchased, along with
bread and dried meat and fruit, on the way out of Lesser Khaim with
the copper coins Djoka had given me.

We were so focused on leaving Lesser Khaim that we didn't notice
the sound at first. But eventually it become unmistakable: hoofbeats
pounded down the road from behind us.

My mother looked back. "Off the road," she ordered us both. "There are city guards coming."

It didn't occur to any of us that the horses rode for us until the pale, awkward Duke Malabaz veered off the stones and into the grass.

"There!" the duke screamed. "These are our thieves."

Five spear tips lowered smoothly from the height of horseback, pinning us with our backs to the cart's rough, gray wood as we cowered in place.

"Where are the gauntlets?" Malabaz shouted. "Where are they? Tell me now!" He kicked his horse forward and looked at the cart, as if we would have left the preciously decorated armor sitting on top of our bundled possessions.

Too cowed to speak, we huddled together as the guards descended to yank everything from our cart and scatter our possessions across the road. I saw the bundle with the gauntlets in it picked up, and the pig iron fell out. But the guards shook things out too quickly to realize what they held, and threw the bundle into the ditch after they stabbed it with knives to shake out only more cheap iron.

My father opened his mouth, but Malabaz had sat long enough watching this. "I knew you useless mud fish wouldn't have the strength to do what was right. I placed a watcher on you. They called me to the forge and I saw what you had stolen. Had you run without my gauntlets, maybe I would not have bothered. But that isn't what you did."

"We are not thieves," my father said. He had seen the bundle tossed into the ditch as well.

The nearest guard had a bracelet on his upper arm that identified him as an officer. He seemed disgusted and annoyed all at once. He looked back at the duke. "They have no jeweled gauntlet, my Duke. They have barely a few coppers, and just some food. If they have harmed you, follow them down the road and take your revenge at night. Or let it be. But you are wasting my time."

I prayed to the gods that this would break the duke's interest. But his eyes narrowed and his rage increased at what he saw only as disrespect.

"Captain, I told you I would haul these thieves before the Majister himself. He happens to have come out a day early to see the clearing of the new estates from the stranglehold of bramble itself." Malabaz saw my father turn pale at the words, and he nodded. "Did you think I made an idle threat? To haul you before him? Bring them, Captain! You will also answer for your insolence."

The guards shoved us across the newly reclaimed fields, the dirt still caked in the ash of recently burned bramble. They prodded us with the butts of their spears whenever we faltered, the metal plug smacking cruelly into the small of my spine and making my eyes water.

My mother said nothing, nor made any sound. She only stared at the ground as if wishing she could become invisible. My father looked ahead in horror. He clutched a pack with our food and some wine in it as he pulled the cart. He would clutch it harder to himself as the guards struck his shoulders to move him along.

Ahead, a figure in long black robes appeared through the ash clouds and setting sun. My chest squeezed down on itself, forcing my heart to skip and race, and I could hardly breathe. It was Majister Scacz. Scacz himself stood before us, flanked by two dog-headed men in city guard uniforms. The flesh where dog met human was seared by magic. The fused flesh twisted and contorted as the lean muzzles turned to stare at us, regarding us with glowing hunters' eyes.

I felt like a tiny sewer rat.

Two beardless merchants stood with the Majister, watching the lines of laborers where the bramble became thick enough it was an implacable wall. Their fine silk robes whipped in the wind, showing the rotund curves of their ever-filled, rich bellies. Behind them stood even more city guards. Though these ones, mercifully, had human heads. Untouched by the Majister's magics.

Duke Malabaz had us shoved before the Majister and his men gleefully. Our knees struck the ash and stirred it up into a cloud that made us choke. The Majister's face pinched and he spared us not even a second glance. He waved the dust away with a gesture. Suddenly the air was cool, clean, and smelled faintly of rogia oil.

"What is this interruption?" he asked coolly.

"Majister!" Malabaz said with friendly exuberance that was not returned, though Malabaz seemed not to notice it. "I've come to demand justice for myself and my house."

The Majister sighed. "Malabaz, as you can see, I'm busy. Send me your request in writing, I will consider it then."

I saw the city guard captain behind the merchants smile with just the tiniest corner of his mouth. I looked over at my father, trying to catch his eye. The duke was not the fearsome creature we thought him. Or at least, not to the Majister.

The Majister was to the duke as the duke to us.

Yellow, I mouthed. But my father was too scared of the dog-headed guards and Majister Scacz to think.

Malabaz's voice rose an octave as he actually wheedled with the Majister. "My lord, you promised support to me, if I held the lands you cleared for me. I have come for your support!"

Majister Scacz cocked his head. "I *did* promise that, Duke. What an optimist I must be, to assume that the lords of Khaim will hold the lands I gift them effectively and with little botherment. Please, pray inform me, how may I *support* you this fine day?"

Malabaz regarded the ground, suddenly realizing now that he had the Majister's full attention. This was the man who could loft bridges into the sky, or refashion human flesh to his whim. Malabaz's voice, now low, mumbled. "I will just turn them over to the captain of the guard, Majister."

"Oh no," said Majister Scacz. "You have already interrupted me and taken my time. That is the one thing we can never unspend, Duke. Time. Now that you have used it, I would be careful about outright … wasting it."

Malabaz quickly blurted, "These blacksmiths have stolen something valuable from me. Gauntlets to fine armor that I commissioned.

I want them punished, Majister. Not killed, they are valuable, of course, but certainly . . . punished."

"All this, it is over some pretty gloves." Majister Scacz fairly tutted. But there was a glowing interest in his eyes that chilled my blood as he turned in our direction. "Forward, blacksmiths!"

The guards threw my parents before him like meat to a dog. But I was young enough they left me in place. I moved to step forward and join them, but the captain who had captured us twitched slightly and moved the tip of his spear over my sandaled feet.

I froze at the feel of the spear point casually pressed against my toes.

Majister Scacz's dog-headed guards stepped forward, sniffing the air and curling their lips at my mother and father. My father had slumped forward, bowing to the Majister, his face completely buried in the ash.

The Majister regarded them incuriously for a moment, and then muttered something under his breath. The air around him rippled slightly. He spoke flatly, as if bored. "Knowing that I can see a lie, and pull the truth from you with my magic, tell me: Did you steal these gauntlets?"

"Yes," my father confessed without even pausing. "Mercy, Majister. They are in the ditch, near my cart, in a bundle of pig iron."

Duke Malabaz glared at the guards.

Majister Scacz shrugged and looked back to the duke. My parents had confessed, and now it was time to sentence them, I saw.

"Yellow!" I shouted, startling the captain next to me.

Malabaz paled.

The Majister turned and looked at me. I stood transfixed in his glare, like a fly drifting toward a white-hot lamp. "And you are an apprentice, or daughter, perhaps?"

"Yes, Majister," I managed, the words awkward in the shimmer of air. "A daughter."

"You like colors," the Majister observed, "and shout them out randomly?"

I'd thought about the words and repeated them in my head several times while I stared at the Majister. They came out in a jumble. "He demanded a suit that glowed yellow, using vitreous ndeza, Majister. I suspect him of using magic, and like all of Khaim, I am obligated to turn him in to protect us all, as you require!"

"No, no, no!" Malabaz screeched as it was his turn to be impaled by Scacz's attention. He dropped to his knees, beseeching the Majister. "It was for my son. It was for my son."

"Glowing. Yellow." Majister Scacz rolled the letters around in his mouth, seeming amused by them. "Duke Malabaz, you wouldn't, perhaps, be considering using magic while surrounded by the glow of yellow?"

"For my son," Malabaz almost sobbed. "I would never."

Majister Scacz frowned. "You speak true. Is that how your weasel of a boy pretends his strength? Interesting."

Malabaz said nothing, doing his best not to implicate himself any further. He just waited.

Majister Scacz looked back to me. "Was the armor truly for his son, and not the duke?"

Transfixed, the air between us wavering with the crackle and sulphuric scent of magic, I could only speak truth. "It was, Majister."

The air rushed from my body when he looked to my parents. He waved a hand, a piece of parchment dropping from his long sleeves into his fingers. He twirled his fingers around the edges of it. The smell of burned spelled paper struck us, and then the Majister roared.

The ground twisted and dropped in on itself, becoming a deep pit where my parents had stood just a second before. I screamed, ran forward, and almost fell over the edge of the great hole the Majister had opened beneath them.

Fifteen feet below me, my father and mother stared up at us.

We screamed one another's names as the Majister silenced our lips with a spell, and then threw magic into the air at the pit's opening. Bramble curled, appearing around the numinous edges of blue light, and then spread rapidly as Scacz continued fill the wind with paper and magic.

The bramble grew thick, hard and cagelike around the pit's walls until it reached up over my parent's heads into a roof that forced both my father and mother to crouch. At first I could see their faces through the lines of bramble. But within seconds it solidified into a wall as thick as any around the farms on the far edge of Lesser Khaim.

Scacz swept his hands again. Dirt rose from the ground, raised by whirlwinds that tore through our party to land on top of the bramble in the pit, sealing it off and returning the land to its ash-caked smoothness.

As if nothing had happened.

As if they had never been standing there, just moments ago.

I lay on the ground and wept as Scacz straightened his robes. "There is your punishment, Duke. I have not killed them, as you requested. At least, not yet. They have some air in there, and if you listen, you can almost hear them weep. It will be days before death will reach them, or they fall into the bramble's sleep. For though I have let them live, I cannot allow the lesser people to go around stealing pretty gloves, now can I?"

"Of course not, Majister," Malabaz whimpered.

"And as for the yellow: I guess a father would worry about a son, when dukes' velvet houses clash in the streets, though I have forbidden such things. Maybe such a son, not from a particularly martial house, would risk using magical trickery to save his neck in the heat of battle?"

"Maybe," Malabaz sniffed.

"Well, if he were ever foolish enough to do such a thing I would have him executed." Majister Scacz looked around, found the captain, and added, "And I would have it done in public, to make an example to other nobility. To remind them all that no one is exempt."

"Of course, my lord."

"It would be like the execution of your wife, wouldn't it?" Majister

Scacz continued with acid in his voice. "What was her name again?"

Malabaz cowered. "I . . ." He couldn't bring himself to say anything.

"Ah, your ability to mentally discard so quickly those you suddenly consider inconsequential has always been something I admired about you, Duke Malabaz," Scacz laughed. "I aspire to forget those who disappoint me as profoundly as you appear to."

The Majister made a sign and the two dog-headed guards snapped to his side. He walked over to his carriage, which was no longer obscured by ash dust. Carved from raven wood and wrapped in iron staves, it crawled with gold and silver serpents that dripped venom from their fangs as they tried to break their tails free of the structure, where they were fused into the very carriage itself. The cinder-horses at the front stamped their feet and kicked up flurries of burning ash.

"By the way," Scacz called out over his shoulder. "Duke, your house color are now yellow. If I ever see you, or your family, in any other color, I will end your bloodline."

His retinue entered the carriage. Once the doors shut, the horses burned a trail of fire wherever their hooves struck until they all lifted off the ground, blazing off back toward the floating palace.

Malabaz turned to me. "You!"

I gathered my linens up in my hands and ran for my life.

Malabaz struck me from his horse with a club and sent me sprawling and tumbling in the ash. Blood spurted from the back of my skull. When I stood to run again, I could barely focus my eyes.

He grabbed my hair, and when I spun to pull him loose, he struck me in the face. I raised my hands to ward off each frustrated, angry blow. He dismounted, then clubbed me back down to the ground and kicked me in the ribs, stomped my shoulders, then kicked me in the head.

He was an old man, yes, but the boots rung hard. Blood filled my eyes and spattered on the ash, turning it to mud.

There was nowhere to flee where he couldn't ride me down on his horse.

This was the way it was for those in Lesser Khaim.

He was velvet. I was mud.

I could only wait until the blows stopped.

Malabaz finally stopped beating me down, panting and resting against his horse. He held his sides and belly, grimacing. He grabbed a spear and limped back over to me when I stirred to try to sit up. He dug the tip into the dirt right by my chin. He leaned on the haft, still trying to catch his breath as I watched him from between my swollen eyes and the steady little rivers of blood stinging my eyes.

The guards stood behind Malabaz's horse and did nothing. I knew that if I ran again they would help Malabaz after me.

I could lift Malabaz. I could snap his arms as easily as I could bend a rod of metal when glowing hot. I could drive my fist into his face with all the strength of my years of pounding at the metal alongside my father, and I would break it.

And then the guards would kill me.

There might be satisfaction there, for a brief moment. But it wouldn't bring my parents back. It wouldn't save me. So I continued to do nothing.

Because I was mud.

"Kill me," I told him, and grabbed the spear's point. "You killed my parents. Kill me now too."

But the fire in Malabaz had been banked.

"No," he said, thoughtful. "You're going to go get those gauntlets. Take them back and continue what your house promised mine. Your parents bragged about your skill. Now you will use it to finish the armor."

I spat blood out into the stirred-up ash between us. "Who cares about the yellowed armor now? It won't hide your son's magics."

"I care!" the duke roared at me. "It will still be great armor, and you owe it to my son. That is why. That is all. I'm a duke and you're a blacksmith's daughter from *Lesser Khaim*. Gods behold, child, you're dirt between my toes. You are part of a transaction and you must hold to your end of it. The suit will be delivered on time. As promised."

I stared at him as if he was crazy for a moment. "Why?" I asked.

Malabaz gaped at me. He even looked around, as if to confirm who the crazy one was. The guard's faces remained blank as they stared thoughtfully off in the distance. They had no interest in this. "Why?" he repeated.

I stood up, my legs shaky, and wiped blood onto my sleeves. I was taller than the duke, I realized. I looked down at him. "What will you do if I refuse? You've already killed my parents. You can order me to do something, but I have no reason to do it. Maybe you will threaten me with something worse than death. I've heard such things. But the moment you do that, when you're done, I'll just give myself the mercy cut."

The guard's captain regarded me for a moment with something that looked like respect, I thought. He gave me a faint nod, and his men suddenly looked interested in the exchange between me and the duke.

Malabaz raised his spear and pointed back the way I'd run. "I'll show you why you'll do it," he said. "Walk with me."

I stood in place, but the guards pushed me forward, forcing me to limp back over my own footsteps to return to the freshly covered pit. Malabaz stepped over the fresh dirt and jammed the spear deep into it. When he let go it quivered and remained in place, a terribly thin post in the dimness of evening's fall.

"You'll do it because I can save your parents," Malabaz hissed. "They yet live inside that pit. Yes, the bramble covers the top of it, but I can still faintly hear their screams. Can't you?"

I stopped wheezing and listened. "I think so."

Malabaz continued. "They can still breathe. They likely will starve. Or give each other the mercy cut, knowing they are trapped alive."

I looked over the butt of the spear at him.

"Oh yes," he said. "I won't threaten you. Instead, I'll promise you something. Give my son the greatest armor and I'll announce it is to mark the changing of our house color. I'll say it is to honor the Majister's request. I will follow his edict, but I will claim it a sign of our special relationship. And I will dig up that field and burn the bramble out so that your parents can go free. The Majister never said I had to leave them in there, only that he had punished them. It's important to listen to what people *really say*, don't you think?"

Malabaz was a devious, wrinkled little thing, I thought. But I nodded. "I have no money to finish the suit."

"Here." The duke threw four gold coins into the ash in front of my feet. "It does not all have to glow, it's original purpose has changed. You can be creative with that, and no more. Make my house proud with armor that will draw envy, but most importantly *protect my son*, and you will have your parents back."

He walked away from me and clambered awkwardly back onto his horse.

"You have four days, or I leave your kin to their death. On the morning of the fifth day, I arrive for my armor. And I will make a hell of your life if it is not ready that morning, for what little of your life will be left!" he shouted as he spurred his horse.

"Four days . . ." The words died in my mouth as the duke trotted away from me, unhearing. The captain ordered three of his guard after the duke with a sigh.

As the ash cloud trail of the duke meandered off across the fields, two guards arrowing in to join him on either side, the captain cleared his throat. "You know he won't ever release your parents. He'll open the hole and throw you in there with them, to see you all suffer once again. To laugh into your faces."

I looked at him through my swelling eye, broken lips, and blood splattered face. "I'm lesser born," I said. "Not stupid."

"Then you should take those coins, right now, and run," he said. He looked at his two men. One of them had lit a torch and held it up between them. "Would you stop her?"

They grinned through the sickly yellow flamelight. "To see that toad of a man spit and huff in disappointment? We would see, and say, nothing."

I bent slowly and picked up the gold pieces, all four of them, and I thought about my future. "I can't, not just yet."

Disappointment flicked through their eyes and I wondered where they had been born. Where did their allegiances truly lay? Maybe they were men who had once known Lesser Khaim, who worked their way up in blood and steel to find themselves in the service of the Majister's wills.

I held up the four coins. "Can you read letters, Captain?"

"I can," he said, curiosity on his face.

"What is your name?"

"Lukat, of the Oskini." A family, I realized, that had once specialized in poling ferries across the Sulong. "My father is Jaiska."

"If I run I'll give a note to someone who can't read. I'll tell them that if I am not dragged back by the guard after a week, they will deliver you that note. It will tell you where one of these four gold coins is. Do you understand my meaning?"

"Leave another note that tells me where you're going and I'd be half tempted to join you just to be at your side on that adventure," the so-far silent other guard said. He had a smile that was too friendly, and yet not threatening to me.

"And I would be tempted to tell you," I said, "but that you don't understand why I can't run is why I won't. My kin lies down in that pit, the people who raised me from birth and sacrificed all for me. Who taught me all I know, and gave me all I have." I wasn't interested in yet another Djoka. A good man ultimately unwilling to fight for what was truly right.

Captain Lukat stepped forward and leaned close so that only I could hear him. "If you run, I will do what I can to frustrate the duke, if the timing works. Particularly if I am the one asked to lead your hunt. But I make no guarantees."

"I understand." I tried to keep the despair out of my voice. I was the one choosing not to run. "I am not sure if I can make this happen so fast. My father, mother, and me would make this suit in four days.

But me alone? Surely the duke knows he's setting an impossible task for me."

Luka glanced around again. He opened his mouth, then closed it, as if thinking better of telling me something. Then he shook his head and whispered.

"Malabaz wants the stilthouses on the mudflats for himself. But the merchants who own them now refuse to sell, particularly now that there hasn't been a Paikan raid in so long. The rents are too good when so many are desperate to seek the safety of a stable, growing city free of bramble. There will be a fight in the dark among the velvet ones soon, as the merchants have a meeting with their financiers. Malabaz will introduce his son to the family trade and make a man of him that night."

Savar was not a natural fighter. He would have needed to have spells to aide his slight frame and protection from his attackers. That was why we'd been commissioned to make special armor.

"Malabaz wants the money from rents?"

"He wants the land."

"It's just mud," I said.

"He will burn the old, infested houses and build new ones. Villas for the newer merchants who can't now afford the old river houses on the other side of the Sulong."

So they could pole across the river without the censori's smoke drifting toward them. And throw whatever they had used up into the river under the cloak of night.

"How do you know this?" I asked.

Lukat grinned. "I have sold my sword to the duke for that night. And when the noblemen need discrete, expert polemen, my cousins will navigate the mudbanks and river runs. As it used to be before the bridge."

"The blood of family, the blood of strangers, and gold. That's what this is all about." I spat bitterness at the ground.

"As it always has been." Lukat swept onto his horse, and then leaned over and held out a hand. "Are you still going to try to do this thing, then?"

I took a deep breath. "They are my family. I must try to save them."

"Then come, let's get those 'pretty gloves' and take you back to your forge."

I looked out toward the road, and then back to his leather gloved hand, and grasped it.

He swung me easily up onto the horse.

He would be good with a blacksmith's hammer, I thought for a second, gauging the grip and strength. Then he spurred the horse, and we were off into the night.

SAVAR SKULKED AROUND THE DOORS AS LUKAT RETURNED me to the forge.

"Father says I'm to keep an eye on the girl to make sure she doesn't run," he said as he glared at Lukat and his guards. "You may leave."

"Are you absolutely sure, my lord?" Lukat asked with full, but utterly false, sincerity.

"I gave an order!"

"Good luck, and be careful with that one," the captain said softly as he helped me down.

Lukat clattered off down the cobblestones into the night, and Savar moved close. He leered when he looked at me, which made me feel self-conscious in a way that made me hate him far more than I had already. All I could see were his father's features in him. The same sneer, the slight wheedling tone of his voice. "The old man really did kick you around like a servant, didn't he?" Savar said.

I walked to the doors and opened them. Savar tried to follow me inside, but I shoved him back. He was skin and bones, birdlike, much as his father. He staggered and stumbled, his eyes narrowed as anger flashed like lightning.

A piece of old parchment fluttered in his left hand in the dirty wind outside the forge. Savar had muttered words under his breath. But he bit his lip and stopped. He slowly gained control of his anger.

"I'll be watching you," he said calmly, tucking whatever spell he'd been foolish enough to consider using out in the open of the city of blue. "I'll check on your progress constantly, until you make me that armor, bitch. Or there will be consequences."

He kicked the door shut.

I walked to the large sink and looked at myself in a polished metal mirror. I had protected myself against the worst of Malabaz's blows. The blackening eye, the split lips, and the cut on my head seemed worse due to the blood. As far as I could tell, he had broken no bones nor hurt anything beneath my skin.

It stung when I washed my face with shaking hands in the dark, but I ignored it. My mind roiled and spat anger and ideas. I crawled around to the edge of the forge to my old bed and lay down.

The forge felt ghostly and empty. The suit of armor lurked in the dark, the coals of the forge barely touching the helmet's serpent heads that roiled together in the demon Takaz's fanged visage.

I balled up my blankets and hugged them. I would have cried, but I had no energy for it. I felt guilty for needing to close my eyes, as all I could hear were Malabaz's words. *Four days.* But I couldn't even stop my hands from shaking. What was I going to do? What chance did I best have to save my parents: make the suit, or try to dig them up somehow?

I needed guidance.

I lay still, staring at the wall, until I couldn't see it anymore.

I woke with purpose. I added wood to the coals, but there was no breakfast to make, so I drank hot water to chase the chill from my aching bones. Then I left the forge. A dirty man in ragged robes I had never seen before watched me lock the doors. I walked over to him.

"I am to prayers," I told him firmly. "Tell your simpering lord I'm at the house of Che. I'll be making an offering to the god for steady hands. You do not need to spy on me."

The wiry man tugged at his beards. "I don't have to follow you to know where you go," he said.

I shrugged. "I am going to the priestly row. Walk with me, or not. It is your morning to waste."

He fell into step behind me, his bare feet padding dust. "You look at me with disgust," he says. "But all I do is tell people truths. The truth is pure. Do the gods not tell us we should only tell truths?"

I ignored him as we passed through the stench of morning workshops belching to life.

"I worship truth. And so it is good to me. It always reveals itself because I honor it by giving it light. Please remember that."

He slipped away from me as I turned the corner for the priestly row, where the temples of Lesser Khaim clustered near the butcher's shops and jewelry stalls packed with glittering images of gods.

I let out a deep breath and walked right past the house of Che.

The priests of Assim blinked at me when I arrived at their doors. Their temple was one of the larger in Lesser Khaim: thick granite walls standing strong against the rundown wooden columns of the other orders. There were no courtyards in the temple of Assim, but small dark, stony rooms with statues of the Assim's harem in the flickering shadows.

Standing in the lobby, I blinked my eyes to adjust to the gloom. I could hear the soft murmur of tens of petitioners muttering as they traced thumbs against sigils burned into the walls by ancient magics. Walls that had been disassembled in the north and pulled by Merciful Monks in their bloodred robes through many miles of bramble-choked mud roads to bring them here.

"Hello, child." A shriveled older man with a bandage over one of his eyes, peeled away from a cluster of waiting priests as I ascended the steps to the first sanctum. His voice quavered with age. "Have you come for mercies?"

I nodded, my mouth dry with fear.

The old priest placed a hand on my shoulder. A calming gesture. "For three coppers off your string, you can speak to the wall and ask for relief from your wounds. . . ." he started to say, looking at my bruised face.

"No." I pressed a gold piece into his palm. "I would speak to a prophet." I needed not just guidance, but all the help I could get. I would speak to the gods of my father and his people.

The priest looked down at his hand, the coin, and then back up at me. His lips twitched. "Ah . . ."

He pulled at my sleeve. "Come. Come here."

Two younger acolytes wordlessly joined us, walking down a small corridor lit by dishes of lamp oil away from the confessional walls. We moved deeper into the temple. The susurration of people's whispered confessions died away, the air stilled, and it became hard to breathe.

We were deep amongst the cells the followers of Assim actually lived in. We passed a small kitchen where robed priests sat at a communal meal of bread and soup; the strong smell of cumin tickled my nose. More still prayed against the walls of their cells, lips pressed against scribed granite, fingertips tracing out swooping symbols of the long-dead priestly language.

At the end of this, the acolytes opened a thick wooden door into another small room. Scented aromatics heaped in large tin plates burned softly, the occasional twig making a faint cracking sound. A young man lay on a divan at the head of the room, naked except for a white linen loincloth. He had obviously become a prophet many years ago, as his skin had not seen the sun since and had paled almost to transparency. His bones pushed up against his skin, which hung loose against him.

High-marked coins lay on the ground around his divan, as well as entire coils of cash strings. Gold, like the one I'd given the priest, and other denominations as well. Jewels and fine sculptures lay among the coins, scattered casually.

"Valka felt called to prophecy four years ago," the priest next to me said, adding my gold coin to the treasure around Valka's emaciated body. "He was bitten by bramble after one full year of preparation. He walks the shadow worlds between gods and man, neither dead nor alive, now. Your words will pass through him to the other realm."

I looked at the corpselike Valka. "But what about signs?" I asked. "I need—"

"If the gods will it," the priest said, "Valka will give you a sign. If your heart is strong. If the gods hear you. Watch closely. It could be the slightest twitch. A motion. You must let your mind go out to the gods and be open to anything. Only then might your prayer be acknowledged. Only then might the Merciful One trick the demons from seeing you. Ask the prophet respectfully your question and seek the signs."

"How long? How will I know?"

"Long?" the priest asked. "As long as you need. We will be outside the door, waiting. When you are ready, knock three times."

"But . . ."

The two acolytes approached with a prayer mat held between them, cutting off further questions. The red threads on it were old and worn, but styled much the same as the symbols of mystery throughout the walls of the temple.

They unrolled it in front of me with a quick snap, and then retreated out the door with the priest. I watched as the thick door slid inexorably shut with a thud. I was left with only the faint crackle of the aromatics and the sound of my heavy, scared breathing.

Here was what we all feared: to be bitten by the bramble. To lie there neither fully dead nor alive. Our body dependent on others to feed it soups, cleanse it, burn aromatics to mask the smell of excrement. Yet this holy man had reached out and rubbed his hand among the fine bristles of bramble and collapsed of his own will. All to try to seek the gods themselves.

According to many holy orders, some priests came back from bramble sleep. When they arose they spread through the countryside, claiming to have returned with the words of gods themselves. Though one had to be careful, as there were many who claimed to wake from sleep to deceive simple country folk.

Here in the city, only a priest who took the kiss of the bramble in full view of twenty or more priests from three different temples could be certified a prophet. Here in the city, on priestly row, everyone knew these were genuine prophets lying in the bramble sleep.

The Temple of the Merciful and Sly Assim had four prophets lying in the dark, waiting to reawaken. None of them had awoken in my life. But my father remembered a prophet by the name of Bylavi who had woken, taken all the offerings surrounding him, and left to spread what he was revealed.

So I gently fell to my knees on the prayer mat and stared at the prophet Valka. It was not the priestly tradition to close a sleeping one's eyelids, so his glazed, milky eyes stared directly at me. Seeing through to my soul.

I lowered my gaze.

"Prophet Valka, I seek a sign," I said, my voice breaking with nervousness. "I'm just a blacksmith's daughter. We are simple people, but hard working. We have done little to offend. But now . . ."

I swallowed.

"Now my mother and father are imprisoned, and I . . ." I stopped again. My hands shook like leaves about to fall from a tree. "What am I to do, Prophet? What should I do?"

I waited in the dim light, staring at the cloud-white skin of his body and into the clouded eyes while waiting for my sign. I counted breaths to a number as high as I could stand, and then moved off my knees to sit more comfortably. I never took my eyes off the prophet as I shifted, though.

Maybe, somewhere in my thoughts, I believed the prophet would blink and speak directly to me. Like I was a hero on a quest given secret instructions.

But he did not.

Time stretched on as I waited.

And waited.

"Some have said I should run," I told the prophet.

The prophet did not respond.

"But there is another idea deep within me, one that may end with us all dead if I follow it," I confessed. "It was in my dreams when I woke. A helm with a glassed visor to protect one from the bramble. Leathers under all the joints. I think I can dig for my parents if I am protected. But—"

The Prophet Valka's right hand seemed to stir slightly.

Yes. I had certainly seen his thumb twitch.

"Prophet," I gasped. My heart leaped into my throat. I moved on my hands and knees and crept closer to the pale body. The skin under the prophet's thumb trembled again, my mouth gaped wide with awe. And then the thumb split apart. Blood and pus trickled down the base of his hand as maggots writhed and tumbled out to the ground.

I leaped to my feet.

"Gods."

This was no sign. His body had lain fallow too long. He might be alive, but the creeping and crawling things of the world did not see it that way. They saw only restful flesh.

I stumbled back and knocked on the door three times.

"So fast?" the priest asked, worry in his features as the acolytes opened the thick door.

I grabbed at them. "The prophet has maggots."

One of the acolytes muttered under his breath and swept into the tiny room, but the priest held up a hand. "It is a sign!" he proclaimed loudly, startling all of us.

The acolytes looked at him, then me, and bowed their heads in agreement. "It is a sign," they repeated.

The older priest took my arm and began to escort me back through the temple. "You have your message," he said to me as we walked back past the sleeping cells. "It is a beautiful thing."

"I don't understand," I said.

"To you or me, maggots are a thing of disgust," the priest said. "A sign of putrefaction. Mess. Garbage. Ruin. But from the perspective of the maggot: It is all life. They live, they breathe, they grow. And you and I are like maggots to the gods, child. Do not forget that. There is the meaning of your sign. Do you understand now?"

We walked on as I tried to grasp the meaning of his words, and what they meant for me.

An instant passed before we stood at the lobby. The murmur of hundreds at prayer once again filled our ears, comforting me. "Life," I repeated.

"You were shown life," the priest agreed, guiding me toward the steps and the bright light of morning on the priestly row, filled with incense and chants. "The prophet gave you the sign. An uncountable gift. Life."

"But what does that mean about what I'm supposed to do?" I asked. Was it seek my own life? Or save my father and mother's? Or try?

"Think on life," the priest said firmly. "And there your answers will be. For we all die, child. It is only the choices of life that make matters."

The priest turned and left me quickly.

Only the choices matter, I thought.

Not the outcomes. The choice. What was the right choice?

The doors to Milaka's opened as the final dregs of morning light finishing dripping in from over the tips of Khaim's buildings. They always unlocked at this moment. Milaka was as precise as her springs and clocks.

She gasped when she saw me, her sunworn face immediately lined with concern. "Sofija!"

"It looks worse than it is," I told her as I stepped inside. There was a clock just as precise as any of the ones Milaka made running inside my head, keeping track of how little time I had left.

I had made a choice as I walked through the clouds of incense. I had a plan. It was dangerous. There was little time. But even before I had visited the monks of Assim it had formed as I drifted to sleep, cooled and hardened in the night, and been a heavy lump in my mind when I woke. Now I had made the choice to follow it.

To seek life.

"Who did this to you?" she demanded, seeing my bruised face.

"A duke. There is nothing you can do against him." I took her bony shoulders carefully in my hands. I hated the lie that would come, but I had to do this for my parents. "Milaka: I hate to ask you this. But you are almost my blood, Djoka is your nephew. If you share my anger, I need one of your secrets. The duke has trapped my mother and father in a pit and will not release them unless I finish a suit of armor for his son. I . . . am so sorry I have to ask for such a thing." For what other wealth did tradespeople truly have, but their tricks and shortcuts?

"I'm an old woman, Sofija," Milaka said, not unkindly. "I've given most of my trade secrets to many of my nieces. Your mother was always generous to me, as well. Tell me what you need."

I sat with her among the brass cylinders and carefully blown glass globes on her shelves. "You told me once about a clockwork hand that you built for an officer who lost his arm to a sword."

Milaka stood up. "It was powered by magic. I cannot do such things anymore. Not without losing my head. You know this."

I held up my hands to placate her. "No, I'm not asking for that. I'm asking for the gears, the springs. How did you make it work? Show me that. I need to make springwork gloves." Something neither Malabaz nor Savar had ordered for this armor, but something I needed if I was to dig through unyielding, dangerous bramble with my own hands.

She calmed. "I can do that. Over the next weeks."

"I only have this morning, Milaka. Time is not on my family's side," I reminded her with a small emphasis on the word "family."

Milaka closed her eyes for a long moment.

Then she stood up and closed the door to her store. It was the first time I had ever seen it so.

"I will show you what you need. Come back here into my workshop. We will get you everything. You will pay me later, or if you can."

Now it was my turn to close my eyes, fighting back tears. "They have some food, and a little watered wine in a pack they had with them. But I don't know how long that will last them. Or if their air will grow stale before then."

Milaka took my shoulders. "Let us hurry."

Even with Milaka's decades of skill with coils of metal and gears, and my fine metal work, it still took a full day and night. When she succumbed to sleep I drank tea and continued on, and she would correct my mistakes when she woke with a stifled groan from her cot.

I slipped out in the early night and evening to keep the fire in the forge glowing. Enough to pour smoke out of the chimney and allow Savar and the rat he'd assigned to spy on me to keep thinking I was inside.

I would never be able to repay Milaka. We both knew it. But I pretended I would, and she pretended to believe me.

I bit my lip, and did not complain about our pace. I remained gracious for the help, knowing that had I only gotten a lesson and some tools, I wouldn't have been able to even make these clever gloves in the days I needed to save my parents.

"Thank you," I kept saying.

But Milaka told me to shut up. "Would you have turned away someone needing your help to save their own blood?" she asked me.

"No. But some would."

"You and I are not 'some people,' are we? We are family. Bound by Djoka's blood. Not high family, like those across the river, but still family. We might be the mud by the banks, but leave us to dry, take the fine things in life, and then temper us in fire, and we are strong bricks." She bent back over the gloves and the crimping tools. The refashioned gauntlets lay on the bench before her, palms and fingers spread out like metal spiders. When she triggered the thumb mechanism, the left one closed into a fist, snapping the firewood I held out to it and crushing it into sawdust. "Sometimes, we are stronger."

She showed me the mechanism, the latch near the elbow and how to lever it back and forth, as if I were winding a crossbow. The cogs and wheels whirred, the tension spreading as the gloves slowly opened. After I cranked the fists to full strength, I would have ten times the strength of any man in my hands.

"The velvet one who lurks outside your forge. People are talking. He could be dangerous to you."

"He only watches to make sure I don't try to run away. He is not very good at it. Or much of anything else for that matter."

"You know that no one would blame you if you did run," Milaka said. "What are the chances your parents will live, even if you finish the suit and hand it over?"

I slid my hand up into the gauntlet. It fit. I crooked my thumb and the mechanisms inside snapped my fingers into a fist, scraping them and making me hiss out in pain. "I imagine the duke plans to kill my parents anyway," I grunted, levering them open again. "And probably me for causing him trouble. The armor is all he truly wants."

Milaka grasped the mechanical fist. "I could help you run," she whispered urgently. "I can help you flee."

"You've risked enough just helping me," I said. "If I were to run, and anyone knew I came to see you, you'd . . ."

"Loti, the weaver, is the only one. She won't speak to anyone."

"I won't run," I said to Milaka. "I have a plan."

She looked down at my right hand. "I notice that your hand fits inside the gauntlet perfectly. Is that part of your plan?"

I finished cranking open my fist and reset the clockwork inside. "Savar's hands are small," I said. "Delicate from lack of work. Spindly."

Milaka wasn't fooled. She stared at me until I blinked and looked back down at the glove. "You will waste your life as well if you attack a duke."

I had a sudden urge to tell her everything as she had come close to sniffing out my designs, but the words didn't come. I feared that to speak my plans aloud would destroy my chances. I didn't want anyone—person, demon, or gods—to know about the intentions I held in my heart. It was my own secret to bear.

I put the gloves in a case, nestled against fur, and hugged her. "Thank you for your help, Milaka. You have done me too much kindness.

She gave me an appraising look. "I wonder if Borzai will weigh it so, when I go before him."

I threw my arms around her. "He must."

"Be safe, my child." Her voice cracked. "Be safe, Sofija."

Savar somehow found me all too quickly on the way back from Milaka's, as I shopped for leathers early in the morning, when sellers still blinked the sleep from their eyes. He shoved at the thick, stiff material. "What is this?" he demanded.

"Padding," I told him as we walked through the spice lanes and my mouth watered. I had not eaten. I couldn't. "Why are you following me?"

"You spent a day outside the forge, you tried to escape my eyes and trick me by keeping your fires on, but I see everything, girl." Savar moved in front of me. "You are wasting time. My family does not have time to waste. I am not here to disappoint my father. Time is of the essence. I need that armor."

"I've been getting padding," I said through gritted teeth.

"Doesn't look like padding to me." Savar jabbed at the extra leathers I had just purchased.

"Shall I get some cotton pillows for under your armor?" I asked loudly. People stopped and looked at us. "Is armor too hard for your delicate shoulders? Maybe some goosedown for your delicate skin...."

"Shut up!" Savar hissed. "Shut up."

"But it isn't protection you need, whatever you're going to do with this armor. You need special help to compensate for your weak fighting skills. What was it going to be? A scroll that would give you the strength to hold a sword in both your hands?"

Savar's face reddened. I'd pushed too far. "My father has taught me. I could breathe words that would strip your skin from you and make your eyes boil," he said.

I looked around at the crowds. Would he dare to do anything like that here, in the middle of a crowd that would delightfully call for the censori?

"The leathers," I explained, holding them up and trying to redirect our words, "sit under the plate. It's like inner armor." And I needed to add enough to cover every gap to protect against bramble if I was going to use this armor myself, as Milaka had suspected. "If you are such an expert on what goes into armor, maybe you should build your own."

"Maybe I would," Savar snapped, still angered. "But *my* parents aren't the ones waiting in a pit, are they?"

He saw me suck my breath in and he smiled.

"Do you remember the townsmen of Horia? How they cut their own children's throats to drink rather than die from lack of water? And when traders burned back the bramble on the road to get to the town, they found nothing but starved cannibals. Will your father drink your mother's blood, or will she his, I wonder?"

I swallowed the hurt. Swallowed it deep down into myself. Because I was born on this side of the river. Because it would only lead to worse.

I ignored Savar and kept walking so that he couldn't see the tears stinging my eyes.

"I'm watching you even more closely, now," he said from beside me. "Do not dare to cross a duke. Your time is running out, blacksmith's daughter."

After the full day and a night at Milaka's, I'd frantically thrown myself into work sealing up the armor's under layer. My second day was now mostly gone. The glass on the visor—that had been tricky. But by afternoon, I'd blown glass from melted sand in the forge. It was not my trade, so it took several tries to get it too cool in the shapes I needed. They were not as clear as I'd hoped for, but after I'd glued the pieces to Takaz's demon eyes, I could place the helmet on my shoulders and move throughout the forge.

I had never worked so fast. The gloves. The leather underlayment as strong as the aprons worn by the men and women who burned the bramble back. The last few plates I had sewn in. My father and mother would have been proud, I thought, as I rubbed my raw hands and massaged my sore back.

But there was another dilemma, I realized as I sat in front of the armor on its straw in the corner of the forge after I placed the fearsome helmet back on. I needed far more plates of steel to finish strengthening the armor. The leathers were a last line of defense. I needed more actual armor.

I placed the three gold coins thrown at me by the duke on my anvil and regarded their dull glitter. Three gold pieces. I could finish the suit. I could get enough metal, barely, to finish the plates tomorrow morning. The coins gave me that.

But it wasn't enough for *my* plan.

I needed a cart. I needed supplies. I needed to pack, and in such a way that it wasn't obvious to Savar, or whoever got a look inside the forge.

One coin would stay with us. I wanted something kept from this hell, some small token of profit.

One coin, as promised, would be left for the guard captain Lukat to delay hunting us down.

Which left a single coin to complete the suit.

It was not enough.

I stared at the suit. The fine engraving. The gold hammered into tiny channels, fashioned into flourishes and swoops that evoked the war demons of Kuchk. My parents were not here to tell me I couldn't strip the frippery and decoration off the suit. Everything they'd feared about that action had come to pass. I was the one making the decisions, now. For better or worse.

"Okay," I said to the dark corners of the forge. It was the choices that mattered.

I picked up a pair of fine pliers and walked to the back of the suit.

I'll start from where the finery sat in the shadows, I thought. I began yanking and digging out the gold to pay for the metal to finish the entire suit. Milaka always needed fine gold for her clocks.

I could trade for her steel scrap and hopefully a little something extra. Maybe I could dance back across from the edge of this precipice.

Milaka's was, oddly, closed an hour early. That the workshop had been shut before sunset puzzled me. I put my ear to the door and heard Milaka's shuffling feet on the other side.

No locks clicked. No bolts shifted aside to welcome me.

"You lied to me," the old woman said from the other side of the stout doors when I knocked at them.

"No." My voice broke slightly.

"You should have told me about Djoka."

"And then what would you have done?" I asked.

"I don't know," Milaka replied. "You never gave me the chance."

I punched at the doors, rattling them. Then pulled them back and hugged myself. "I'm sorry, I shouldn't have done that. I'm desperate. My mother and father are dying in a pit, Milaka. I have to save them. I need help. I need help."

I pushed my forehead to the door, my eyes stinging hot with tears. But the doors remained barred.

"You said my mother was kind to you. Does kindness count for nothing in these days?"

"What is it you need?" Milaka asked.

"I have gold. Fine gold you can use for filigree and decoration. I need steel for it. And supplies."

A finger tapped the other side of the door. "Sofija, you know I have seen much. Djoka may not be yours any longer, and you will not become my blood. But you are a good child. So hear me. You need to run. Take the gold you want to give me and *run*. Now. Get onto the road. Use it for a dowry and find a nice man who will treat you well. Leave your family to their fate. Or you will share it. That is all I can do for you."

"No. I have made a choice. I will follow it." I heard her start to shuffle away from the door. "Wait! If you can't help me, at least tell me the name of a jeweler who will take the gold."

Milaka stopped. Her distant voice barely made it through the door. "You'll want Zlatan. But he will likely betray you for extra coin as soon as he is able. And no, no one else will touch your coin. They've all seen the velvet child's servants shadowing you. You are tainted."

"All I need is a day," I said.

Zlatan the jeweler stood for a moment, blinking in the lantern light at me, before looking down at the dirty cloth I had the lump of melted gold in.

"Inside," he hissed, yanking me into his small apartment, his precise fingers digging hard into my collarbone.

I broke free of him, shoving him back hard enough he clutched his chest and wheezed. "Do not put your hands on me," I growled.

"Hush!" He shoved the wooden door closed. "Do not wake my family," he whispered. "Or the neighbors."

"Do you not trust your own family?"

Zlatan shook his head as he guided me downstairs by candle-light into the back of his shop. "You are here in the dark of midnight, with melted gold. Children tell tales, wives have friends they share their secrets with, and thus the circle leaps ever outward like ripples in water. A secret is only safe with one person. It is barely a secret between two. It is never a secret between three."

He walked over and pulled a set of small jeweler's scales out, taking the lump of gold from me. He inspected it, bit it, then weighed it. Then offered me a third of the lump's worth in tradable coin.

"That's an insult," I said. I'd weighed it myself. I'd purchased some of it myself. "What I handed you is worth three times that coinage."

"This is its true worth," Zlatan whispered. "Unless you could hand slivers of gold over to merchants yourself. Why don't you go and do that?"

My face fell.

Zlatan nodded. "Exactly. You are here in the dark of night, and you don't want anyone to know you are trading tiny slivers of gold. So you take less to get my coins, which you can then use tomorrow morning."

I glowered. It would barely cover the metals I needed and there would be none left over as I'd hoped. "I'll do it. But you must give me a day," I told him.

Zlatan frowned. "What do you mean?"

"Before you sell the information that I was here. You have your two thirds. Wait until dusk tomorrow. That is all I ask."

Zlatan ground his teeth. "I did not get where I am by selling information, no matter what you may have heard from others."

"Please. It isn't my life, but my mother and father."

"I know what has happened," Zlatan said kindly. "The streets tell their tales. And I will give you the time you have asked for . . . if not much longer. We are Lesser Khaim, are we not? If we do not help one another, then can we call ourselves neighbors?"

"Thank you," I said warily.

"Now, it is time for you to leave."

I walked toward the door and Zlatan grabbed my arm.

"The back door," he said firmly. "Leave through the back door, child."

Before he closed the door he'd shoved me through, I looked back at his brown face flickeringly lit by the candle he held. How long before he would truly give me up? How long would it take for word to trickle back to Savar?

I had made a choice, but I could feel the coils of the clock winding down for me.

Zlatan shut the door and latched it behind me, and I was on my own in the city's deep night.

~(~

Savar shouldered his way past me to look at the suit the moment I opened the doors at dawn. I fought panic as I stepped in front of him.

"This is your last full day," he said. "It needs to be done by tonight. My father will be here in the next morning."

"Then I have work to do." I pushed him back out.

"It is my right," he said. "It is mine to look at."

"If you want it done by tomorrow, then do not cross the threshold," I hissed. "Do not interrupt my work or it will take longer. Come in, and I will stop work."

Savar stepped back, but prowled around the threshold anxiously. I thought about it. He knew he couldn't use magic. But he knew he would be following his father into a fight of some kind tomorrow night.

He wanted his armor.

"I will leave the door open, though, so you can stare as much as you'd like." He could watch me sweat as I hammered shapes out on the anvil.

"Your parents do not have forever," he said coldly as he backed away. "Do not delay me what is mine."

Servants waited outside with a palanquin for him. Savar avoided the rising morning sun for the next hour by sitting inside its shade on comfortable tasseled cushions, sipping teas and making my stomach growl as he had sweet meats delivered fresh from the markets by men he would whisper to, then dismiss with a flick of his wrist.

I could not remember when I'd last eaten.

Savar would stare at me as I paused for a drink, or pushed the sleeves of my tunic up. I knew that, once the sweat began to drip down my arms, chest, and sides, the tunic stuck to me in a way passing men found hard to ignore.

Let him stare, I thought as I shaped the metal. As long as he didn't get inside to look behind the armor. Or see the supplies I had packed away under the tool trays throughout the forge.

A woman in dirty robes slid next to the palanquin halfway through the morning. She whispered to Savar. She carried nothing with her, but her words changed his whole body. He stiffened.

Savar slipped off his feathered cushions, brows furrowed, and stalked toward the forge.

As Savar walked toward the forge he pointed at the nearby guard posted by the palanquin. "Leave," he said, his voice filled with the assumption that his command would be followed. "Now."

The guard looked at me standing by the glow of the forge's fires, at Savar, and then melted away.

I ran to shut the door and bar it, but Savar got there first and slammed his back against it. He lowered the bar down with his left hand, facing me.

"Get out of our forge," I said. But I thought, *gods, I've made the wrong choices.* I hadn't understood the signs given to me by the prophet lying in the room deep inside the temple. I was supposed to save my life. To run. "Savar, leave!"

Savar ignored me and walked toward the armor. For a second I was torn. Try to stop him from seeing the armor? No, if I did that, he would know something was wrong for sure.

He had left me at the door. I could run. Lift the bar up, yank the door open, and run.

With nothing but the sweaty, dirty clothes on my back.

I would die, begging for scraps somewhere along the road out of the city. Or I could try to hide in the city, always looking over my shoulder for one of Savar's agents hunting me.

Or I could stand here, arms crossed, hoping he didn't circle around to the back of the armor. Hoping that, whatever he'd been told, he wasn't going to peer into the shadows.

"Savar." I tried to draw his attention back to me. But Savar ignored me and leaned around the armor.

I sucked my breath in.

"You lowborn piece of shit," he said. His voice was almost reassuringly soft. "The man I set to follow you around was right, despite his babbling about truths. You haven't finished the suit. You are stripping gold away from it to sell."

"Zlatan," I muttered angrily.

"I don't know who that is. Is that the name of the old woman?"

Milaka? I slumped, the betrayal sucking the energy out of me. I was already so tired from not sleeping.

"That one crumbled when offered our gold and favor." Savar looked thoughtful. "But, seeing as that she was stupid enough to help you, I think instead we will send the city guards over to her shop and arrest her as an accomplice when I am done here."

I opened my mouth to protest. But Savar was a duke's son.

"That old woman; those brittle bones will break so easily when they make her pay the price for an offense against my father," Savar continued.

Milaka had betrayed me, but those words still struck me. "You can't. She was just trying to help."

"Help cheat me." Savar pulled out a slip of parchment tucked into the sleeve of his tunic. I had seen that spelled artifact before. He wouldn't dare. Or would he? He had sent the guards away. The forge was locked. I moved my back against the door and felt for the bar. "Cheat me of the armor you had until tonight to create. But it isn't finished. Not only that, you have continued to try to steal from me, just as your parents tried to steal from me."

I grabbed the bar to the door and shoved it up. Savar leaned forward and blew on the parchment, holding it in both his hands. The smell of citrus blasted through the room.

The bar slammed back into place. My fingernails scratched at the wood as I tried to hang onto it.

I forced it back up, but it felt like invisible hands were shoving it down. I glanced over my shoulder. Savar stood by the demon-headed armor, his hands and wrists glowing with parchment dust and the black ink of ancient symbols writhing on his skin.

"The price of thievery is to lose your hands," Savar said. "But I'm going to rip the skin off them first and watch you scream. You're an oaf. An ugly, thick, muddy, lowborn bitch who can hammer things. You can shove me out of a door, but I can rip you apart."

Cold hands grabbed my neck and yanked me free of the door. I struggled to breathe. "Blue . . ." I gasped. "You can't . . ."

Savar swung his hands to the side and my head struck the stone wall. My vision wavered and I staggered.

"There are no censori here tonight." Savar made a fist and punched the air. I doubled over, clutching my stomach. "And when I am done, my men will come, wrap me in blankets, and put me in my palanquin to bear me home until the magic fades and I am safe again."

Blows smacked my head and face. I tried to hold my hands up to block them, but I couldn't see where the next invisible attack came from.

I lurched at the forge.

"Tomorrow night my father will fight without me. He'll be disappointed." Savar's voice cracked slightly. "But I'll show him I'm still a man. I'm still strong. I'll show him what I do to a thief."

I spat blood that sizzled as it hit the hot brick around the forge fire and tried to reason. "You left me with so little to make this armor I had to take the gold from it, but the steel plates to finish it are right here, there's still time . . ."

"You have stolen gold from a True Family!" Savar shouted, moving closer. "Your *life* is forfeit."

"There was nothing else I could do," I protested.

"Your . . . life . . . ," Savar repeated. He slapped my face with his free hand from the other side of the forge fire.

I rocked back, pulling away from him as I blinked tears out of my eyes. Savar and his father, they had always planned to kill us. We'd struggle to finish the armor, they'd accuse us of stealing, then kill us so no one knew anything about the armor.

Because who would miss us? We lived on the wrong side of the river, after all. This was our fate. I knew I couldn't fight it. But I had hoped to save my parents and myself anyway. I had hoped to run from it. But I couldn't.

Maybe Borzai would judge me well and I would have a good afterlife. In the balance of my life, I had done many small injustices that would weigh against my soul, but had there not been enough done to me to compensate? Had I not worked hard for my parents, hammer in hand, day in and day out? My once-small hands had been blistered at first. Now my fingers were rough and callused.

I circled the bricks around the forge, a rabbit trying to flee, and looked back at Savar with my head hung low. There was something in his eyes as he jumped up onto the bricks to look down at me. A feeling that had broached from deep within a fetid soul.

It was hatred. Anger. And glee. He was looking forward to torturing me.

I would be another mutilated body that floated down the Sulong.

"The armor is almost finished." I tried to placate him one last time. "Come back in a few hours and it will be done. It will be amazing. Believe me . . ."

He was so close, just on the other side of the hot, rippling air of the forge. He raised his hands.

"There are other blacksmiths we can pay to finish it by tomorrow. But for you, there is no tomorrow!" Savar screamed as he raised a fist. The next invisible strike knocked me back from the bricks and to the floor. My fingers brushed a pair of tongs and I grabbed them without a second thought.

Savar stepped around the circle of bricks, massaging his hand. "Do you know what happens to those who steal from a duke in the Blue City? Have you ever seen it? Majister Scacz is always on the lookout for fresh bodies. What kind of animal will he place on your neck with his magics? I think a pig. No! An ox. Dumb and strong."

I jumped backward, tongs in one hand behind me.

"You are a thief, and you will get the thief's reward." Savar punched me in the stomach.

"Please," I begged. "Please, my lord."

"By my family's right, your head will sit on a pike by the bridge yet today," Savar spat.

I threw the tongs at him and ran.

I was leaving the forge, my tools, even the gold. I was leaving my plans. I was abandoning my parents. But it was the only thing I could do.

But Savar was surprisingly quick. He dodged the tongs and those invisible hands grabbed my hair and yanked, hard enough to pull me right off my feet. I hit the floor hard, gasping, but saw him stumbling forward.

He had spelled hands, but he hadn't gained strength. I stood up.

"Stop this," I said, my voice strong and clear.

Savar pulled a dagger out from his waistband. It glinted as a stray beam of firelight struck it.

This was it. This was the path of the road we were on. Savar's fingers clenched the handle and took a deep breath.

"No," I said, and ran right at him.

Savar hit me, each strike knocking me off my stride. But all they did was slow me. Savar sneered, hit me one last time, and then raised the dagger.

He stabbed at me with it. But I grabbed his forearm and stopped the blade halfway to my throat.

"No," I said again, firmly.

He struggled to pull free of my grip, but my fingers were accustomed to the strike of hammer on metal. They were thick and strong. Anger grew in his face, but he couldn't free himself. "Let go!"

I wrenched his arm to the side and hit him in the face. The crunch of knuckle against nose sounded like a walnut being cracked. Savar jerked back and yanked free as blood flowed from his nose.

We stared at each other, him unsteady on his feet and quivering with rage, me with my feet planted solidly. The symbols on his arms were starting to fade, and the parchment dust turned to sweaty ash on his forearms.

"Go," I said. "Leave my forge."

I had done the incomprehensible. I'd struck a duke's son. He would run and come back with guards. But I would have time to grab a few things and run as well.

And we would both live.

But Savar could not hear my words. Rage burned uncontrolled through him as he shrieked. "You are mud. I am a lord! You *will* die. Stop fighting. Your life is nothing." Tears leaked from his eyes as he pulled out another dagger, this one crusted with diamonds around the hilt.

I stepped back as he stabbed again at me. The blade nicked the tunic and sliced my shoulder. Blood ran down my upper arm as I jumped back toward a tool bench.

Savar slashed at me. Not at all the delicate swipes I'd seen when knife fighters brawled in Lesser Khaim, but enough to force me to keep backing up against the bench. I grabbed one of the forge hammers by the handle.

The worn, smooth wood felt comforting against my callused palms.

Savar swung his glittering dagger. Metal clinked against metal as I knocked his weapon away with my wedge-shaped hammer.

I tried to warn him away, but my words died as he lunged. He tried to stab at my heart and grab at my shirt with his free hand. I grabbed his wrists and kicked him back hard.

The duke's son sprawled on the floor, his robes fluttering and pale legs flopping on the ground, and for a second I felt horrible about what I had done. I wanted to take a step forward.

Savar scrabbled backward and pulled out yet another piece of parchment. Gods, the forge was going to glow if the censori ever approached. It was sick with it now.

He balled the paper up and bit it between his teeth. Then with a satisfied smile, he began to chew.

The smell of sulphur made me cough, and a dark green glow built inside the wet wad in Savar's mouth. He stood up, brushing his robes off and putting the dagger back into the hilt inside his thick belt.

A wind stirred inside the forge as the power between Savar's mouth began to suck the hair from around us toward itself. He raised his hands and they seemed to glow.

This minute, I realized, would only release one of us alive.

I rushed toward him as the hair on my arms stood up and began to dance with a pale fire. I ignored the searing sensation. I ignored Savar's hands rising toward me, burning my flesh as he tried to stop the impact.

I slammed my hammer down as if Savar's head were a glowing strip of steel.

The hammer didn't bounce, as it did whenever it struck metal. It did not require the steadying of my forearm. It just buried itself deep into a wet explosion of blood.

An explosion of heat threw me onto my back.

I dropped my hands away and looked at Savar.

The hammer remained in his forehead, the handle sticking up into the air over his dripping red face. He screamed, spitting more blood and pieces of parchment, and staggered toward the door before he fell to his hands and knees.

His eyes looked beyond it, though. To another realm. To something I couldn't see as he crawled forward, dripping blood on the forge floor.

I couldn't let him leave. Not keening like that. Someone would hear it the moment the thick doors opened.

I dragged him back from the entrance.

He pawed at me with one hand, smearing me with blood. His words sounded real, but made no sense to me, despite their earnestness.

"You can't go," I said. "It's too late. You can't go now."

Savar looked over my shoulder at the thick beams of the roof and screamed. Screamed like one of the cats I had seen the riverboys throw in the Sulong for amusement, then pelted stones at it until they stopped struggling and slipped under the oily surface.

I cupped my hand firmly over his mouth. "Be quiet."

A loud gurgling sound bubbled up through my fingers. I looked away. I had to find a cloth to stuff down his mouth, and then rope to bind him with. Then I could run.

Then I could run.

All this because of gold filigree. All this over the suit of armor.

Savar shook his head and screamed again with those strange, nonsense sounds.

I was already dead. I couldn't walk away alive from this. But if I moved quickly, I could save Milaka from him. I might yet be able to free my mother and father.

Looking slightly off to the side, I yanked the hammer free of Savar's face and raised it again. I smashed it into his face and he screamed even louder. So I hit him again. And then again. And again. Until he stopped screaming and blood dripped softly from around the edges of the dying wad of light he clenched between his teeth.

I watched dust motes sparkle in the morning air above the coals of the forge as I sat on the floor and trembled. What had I done?

What had I done?

I panted like a dog, suddenly unable to draw a full breath. I scrambled on my hands and knees around the forge to put the warm bricks between me and the body of Savar.

For long minutes I waited for the door to splinter. For city guards to spill in and drag me out into the dusty street.

For anything.

But there was only the still, slowly warming air of the forge.

My face still felt numb from his slaps, my shins ached from his kicks. But he was dead on the floor, now, on the other side of the forge from me.

I peeked around the bricks. A red pool of blood grew around his ruined head, the hammer still buried so deep into his face. I kissed my thumb and little finger and touched them to my stomach. "Assim. You gave me a sign. So why is this happening to me? Have I made the wrong choice?"

Assim did not respond.

After my breathing slowed I struggled back up to my feet and walked to the door. I cracked it open to look outside. Savar's palanquin sat untended at the corner of the street, beaded wet with late-morning mist that the sun had long since burned away. The city's air was now filled with squawking chickens, hawkers, songs, bells, and all the cacophony of a city well into the swing of its day.

No one was coming for me. Savar had sent them all away.

I shut the door, barred it, and put my back to it.

But what would happen when the guard came to look for his lord? How long would it take for them to think of me as the killer, and to come hunting for me? A day? Half a day? The pool of blood around Savar flickered as fire licked higher into the air in the forge.

A fly landed in the blood and started licking at it. Life can be found, even in death, I realized. I needed to stop thinking about things that may or may not happen and make choices.

The fly, heavy with blood, took to the air as I shifted.

"Soot," I said. My father hated it. We kept the floors scrubbed. But most forges were caked with soot.

"It covers everything, sticks everywhere, unless you keep a clean shop," my father had said.

His words echoed inside me as I looked around. If I hid Savar behind the woodpiles, maybe the guards would not spot him. And if I spread soot around to soak up the blood, maybe it would just look like a dirty blacksmith's shop.

I glanced at the forge. It was not big enough to accept a whole body. I would have to chop it up piece by piece to feed it to the fire. The smoke would discolor, and the smell would betray me to any passersby. It would take too long to do it correctly, and I wasn't even sure if I had enough wood to finish the suit as well as burn a body.

So I needed to hide the body quickly, finish my work, and then don the armor to execute my plan.

I grabbed a firepit shovel and approached the coals for ashes and debris to spread around the floor.

I stopped when I reached Savar's body and looked down at his hands. They lay unmoving on either side of his body. A good soul would put that jeweled dagger of his in his palm. That way Savar could offer one of Borzai's godlings a fine price to whisper sweet praises to the judging god's ear before he weighed Savar's soul.

Well shit on that, I thought, and raised the shovel. Savar and his father had destroyed our lives. Beaten us. Tried to kill us. May yet kill us. Why let his soul be judged with coin on the other side of the scales for Borzai? I slammed the point of the shovel down into his left wrist, twisting until the blade of the shovel separated the hand from his forearm.

I repeated the act of butchery on the other arm.

Now Savar would be unable to press valuables into any godling's hands on the other side. When they buried the little lordly rat, he would be unable to help his soul weigh anything other than true. He would be no different from any of the lowborn criminals hanging without their hands along the Avenue of Justice.

I threw open the windows to the noon sun as if I had nothing to hide. As if there weren't the body of an actual lord limp behind the woodpile.

And then I threw myself into the last day of work before me. The last of the plates needed to be shaped and connected. The armor's springs needed to be hooked together, and the pump latches on the forearms installed. After that, the cart in the shed would need to be packed up.

I moved as if I were possessed. I did not think about the future as I saw the guard return to the palanquin: I hammered metal.

"Girl!"

I turned, throwing sweat from my forehead to the ground with my hand. "What? What are you interrupting me for?"

The guardsman looked puzzled at my anger. "Where is the duke's son?"

"I don't know." I turned back to my work.

"He was in here this morning when I left."

"He was." I turned to show him the bruises on my face. Then I peeled my sleeves up to show him the cuts and marks on my arms. "He did what he came to do. And now I must get to my work, or when tomorrow dawns worse will happen."

The man swallowed. "Where did he go?"

"I assume he left to go beat someone else," I hissed. "Sir, I must finish my work. Look around the forge. He is not here."

The sweat that dripped from my brow was no longer just from the heat.

I returned to my work as the guardsman searched, even poking around the edges of the wood pile. But he saw nothing, Savar was at the very bottom of all the cut wood.

As he left, I pointed my hammer at the man in the ragged robes waiting near the palanquin. "Ask him. He'll know."

The guard ran off to consult with Savar's pet spy while I continued my work.

Throughout the midday they continued to come and go, their search expanding until two men dressed in house color strode angrily down the street to hassle the bodyguard. They hauled him away as he protested, off to go explain where the missing boy was.

"The duke will deal roughly with him," the informant so very obsessed with truth said casually to me from the edge of the forge, seeing my interest.

"It's never smart to take up with the velvet ones," I said.

"The boy has seemingly disappeared into thin air."

"I wouldn't be killing myself to finish this armor if that were true," I replied. "Now come in and search, like the guard, or leave me to my work."

The ragged robes shifted in the wind as he considered my offer. "No, I have other haunts to investigate. But if you hide the truth from me, know it will come out."

"By morning I'm sure the mystery will be solved," I said, with absolute certainty. Then I turned my back to him and picked up the hammer.

When the light paled, calmly, as if it were any other night, I closed the windows, doors, and banked the fires. I cleaned up my tools, setting them all in a neat row on the main bench. Water to douse the last embers was drawn from the trough. Water to wash my face in the second bucket.

It felt like any other night in the forge.

Until I faced the armor and stared into its glassy, blank eye-slits covered in glass. The dark, demonic eyes of something that had pulled us all into its fold.

"You've taken so much from us," I told the unmoving statue that silently watched everything in the forge. I reached forward and pulled the helmet with its carved serpents off its shoulders. "Now please give me something back."

I'd need to pull the armor on now, because who knew what time I would have once out on the open fields. I had to leave the forge in full armor, and hope the night hid me enough from curious eyes and guards who would challenge me.

I pulled each segment on one at a time. It was a difficult thing to seal it properly, but I'd worked hard on that as well. There were buckles and catches all around the outer pieces that pulled each piece into place. But it was slow, sweaty work, with a lot of fumbling.

When I finished I stood still for a moment. I'd never put all the pieces on, just tried different parts. It felt strange to stand here, dressed like a fully blooded lord in armor. It shifted slightly as I walked, the leather and plated armor skirts over my steel-cased legs swinging with me as I swayed from side to side, getting used to the restricted movement.

I could walk around well enough. Even hop. The weight wasn't that much worse than carrying a shouldered piece of plank and seven or so full buckets of water for the trough. My back held up easily.

With care, I took the helmet up with my gloved hands and pulled it on.

I breathed with relief as it settled over my neck.

Now, for the first time, I could actually begin my plan. The heavy weight I'd been carrying melted from my shoulders.

There was nothing left to do but go out to the burned fields and ash where my parents were buried alive.

The night had cooled, thankfully. The moon hid somewhere out of sight, leaving me to navigate down the dirt roads of Lesser Khaim by the occasional flicker of the night torches. But my feet knew the roads, even without light.

I still had to take the helmet off right where the road turned to cobblestones, as my hot breath fogged the glass slits near my eyes and I did not want to stumble over the stones.

Not a soul challenged me. By the banks of the Sulong only the occasional drunken worker passed by, on their way to a late collapse into their home. If they had one. Some stared at me. But the heraldic symbols and obvious wealth of the armor kept all at bay. Some shook their heads and fled, sure they were seeing a demon walking the night streets.

This was what it felt like to be one of the people from higher up the hill, I thought. People avoiding my eyes, looking to the ground. Giving me a wide berth.

Only the cart I pulled behind me made one tavern keeper throwing a bucket of slop onto the street frown and stare after me, trying to work out what I was about.

But then he shook himself and continued on.

I reached the fields soon enough, bumping my cart along in the dark. I stopped again, this time to prime a shop lantern and hang it from a pole I fixed to the handles of the cart so it could swing above me and light the path. With the day's bramble burning done, there was nothing but me and the ash my feet stirred up. It swirled like gray snow flurries in the orange light of the swinging lantern.

It took several passes of the field to find the spear Malabaz had thrust into the ground.

I put my helmet on and tightened the buckles holding it to my neck. The spear quivered slightly in the wind as I approached and touched my helm, my heart, and offered a prayer.

Then I took out a shovel from the cart and dug.

The bramble Majister Scacz had summoned appeared after I cleared away the dirt, like the ribs of a skeleton appearing from under a shallow grave. I cleared the brown clumps away, then stepped down onto it with a shudder. My copper and steel-shod feet crunched against the fuzzy tendrils, and the thicker, bonelike netting of bramble under that did not give as I stomped on it.

I took a deep breath and reached my gauntleted hands in.

For as long as I'd known anything, I'd been taught to be scared of bramble. Do not touch it. Destroy it with fire. Chip it off the nooks and crannies of a building with long-handled tools and thick leather gloves.

The burn teams destroyed it with fire, and then axes.

But if I lit a fire in the night, people would come running. It would sear my mother and father with sap or burn them up.

So I had to break through it myself.

My metal fingers gripped bramble, my arms shoved deep into the killing branches. And then I triggered the gloves and ripped bramble apart by the fist-full, careful to keep hold of the pieces and toss them to the side so they didn't fall down. Bramble pods burst and filled the air around me. Sap hissed and burned at my forearms and gloves. But it didn't burn through the metal, or through the leathered joints underneath.

With each ripped-out handful, I had to stop to crank the levers on my forearms to prime the gauntlets. It was slow work, but handful by handful, a sizzling pile of curled bramble grew next to me.

I clawed until my fingers felt like they would crack. Sweat spilled from my pores, soaking the armor's padding. But I'd become a badger-dog, digging and clawing with a single-minded ferocity that took me over.

The acrid, oily smell of bramble sap filled my helmet, choking me. Even in my armor, I wasn't fully protected from everything the bramble could do to me.

A loud snap startled me, and my right forearm blazed with pain as blood trickled down toward my fingers.

"No," I hissed. The clockwork Milaka and I had built, broken and no longer able to help drive ten times my own strength to my hands, dug into the skin of my arm.

I looked up at the stars and swore at whatever watching gods looked at me. "I do not know if I am on the right path, but I will not stop!"

I ignored the pain and began to dig with only my left arm, pumping the lever as fast I could to make up for the lost time. I ripped out more desperate handfuls and threw them out onto the field.

"Mother!" I screamed down at the bone-white bramble. "Father! Hear me!"

The left arm's clockwork snapped and I screamed as blood trickled down my arm. I leaned back on my legs, eyes closed.

I couldn't stop. I couldn't go back to try to fix it. There was no time, Savar might be discovered. I couldn't fix the suit here.

I screamed at the bramble and raised my hands high in the air and struck the bramble hard, then pulled. Without clockwork, my forearms strained and my back tore as I yanked with everything I had in me. Every muscle that had been built over the long years of working metal. And I was rewarded by the satisfying sound of ripping bramble.

I kicked, pulled, sobbed, and ripped the bramble out, inch by inch, until a small hole grew in front of me. Wide enough to put a ladder through, and just wide enough for me to shove and kick my way down through with a lantern.

The moment my feet touched dirt I spun around and removed my helmet. "Father? Mother? It's me. I've come for you."

I raised the lantern with my other hand.

They lay together, not having stirred despite all the noise I'd made screaming my way through the bramble. My hand shook, the light twisting about because of it, as I approached them.

My father had his strong hands wrapped around my mother's waist as they curled together on the dirt. The last of their bread lay close next to an empty water skin. At first I thought the water had spilled around them. Then I realized why the dirt looked a different color.

They'd given each other the mercy cut. I could see the knife held in both their hands, clasped together. The small, precise wounds on the forearms. Their ashy faces. Their closed eyes.

They'd seen no other option. Their food had run out. They were trapped in bramble.

I lay down, bereft. In the soft flicker I crawled over, rested my head carefully against my mother's side, and cried.

AFTER MY TEARS MINGLED WITH THE BLOOD ON MY parents' tunics, and once I could no longer find the energy for another single sob, I used a water skin to carefully wash their bodies. I wrapped them in fresh linen sheets, sweating inside my armor as I moved their still forms up the ladder and to the cart.

I took my mother up first, her thin body no heavier than a sack of yams. My father still weighed more like a barrel of ingots. Bramble scratched at their skin on the way up through the sheets, but it didn't matter anymore. I brushed the deadly threads away from my father's death wrappings with my dirty gauntlets.

After digging in the ground, weeping, then preparing my mother's and father's bodies, the world above the pit had started to lighten. A rosy line of light glinted behind Khaim's buildings. Smoke rose from markets where vendors would be skewering meat and baking bread for morning workers. Lesser Khaim awoke.

"Identify yourself!" a voice laced with cruel authority snapped. One of the city guard, heavy and sweaty, his boots covered in mud and ash, pointed a poorly fashioned bronze spear at me.

He flinched when I turned to look directly at him. The fearsome helmet's demonic faces unnerved him. I considered taking it off, but then that glinting spearpoint was only a foot away from my head. "I am . . .," I said, and faltered. What would I say next? Would I say I was Sofija, the daughter to Cedomill, the blacksmith, and Natazia, his wife?

And what would he say then?

What could he see through the glass-plated slits in my helmet? Was he even looking that closely?

I lowered my voice and filled it with the same authority I would use on anyone at market trying to cheat me out of the true weight of a copper ingot. "I am Savar, son of the Duke Malabaz. What I do is my business. Get out of my way."

"My l-lord," the guard stammered. "I, uh, need you to come with me. There are many looking for you."

I grunted and moved my father's body up onto the cart, ignoring the city guardsman.

"Lord, you at least need to explain what is happening here."

"I need explain nothing to you," I growled at the man. "But if you insist . . ." I was thinking furiously, sweating and nervous. He was going to figure out something was wrong. He was going to realize my voice was cracking inside the helmet. Surely he could hear that my accent was not velvet, even though I tried to imitate Savar's wheedling voice.

But what could scare him off any more than a duke's son?

A majister.

"Maybe," I said, my voice dropping, "you're interested in finding out more of what Majister Scacz does in those rooms with blood-grooves in the floor? Will you be coming with me?" I pointed at the bodies.

The guard swallowed and looked at the bundles under my parents' bodies. "No."

"Then leave me while I wait for the majister. Better yet, run from here before I decide to tell him you have asked too many questions. Or do you want just your headless body to show up in the Sulong tomorrow?"

He fled, his feet kicking up ash.

I waited until his figure disappeared between the farm shacks at the edge of the field, then picked up the cart and pulled it with me. Exhausted from digging, my head swirling with exhaustion, I stumbled more than ran.

But no one bothered a noble in armor stumbling away from Lesser Khaim along Junpavati Road, pulling a small cart behind.

Out on the road, only a few refugees approached the city from the hazy distance. I stopped, ignoring the bramble-choked trees that crept toward the road's edges, and quickly pulled a ragged, patchwork cloak on over my armor. I hid the helmet under my parents' bodies. I didn't have time to pull the armor off, not with all the buckles and layers. The cloak would have to do. I used a butchering knife to cut my hair short, nastily and quickly. My cut hair drifted down to the dirt.

I flung a small tarp over the cart and hung a few cups and spoons off the edge to clank against one another, I looked like any other refugee, or tinker, wandering the roads.

Only this tinker kept glancing over a shoulder every ten steps and walked *away* from Khaim.

I walked the entire day. I pulled the cart through mud and ruts. I struggled over grass knolls, swearing when my feet broke through small burrows in the ground. But in time, Khaim fell farther away. At the midday, as the sun hung high overhead and beat down on me, I trudged wearily through a tiny huddle of abandoned buildings that had once been a post station.

I left the road for a hill far behind the stone tower, reasoning that I could use it as a landmark to find my way back to the road. Bramble covered the land, growing thicker on the ground as I left the cleared road behind me. The gnarled trees here succumbed to the gray, ropey fingers of it.

Since man had fled here, bramble didn't grow as strongly as it did near the towns where it was fed by constant magic use. Out here in the wastes, only the distant effluvia of magic blowing in on the winds from afar gave it continuing sustenance.

At the top of the hill, several miles from the tower, I found an open space of soft dirt. This would be a good place. A fine hill that my parents could see from the afterlife, a grave they would be proud of.

I dug deep and laid my parents out in the broken dirt. In an hour the sun would set. I would spend the night here, watching vigil over them. When morning broke, I would kiss the ground they lay in, weep one last time, and then leave all this behind me.

We would all be at peace.

I looked over at the cart and wondered what Borzai's price should be. The gold coins? The other left over pieces of fine materials for the armor I'd packed away?

As I mulled it over, the muffled thump of a churning drifted to the top of the hill. Horses. I ran around the cart. Three men in city guard cloaks rode their way up the hill. The horses' legs glinted harshly in the setting sunlight, clad in metal and heavy leathers to protect against the low-lying bramble.

Like a startled rabbit, I took a few steps left, then right, trying to think which direction I could bolt in. But then I looked back at my parents' graves. I stood frozen by the cart as the men thundered into the small grave space, their faces dark as they reigned their horses in and leaped to the ground around me.

I recognized Lukat, the sympathetic guard captain from earlier. He had a hand on his sword's hilt as he walked toward me. "I'm here to take you back to Khaim," he said sadly.

"The gold coin . . . ," I said. "I did leave it for you. Like I promised."

Lukat shook his head. "Even a gold coin isn't enough to stay my hand when it comes to a lord's murdered son. They gave us horses to track you. There are more out on the roads. Malabaz himself paid the stables."

My eyes burned slightly, but I had cried too much over the last few days for anything to trickle out. I merely nodded. I felt somewhat relieved to realize it was all ending. "I will come. Just, please give me time to fill my parents' graves."

But Lukat looked down at the ground and shook his head. He pointed at the graves. "Fetch the bodies," he ordered the two younger guards.

They moved forward and I shouted, "No!"

"I'm sorry," Lukat said. "Malabaz ordered that your entire family be returned to him. Regardless of your conditions."

I grabbed the helmet and my hammer from the cart and moved between my parents' graves. "You will not desecrate the grave of my mother and father." Not after all I had done.

"You desecrated the boy," Lukat said. "He will never find peace. The lord demands his retribution."

"He should have lived a life better suited for the scales."

Lukat shrugged. "True. But we are still here to take your family."

"You will not have my parents," I said firmly.

Lukat looked pained. "I have no choice here. These are the duke's orders."

"Piss on the duke!" I shouted, startling them all. But I was furious, desperate, and deep inside myself I begged for Lukat to see the obvious path my words beat toward. "We're outside Khaim now. You can make any choices you want. Let us choose life."

I was thinking back to the priest's words.

"Bind her," Lukat ordered, his voice catching. "Then we'll deal with the graves."

I looked at him, angry to see the sorrow in his eyes. "You'll have to fight me first." I pulled the helmet on, buckling it in place with a single hand while stepping back even farther.

"You're a girl, not a guard," Lukat said. The two guards on either side of the graves pulled their swords and looked back at Lukat, wondering what to do next.

"I am a girl wearing armor," I said. I shrugged my cloak off to fall by my shod feet. "Your swords will struggle to pierce it too. I'm a damned good craftsperson. I'm my father's daughter. My family's armor is well known for its reputation against a blade."

Lukat's lips curled with frustration. "Then we will bash you senseless in your armor."

"You, maybe." I looked at the other two guards. "But these two *boys* you have with you? They've barely held these swords for a full year. I have been swinging my own hammer since before I could walk. Look at their arms, Lukat: they have no rope on them." They were skinny little things, unaccustomed to hard work. Hell, they didn't even have calluses on their fingers.

I raised my hammer. Lukat shook his head. "Get her," he ordered, waving them forward.

I did not wait for the nearest one to move at me. I ran for him. He raised a hand, thinking to block me, somewhat shocked at my presumption. I swung the hammer hard and it clanged against steel as he struggled to bring the sword up, suddenly realizing his hand would do nothing against armor and a hammer.

He punched at me, howling as his knuckles bounced off armor. I smacked him with a fist against the side of his head. It was as sure a hit as any: my arm tingled from the impact.

Dazed, he stumbled back and grabbed at his ear, looking shocked to find blood flowing down to soak the collar of his tunic. Then he sat down and coughed, unable to keep to his feet.

"Go, now," I begged them all.

But the second guard came at me, grabbing me in a great hug as he tackled me from the side. We struck the soft dirt. Air huffed from between my lips.

I rolled away from him and crouched on my hands and knees. As I drew in a long breath the guard reared up, his sword held in two hands for strength, and struck my helmet with the butt of his sword.

My head snapped and I shut my eyes as the glass behind the slits in the helmet shattered. Shards dug at my neck as I stumbled to my feet. But the helmet had taken his strike and remained intact.

He swung at me, the sword high over his head for another brutal strike. I walked into it, my head bowed and hammer still in my hand. He struck the helmet again. I struck his side. As the sword bounced off my helmet and shoulders, he crumpled, his ribs broken. Blood stained his garments, soaking the dirty gray material quickly, as I hadn't used the blunt side of the hammer. The tip had shattered his ribs and pierced deep between them.

When I yanked the hammer away, flesh and fabric tore free.

"Leave me be," I begged again.

"Akash!" Lukat shouted. He ran at both of us, sword out. Any hesitation he had about fighting me had fled, there was nothing but rage in his movement. I'd hurt his fellow guardsmen.

Behind him one of the horses whinnied, panicked by the shouting. It yanked at the tether Lukat had staked to the ground, but as it tried to turn and move, it tripped in the leathers. It stumbled out into one of the many patches of bramble surrounding the hill.

I wasn't going to be able to scare these men away, I realized as the horse thrashed and screamed in the bramble. Lukat rushed me as the other guard wobbled to his feet, holding an unsteady sword in the air with one hand, his head with another.

"Malabaz orders this." On his knees, the guard I'd hit stabbed at my feet with the sword as he wheezed the words.

I turned back to him as he raised the point of his sword, trying to aim for one of the joints between my thigh plates and my hip. There was nothing but determination in his eyes. They would kill me if they had to. Then drag all three of our bodies back to the duke. I let the sword hit and work in. But it stopped as it hit the plates underneath.

"Please stop," I begged yet again. Lukat loomed close. The both of them would overpower me at any second.

I screamed and slammed the hammer between Akash's eyes as Lukat struck me, knocking me free of both his guard and the hammer. He hit the helmet with his sword twice, knocking my head about in it. Glass shards dug hard into my collarbone, and blood wet my shoulders.

Lukat pinned me to the ground, using his weight to hold me in place as he pulled out a thin dagger. "I've fought men in armor before," he hissed.

He was levering the tip of the dagger in between the joints under my arm. Metal creaked and scraped as the edge of the dagger pierced the chain slightly.

Lukat pushed harder, his face red from the effort. The bite of metal stung as it broke my skin. Blood trickled down my armpit as I struggled to get free of him.

I hit him with my other hand. One metal gauntleted punch after another in his side as he kept trying to drive the dagger in farther. Each time I rocked in the dirt slightly. I could glimpse the graves of my parents each time.

Then I was able to roll him. We tumbled right into my father's grave, the dip in the ground being just enough to separate our bodies as we fell into the shallow pit.

Lukat howled as I drove my plated knee into his groin.

I scrabbled out onto the dirt, a split second ahead of him. I was half standing, sprinting away, as he struck me again.

But I was hoping for it. I grabbed him and kept stumbling, letting him beat at me as I held us both together and ran us away from the dirt.

He didn't understand why I didn't fight the dagger stabbing up under my arm again, or his punches. I was only worried about moving us both along in a spinning, spinning dance that he did not lead.

And then his eyes focused not on me, but on the world whirling past. He oriented himself, tried to break free of me. I only crumpled with him in my arms. We struck the ground in our embrace and Lukat flailed, trying to get back to his booted feet.

It was too late.

I rolled with him on bramble. I crushed strands and thready needles under my armor as I fell on my back. They stuck to Lukat as he flailed around with me. He shrieked when he pulled free of me, horror in his eyes. He yanked at bramble needles stuck to his skin and swept desperately at his cheeks and fingers.

Then his eyes rolled up and he stumbled forward.

He swayed, then fell forward into the mat of bramble I'd thrown us both into. Near the still body of the horse that had also fallen to the bramble's touch.

I stood up unsteadily, terrified that bramble had poked through my broken helmet. Only a single needle hung limp on the edge of a slit that had once been glassed over. An inch from my eye.

Ever so carefully I undid the straps to the helmet and pulled it off, leaning forward so that any bramble attached to it would fall away from me.

When I strode out of the bramble, helmet in my hands, the last guard dropped to his knees. "Mercy," he said, and threw up. "I won't tell anyone anything...."

"But you will, when the Majister spells it out of you," I said. I wrapped my guantleted hands around his throat and squeezed until he could see me no more. "Mercy? There is no mercy in Khaim."

I dug more graves.

One for Lukat. Another for each of his fellow guards. I did that in armor as the sun set orange over the plains in the distance. I put coin, which I could barely spare, in each of their hands for Borzai. We all made choices. They had chosen to follow lords and Khaim, even into death. But there had been some kindness, far enough back, that maybe Borzai held them in fine regard. I would not harm their afterlives, not even after what today had brought.

This would be done right. Because I wanted things to change from here.

I stripped the armor off and buried it carefully for my mother and father to hold.

That was a price for a lord, a fit price, and one my parents could proudly present to the afterlife.

For what would I do with it? Bring more blood to my hands?

I wanted to *make* things. To hammer them out with my hands. Tap designs out with my fingers. I wanted well-worn tools by my side. I'd spent a life working by my mother's and father's sides to learn these things. My hands knew them by instinct. I was not a killer, I swore it. I had been backed into a corner. Turned into an animal by the true animals of Khaim: the velvet ones.

I was glad to see dirt cover that damned armor.

When all were buried, I built a spell I'd learned as a mere child, long before the blue hung over all Khaim and the nobles died at the hands of the Majister. Paper and oils, and the scratch of symbols I barely understood. In the old days, before bramble choked the land, we'd used this spell to light the forge fire quickly. I lit the paper with a fire strike and threw it on the ground.

I took the two remaining horses with me. I'd reloaded the cart's contents onto one of them, and I rode the other. They picked their way down the hill happily. With a horse, now only the Majister himself could fly overhead to catch me. And I doubted he would bother to hunt me down.

There were bandits out on the roads, I'd been told. But I wore the boiled leather from the armor's underlayer. I had my strength, my mind, and my hammer looped in a belt by my side.

Behind me the top of the hill glowed, flashed, and sparked. A funeral pyre of magic flame burned which made bramble quiver. Vines of threaded stalks crept closer to the disturbed dirt I'd thrown the spell on, lacing themselves over the graves as I reached the road and turned to put Khaim to my back.

When I found a village with need for a blacksmith, I would stop. Or maybe I would head all the way to Paika, where I knew they had need of blacksmiths to forge axe heads. And they might ask me where I came from. I would not say I came from the city of blue. I would tell them I came from the city of blood, and I would tell them to stay far from it.

AFTERWORD

The creation of a place like Khaim requires a great deal of support that often isn't seen by readers but is vital to us as authors. Firstly, we'd like to thank our families for their patience and support as we spent many hours on Skype brainstorming, chatting, and (let's be honest) drinking, as we created this world and the people who inhabit it. We'd also especially like to thank Steve Feldberg at Audible.com for his support of our first experimental forays into Khaim; Bill Schafer of Subterreanean Press for bringing early parts of it to print; and Joe Monti, our editor at Saga, for championing this deepened and much-expanded work that you now hold in your hands. Special shout-outs also to our agents, Russ Galen and Barry Goldblatt, for their unceasing support of our imaginative explorations. With luck, we hope to have many more opportunities to revisit Khaim and its many tangled stories.

—PB and TB